Playing
BY THE RULES

Playing BY THE RULES

New York Times Bestselling Author
MONICA MURPHY

Entangled Publishing, LLC
644 Shrewsbury Commons Ave., STE 181
Shrewsbury, PA 17361
rights@entangledpublishing.com

Amara is an imprint of Entangled Publishing, LLC.

Visit our website at www.entangledpublishing.com.

Edited by Rebecca, Fairest Reviews Editing Services
Cover illustration and design by Elizabeth Turner Stokes
Edge design by Elizabeth Turner Stokes
Stock art by Muneeb Designer/Shutterstock and anggapajar23/Shutterstock
Interior design by Britt Marczak

ISBN 978-1-64937-871-2

Manufactured in the United States of America

First Edition March 2025

10 9 8 7 6 5 4 3 2 1

I need to thank Taylor Swift for Folklore.

I've written a lot of books to songs from this album and now those songs leave me an emotional wreck.

'Mad Woman' really helped a scene in this book and I needed that so thanks…

Playlist

"Wasting My Time" - Hannah Cohen

"Dreams, Fairytales, Fantasies" - A$AP Ferg, Brent Faiyaz, Salaam Remi)

"T Love" - Quarters of Change

"Hit Me Where it Hurts" - Caroline Polachek

"Sugar" - Remi Wolf

"All I Really Want is You" - The Marias

"Spectra" - Pink Skies

"Mad Woman" - Taylor Swift

"Even when I'm wide awake
I'm in a dream, fairytale, fantasy
When you're around me"
— A$AP Ferg

1

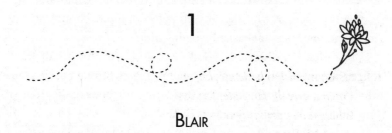

BLAIR

I am in love with a man who doesn't know I exist.

Wait a second, scratch that. He knows I exist. He just chooses to ignore me. Which hurts even more.

Oh, and by "in love with him," I mean I think he's super-hot and sweet. A phenomenal athlete with strong, silent type-vibes, and I want to have sex with him.

I don't admit that to anyone though. Not a single soul. Camden Fields, hotshot quarterback at Colorado University, best friend to my overprotective big brother Knox, fuel for my filthiest sexual fantasies and dreams, is my secret.

I first met Cam before I was a senior in high school. Knox brought him home with him in the middle of summer one weekend. They were already at college, preparing for the upcoming football season, and Cam wanted to meet our dad. Or Knox wanted to show off that our father is a retired NFL player.

Whatever the reason, Camden walked into our house and my jaw literally dropped. He was the most gorgeous guy I had ever seen, and

I still stand by that statement.

Worse? He was nice. Funny. My parents loved him. He was kind to Ruby, our little sister, who can be a total shit. And when he appeared in a pair of swim trunks to go swimming in our pool? Forget it.

I was drooling.

Kind of like how I'm currently salivating as I lurk on the second floor of the library on campus, spying on Cam sitting at one of the tables nearby. It feels wrong, watching him when he's unaware, but I need a few seconds to gather myself before I approach him, so why not spend that time unabashedly ogling him?

The man is ridiculously good-looking. Dark brown hair that's longer on top, which he keeps raking his fingers through as he reads whatever extremely thick and intimidating textbook is in front of him, and I wish it were my fingers in his hair.

I stare at him with longing, grateful he hasn't noticed me yet as I continue to mentally catalogue his features. Those dark brown eyes and a big smile with the straightest teeth. Strong jaw and chin, with cheekbones that could cut glass. He's tall because, of course he is, as well as broad and built. Big hands that know exactly how to throw a football. Bet they know how to do other things too.

My entire body flushes at the thought.

"Excuse me," a guy murmurs from behind me, and I step aside when I realize I'm in his way, offering an apology before my gaze returns to Cam.

To find him looking straight at me, surprise etched on his handsome features.

Oh shit.

Smiling faintly, I offer him a lame wave and slowly make my way toward his table, telling myself it would be rude to ignore him. I stop on the other side of it, reaching out to grip the empty chair directly in front of me, so I have something to hold on to. "Hey, Camden."

"Blair." His deep voice washes over me, making me tingle all over. "Surprised I haven't seen you sooner."

I've only been here for about a month—after two years at

community college back home, I transferred to Colorado University.

And what, did he expect me to chase after him?

"I thought you'd stop by our place by now to see Knox," he continues, probably because he notices my confusion.

"Oh. Yeah, no. Knox and I have met a couple times for dinner, but I haven't stopped by your guys' apartment yet." I was always secretly disappointed Knox didn't bring Cam with him to dinner too. "I've been busy."

"I bet." His slow, sexy smile makes my panties feel like they're made of dissolvable fabric. "How are you liking it here?"

"I like it a lot! It's great!" I am chirping. I sound like an idiot and need to tone it down a notch or ten. "My class load is kind of tough, but I'm getting used to it."

"Oh yeah?" He frowns, inclining his head toward the chair I'm currently holding on to for dear life. "You should join me. Unless you need to be somewhere?"

"No, no. I don't need to be anywhere." Now I sound like a loser. This man turns me into an absolute fool, just being in his presence. "My next class is in like…forty-five minutes."

I let go of the back of the chair and he kicks at it, making the chair skid across the floor, nearly bumping into me. I grab it, settle in and drop my backpack at my feet, inhaling discreetly.

His spicy cologne hits me like a drug, slipping through my veins and making me want to sway in drunken pleasure. No one should be allowed to smell this delicious. To look this delicious. Everything about this man just lights me up. It's criminal, how much I want him.

How much he doesn't realize it.

"What are you reading?" I ask, needing to distract myself.

Cam holds up the book, so I can see the cover with the title, *American Political Thought*, on the front of it.

"Sounds boring." I wrinkle my nose.

"It's not so bad." He shrugs. "I'm a poly sci major so…"

Great. I just insulted his choice of major. "Oh right. Sorry. I forgot."

Actually, I didn't even know. Not like Knox and I discuss Cam beyond him mentioning Cam's name here and there. Mostly in reference to football and the team and stats and all the bullshit that comes with it.

I shouldn't describe it like that. Football is our family's life. Dad always says, it's a part of our legacy. He fully expects Knox to get drafted into the NFL, predicting he'll get picked by the fifth round, and I don't doubt it'll happen. I'm related to a bunch of guys who are currently playing in the NFL, both by blood and through marriage. We are just *that* family.

"It's okay. You shouldn't care what my major is." He slams the book shut and pushes it aside, before he rests his arms on top of the table, contemplating me. "So, how's it going?"

"How's what going?" I stare into his eyes for a beat too long, trying to calm my breathing. My rapidly beating heart. Pretty sure this is the closest I've ever been to Cam, beyond that one moment when I got to hug him after a football game last season.

That experience about did me in. My emotions went into a chaotic spiral the moment I felt his arms close around me.

Or maybe that was just my hormones kicking in, reminding me that I'm extremely attracted to this man.

"School. Life." He shrugs, leaning back in his seat, sprawling his legs out. He's dressed in a Golden Eagles Football T-shirt that stretches tight across his wide chest and a pair of black basketball shorts. The outfit is nothing special, but heaven help me, he looks amazing. "Knox mentioned you're doing well since you got here."

"I am." I nod—a little too enthusiastically. "I just—I don't have a lot of friends yet."

He frowns, seemingly concerned. "Oh? Well, you did just start here."

While the campus is crowded and my classes are full, I haven't really been able to fully connect with anyone.

Yet.

"Right. Well, I have my roommates." Rita and Cheyenne are

perfectly nice, but I don't really know them, and they are already super close since they've roomed together since freshman year. Which means, most of the time, I feel like a third wheel when I'm hanging out with them. "And they're nice. But I haven't really talked to anyone in my classes yet."

"Ah." Cam nods. "Well, at least you have your brother."

I roll my eyes. "He doesn't count."

That smile is back, closed-lipped and absolutely adorable. "You have me."

My heart drops, landing between my legs. *You have me.*

He can't say things like that unless he means them.

"I'll be your friend," he continues. "Knox did mention to me recently that he needs my help."

Be my friend. Would he freak out if he knew what I truly wanted from him? It's definitely not friendship.

"Help with what?" I ask warily.

"Watching over you. He says I'm the only one he can trust on the team not to make a move on you." Cam shakes his head.

And just like that, my heart returns to its normal spot in my chest, all tingly feelings occurring between my thighs disappearing. Great. Cam views me as the little sister he never had, thanks to my completely over-the-top brother.

"Wow, can't wait to have *two* overprotective brothers on campus watching out for me," I say, heavy on the sarcasm.

Cam scratches the back of his neck, seeming a little uncomfortable. "Is Knox too much sometimes?"

His question opens up a dam of opinions. "Too much? If he could put me in a cage and keep me under lock and key for the rest of my time here on this campus, he totally would. It's ridiculous. *He's* ridiculous. I don't know why he thinks I'm incapable of making rational decisions, but for whatever reason, he believes I'm going to put myself at risk on a daily basis, like I'm stupid."

"Knox doesn't think you're stupid," Cam says, ready to defend his friend, which is a little annoying. Though not annoying enough to make me think he's awful. I could never think Cam is awful. "More like he doesn't trust anyone else."

I raise my brows. "Meaning?"

"Like all the guys. Everyone we know. The team, mostly." He crosses his arms, making his biceps bulge. Good lord. It's hard not to blatantly stare at them. "He knows what we're all up to when we're not playing football, and doesn't want his little sister exposed to our terrible ways."

"Are you all just a bunch of dirty dogs deep down?" Dirty dogs? What in the world am I saying?

Cam chuckles. "I would say the majority of us think with our dick first, can't lie."

Okay. The tingle is back between my legs because hearing Cam talk about his dick is just a bit exciting, which makes me feel a tad pathetic, but whatever.

"Oh, come on. You're deeper than that, right?"

"Not really." He shrugs again.

"Says the man who's reading about American politics."

"I have to for an assignment in the class," he explains, that smile still on his face.

I'm getting the sense he's enjoying this conversation as much as I am, though maybe that's just wishful thinking on my part.

"You're telling me then, that when you first meet a woman, you can't help but think about having sex with her?"

"Well, yeah." He looks sheepish. But not enough to hold back being honest. "Most of the time."

"Every woman?"

"If I find her attractive, definitely." He shrugs, seemingly uncomfortable.

Huh.

The words leave me before I can even think about them, which isn't normal.

"What about me?"

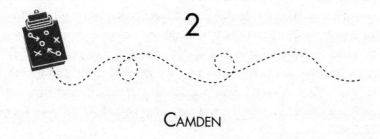

2

CAMDEN

I stare at Blair Maguire's beautiful face, dumbfounded.

Did she say what I think she just said?

"Never mind." She waves her hand, her cheeks turning the faintest shade of pink. "Forget I asked that."

The problem is, I don't think I'll ever forget she asked that. I have always found her attractive. Even when Knox and I were incoming college freshmen and she was going to be a senior in high school, and I went to her house that one summer, eager to meet their dad. She was cute then. Blonde and green-eyed and always wearing a friendly smile, yet rarely wearing much clothing, considering how hot it was that weekend. I stayed at her family's house for three days that first summer I met Knox, and by the end of the stay, I realized something.

My new friend's sister had a crush on me.

That's not my ego talking either. I'd always catch her staring at me. She followed me around—a lot. Made sure she was always sitting out by the pool when we were out there too, wearing some little bikini that barely covered her. She has perfect tits and a tiny waist and flared hips. Curves in all the right places that I would mentally tell myself not to look at.

I told my mental, nagging voice to fuck right off every single time I caught myself checking her out. Even though I knew it was a bad idea. As in, me and Blair.

We're a terrible idea.

The worst part of that one short summer visit? How her sweet voice would always turn softer when she spoke to me, those big green eyes drinking me in. Like she couldn't get enough of my presence. She'd try to make conversation with me every chance she got.

Can't lie, it felt good to have such a pretty girl seemingly crushing on me, but she was young. And I wasn't interested. Not really. One, the age difference—well more the school difference—and two, she was Knox's sister. And he warned me straight out that his sisters were off-limits.

Having her sit in front of me now, looking prettier than ever and asking me if I ever thought about having sex with her? Fuck.

My answer would be a hell yes, but I can't say that out loud.

Can I?

I might've told myself back in the day I wasn't interested in her, but it was a lie. I always thought she was beautiful. I would've totally made a move on her if she'd been older and not Knox's sister.

Still can't make a move because...yeah.

Blair is Knox's sister.

There are rules Knox has laid down and boundaries established. We can't touch Blair.

Period.

"Yeah, I've thought about it," I finally mutter, so low she almost didn't hear me.

But she definitely did. I see the realization dawn. The slow smile that curls her lips, immediately erased, like she didn't mean to do it.

"Camden Fields," she softly chastises, her eyes twinkling with mischief. "Really?"

She sounds surprised, but come on. Has she looked at herself in the mirror lately? She's fucking gorgeous. All that blonde hair and smooth skin. Those pink lips that are perfectly shaped. Not to mention she has a great body. A perfect ass that I've stared at more than a time or two.

I scrub a hand over my face, trying to keep my thoughts under control.

"I shouldn't be talking with you like this." I sit up straighter, clearing my throat. "Your brother would have my ass."

"I won't tell him if you don't," she promises, her voice...sultry?

Well, damn. What do I say to that?

"Look, I should go." When she rises to her feet, I recall her saying she didn't have to be at her next class for another forty-five minutes, which was like...ten minutes ago. Tops. "It was nice seeing you. Hopefully we'll run into each other again sometime soon."

Before I can say anything, even goodbye, she grabs her backpack and she's gone.

Without hesitation, I shoot out of my seat, leaving everything behind at the table while I chase after her. She might not be tall with a long stride like me, but she's fast, seeing as she's practically to the side doors of the library when I curl my fingers around her upper arm, stopping her.

She whips around, surprise in her eyes when she realizes I chased after her.

"If I made you uncomfortable, I didn't mean to," I say, suddenly sweating. I don't want to piss her off or offend her. And this has nothing to do with Knox. I know he'll kick my ass if I did something rude to his sister, but really?

I respect Blair. I like her. And I don't want to hurt her feelings.

Something dawns in her gaze, something I can't quite figure out, and her lips curve into the tiniest smile. "You didn't make me uncomfortable, Cam."

Thank Christ. "Okay, good."

"It was—interesting though, what you said."

I'm frowning. "How so?"

"That we're having the same thoughts about each other."

I blink at her, the meaning behind her words sinking into my brain.

"I've wondered what it would be like with you too." She blasts me with the full wattage of her smile, before she turns and pushes her way through the double doors, disappearing out of view.

Leaving me at a complete loss.

. . .

Practice is a bitch. My arm aches from constantly throwing and that son of a bitch Derek tackled my ass out of nowhere, taking me down to the ground. The coaches went apeshit, screaming at him, and Derek apologized over and over again, making me feel bad for being mad at him.

Still am though, even if it's unreasonable.

Once I'm dressed and ready to leave, Coach asks me to come into his office, which I do, settling in the chair across from his desk.

"Maguire waiting for you?" he asks. He knows our living situation and how we usually go to practice together.

"He is," I answer.

"I'll make it quick then." He scoots his creaky old desk chair closer, resting his arms on the edge of the desk. "We need to protect you at all costs."

"Protect me?"

"Your arm. That asshole Derek." Coach rubs his jaw, his lips firm. "I'm sorry that happened."

I'm in shock Coach would apologize. "You had nothing to do with it."

"Still. You're the best fucking QB we've had in years. I can't risk losing you, not this year. You and Maguire are powerhouses. You two keep this up and you're on your way to the NFL for sure."

I refuse to get my hopes up. That is the ultimate dream. But I'm not part of a legacy like my friend. With his retired NFL-playing father and uncle, he's got an automatic 'in' that I will never have, and while I'm not jealous of it, I sure do wish it was me sometimes.

"Thanks, Coach," I say when I realize he's done. "That's all you wanted to tell me?"

"That and I wanted you to know how much I appreciate you. The entire coaching staff does. Your calm demeanor keeps everyone on an even keel which we appreciate. Those boys listen to you, son. Your quiet leadership is outstanding. You are an asset to this team, Fields." He nods once, and I leap to my feet, taking that as my dismissal. "Don't fuck it up."

The same words linger in my brain the entire drive home. I give noncommittal answers to Knox, while what Coach said is on repeat.

Don't fuck it up.

Talk about freaking me out. I am bound to fuck it up. I'm not perfect. Not even close. And I have a feeling I will do exactly that at one point or another during the season.

"What the hell did Coach say to you to put you in such a funk?" Knox demands.

I send him a look, afraid to repeat anything out loud. "Just tried to pump me up."

Knox grins, the cocky bastard. "I take it that it wasn't a success."

"More like freaked me out."

"Well, put his words out of your head. Don't let him get to you." He pauses, and I know he's thinking about how this sort of thing always messes with me. "We have a game this weekend. It's going to be great."

"You really think so?"

"I know so," Knox says firmly. "Think about something else. Think about...the pretty girl you ran into on campus today."

My defenses shoot up. "How do you know I ran into a pretty girl?"

"Because you always do, asshole. It's that face of yours." Knox slaps me on the shoulder, making me flinch.

The only pretty girl I ran into just so happens to be related to my best friend and roommate. Blair's face pops into my brain, her tantalizing words now on repeat, replacing Coach's.

I've wondered what it would be like with you too.

Seriously, what the fuck is she saying? She had a crush on me a while ago, but was she implying she's still into me?

Hard to believe, but I don't think she was lying when she said that.

Wild.

Not like we can act on any urges we might have for each other. Knox would chop my nuts off with a machete and make me wear them around my neck as a reminder of what not to do. Blair is untouchable with a capital U. I'd be an idiot to even consider getting involved with her.

And when I mean involved, I use the word loosely. I am *not* the commitment type. I just don't have the time and most of the women I've spent time with aren't out for a real commitment either. They just want to have a good time. Same as me.

Relationships aren't my thing. I'm not ready to have one. I don't know if I ever will be. I saw the way my parents went at each other's throats every chance they got through their divorce. My older brother got the hell out of the house the moment he graduated from high school and never looked back. I did pretty much the same. Dad will show up to my football games from time to time, but I don't talk to him much beyond those encounters. We're not close. I'm holding on to too many old memories of him yelling at us, drunk off his ass and pissed at the world.

No thanks. I'm doing my best to make my life positive. I don't need his negativity to bring me down.

"You all right?" Knox asks, once I've pulled into our assigned spot in the apartment parking lot. "You seem…preoccupied."

"Just got a lot on my mind." Which is the damn truth. I feel like I'm going to cave under the pressure at any moment. From school. Football. A hot girl I shouldn't fantasize about.

I need to let loose. I need to get out and forget about my troubles, even for a few hours. "Want to go to Logan's tonight?"

"Nah." He makes a face. "Still not over what happened last time I went."

When he saw that one girl and she sat on his lap after he tried to snag the same chair she wanted. I think he's got a thing for her. The girl who works at the bookstore or whatever. She's cute. Not necessarily my type, though I try to rile him up by acting like I'm interested.

Sometimes I'm a prick, but it's all in fun. Everyone on the team loves to give each other shit.

"Your loss," I tell him, envisioning a cold, crisp bottle of beer waiting for me at the bar. Hopefully a cute little blonde will be there too, one who doesn't have green eyes or the last name Maguire.

That would be the best scenario. Doesn't matter how much I'm interested in her, I can't have her. Blair Maguire may as well have a sign across her face that says...

Hands off.

3

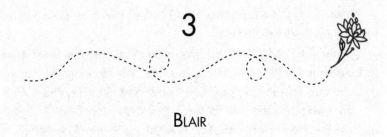

BLAIR

"Girls, we are so going to the bar! Logan's, watch out, here we come!" Rita starts clapping, her red nails flashing every time her hands fly through the air.

Cheyenne yells out an extra loud whoop, making me jump. "Yes, girl, YES. I am so sick of sitting in the library studying every night."

Please. They don't sit in the library every night. Every time I'm in there, I never see them, but the building is large and multi-leveled, so maybe they are?

Huh. Doubtful.

"Let's go find some men tonight," Cheyenne finishes with a big grin.

"Stat!" Rita adds because she's been on a *Grey's Anatomy* kick and likes to talk as if she works at a hospital every chance she gets.

I watch them with trepidation in my chest, wondering how I can get out of this. Don't get me wrong, I like Rita and Cheyenne, but they are so high energy while I'm…

Not.

I leave that sort of behavior to my sister Ruby. She's full of it. Loud and obvious and wanting all the attention, all the time. She would adore Rita and Cheyenne. They'd become fast friends. Maybe I should call her.

"Blair!" I nearly jump out of my chair when Cheyenne screams in my face. "You're going with us, right?"

My gaze goes to Cheyenne, then to Rita, and back to Cheyenne. I can tell from the looks on their faces, they won't take no for an answer.

But I gotta try anyway.

"I don't know..." I let my voice trail off, grimacing slightly. "I have a test tomorrow."

"Oh, please." Rita rolls her eyes, reaching for me. "You'll have to take a bazillion tests. That first one of the semester doesn't count."

I back away from her grabby red claws. "It definitely counts."

"Come on, Blair. Please?" Cheyenne puts her hands together like she's begging. Praying. With those big blue eyes and the subtle lash extensions that she's currently batting at me, she's hard to resist. "It'll be so much fun."

"Plus, maybe you can introduce us to your brother's teammates." Rita and Cheyenne share a look. "They're always at Logan's."

My heart sinks. They're using me to get closer to the guys. Not because they want to hang out with me and get to know me better.

Ouch.

"I don't really talk to them," I start, but Rita cuts me off.

"Please. Girl, you talk to them all the time. Knox Maguire is your *brother*. We want the connection. I've been dying to meet that dude since freshman year, but he doesn't pay any attention to me."

"Maybe if you let him feel you up in a bathroom at a frat party he might notice you," Cheyenne jokes, making me wince.

I don't want to think about my brother feeling anyone up in any sort of bathroom, eww.

"God, Chey! I let one frat boy feel me up in his bathroom and I never hear the end of it!" Rita goes stomping off, leaving Cheyenne and me alone in our tiny living room.

Cheyenne shrugs, her eyes a little wild. "I didn't mean to make her mad."

Before I can tell her not to worry about it, Cheyenne is bolting down the hallway, banging on Rita's closed bedroom door. "Come on, Rita! Let me in! I was just kidding!"

I scoot past her and continue down the hall, locking myself in my room and collapsing on my double bed with a loud sigh. Thank God I have my own bedroom, so I can lock myself away from the chaos that is my roommates.

They love each other fiercely, but they're like sisters, which means they fight fiercely too. And witnessing their chaotic relationship makes me miss my sister.

Grabbing my phone, I FaceTime Ruby. She picks up on the second ring, though her face doesn't appear. I can tell she's in her dorm room. I see movement in the background and I assume it's her roommate, Becca.

"What are you doing?" I ask, frowning when I hear something crash.

Ruby's head pops up, a big smile on her face. My sister is gorgeous. Her sparkling personality makes her even more appealing. Guys have been chasing her since she was twelve.

Twelve.

She's never interested in any of them. Not really. She's dated guys, here and there, but it never turns into anything, which always makes our dad happy. He thinks we're all too young to settle down—well, us girls at least.

Doesn't matter that he got with Mom when she was only eighteen and they're still blissfully happy, but whatever.

"Sorry, I just dropped my pencil box and it spilled everywhere," Ruby says.

Ruby likes to draw. She's always sketching something, though she insists it's just a hobby and she can't make a business out of it. I beg to differ, but she doesn't listen to me ever. I'm just her big sister, always trying to tell her what to do, according to her.

"How's it going?" I smile at her, watching as she settles into her desk chair, brushing the wild blonde strands away from her face.

"Good! Busy." She glances over her shoulder, waving at her roommate before she turns to face the camera once more. "I hate it here."

I frown. "What do you mean?"

"I'm bored. Campus life is dead. I thought it would have more of a nightlife but nope. The sidewalks roll up at nine and there's nothing going on, ever. Plus," she leans her head closer to her phone, "I don't like my roommate."

"Ruby!" I press my lips together, hating how loud I just was. I'm reminding myself of my roommates. "Isn't she right there?"

"She already left. And it doesn't really matter. I don't think she likes me either." Ruby leans back, exhaling loudly. "I didn't think it would feel so good, confessing that. It's like a weight just lifted off my shoulders."

I shake my head. "Is it really that bad there?"

"Worse than you can imagine. At least for me. You know how I am. But enough about me. I always make it about me."

This is *not* a lie. Ruby used to be one of the most self-centered people I knew, though that might have something to do with the fact that she's my little sister and was always in my business, in my stuff, in my face, all the damn time when we were younger. But at her core, she cares about others. Her circle is small, just like mine. Just like Knox's.

I prefer a smaller group of friends. People I adore and trust. People who don't care that once upon a time, our dad was famous. My brother and sister feel the same way.

"What are you up to? How's school? How are your roommates? Met any cute guys yet?" Ruby asks.

"Nothing much, school is going well, my roommates are okay, and no, I haven't met any cute guys yet." Cam doesn't count. I've known him for a while, so I can't put him in the 'just met' category.

"Why aren't you hanging out with Knox and all his friends?"

I roll my eyes. "Because the majority of them are ridiculous. And Knox doesn't want me hanging around them. He's afraid I might run off and hook up with one of them, as if I have no control over myself."

"Like Cam?"

Her question hangs heavy in the air, and as always, I regret that I ever told her I was interested in him.

"That was years ago. I'm over him," I say, but I sound unconvincing even to myself.

"Liar." Ruby laughs when I give her the finger. "It's okay that you still have a crush on him, Blair."

"Not when he doesn't notice me." I think about what he said earlier, and what I told him. I then spill my guts to my little sister, giving her an entire replay of the encounter that I had with Cam at the library.

"So, he actually said he's thought about having sex with you?" Ruby sounds scandalized.

"And then I basically admitted the same thing." I pause, all my insecurities rushing through me. "Was that a mistake?"

"No, not at all. I'm proud of you. How long have you been lusting after this guy again? And you only just now put it out there?"

"Stop. It's not easy for me to say stuff like that." I'm embarrassed. I feel like a child with a crush on some unattainable teen idol or something. Which is fairly accurate when it comes to my relationship with Cam. He feels completely out of reach. He always has.

"I'm not trying to make you feel bad. I'm trying to lift you up. It's been a long time that you've felt this way about Camden Fields. I feel like you're finally making progress."

"Nothing happened, Ruby. You're making a big deal out of nothing."

"We all have to start somewhere, and this is your start with Cam. When do you think you'll see him again?"

"I don't know." I think about the roomies going to Logan's. "There's a chance I could run into him tonight if I go out with the girls."

"For all you know, you might still be on his mind. Right now is the perfect time to go out and hopefully run into him."

"I feel like Rita and Cheyenne only want to drag me along with them because of my connection to Knox." And I don't like feeling used. It's not fun. Not at all.

"So? Use that to your advantage to get closer to Cam," Ruby points out.

"Right, only for Knox to ruin it because he's so overprotective that he'll drive Cam away forever." I sound morose. I *am* morose. Our brother has this way of ruining everything when it comes to guys.

Poor Knox. I know he means well, but he's too much sometimes.

Okay fine, most of the time.

"Ugh, forget him. He can say whatever he wants, but ultimately, he doesn't control our lives, right? I say go for it. Let Cam know you're interested."

"But that's so…" Scary. Intimidating. Terrifying.

All the above.

"It's what you need to do," Ruby says firmly. "How else will Cam know you're interested, if you don't tell him?"

I wish I had even an ounce of Ruby's confidence.

"Maybe he isn't interested. Maybe he just said that for…whatever reason. I don't know what to think. But it's hard for me to put myself out there like that. I mean, he's the freaking college quarterback, and he's gorgeous. Everyone knows who he is. He could have whomever he wants, and I'm just—"

"You're Blair fucking Maguire, that's who you are. Have you taken a good look at yourself lately? You're smart, you're kind, you're gorgeous. Cam would be an idiot not to be interested in you."

We may have fought like cats and dogs when we were younger, but Ruby is the best hype woman ever. "I wish you were here right now."

"Me too. I'd make you talk to him tonight. I'd probably make you text him right now, if I was with you. In fact, you should totally do that."

"I don't even have his number," I mutter.

"One text to our brother and you'd have it."

"Along with a ton of questions I don't want to answer."

"True that." Ruby's smile is soft and encouraging. "Just go out with your wild roommates to that bar and see what happens. You might run into him."

"And then again, I probably won't. Or he'll be there surrounded by a ton of gorgeous girls and he won't even notice me."

"Please. How could he not notice you?"

After I get off the call with Ruby, I venture out of my bedroom to find Rita and Cheyenne in Rita's bedroom, Cheyenne lounging on the bed on her phone, while Rita searches through her closet. I stand in the open doorway, take a deep breath and announce, "I'll go out with you tonight."

Rita whirls around, a giant smile on her face. "You will? That's great!"

"But I have one condition."

"What is it?" Cheyenne asks.

"I'd love to introduce you to my brother." Not really. That sounds like torture. But I have to say this. "But I can't guarantee it's going to happen. Or that he'll even be there."

"He goes to Logan's a lot," Rita says with complete confidence. "And hey, I get it if you can't help us meet Knox. He's a popular guy."

"Right." Was that an insult? "Let's just go to Logan's and have fun, and if we run into Knox and his friends, well, lucky us, right?"

"Lucky us!" Rita does a little shimmy, waving her hands above her head. "We need to pre-party first. I refuse to spend too much money on alcohol."

"Perfect. I'll go make us some shots." Cheyenne is off the bed and out of the room in seconds.

"Hey, Blair," Rita calls when I'm about to turn and head back to my bedroom.

I glance over my shoulder. "Yeah?"

"Thanks. I know sometimes we can be...a lot. And you probably think we're just using you for your connection to the football team, but I swear we're not. We like you." Rita smiles and I smile in return. "You're a true homie though, going out with us tonight."

"Thanks for including me," I tell her before I go to my bedroom, shutting the door behind me and leaning against it.

I want to believe Rita, but there's a tiny part of me that makes me think she is just using me to get closer to Knox. It's happened before. Actually, it used to happen all the time when we were in high school. That's the main reason I like keeping my friend circle small.

Hopefully, my instincts are wrong.

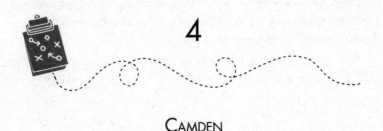

4

CAMDEN

I should've never gone to Logan's.

I'm here with Derek and a bunch of other guys from the team, including Ace, my backup quarterback. The kid is amazing. Fast. Not afraid to run the ball if he can't find anyone to throw it to. He's taller than me, wider than me, and charismatic as shit. I refuse to let this kid make me feel less than, but it's tough. The one thing to my advantage?

I'm on top of my game and set to play the best season of my football career.

Ace will get his shot—after me. He's a sophomore and set to take over my position next season. He's currently chomping at the bit to take my place right now, but the fucker needs to learn his place. Luckily, my teammates feel the same way, and we've been giving him endless shit all night.

Oh, and I'm well on my way to being buzzed. Drinking my third beer and not in the mood to stop. Girls come around the table every few minutes, all of them overly flirtatious and dressed to kill. As in, showing off all of their physical assets in the hopes of enticing us.

Not cappin' on them, just stating facts.

We've got groupies, and most of the time, I'm interested. In fact, ninety-nine percent of the time I'd already have my sights set on one and I'd currently be trying to figure out a way to get her to leave with me. A hookup in the back seat of the Challenger happens more often than not, or I go back to her place. It's a rare occasion that I bring her back to my apartment. I don't like doing that.

They don't deserve to see my inner sanctum. Worse, they get kind of weird and start having expectations. Like maybe they could move in.

What the actual fuck?

For real, I had that happen once, which Knox thought was hilarious. The fucker. He doesn't really bring girls back to our apartment either.

The groupies tonight though? They're not interested in me—they're all swarming Ace. It doesn't matter that he's not twenty-one yet and currently drinking copious amounts of beer, thanks to the fake ID he has on him that says he's from Louisiana. He doesn't even have an accent.

The asshole is from Washington state for God's sake.

The groupies aren't bothered by the fact that he's only twenty either. The girls are digging him, and I just don't get it. I guess he's decent-looking. Doesn't seem to say much to them, just grin like an idiot, but they're still fawning all over him. The rest of us are giving him grief and he takes it all good-naturedly, which is even more annoying. I play along and steadily sip from my beer, my mood shifting. Darkening the longer the night goes on. I hate being a jealous fuck but...

I'm a jealous fuck.

Until I see *her.*

The moment I lay eyes on Blair Maguire, every hair on my body feels like it's standing on end, completely aware of her presence. My heart rate kicks up and there's a sense of relief, knowing that she's here.

Within reach.

Not sure when she slipped into Logan's, but there she is, as beautiful as I've ever seen her. Her blonde hair cascades down her back in soft waves, and she can't stop smiling and laughing at whatever the other two girls she's with are doing and saying. She's currently wearing baggy jeans—the girls rarely wear skinny jeans anymore, which I always appreciated because I'm an ass man—and a cropped black T-shirt that shows off the flat expanse of her stomach and emphasizes the generous curve of her tits.

I scrub my hand over my face, like maybe my vision is blurry, and it'll change, but nope. There she is. Fucking gorgeous and oblivious to my existence.

All thoughts of the rules I made for myself in regards to Blair Maguire fly right out the window at seeing her. I want to go talk to her.

Touch her.

Shit.

"What's your problem?" Derek slaps my chest, and I glare at him, wishing he'd leave me the hell alone. "What, are you jealous of Ace getting all the ladies' attention?"

"Of course not," I mutter.

"Oh. Because I am. That little fucker doesn't deserve it." Only Derek would call the six-foot-five, two-hundred-and-ten-pound backup quarterback little. That's because Derek is bigger than Ace. "With that pretty boy face and the *awe shucks* attitude."

"He's fine." I wave a dismissive hand.

"He thinks he's the shit."

"He *is* the shit." I don't bother denying it. What's the point?

"You're better."

"For now. Once I'm gone, he's still got two years to go, and he's already impressive." I hate feeling subpar, but I'm wallowing in it tonight, something I rarely do. But shit, when you've got a constant reminder that you're on the way out and your replacement is dying for you to leave?

It's hard not to focus on that.

"While you'll be in the NFL, number one in the league and

winning championships," Derek says with way more confidence than I'm feeling.

"Sounds like a dream, bud." I grab my bottle and bring it to my lips, tipping my head back and taking a swallow, my gaze never straying from Blair.

She glances over at me, our gazes locking, and I don't look away. Neither does she.

It's like I can't. We can't.

I set the bottle on the table in front of me as a slow smile curves her lips, and we're still staring at each other. I feel that smile all the way down to my balls. I smile in return and she looks away, like she's embarrassed or some shit.

Come on. I've known her for years. She needs to get over it and come talk to me.

"Oh fuck, there's Maguire's sister." The panic in Derek's voice makes me chuckle.

"So?"

"I don't even want to be near her. Knox will kill us." Derek ducks his head as if he's in hiding.

"No, he won't," I drawl. I stare blatantly at Blair, wishing she'd look in my direction again. Her friends keep glancing over at our table and I can't help but wonder if they're talking about us.

Is Blair talking about me? In my fucking dreams. And who are those girls? Her friends? Roommates?

"Oh shit, I think she's headed over here right now." Derek sounds completely freaked out. "Who is she with? The dark-haired girl with the long red nails is hot."

Jesus. Derek bangs anything that walks, I swear.

I play it cool as Blair comes closer, but deep down, I'm agitated. Nervous. The girl makes me feel all sweaty-palmed and ready to make a fool of myself. And when she finally stops right next to me, a friendly smile on her face, her perfume flooding my senses and tempting me to bury my face in her neck so I can inhale her, I brace myself.

"Hey, Cam." Her sweet voice wraps around me, leaving me dizzy, and I tell myself it's just because I drank too much beer.

But I know the truth. It's the girl.

It's always been the girl.

"Blair." I nod, trying to maintain my calm façade. "How are you?"

"Great. Haven't seen you in a while." She's teasing. Her cheeks are flushed and her eyes are sparkling, and I'd guess she's had a few drinks already.

When the hell did she sneak in here anyway, and how did I miss it?

"Right. Only a couple of hours." I glance over at Derek, who's watching our interaction with a mixture of curiosity and fear in his eyes. "You know Derek, right?"

"I don't think so. Hi." She holds out her hand, leaning across me as she does, her tits brushing against my arm, my chest.

Fuck.

"Hey." Derek shakes her hand, releasing it quickly like she might bite. "Knox's sister, right?"

"Right."

"Speaking of Knox." The dark-haired girl with the red nails suddenly appears behind Blair. "Is he here tonight?"

"Afraid not," I say.

The disappointment on her face is clear, but it's also gone in an instant, her focus shifting to Derek. "Aw, that's too bad. I'm Rita, by the way."

"Derek."

"We had Intro to Communications together," Rita tells Derek, moving over, so she can stand right next to him and continue their conversation.

Blair glances over at the other girl standing just behind her, indicating she wants her to scoot closer. "This is my other roommate, Cheyenne."

"Cam. Nice to meet you." I shake the girl's hand, who's watching me with wide eyes, like she can't believe she's in my presence.

"Nice to meet you too," she squeaks like a mouse.

Oh boy.

"When did you get here?" I ask Blair.

"About an hour ago or so." Blair brings the glass, that I just notice she's clutching, to her lips, sipping from the skinny black straw. "It's packed tonight."

"It's crowded every night," I say, glancing around the busy bar. Everyone comes to Logan's. They have the best drink specials and they're not too strict when it comes to the fake-ID situation. This is why Ace is having the time of his life tonight.

Cheyenne touches Blair's shoulder. "I'll be right back."

We both watch her go, silent for a moment, Blair continuously sipping from her straw, which is giving me all sorts of thoughts I shouldn't be thinking. Like how good her lips would look wrapped around something...

Thicker. And attached to my body.

Shit. I need to say something. Maybe even make a move, but Knox's face is suddenly looming in my mind, reminding me of what he'll do to me if he finds out I was talking to his sister while thinking all these pervy thoughts, which keeps me silent.

"I was hoping I'd run into you here," Blair finally says, shocking me.

"You were?"

She nods, her cheeks pinker than normal. "Yeah."

"Why?"

She blinks, seeming at a loss until she says, "I forgot to tell you earlier when I ran into you at the library."

"You forgot to tell me what?"

"I had a dream last night and you were in it." She says the words all at once, so they sort of run into each other, and it takes me an extra couple of seconds for my brain to compute.

"Oh yeah?"

"Yeah." Her voice is a whispered rasp. "Yep. Yes."

"Well, what happened?" I'm curious. Now this girl is dreaming about me?

That's promising.

"What do you mean?"

"What happened in your dream? What did we do?" I pause, giving in to my curiosity. "Did I do something to you?"

I can think of about a bazillion things I'd like to do to her in my dreams. And my reality.

"Oh…" her voice fades, and she swallows hard. "You were, uh, chasing me across a football field."

"No shit?" I don't know if I believe her. Maybe she's just saying this to make conversation.

"Weird right?" She laughs nervously. "I don't know why you were in my dream."

If she wasn't Knox's sister, I would take the opportunity to explain that I'm in her thoughts because she's into me, but I keep those observations to myself simply because of her last name.

But then I go ahead and do it anyway.

"Can't stop thinking about me, huh?" I raise my brows, pissed at myself for even bringing it up.

I shouldn't carry on this conversation with Blair, but it's like I can't help myself.

"Maybe." She scoots closer, so she can set her glass on the table in front of me, her shoulder brushing mine, and it's like an electric jolt to my system, making me aware of how close she is. How warm she is and how sweet she smells. Fuck, what perfume is she wearing? "I've known you a long time, Cam."

"A few years," I agree with a nod, grabbing my beer bottle and taking a giant swig. I hold the bottle in front of me like a shield of armor.

"And we've never really had any…deep conversations."

"I don't know you that well. You went to another school."

"Right. And you're busy with football."

"Extremely."

"Plus, you're my brother's best friend."

"Damn straight." I bring the bottle to my lips once again.

"Which is probably preventing you from making any type of move on me, right?"

I nearly spit out the beer currently in my mouth, instead swallowing it down with extreme difficulty. "Blair..."

"Or maybe you're not interested. I get it. I'm just me while you're you and you can have any woman you could ever want. Take your pick." She laughs, but it sounds nervous, and she's waving her hand around the room, indicating all the other options I supposedly have. Like I'd rather be with anyone else than her.

The woman is obviously mistaken.

"Blair."

Those big green eyes meet mine once more, blinking at me in seeming confusion. "You don't have to let me down easy. I've got liquid courage flowing through me and I had to say something."

"To me."

"Yes."

"That you're into me?"

She blinks again, but doesn't say a word.

"Or you could be into me?" I amend.

She shrugs one shoulder.

"Don't you think that's a terrible idea?"

"Why would you say that?"

"Your brother will kick my ass if I disrespect you."

Blair shifts closer, her sweet floral scent getting stronger as she tilts her head toward mine, her mouth right at my ear. "Maybe I want you to disrespect me."

5

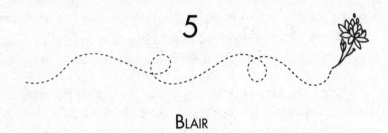

Blair

I cannot believe I just said that to him.

Slowly—reluctantly—I pull away from Camden, a lump the size of a boulder stuck in my throat. I watch him, holding my breath, terrified he'll push me away or worse…

Laugh in my face.

He does neither of those things, thank God.

"I don't think it matters what you want, or what I want," he finally says, his deep voice so low I have to scoot even closer to hear him. "Knox will rip my heart out of my chest if I lay a single hand on you."

The blood is roaring in my ears and I swallow past the disappointment coating my throat. "No, he won't."

His smile is small. Almost sad. "Yes, he will. And you know it."

An irritated noise leaves me and I take a step back, needing the space. "That's so annoying."

"What, me telling you no? Or your brother being the problem?"

"Both. If you ask me, it sounds like you're just making excuses." I reach across him to grab my glass and drain the last of my drink with a furious sip from my straw—I am so ridiculous—before leaning over Cam to set my glass back on the table. His body is like a solid wall of heat and muscle. Touching him in even the most innocent of ways sets off a fiery path of tingles all over my skin.

Which makes me even more frustrated.

"You know how he is." I refuse to look at him, averting my gaze. Taking in everyone else around me, but the guy sitting too close. The guy who I've had a massive crush on for months. No, *years*, and who just let me down easy. "Blair. Look at me."

I hate hearing him say my name because it sounds so good coming from his lips. I barely glance in his direction, noting the pain in his expression. Like he's hurting too.

Please. He can't be hurting that badly.

"You're afraid of my brother," I retort.

"I'm afraid of myself," he returns, his response making me frown. "I'm a shithead. I treat girls like garbage."

"I don't believe that." I make a dismissive noise. "And you've never treated me like garbage."

"You're different. I know you. You're my best friend's sister." He pauses. "And that's the reason why we can't do this. I don't do relationships, especially with a girl who's related to someone I'm close to."

I roll my eyes. "Why do all men assume that's what we're looking for?" When he sends me a questioning look, I explain further, "Relationships."

"Because you're the type of girl who deserves nothing but the best. A casual hookup with some asshole will only leave you feeling...empty."

Cam is right, damn him.

An irritated noise leaves me. "Woman."

He frowns. "What?"

"I'm not a girl, I'm a woman. I'm twenty-one. I don't think you can call me a girl anymore."

"Trust me, you're definitely a woman in my eyes." The knowing look on his face makes me want to smack him. Or kiss him.

Take your pick.

"Well." I cross my arms. "You got the 'some asshole' part right."

He grins. Actually grins. Like I amuse him. "You're kind of cute when you're angry."

"Do not say nice things to me right now." I thrust my finger in his face and he grabs it, sending an electric current down my arm, but he immediately lets me go, like his body just had the same reaction. "I can't believe I tried to hit on you and you turned me down."

"Would you believe me if I said it was painful to do that?" He raises his brows.

"No," is my immediate response.

"It was," he reaffirms. "You're beautiful. You're smart. You're brave. And I'm a dickhead."

"It's getting old, Cam, hearing you call yourself names. Trying to imply that you're not good enough for me."

"I'm not. That's why you're better off." He opens his arms to me. "Now come here."

I go to him as if in a trance, not about to turn down a shot at being hugged by the one and only Camden Fields. I let him pull me into his embrace, sliding my arms around his solid torso, turning my head so my face is pressed into his neck. He wraps his arms around me, his fingers teasing my bare sides, just above my hips, and lord help me, I might pass out just from that singular touch.

"I had to get one more hug out of you before you hate me forever," he murmurs close to my ear, his moving lips brushing against my sensitive flesh. "I'm a fucking idiot."

"Yeah, you are." I pull out of his arms, immediately missing the solid weight of him pressed against me. "You don't know what you're missing."

"That's the problem," he murmurs, his gaze skimming over me slowly, lingering on the places where I tingle the most. "I'm pretty sure I know exactly what I'm missing."

We stare at each other for a moment longer until I can't take it anymore.

I have to get away from him. As Rita would say, stat.

With an annoyed huff, I turn and walk away, holding my head high, my posture perfect. Trying my best to remain composed versus completely falling apart like I really want to do. I take one step in front of the other, moving through the crowd, making my way toward the bathroom, and once I'm in there, I crumple, leaning against the wall and covering my face with my hands.

Taking a deep breath, I drop my hands and scream, startling every single woman that's in the bathroom with me, and there are a few. A couple of them scream along with me. Some of them even start laughing.

Only one approaches me, a knowing look in her gaze when she reaches out and rests her hand on my arm.

"Was it a man?" she asks.

"Isn't it always?" I respond.

She pulls me into a hug while everyone claps around us and I can't help it.

I start to cry.

• • •

Twenty minutes later and I'm back out in the bar, like nothing ever happened between Cam and me. I've got my shit together. No evidence of tears remains on my face and I'm completely composed.

Well, composed might not be the right word to describe my current mood. I'm another two drinks in and complaining about life in general with Cheyenne, who nods in agreement with everything I say and keeps downing screwdrivers with the logic that it's the only way she's going to get screwed tonight.

I laugh every time she brings it up.

We've lost Rita to a group of hockey players, who are on the other side of the bar. She flirted with Derek for a few minutes, but she said he wasn't into her, so she bailed on him, coming over to fill us in before she found some hot hockey players and ditched us completely.

"I hate men," I announce, slamming back a shot of whiskey before I practically drop the glass on the table.

"You're talking about one man in particular, right?" Cheyenne sips from her shot, making a face as she quickly sets it on the table next to mine.

"No," I say way too quickly, shaking my head. I immediately stop that because my brain feels like it's scrambling. "They're all terrible."

"Not a bad assessment," Cheyenne gives me. I grab my other drink and sip from it. "But I'm pretty certain you're referring to Camden Fields."

I spit out what I just slurped up back into my glass, grossing myself out. "Not at all. There's nothing between us."

"If you say so."

The doubt in her voice is obvious. She doesn't believe me.

I don't believe me.

"Seriously. We're just—friends." I can't even call us that because if I can't have him, I don't want to be anywhere near him. It's just too hard on my heart and all of the other lustful parts of my body. Denying myself him when he's right there in front of me sounds like a special type of torture.

But the asshole is denying me as well so…

"Friends, right. Keep telling yourself that."

The tone of her voice has me on edge. "What do you mean?"

"You two were full of tension when you were talking earlier. Like, the way he looked at you. The things he said. When he touched you." Cheyenne fans her hand in front of her face. "Hot."

"Not hot. Cold. Totally cold." I'm in complete denial. "He's not interested in me like that."

"Oh, he is," Cheyenne argues. "But I get it. You need to keep your distance from each other or whatever."

"Right," I say weakly, wondering why we're keeping our distance from each other.

Well, I know why. Cam gave me an entire list as to why.

Knox is my brother.

Knox is his roommate.

So that equals a conflict of interest in his eyes.

Cam doesn't do relationships.

I have relationship written all over me in invisible letters.

While we both know he'd mostly likely hurt me and eventually break my heart.

How does he know I only do relationships? The last time I was in a relationship, I was a freshman in college, and it lasted for approximately six months with a dude named Randy.

We had Intro to Statistics together and that class was super difficult, which allowed us to bond together while we whined about how tough the subject was. We started studying together, spending a couple of hours in a local coffee shop pouring over our textbooks and trying to figure out what we were doing. Then we started talking. Talking led to going out to dinner, to going to the movies, to going back to his house and messing around.

I broke it off after the class was over. I realized I didn't particularly care for his giant ego and vaguely pretentious ways.

Before Randy, there was my high school boyfriend, Travis Strickland. Football player. Good looking and popular. My father *loved* him. They would talk football together, ad nauseam, every time he came over, and I remember being so bored. But also, I was grateful Knox wasn't around because he would've completely taken over the conversation and my dad was bad enough.

Oh, Knox also would've threatened poor Travis and told him to watch it or he'd have to kill him, which is what has Cam currently running.

Travis was my first love, my first heartbreak, the first boy I ever had sex with, and while it was all right, it wasn't much to brag about. Randy was better in bed but not by a whole lot. Neither one of them necessarily rocked my world, so to speak.

I definitely never felt all aflutter and ready to sink to my knees in front of a guy like I do around Cam. He gives me a look and I'm breathless. He touches me in the most impersonal way and I think I might keel over. And when he hugs me, like he did approximately an hour ago?

Forget it. I'm surprised I'm still functioning.

The hairs on the back of my neck start to tingle and I lift my head, glancing around as inconspicuously as possible, my gaze landing on Cam, who's still sitting at the same table, his dark gaze on me.

I don't look away. It's as if I can't. I stand up straighter, thrusting my chest out, giving him a good look at what he's missing, and then with a huff, I push away from the table, marching directly toward him.

The panic on his face is almost amusing. I can see it flare in his gaze and he looks down at the table, like he can't even face me.

At the last second, I dodge right, returning to the bathroom, his gaze trailing after me. I can literally feel it, hot and intense, and I look over my shoulder, making sure he's still watching before I duck into the single unisex bathroom.

Leaving the door unlocked.

My heart racing, I go to the sink and wash my shaking hands, hopeful that I didn't misread the situation. If he sneaks into the bathroom with me, then I have a chance, but if he doesn't...

I'll stop. I won't bother him again. I'll let this be and move on.

Seconds turn into minutes and my chest begins to ache. He's not coming. I was wrong. He told me how he felt and he one hundred percent meant—

The door swings open and Cam barges his way in, locking the door behind him. He stops short when he finds me standing in the middle of the room, a crumpled paper towel still clutched in my hand.

I quickly toss it into the wastebasket, gasping when Cam grabs a hold of me and takes me with him, backing me up into the wall. My butt hits it first and he braces his hands on either side of the wall, caging me in. Trapping me.

"You're trying to drive me out of my fuckin' mind, aren't you?"

"No, I'm no—" I can barely get the full word out when he's dipping his head, skimming his nose along the side of my face. A gasp leaves me and I close my eyes, overwhelmed by his nearness. The way he's—smelling me.

It's almost primal, his behavior. I swear I can feel his restraint. How he's holding himself back from unleashing all over me and I open my eyes to find him staring straight into them, anger filling his gaze.

"You are," he says accusingly. "And it's working, Blair."

Everything inside me goes loose and shaky at the way he says my name. He's so close. Kissing close. I stare at his lips, how full the lower one is. It's plump and perfect and I'm tempted to bite it.

I don't though. I don't have the nerve. I'm not as brave as he thinks.

"It wouldn't bother you if you didn't care." Giving in, I reach out, drifting my fingers down the front of his chest, his heat seeping through the fabric of his T-shirt. He's so hard. I've seen him without his shirt on, but it's been a while, and I've certainly never touched his naked chest.

I want to. Badly.

"You think I don't care?"

"You basically said that to me earlier." I lift my gaze to his, not daring to look away.

"I never said I didn't care. I said I *couldn't*. Big difference." He leans in again, his mouth at my ear, his hot breath blowing across my skin and making me shiver. "I care too fucking much. That's my problem. I'm pretty sure you're going to be the death of me."

We don't move, our heavy breaths mingling, my heart beating so loud, I'm positive he can hear it. I can't believe this is happening. I want him to kiss me. I want his hands all over me and if he said he wanted to fuck me in this not-so-sterile bathroom, I'd say yes.

I would. I wouldn't even hesitate.

"Are you going to stay away from me?" he finally asks.

I slowly shake my head. "No."

A frustrated breath leaves him, and he slowly backs away, almost reluctantly. "That's too bad. I don't know if I can be responsible for what happens if you keep coming around."

I smile at him, savoring the power currently sweeping over me. "Guess we'll have to wait and see."

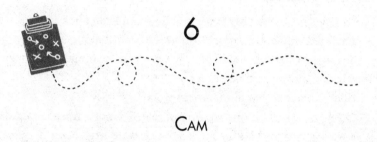

6

CAM

"Hey, what are you doing right now?" Knox asks me when we're in the locker room, getting ready to leave after practice.

"Uh, going home with you? You are my ride, after all," I remind him.

"Right. Well, what if I told you I could get us a home-cooked dinner tonight?" Knox grabs his duffel and slams the locker door with a loud clang.

"I'd say I'm down. Who's making it?" If this is his new girlie or whatever she is to him, then she's a smart woman because there is no quicker way to Knox's—and my—heart than our stomachs. We love to eat.

And we get real sick of the fast-food places around here. We try to make our own meals, but sometimes, fine, most of the time, that's a complete pain in the ass.

"My sister. Weirdest thing. Blair texted me earlier and said she missed cooking, so I, of course, suggested she make us something and she was like, 'I'll have your dinner ready by the time you come home from practice.'" Knox shakes his head, smiling. "Just like my mom used to do."

Fucking Blair. She's a sneaky one. "What is she making?"

"Homemade chicken tenders, french fries and a salad." Knox slings his duffel across his shoulder, rubbing his hands together. "My mom's special recipe she used to make us all the time when we were little. You're gonna love it."

"Sounds delicious." My voice is hollow and I can't lie.

I'm filled with anticipation. I get to see Blair tonight.

She knew what this would do. She's not making dinner for Knox. I may sound like an asshole but...

Blair is making that dinner for me.

"Practice was good this afternoon, yeah?" Knox's voice is casual as we walk out to the parking lot, heading toward his truck.

"It was great," I reassure him, knowing exactly why he's asking. "Your knee seems better."

"It is. I've been going easy on it and I managed to go to a PT session this morning. It seems to help." Knox stares off in the distance, his expression thoughtful. "I can't fuck this knee up, man. I need to be careful."

"You've got this," I say, casual as shit. I'm not worried about Knox. He's going to have a stellar season and then when it's over, he'll go on to the NFL draft, get picked for a team and his life will be perfect.

"I still gotta be careful," he says, hitting the keyless remote and unlocking his truck. "You're looking good out there."

"Better than Ace?" Saying his name leaves a bitter taste in my mouth. I shouldn't let that kid bother me but...

He bothers me.

"What the hell, man? Yes, of fucking course, you're better than Ace. He's good, but he's no Camden motherfuckin' Fields." Knox grins as he opens the driver's side door.

We climb into the truck and head back to our apartment, nerves making my knee bounce up and down. I try talking about football. Hell, Knox is *still* talking about football, but I'm just giving him one-word answers while I stare out the passenger-side window.

I can't stop thinking about Blair.

How sweet she smells. How fucking tempting she is. How I followed her into the bathroom at Logan's like a trained dog a couple of nights ago, giving her exactly what she wanted.

The satisfaction of knowing that she still holds some sort of power over me.

I could've kissed her. I could've mauled her and she would've probably loved every second of it. I would've loved it too, but how do I face her after doing that?

How do I face the very guy sitting in the truck with me?

Yeah, I can't. And that's why I backed away. Why I left her in that bathroom and strode out into the bar and told Derek I was leaving. I might've been buzzed before that encounter, but after? Stone-cold sober. I drove home as if I hadn't had a drop to drink, took a shower, jerked off to thoughts of me fucking Blair against that cold tile bathroom wall and fell asleep, only to have fucking dreams about her.

Just like she said she had dreams about me.

The girl—excuse me, *woman*—is driving me out of my fucking mind. And now I have to face her in a few minutes. She'll probably be wearing a smirk, her eyes dancing with mischief, and while I know I'll enjoy her home-cooked meal, it's also going to be tough, trying to act like she doesn't affect me, while sitting there with her overprotective brother.

Fuck my life.

We're back at the complex in record time and the moment we walk into our apartment, the scent of something cooking that isn't ramen or microwavable bullshit hits my nose, making my mouth water.

"Smells good, sis," Knox calls as he heads to his bedroom to get rid of his stuff.

I drop my bag on the couch and make my way to the kitchen to get seeing Blair over with, stopping short at the vision that greets me.

Blair bent over and peering into the oven, her ass in perfect alignment for me to stare at. She has on denim shorts that show off her long, tanned legs and a white T-shirt, and oh Jesus, she's got a freaking apron on, the cloth belt sitting in a neat little bow right at the base of her spine.

I scrub the back of my head, unsure how to proceed.

She stands up straight, closing the oven door partway before she bumps her hip into it, making it slam shut as she settles the glass baking dish on top of the stove. She's completely oblivious to me watching her, and once she's no longer handling anything hot that could burn her, I clear my throat to announce my presence.

"Oh." She turns to face me, and yep, there's the smirk. "Hey."

"A home-cooked meal, huh?" I raise a brow, crossing my arms as I lean my shoulder against the wall.

"I thought you boys would like to eat something other than takeout or whatever else you two consume." She turns away from me, poking at whatever is in the baking dish, and I glance over my shoulder, making sure Knox is nowhere around before I quickly walk right up behind her.

"Boys?" I shift closer, looming over her shoulder, my front brushing her back, and she goes completely still. "Don't you mean men?"

She stares straight ahead for a beat, then turns her head to meet my gaze. I'm standing way too close to her, basically invading her personal space, but I don't give a shit. I like being this close to her.

Way too much.

"Sorry," she murmurs. "I meant to say men."

"That's more like it." I check out what's in the dish. A bunch of homemade, lightly breaded chicken strips that are sizzling, they're so hot. "That looks delicious."

I could be talking about the food. I could be talking about her.

Take your pick.

"Dinner ready yet?"

Knox's booming voice comes from behind us and I smoothly edge away from her, turning to find him striding into the kitchen with a smile on his face. "Smells good, Blair."

"It's almost done," she says, bustling around the kitchen. I step out of her way, ignoring the look she sends me as I mosey out of the kitchen and settle onto a barstool at the counter, covertly watching her while I pretend to mess around on my phone.

She makes small talk with Knox, catching up on family drama. Why their mom and dad are acting mysterious lately and how they both think their parents are up to something. Blair asks him about the girl at the bookstore and Knox immediately clams up, which has Blair sending me a knowing look. I return it, enjoying the moment, feeling like I'm a part of a secret club, which is some stupid shit, but I can't help it.

There's something so comforting about hanging out with the Maguires. Even if I want to get Blair naked and under me and am denying myself the pleasure, I can still enjoy spending time with her.

It's torture, but I'll take what I can get.

"What's going on with Ruby?" Knox asks after Blair hands him a glass of water.

She gives me one too before she says, "Ruby isn't happy where she's at."

"What do you mean?"

"Um, she says she's not enjoying the college life there. Called it boring."

"She should come here then," Knox says, as if that's the most logical answer to Ruby's problem.

"I doubt very much she wants to come here."

"Why not? You and Ruby could get an apartment together next year. Or even next semester."

Blair returns her focus to the oven, pulling out a cookie sheet covered with french fries. My stomach growls when the smell hits me. "I already have roommates. And it's not like Ruby can drop everything and come here. She's just feeling lonely. Homesick."

"Do you ever feel lonely and homesick?" Knox asks his sister.

She keeps her back to us, grabbing a spatula and stirring the fries around on the pan as she salts them. "Sometimes."

I hate hearing that. It makes me want to go comfort her, which is some sappy shit.

"You know you can come over here anytime you want and we can hang out." Knox always the protective big brother.

Though I'm not sure how comfortable I would be with Blair hanging out over here all the time, just because she's lonely.

Talk about temptation.

"That's very sweet of you, but I swear it gets easier every day. Plus, it's always an interesting time, hanging out with my roommates." She laughs almost to herself, which gets Knox's attention. And mine.

"Why do you call it an interesting time?"

"Because Rita and Cheyenne are...interesting people."

"That sounds suspicious." Knox glances over at me. "What do you think?"

I throw up my hands in front of me in a defensive gesture. "I have no skin in this game."

"Oh, please. They're harmless. You met them, Cam," Blair reminds me. "Or did you forget?"

I didn't forget. I don't forget a single damn thing when it comes to Blair and what's going on in her life.

"I met them," I confirm.

Knox's brows draw together, his expression suddenly thunderous. "When the hell did you meet Blair's roommates?"

"At Logan's a couple nights ago."

Knox whips his head in Blair's direction. "Why were you at Logan's?"

"I went with my roommates. The ones that are interesting."

"I hate how you keep calling them that," Knox practically growls.

Blair's mischievous gaze meets mine. "It's the best way to describe them, don't you think, Cam?"

"Sure," I say with trepidation, keeping my gaze fixed on her beautiful face.

"Tell me you watched over her," Knox says to me. "And you made sure no one harassed my sister."

"No one harassed your sister," I automatically say.

Blair snorts.

Knox glares.

And me? I keep my composure, though I send her a look that says *watch it.*

Blair changes the subject and asks Knox about his class load, while she serves us our dinner. She delivers a plate to me first, which has Knox groaning.

"I'm starved."

"Oh my God, stop whining." She sets his plate in front of him and he immediately starts eating. "You need anything else before I sit down?"

Knox mumbles no. I shake my head, waiting for Blair to sit before I start eating. She grabs her plate and her water bottle and settles onto the stool next to mine, brushing against me with the movement.

Despite the delicious smelling food, the scent that hits me the hardest is her perfume. That sweet floral scent smells like she rolled in a field of wildflowers, which immediately has me thinking of Blair lying naked in a lush green meadow, her body covered in colorful petals.

I seriously need to get a grip.

The chicken tenders are melt-in-your-mouth good, and she even put together some homemade ranch dressing. The fries were frozen, but she cooked them perfectly and the salad has all my favorite things—avocado and red onion but no tomatoes. It's like she knew exactly what I like.

Huh. Does she? Has she paid that close attention to me? We don't spend that much time together, so I don't know how she'd know.

Knox inhales his meal in record time, leaning back and patting his flat stomach when he's finished. "That was fucking delicious."

Blair laughs. "As good as Mom's?"

"Definitely. Maybe even better. Don't tell her that though," Knox says, sounding vaguely panicked.

"What did you think, Cam?" Her pretty green eyes land on me, and I stare into them for a few seconds, getting lost. She has the prettiest eyes I've ever seen.

"Really good," I finally say, slipping off the barstool before I start gathering up the dirty dishes. "I'll clean up."

"Oh, you don't have to do that." She rests her hand on my forearm as if she's trying to stop me when I reach for her dish, and I send her a look, trying to ignore the way her touch burns my skin.

It's a pleasant burn. A *God damn, what would it feel like to have her hands all over my body* – kind of sensation.

I need to push that thought out of my head. We are not turning into anything. I don't care what she tries to do—like coming around here making me dinner. I can't succumb to her charms.

And she's charming as fuck, not gonna lie.

"I want to. It's the least I can do. You made us dinner, I'll clean up." Her hand falls away from my arm and I grab her plate, stacking it on top of the two I'm already holding.

"Oh. I should, like, wipe down the counters."

"Stay where you're at," Blair tells her brother. "I'll take care of it."

"Well, if you guys got this handled, then I think I'm going to take a shower." Knox stands, pushing his barstool in.

"Didn't you already take one after practice?" He did. I know he did.

"Yeah, I did, but it lasted for all of five minutes." His expression turns sheepish and I realize I don't want to know what's going to happen in that shower. He can go right on ahead and do whatever it is he needs to do.

"Go take your shower," Blair chirps. "We've got this."

I take the dishes to the sink and turn on the water, waiting while it gets hot. Blairs puts away stuff in the fridge and tosses a few things in the trashcan. I'm aware of her every movement, growing tense as she draws closer, and next thing I know, she's standing right next to me at the sink, grabbing a dry wash rag and dipping it under the water, leaning into me as she does.

She's pressed right up against my side, warm and soft, and fuck, her scent. I can't take it.

"I hope you enjoyed dinner," she says softly.

"It was good," I say as I open the dishwasher, scooting away from her. "Thank you for making it."

"Just trying to show off my culinary skills."

"I thought you were trying to keep us from eating too much junk food." I start rinsing off the dirty dishes with hot water, loading them up one by one.

"I was hoping I would dazzle you with my amazing cooking skills, but I guess you're immune."

She's teasing, but not, so I remain quiet as I finish loading the dishwasher, then grab a cleaning brush from the dish drain and start scrubbing the glass baking dish she cooked the chicken in.

Blair sighs, folding the damp washcloth before she starts wiping the counters clean. "See? Immune."

"Blair."

Now it's her turn to ignore me, and I keep scrubbing the dish, taking all my aggression out on it. I'm holding my breath when she draws closer yet again, doing my best not to inhale her delicious scent, but there's no fucking use.

"What perfume do you wear?" I ask, like the idiot I am.

She goes still, leaning against the counter as she watches me. I finally give in and reach over to shut off the water, turning so I'm facing her.

"Why do you care?" She sounds suspicious. Like she's on to me.

I shrug, desperate to play off my question. "I don't know. Thought I might buy some for my mom. Her birthday is coming up."

The very last person I want wearing the same perfume as Blair is my mom.

Blair's smile tells me she knows I'm full of it. "It's by Gucci."

Of course, it is.

She lifts her wrist to her nose, taking a deep inhale. "It's hard for me to smell it anymore, which is a shame because I love it. I am definitely the type that wears perfume for me and not for anyone else. Though if you think I smell good…"

Her voice drifts, sounding vaguely suggestive, and I tell myself to ignore the part of me that stirs.

"Uh huh." Gucci what, is what I want to ask her. She's being way too vague.

"It's in a turquoise bottle. Gucci Gorgeous." She frowns. "No wait. Gucci Flora Gorgeous. Jasmine."

"Gucci Flora Gorgeous Jasmine?" I repeat as a question. That's a mouthful.

She nods, approaching me with her wrist thrust out. Like she wants me to smell it. "Yes, that's it. And make sure you remember it's jasmine. There are other scents, but I have the jasmine one in the blue bottle."

I give in and gently grab her arm, bringing her wrist to my nose so I can take a deep whiff. I feel like a drug addict, who just took a big snort of cocaine. The moment the scent hits, I close my eyes, savoring it. She smells *so* fucking good.

"You like it?" she whispers.

My eyes pop open and I let go of her arm. "Yeah." My voice is scratchy and I clear my throat.

"For your mom, huh?" She absolutely knows I'm full of shit now. My reaction confirms it.

"Sure."

"Mmm hmm." She returns to the sink, turning on the water and running the rag beneath it a couple of times before she shuts the water back off. "Thank you for helping me."

"Thank you for dinner."

"I'm glad you enjoyed it. I'd offer to make you dinner again, but I get the feeling you'd turn me down."

"If you want to make Knox dinner and include me in it, I'm never going to turn you down."

"So, you'll turn *me* down but not my dinner offers?" She keeps her back to me, wiping at the same spot on the counter over and over, emanating frustration.

I'm just as frustrated and I let out a ragged exhale, running a hand through my hair when she turns to face me.

"You saw the way your brother just reacted over your 'interesting' roommates. Imagine if he found out we started hooking up without his knowledge?" I toss at her.

Blair frowns. "First off, I would make sure my brother doesn't find out that we're hooking up. It's none of his damn business, what I'm doing."

"It is if it involves you and his best friend."

"I won't tell him if you don't."

"I have to tell him." Doesn't she get it? "I live with him. I couldn't keep living that lie every day."

"Where's the lie in it? There is no lie. You just…don't say anything at all."

"It's not that easy."

"Right. And you're making it extra hard. God, Cam." She marches over to the sink, hip checking me, so I immediately shift out of her way. She turns on the water and drops the rag in the sink, then washes her hands. "Are you implying that you're scared of my brother? Is that your problem?"

"I'm not scared of Knox."

She laughs, turning off the water and drying her hands before she turns to face me. "Please. You're terrified of his reaction, which tells me that you're scared of him."

I crowd her, trapping her against the sink with my hands braced on either side, her back against the counter. "I'm not scared of Knox."

Blair tilts her head back, her glittering eyes meeting mine. "What is it then? Are you afraid of me?"

Yes, I want to tell her. *You terrify the shit out of me.*

Worse?

The way you make me feel is the most frightening thing of all.

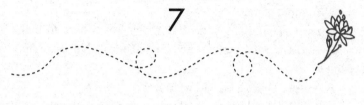

7

BLAIR

I am completely surrounded by Cam, his big body pressed against mine, his hands on either side of me gripping the counter's edge. He's as solid as steel, muscly and hot, and I swallow hard when I note the determined gleam in his eyes. I basically accused him of being scared of me, when I'm sure that's the last emotion he's feeling. How could I scare him? I'm not that important to him. Not at all.

He's more than proven that.

Though, what was with him asking me what perfume I wear? So he can get it for his *mom*? Give me a break. I don't believe that at all. But why does he care? Supposedly, we're just friends, if I can even call us that. Meaning it shouldn't matter what scent I wear. I don't affect him.

Cam still hasn't moved. He hasn't said a single word, so feeling brave, I reach out, resting my hand against the center of his chest. His heart thunders beneath my palm, his eyelids wavering when I touch him, and I realize something.

I *do* affect him. Just by his minimal reaction, I can tell.

Heady power courses through my veins, and I press my hand against his chest more firmly, absorbing his heat. His strength. He doesn't move. Doesn't so much as twitch. It's only when I clutch the fabric of his T-shirt in my fingers that he finally pushes away from me.

"We can't keep doing this," he says.

"Doing what?" Oh, don't I sound innocent and sweet?

"Blair." His voice is firm and full of annoyance, and he rests his hands on his hips, looking far more handsome than he has any right to be. "No more games."

"I'm not playing any games, Camden. I was here to make my brother and his roommate a homemade meal. No other motives behind it."

Okay, fine. That's a lie, but whatever.

I exit the kitchen, satisfaction curling through me when he follows after me. Right now, he's behaving like a silly boy, and even though he's a year older than me and probably has far more experience with women and relationships, or whatever he wants to call them, I feel like I'm more mature than he is.

"Where are you going?" he asks.

"Home," I toss over my shoulder, as I grab my backpack from where I left it by the front door. "I have homework to do."

I open the door and exit the apartment, Cam still hot on my heels. "How are you getting home?"

"Walking." I turn to face him, both thrilled and annoyed that he followed me outside. I walked over to their place, even with the groceries. I didn't have that much stuff with me.

"You're walking? At this time of night?"

"It's still light out." I wave a hand at the pinkening sky. It won't be light for much longer, but I don't live that far.

"It's not safe." He crosses his arms in front of his chest, looking like a grumpy badass. "I'll drive you home."

"Absolutely not." I grip the strap of my backpack and start walking down the sidewalk, heading toward the street.

"Blair!" he calls after me, and I can't help the satisfied smile that curls my lips. "Let me drive you home."

"Only if you tell Knox," I throw back at him, testing him. If he can't even mention to my brother that he's driving me home, then he's a giant pussy.

He says nothing and I turn around to face him, watching as he taps away at his phone, then holds it up for me to see.

It's a text thread between him and my brother, with his latest text saying:

Left to drive your sister home. Be back in a bit.

Giddiness rises up inside me, but I mentally try to tamp it down. "Fine. You can take me home."

He smiles, and it's like a shock to my system, pleasure rippling through me at the sight of it. He is too sexy for his own damn good, and I both hate and enjoy seeing how pleased he is at my giving in.

Like he wanted to drive me home just as badly as I wanted him to take me.

What the hell are we doing?

I follow him to his Dodge Challenger, rolling my eyes once we're settled in our seats and he's revving the engine. God, he's such a show-off.

"I can't believe you walked over here," he mutters, as he's backing out of the parking spot, his arm stretched out, his hand resting on my headrest, long fingers briefly tangling in my hair.

"It's not that big of a deal. I basically live down the street from you guys."

He tugs on the end of my ponytail, making me yelp. "You're mouthy."

"You like it," I retort. "And you shouldn't do that unless you mean it."

"Do what?" He pulls out of the parking lot with a roar of the engine, his tires squealing.

He's not driving that fast, yet he still manages to make a complete scene. "Pull my hair. Don't make a promise you can't keep."

I gulp past the sudden panic that flares up my throat. I probably shouldn't have said that. Hopefully he doesn't get what I'm meaning. Not that I've ever had a guy pull my hair or slap my ass or whatever other kinky things happen while in the midst of sex. I never thought about it enough to wonder if I'd like that sort of thing or not.

But Cam's fingers wrapped around my hair sends an automatic vision in my head of him looming over me. Intimidating.

Sexy.

Curling my hair into his fist and giving it a hard pull, yanking my head back only for him to settle his perfect mouth on mine and devour it.

A full-blown shiver moves through me at the thought.

He's quiet long enough that the tension grows between us, in the close confines of his car, to the point of it almost suffocating me when he finally speaks.

"What the hell are you talking about?"

I glance over at him to find he's already watching me. More like he's keeping one eye on the road while also trying to look at me, his face full of confusion. Then realization.

"You know."

That's all I say. And that's all that's said for the rest of the drive to my apartment. He pulls into the massive parking lot a few minutes later, somehow parking almost directly in front of our building, though he's never been there before. I'm reaching for the door handle as soon as he comes to a stop, eager for once to get away from him, already halfway out of the car when he speaks.

"You into that sort of thing?"

I freeze, one leg on the ground, the other still in the car. Slowly, I turn my head to look at him. "What sort of thing?"

"Hair pulling."

"If you were the one pulling my hair, yes." I scramble out of the car as fast as I can, slamming the door shut and practically running to my front door. Never once looking back because how can I face him after saying something like that?

I've got nothing to lose, I think, as I frantically stick my key in the deadbolt and unlock it, pushing my way into our apartment. I shove the door shut, falling against it with all my weight, my backpack dropping at my feet.

Rita and Cheyenne are both sitting on the couch, watching me with confusion and concern in their eyes.

"Are you okay?" Rita asks.

Closing my eyes, I nod, trying to remember the look on Cam's face when he asked me…

You into that sort of thing?

Yes, yes, yes! I wanted to shout at him. You can pull my hair and slap my ass all you want.

"Blair." Rita's voice is sharp, and I open my eyes. They're both watching me as if I just lost my mind and they're witnessing me falling apart. "Was someone chasing you? You're breathing really hard."

Cheyenne whips out her phone, her fingers poised above the screen. "I'll call 9-1-1 right now if you want me to."

"Put your phone away, I'm fine." I offer them both a brief smile and push away from the door, not willing to describe what just happened to me.

"Where were you?" Rita asks me as I walk through the living room, heading for the short hallway, so I can hide away in my bedroom.

"I went to my brother's place."

I'm just about to shut my door when I hear Cheyenne giggle before she asks, "Was Cam there?"

I press my forehead against the door and briefly close my eyes. Damn it, she remembers our conversation. She knows.

"No," I lie, shutting the door.

• • •

I'm on campus a few days later, at the quad by the student center between classes, grabbing something to drink. I pick up an iced white chocolate mocha from the little coffee shop that's inside the building, constantly searching for one face in particular.

My brother's.

Wherever Knox is, Cam is most likely with him. Those two stick together. If I see them, I'll approach Knox like I need his help, but what I'm really doing is trying to get under Cam's skin.

Like he's gotten under mine.

I cannot stop thinking about him since our last encounter. Being in his car, his warm, spicy scent wrapping all around me. The gravely sound of his voice when he asked me if I was into that sort of thing. Then I remember what I said to him in response and I sort of want to crawl into a hole and die.

Embarrassing. But also liberating, if I'm being real with myself. I am so into Cam I would be willing to do just about anything he'd want me to. It wouldn't be difficult for him to convince me.

When it comes to Camden Fields, I am just that easy.

My gaze drifts around the tables in the quad and I spot Knox sitting at a table with Cam and that big burly guy Derek, who is currently staring me up and down like he's got X-ray vision and can see everything.

The perv.

Putting on a brave smile, I hitch my backpack higher on my shoulder and approach them with determined steps. Cam glances my way after Derek says something, his expression shifting into pure anger, and then Cam says something to Knox. Derek looks like he'd rather die than deal with the two of them.

Huh.

Knox smiles at me when I stop in front of them. "Hey, sis."

"Hi, Knox." I glance at Cam. "Camden."

"Blair." Cam nods, barely looking at me as he gathers up his trash and shoves it into a to-go bag as he stands, pulling his backpack onto his shoulder. "I'll see you guys later."

He's gone, never once looking at me.

I settle into the spot he just left, sitting directly across from my brother who asks, "What's his problem?"

"Who knows? He always acts like he has a stick up his ass around me," I mutter, annoyed.

Damn it, my entire plan is ruined, thanks to Cam bailing on us.

"Blair," Knox chastises then sends Derek a dirty look, immediately shutting down Derek's chuckling.

Clearing my throat, I decide to try my plan out on Knox anyway since it is something I should do today, which means I may as well get it over with.

"I was hoping you could help me out." I smile at him, putting on the sweetness.

"With what?" Knox asks warily.

"I need a new laptop. Like, yesterday." Mine has been acting up on me. I've had it forever and keep putting off getting a new one, but I finally have to just do it before the thing completely takes a crap on me. "And Dad said the only way I could get one today is if you go shopping with me."

I can immediately tell Knox isn't down to helping me. "I can't leave campus this afternoon. I only have another—"

"Forty-five minutes until your next class," I tell him. "Mom sent me your schedule."

We talked last night. I called her to complain about the laptop issue, knowing she'd say I should go get a new one. I am so grateful our family has the type of money to take care of my needs when I'm in college, and I realize I'm lucky.

But here's the deal. I don't need Knox's help and Dad didn't say I needed his help either. I never even talked to our dad about my laptop. I'm just saying this because I wanted a reason to come to their table in the first place and the real person I was going to ask would've been Cam. But he ran off like the chicken shit that he is.

"Yeah, and that's not enough time to go anywhere." Knox shrugs, as if saying there's nothing he can do.

I'm not letting him get out of this. I mean, come on. He can help his sister out for a few minutes.

"They sell Apple laptops at the campus bookstore," I say, my smile growing. "Just come with me there, okay?"

He blows out a harsh breath, but there's something in his gaze that's telling me he's changing his mind literally right in front of me. Guess he doesn't hate the idea of going to the campus bookstore with me after all.

"Okay, but I can only stay with you for a few minutes. Then I gotta go."

"Perfect!" I jump to my feet, noting that Knox is moving pretty fast too. "Let's go."

We walk over to the bookstore together, making small talk about nothing at all, my gaze constantly scanning the grounds, looking for Cam. He's nowhere to be found.

Annoying.

Once we're in the bookstore, we head toward the Apple section, Knox constantly looking back at the checkout counter, as if he's searching for someone.

"Can I help you?" the Apple specialist asks me, and I launch into my speech about my crappy laptop and how I need a new one. He takes me over to the display laptops, asking me what I use it for. Knox pretends for all of two minutes that he's interested in the conversation until he finally says, "Hey, uh, there's someone here I know. Care if I go talk to her for a few?"

Her? Hmm.

"Yeah, go ahead." I smile at him, startled when he leaves without another word, heading straight for the checkout counter, where a dark-haired girl is currently standing.

I choose the laptop I want and the guy tells me it will be here in the next couple of days, which has to be fine since I don't really have a choice. He escorts me over to the register in his section, ringing me up, and I'm grateful that my parents help me out as I hand over the credit card they let me use for necessities.

I'm fortunate and I know it. My dad had a lot of success playing for the NFL when he was younger. I have distant memories of watching him play, being in the box seats and sometimes even hanging out on the sidelines. I remember watching my Uncle Drew too. I'm used to the football scene. It's pretty much all I know, which is why it makes sense that I'm crushing on Cam.

Though, really, it's probably more than a crush. That seems like such a light and fluffy word for what I'm feeling for this man.

And he is all man. I can verify that, after having him pressed up against me last night. Oh, and a couple of nights ago too. The guy keeps telling me he's not interested, but he doesn't necessarily push me away either.

I hear horrible singing of a vaguely familiar country song and I glance up to see my brother basically making an ass of himself as he's walking backward in the store, all smiles as he croaks at the top of his lungs. Knox has many talents.

Singing isn't one of them.

I glance over at the checkout desk on the bookstore side, that same dark-haired girl standing there with a silly smile on her flushed face. Knox is completely flirting with her—in a really awkward way, but it's still flirting.

I can tell.

Interesting.

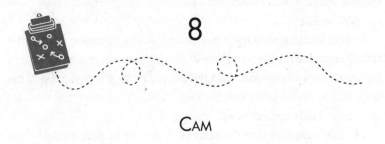

8

CAM

I had to get away from her. It was like an automatic response. As if her mere presence triggers me into action. Like I either want to run away from her or get closer. I don't know why Blair affects me so much, but fuck.

It's bad.

I find another picnic table to sit at that's far away from the quad, close to a grove of pine trees that rustle pleasantly with the cool breeze. The sun is shining and the temperatures are still up there, but I can feel it.

It's September, which means fall is almost here. My favorite time of year.

In my life, autumn equals football. Some of my fondest memories are wrapped up in this time of year and football, as well as some not so fond memories. Like the times my dad showed up to watch my games drunk off his ass. One time he was even asked to leave one of my games, he was making such a drunken scene.

That sucked.

There have been a few injuries here and there over the years. One time, I got knocked unconscious. I was a sophomore in high school, skinny as fuck, working out constantly and not eating properly. Meaning, I consumed junk food and soda instead of protein and water. Of course, my ass got knocked out. My mom had been so freaked out, she gave me a huge speech when I got home about how she lost my father and my older brother. Dad left her and so did my brother the minute he could get away.

She wasn't about to lose me too. Not if she could help it.

My mother is not a bad person. She's just a reminder of the past that I'd rather soon forget. Stuck in the old house, stuck on trying to get money out of my dad, though it's a futile effort on her part. He feels as if he doesn't owe her shit. He paid child support when he had to and the moment that was over, he didn't give her another dime.

So she struggles, and she does what she can. If I ever get into the NFL, the first thing I'm doing is buying her a new house and a new car. I will set her up for life, so she doesn't have to worry about any of that shit anymore.

Thinking of her makes me want to call her because we haven't talked in a few weeks. And because I'd rather do anything but work on class assignments, I pull up her number on my phone and give her a call.

"Camden," she breathes into the phone as her greeting. "You're alive."

I chuckle, a little uneasy. She always likes to give me shit when I don't talk to her for a while. "Hey, Mom."

"How are you? How's football? How's the team? Are you enjoying your classes?" I hear a dog yip in the background, followed by a bird chirping and I can tell she's outside.

"I'm good, the team is great, we have a home game this Saturday, and my classes are all right," I say, answering all of her questions.

"How's Knox?" Mom loves Knox. She thinks he's a good influence on me, which is funny because if anything, I'm probably a better influence on him. At least I try to be.

"He's doing all right." I stare at the roughened top of the picnic table, unsure of what to say next. This is my problem with my mom. We don't know how to communicate anymore. Once I went away to college and found new interests and new friends, it felt like she was stuck in my past life.

A life I don't really want to acknowledge any longer.

It's not like I hate where I came from, or that I had an extra rough childhood. I wasn't physically abused. But it was…hard, witnessing the demise of my father. The way he destroyed his marriage thanks to his addictions, and how he treated my mother. The things he said to me. He never once tried to lift me up. He always preferred tearing me down.

And it sucked. He sucks.

He's the one who pays for my college and supports me financially while I focus on football, and it's the least he can do after what he put me through. I'll gladly take his money, even though I want nothing to do with him.

"It's good to hear your voice," she says, forcing me out of my momentary funk.

"It's good to hear yours too." I clear my throat. "How are you?"

She tells me about her dog and her job working as a server at a local restaurant in the town I grew up in, offering a funny story about an encounter with some customers.

"I've started dating someone," she adds casually, just when I'm about to wrap up the call.

"You have?" I'm stunned.

"Yes. He's a very nice man, who's a regular of ours at the restaurant. His name is Greg," she says.

"How long have you been seeing him?"

"About a month. Maybe longer."

"And you're just telling me about him now?"

"I wasn't sure it would amount to anything and besides, we don't talk that often, you and me."

Ouch.

MONICA MURPHY   63

"Well, if he makes you happy, I'm glad, Mom. You deserve happiness."

"So do you, Cam," she says softly.

I frown. "What do you mean by that?"

"I mean that you work so hard and do so much, yet you never really tell me much about your—feelings." She laughs, the sound nervous. "I don't know how you're really doing most of the time, and I can only hope that you're happy. You're still young, with a lot of life ahead of you. I hate to think of you miserable. Like your father."

Her words stick with me long after we end the call. Am I miserable like my father? I'm not a drunk, I know that. I like to go out and party like anyone else, but I don't feel the need to get constantly shit-faced.

I keep women at arm's length, so I don't get too close to them. A relationship is the last thing I want or need. I have to get out of college first. Get myself established doing...something. If it's the NFL, then let's fucking go.

But what if it's not? The potential is definitely there for my dreams to not come true. I might not go pro and I have no idea what to do with myself if I don't.

Glancing up, I catch sight of a blonde woman heading my way. From the shape of her body and even the shape of her face, I know immediately that it's Blair.

Fuck.

She doesn't even slow down in her approach. Just marches her way toward the table and settles onto the bench across from me. I don't say a word in greeting, just watch her watch me and she shakes her head, a little laugh escaping her.

"You're so weird."

I'm frowning so hard my forehead hurts. "What the hell are you talking about now?"

Her laughter stops. "Why did you leave earlier?"

"Leave where?"

"Stop being obtuse." She leans across the table, the neckline of her T-shirt slipping, offering me a glimpse of her chest. Oh, fuck me,

I can see that she's wearing a black lace bra. "When I came over to your table earlier in the quad and you bolted out of there like you saw a crazed groupie."

"Maybe I did." I shrug, hating how nervous she makes me feel.

Like I'm going to screw something up or say the wrong thing. She has me walking on eggshells, pretty much every time I'm around her, and I don't get it.

"Cam." Her smile is small, her shirt slipping off her shoulder, so I can now see the black bra strap. "You're definitely afraid of me."

"Not at all."

"Then what's the big deal?" She sits up straight, all views of her bra disappearing. "Can't we be friends?"

It's my turn to bark out a laugh. "Friends? You've got to be kidding me."

"What?" Her frown is deep. "You don't like me?"

"Like you? *Like you?*" I'm repeating myself, but I don't give a damn. "That is definitely not the problem."

"What is it then?"

I grab my backpack and climb off the bench, ready to hightail my ass out of there, but Blair is just as fast, right on my heels, never letting up on me.

"You run every time I get near you, and I don't get it. Am I a hideous troll? Can you barely stand looking at me?"

I snort, shaking my head. She has to know that isn't the problem.

"You hate me? Do I smell?"

She smells fucking amazing. Good enough that I even looked up the damn perfume she wears online, just to see what the bottle looked like.

What's wrong with me? Why would I do that?

"What is it, Cam? If all you can say is that you don't want to make Knox mad, that's not a good enough reason."

I come to a sudden stop and turn on her, forcing her to stop as well, her eyes wide with shock. I practically thrust my face in hers, letting her see just how angry and frustrated I am with her. With myself. "It's a good enough reason for me, Blair. Your brother is my best friend. I live with him, we play together, we spend a lot of time together, and he's told me before he trusts no one he knows to treat his little sister right. Which means he doesn't even trust me. I can't mess around with his little sister when he told me I can't. And because I know I would fuck it up—I totally will. Trust me. I will fuck everything up between us and you'll end up hating me, and that's the last thing I want, is you hating me. Your opinion of me matters, Blair, and I don't want to ruin it. I'm shit when it comes to this stuff. Relationship stuff. My parents were all fucked up, and I witnessed their mess my entire life. They weren't a good example of what a loving, respectful relationship is, and they're all I know. Which really means I don't know shit."

I'm breathing hard, surprised that I said so much, and she's staring up at me like I've lost my damn mind, which I sort of feel like I have.

Taking a step back, I thrust my fingers in my hair, pushing it away from my face before I clasp the back of my head with both hands. My heart is racing and I swallow hard, pissed at myself for saying too much.

"You're not a bad person," she murmurs, and when I look at her, I see an understanding glow in her eyes, like she gets it. As if she gets me.

Please.

Little Miss Golden Girl who's never had to deal with anything bad or awful or ugly her whole life. She's lived a perfect existence and she has no idea what it's like, dealing with a drunk dad and a sad mom and an older brother who wanted nothing more but to get out of that house and never look back.

That's me. I'm the same as Samuel. He bailed. I bailed too. We barely talk. He lives clear across the country and has very minimal contact with any of us. At least I still call Mom. He doesn't even bother reaching out to her.

"I'm not a great person either," I tell her. I need to be real with her. She has to know. "I'm not worth trying to fix."

"You don't need to be *fixed*, Cam." She sounds so logical. Like what I'm saying is absolutely ridiculous. "You just need to be... shown."

I'm confused. "Shown what?"

Her smile is blinding. "Love."

Damn it.

I'm completely fucked.

9

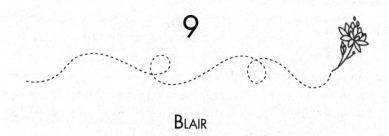

BLAIR

Two days after Cam's little outburst and I'm back at Logan's, eager to spot him. I came with Rita and Cheyenne, who are both in good spirits and not at each other's throats, so we're at peace for the first time in days.

They argue a lot and it's so exhausting. I hide away in my room most of the time, avoiding their screaming fights. I don't particularly enjoy living with them, but what else can I do? Where else can I go? I was assigned this apartment and it's hard to find another place around here since housing is limited. And I really don't want to look for somewhere else to live.

I texted my mom, of course, unloading on her all of my worries and concerns, and she said all of the right things, but nothing beats actually having her with me. Giving me a hug when I'm feeling down.

I miss my parents. I miss my sister. My brother?

I'm kind of sick of him right now, ha.

"The boys are out tonight!" Rita lifts her tequila shot in celebration, and Cheyenne clinks it with hers, the liquor sloshing over the rims of both their glasses. "Where's your shot, Blair?"

I shrug, offering a helpless smile. "I'm the designated driver tonight."

Rita throws back her shot, wiping at her mouth with the back of her hand. "We took an Uber here."

Shit. Not like I can explain to these two that I would rather be sober when I encounter Cam, but they would never get it. "I don't feel like drinking tonight."

"Why the hell not?" Cheyenne retorts. "It's been a tough week."

The fact that we're in school seems to have kicked into overdrive for all of us. Assignments have been piled upon us. Big tests are looming. It's getting serious and I am thriving. I've been keeping up with all of my reading, assignments and papers. I've taken copious amounts of notes. I am ready to tackle just about anything school-wise, while my roommates act like they're drowning.

Rita is a STEM major, and major kudos to her, I don't know how she does it. Cheyenne wants to be a teacher, and I can't imagine her being patient with children, but it's none of my business.

Me? I'm a psychology major. I want to be a relationship therapist. This is partly why Camden fascinates me so much. That speech he gave me—swear to God that's the most he's said to me in one sitting, ever—has been interesting to mentally dissect the last couple of days.

He doesn't believe he's worthy of love. He doesn't do committed relationships because he's afraid of them. Afraid of who he might turn into once he's in one—his mother or his father. I assume his father, though I'm sure he has some of his mother's tendencies.

He's a good guy with a good heart. He's a strong leader of his team, always there for Knox when he needs him, and he's kind. I've never seen him be mean to anyone, though it's not like I spend a lot of time with him to even know.

But I have to trust my brother's opinion of him. Knox wouldn't be friends with an asshole—and Cam is Knox's absolute best friend. They're close. They live together. There's a reason for that.

And that reason is good enough for me to pursue Cam, despite all of his protests. I know we would be good together. I wish he could see it.

"I just don't feel like drowning all of my woes in alcohol," I finally answer truthfully.

Cheyenne grabs the shot they got for me and throws it back, gasping once it's down. "Well, I do. Guess you'll be stuck with our drunk asses tonight."

Rita high-fives her, the both of them laughing, and I remind myself there is no way in hell I'm going to allow myself to be stuck with them tonight. The moment I spot Cam walk in, I'm going to approach him. Even if he doesn't show up, I'm hoping Knox will be here. At the very least, I can spend a little time with my brother before I bail, disappointed.

I tune my roommates out as they gossip about the cute guys at the bar, my gaze constantly searching for the only one I want to see. Every time the door swings open, hope rises within me, crashing down when I realize it's not Cam.

The hours tick by. It's past ten-thirty when I give up and slide off the barstool, fighting the sadness that wants to wrap around me.

"I'm leaving," I announce.

Rita and Cheyenne give me matching odd looks before Rita speaks for the both of them. "Why? It's not even eleven."

"Close enough. I'm tired." And bored. But I don't say that. "I'll see you guys later."

I use the bathroom real quick before I leave, then push my way through the thick crowd of people in the bar, nearly jumping out of my skin when strong fingers curl around the crook of my elbow, stopping me.

Turning, I find Cam standing there, wearing a serious expression on his handsome face, and I nearly collapse in relief at seeing him. The only reason I remain standing, I swear, is because of the grip he has on me.

"Where you off to?" he asks, perfectly normal. Perfectly friendly. Like he didn't just blow up on me only a few days ago and basically rejected me to my face.

He has no idea that I'm far more determined than he realizes. I'm my father's daughter, after all. Knox and I are made of the same stuff. Ruby is exactly like us too. None of us are quitters.

Not even close.

"Home," I say with a sigh, trying to play it cool, despite the way he's currently gripping me sends shivers up and down my arm, his fingers burning into my skin. "I've already been here for hours."

"I just got here." He tugs me a little closer when a group of girls try to move past us, my body gently colliding with his. Goose bumps erupt all over my body. "How are you getting home?"

"I'm taking an Uber. Or Lyft." I hold up my phone.

He slowly shakes his head. "No way. I'll take you home."

My skin prickles with awareness. He still hasn't let me go. But I pull out of his grip anyway, not wanting to look like a pathetic loser, who longs for the elusive, unattainable man to keep touching her. Which is actually how I feel, but he doesn't need to know that.

"It's okay. I don't want to bother you." I offer him a casual wave and with a closed-mouth smile, I leave him where he stands.

On purpose.

I make my way to the door, and I swear I can feel Cam's heavy gaze following my every step. When I finally dare to glance over my shoulder, I find he's already watching me.

The moment our eyes connect, he launches into action, heading toward me, while ignoring everyone who tries to speak to him as he passes. I face forward, rushing toward the door, my heart beating a million miles a minute, and the moment I reach out to push the door to the bar open, a giant hand slams on the glass, stopping me.

Slowly, I turn to face him, my body brushing against his, since he's standing so close. I tip my head back to find him glowering at me, confusion swirling in his gaze.

This man. Can't he see?

"You don't want to bother me?" His voice is pained. I almost want to laugh at how tortured he sounds. "You've been bothering me all damn week."

I huff out a breath. "What in the world are you talking about?"

"Don't leave yet." His hand drops from the door to settle on my waist. All of the air stalls in my throat, making it suddenly hard to breathe. "Stay with me."

Those three words are like magic, weaving their way into my skin. My heart. The solemn truth I hear behind the request. I'm probably overreacting, but it feels like he actually wants me to stay.

With him.

"Here at the bar?" I ask because I don't know what else to say.

He glances around. "There are a few tables in the back. We can sit there."

"And do what?"

"I don't know…talk?" His hand drops from my waist and I can breathe again. "I feel bad."

"About what?" Oh shit. He better not feel…sympathy toward me. I don't want his pity.

A frustrated sound leaves him and he grabs my hand, pulling me through the crowd as he leads me to the back of the building. "I'll tell you when we sit."

I let him drag me through the bar, smiling at a few people I pass by, confused why so many of them are frowning, most of them female. It dawns on me quickly that they look that way because they're probably jealous. Every girl on this campus seems to want a chance at Camden Fields, star quarterback.

Including me.

I have a moment of sudden crisis, my self-confidence crumbling the deeper we get into the bar, all of those negative thoughts filling my head, though I'm not exactly sure why.

Maybe I'm only fooling myself. There is no real reason Cam would be interested in me. People might think I have an advantage because I'm his best friend's little sister, but Cam most likely views me as the girl with the stupid crush on him. He's only nice to me because I amuse him. I'm that annoying little sister who ogled him like some sort of weird perv that one summer he came to our house, and now he puts up with me merely because Knox told him to.

And that is the absolute worst.

Once we're seated at a tiny table in the darkest corner of the bar, my knees knocking into his since we're sitting so close, I'm on the verge of tears.

He is going to let me down easy in a very public setting, which is smart on his part.

"Hey, what's wrong?" The concerned look on his face is undeniable, and I'm sure he's feeling that way only because he knows Knox will kick his ass if he hurts me in any sort of way.

"Nothing." I shake my head, sniffing loudly. *Suck it up, buttercup.* I used to say that to Ruby, right before she fell apart for no good reason, which was often back in the day.

I need to take my own advice.

"What did you want to talk about?" I ask, once I'm a little more composed.

He scratches at the back of his neck, seemingly uncomfortable before he finally blurts, "I'm sorry I unloaded on you."

I blink at him, shocked he'd apologize.

"A couple of days ago," he adds, like I might've forgotten.

"Oh, I remember when it happened."

"Yeah." He rests his arms on the tiny table, his hands close enough to touch me. He stares at them, as if he doesn't want to meet my gaze. "I kind of lost it."

"It's okay," I say gently, reaching out to pat his hand with mine. I jerk my fingers back the moment I make contact with his warm skin. "We all have our moments."

"I never have a moment. I'm always chill."

"Chill? I don't know if that's the word I would use to describe you."

"How would you describe me, then?" He lifts his head, fixing his gaze on mine.

"Intense? Quiet? High strung?" I threw the last one out there just to bug him.

It works. His face turns a little redder and he shakes his head. "I disagree."

"But we both agree that you lost your cool a couple of days ago."

A long, drawn-out exhale leaves him and he stares at the table once more. "Yeah, I definitely did. And like I just said, I'm sorry."

"Thank you for apologizing."

He glances up. "Thanks for putting up with me."

"It's never a hardship," I murmur, settling my hands on the edge of the table, needing to grip something.

"You always make me feel like I want to spill my guts," he admits.

"I do?" Okay, that's surprising.

He nods. "Yeah. Even when I'm mad at you, I want to tell you everything."

His words echo in my head in time with the steady beat of my heart. "Everything?"

His smile is faint. "I shouldn't want to."

"You get mad at me?" What does he even mean by that?

"More like I'm frustrated with myself because of you," he explains.

"Here we go again." I roll my eyes, though I'm secretly thrilled.

At least I'm getting a reaction out of him.

"You know what I'm saying. I'm drawn to you despite everything. Despite my worry and my feelings of disloyalty to my best friend. I'm breaking a promise to Knox, you know. Yet here I am, chasing you down in front of everyone at Logan's. Word will get back to your brother and he'll ask me about it. He'll probably be pissed about it too."

"Oh, come on. He doesn't care that much."

"He does," Cam says without hesitation. "You're not worried about him because he's your brother. You've dealt with him your entire life—"

"Look," I interrupt him, "we've been going round and round like this for weeks. I'm over it. I don't want to get strung along, Cam. I meant what I said a few days ago. You're worthy of so much more than you believe, if you just give yourself a chance. It doesn't have to be like this. Knox won't kick your ass for having sexual relations with me."

The expression of pure misery that crosses his face is undeniable. "Come on, B. Sexual *relations?* Why you gotta phrase it like that?"

"You know what I mean." I roll my eyes, trying to play this off, feeling a little embarrassed. "The two of us together. Having sex or whatever."

"Or whatever?" He lifts his brows.

"You know." I wave a hand.

"No, I don't. Please explain."

He's enjoying torturing me. The jerk.

"Look, my sexual experiences so far?" He nods, encouraging me, and I can't believe I'm even admitting any of this. "They haven't been that exciting."

"Why not?"

"They only ever covered the basics." I send him a meaningful look. "I think I need a little excitement in my life."

"And you believe I can do that for you?"

He swallows hard. I see the movement of his Adam's apple, and because I'm a sadistic bitch, I decide to take this conversation a step further. "I know you can."

His smile is small yet arrogant. Like he knows he can rock my world. "I know a few tricks."

"I'm sure you do," I murmur. "Maybe you could show me?"

Yikes. Where did that question just come from?

"You're a bad girl tonight, B," he gently chastises, shaking his head.

"You're bad all the time," I return. "And you flirt with me constantly."

"I do?" He rests a hand against his chest, like he's shocked. "More like you flirt with me."

"We flirt with each other," I amend. "Though it's been...worse lately."

"What do you mean?"

Oh, he sounds so curious. This is perfect. "Ever since the—hair pulling conversation, I can't stop thinking about you...pulling my hair."

"Huh." His pupils get bigger, swear to God. "When you imagine it, what are we doing when I'm pulling your hair?"

"Wouldn't you like to know." My smile is hopefully mysterious, and his lips part, like he's ready to launch into about a thousand questions.

A waitress appears at our table, exasperated and sweaty around her hairline. "You guys want anything?"

"Just water, please," I tell her.

"Same," Cam adds. "And I'll give you a tip. Don't worry."

She smiles in relief. "Thanks. I've been hustling my ass around here all night."

The moment the waitress is gone, Cam is shifting in his chair, looming nearer. His hands stretch out toward me, getting closer and closer to mine, and I'm tempted to move them into my lap.

But I don't.

"That was nice of you," I say when he still hasn't spoken. "Offering her a tip on our free order."

"It's the least I can do." He shrugs.

"Why aren't you drinking tonight?"

"Why aren't you?"

My smile is serene. "I asked first."

"I wanted to be sober."

"Why?"

"Because here I am, talking to you. And I didn't want to make an ass of myself when I apologized."

"You didn't make an ass of yourself," I reassure him.

"Gee, thanks." He smiles, and the sight of it goes right to that needy spot between my thighs, leaving me throbbing.

"You also changed the direction of our conversation."

"What do you mean?"

"You don't want to talk about the two of us having sex."

He leans back in his seat, his arms sliding off the table. I regret not touching him, but I'm also enjoying the view of him sitting with his legs sprawled, his hands resting on the inside of his knees. He's wearing black joggers and a Golden Eagles T-shirt and he's never looked better. "Jesus, Blair."

"What?" I put on my most innocent face. "What's wrong?"

Cam glances around, like he suspects someone is listening in on our conversation. News flash—no one is. "You can't just drop a *we're having sex* bomb like that."

"That's not what I said, and why not? I think about it." I prop my elbow on the table, resting my chin on top of my curled fist. "I think about it all the time."

His lips part, but he doesn't say anything.

"And I think we'd be really good together. I get this feeling I'd be up to…anything you'd ask me to do."

He is literally starting to sweat. "Anything?" he practically chokes out.

"Anything," I reassure him with far more confidence than I feel.

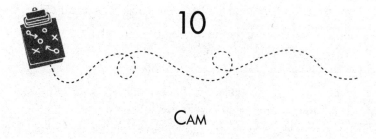

10

CAM

What the hell am I doing? I only came to Logan's in the hopes I'd see her. Just a glimpse of her pretty blonde head and her even prettier face with flashing green eyes and lips made for sucking dick.

Wait a minute. I shouldn't think like that, but damn it, she has a great mouth.

The moment I do spot her, she makes like she's going to leave, and I chase after her like the idiot I am.

I told myself after my unexpected outburst a few days ago that I wouldn't do that again. I wouldn't go off on her. With her. Whatever way I should describe it. I swore I wouldn't dare share even the tiniest detail of my life with her because when it comes to Blair Maguire, I need to keep the walls up. She's slowly but surely working her way into my life and I shouldn't want that. No matter how hard she tries, I should warn her off.

Keep my distance.

Torturing myself further, I go and force her to sit with me and apologize and grovel like the simp asshole I am. One look at her beautiful face and I'm a goner.

When she talked about hair pulling and how she imagines the two of us together having sex? It's obvious she's trying to torment me.

"I mean it," she says when I remain quiet, trying to process what she said. "Though I haven't done much, I think I could be into...all of that."

Sitting up straighter, my gaze bores into hers, like I can see inside her brain and know exactly what she's thinking. "Blair."

"Let's be real with each other, Cam. What's the big deal? We're adults. We can share details from our sex lives, right?" She scoots her chair closer to the table, her knees colliding with mine and I spread my thighs, capturing one of her legs between both of mine. Her breath hitches, and she tries to withdraw her leg from mine, but I don't let her.

I've got a solid clamp on her.

"You really want to share details about our sex lives with each other?"

The waitress shows up with our waters, and once she sets the glasses on the table, I give her a twenty-dollar bill for her trouble. She leaves quickly, not having the time to linger, and the moment she's gone, Blair starts talking.

"I've had two serious boyfriends, but I've messed around with... four guys. I don't have what I would call a ton of experience."

Jealousy spreads over my skin, sinking into my gut. I don't like the idea of her with one guy, let alone *four*.

Fuck those guys.

"How about you? How many girls have you been with?"

"I am not sharing my body count with you." I press my lips together, not about to admit how many women there have been. Not as many as some of my fellow teammates have been with, but my number is definitely more than four, that's for damn sure.

"I'm guessing you have a lot of experience then." Her smile is sweet as can be when she reaches for her glass and takes a long swallow. I stare at her the entire time, unable to look away, focusing on the elegant arch of her throat. Her skin is smooth and I'm filled with the urge to kiss her there. Right at the spot where her pulse beats.

"Define 'a lot of experience.'" I immediately hold out my hands. "Wait, don't respond to that. I don't want your definition."

She laughs, sounding very pleased with herself. "See? This is fun."

It's not fun at all. I'm fucking miserable, but I can't let her see that.

"This conversation is pointless," I mutter, grabbing my glass and draining half of it in one go. "I don't know what you're trying to do, Blair, but it won't work."

All the happiness is zapped from her expression just like that. "I'm so over you. Seriously, I'm done."

She rises to her feet, gives me the finger, and then turns tail and marches away from me with her head held high.

It takes me a second to realize she's left, and by the time I'm scrambling out of my chair and pushing my way through the crowd, I don't see her. She's already gone.

Panic racing through me, I barge through the front door of the bar, the cool evening air like a slap on my hot face. I glance around, first to my left, then my right, looking for her, but she's nowhere to be found.

I round the side of the building that's closest to the parking lot and there she is, leaning against the wall, aggressively tapping away on her phone. She glances up as I approach, doing a double take when she realizes it's me that's in front of her and an irritated noise leaves her.

"Go away."

"No." I'm still walking toward her, getting closer and closer.

"Look, I promise I'll leave you alone, okay? You don't have to worry about me anymore. I'm not into you."

Meaning she's totally into me, and she's pissed because I won't reciprocate her feelings. Even though I want to.

Even though I feel the same exact way.

"You're into me."

She rolls her eyes. "Your ego is ginormous."

"You're just mad at me."

"With valid reason. You're fucking annoying, Cam Fields. Oh, and you're also blind."

"Blind to what?" I'm close to her. Close enough to touch her and I do, pulling her into my arms. She goes with a bit of a fight, struggling when I slip my arms around her waist and haul her into me, but she slowly relaxes, as if she's melting. All those lush curves snug tight against me.

My dick twitches, ready for action, the bossy fucker.

"Blind to me. Blind to us." She rests her hands against my chest, one hand crawling upward so fucking slow, until she's curving her fingers around the side of my neck. "Would it really be that bad, being with me?"

It would be fucking heaven. I know I could fuck her into oblivion and it still wouldn't be enough. I could have her every way I want her and she'd just burrow deeper into my system, instead of working herself out of it.

"It wouldn't be that bad," I admit, my gaze dropping to her chest, which is currently rising and falling at an extremely rapid rate. She's turned on. Or infuriated. There's a fine line between those emotions, especially when it comes to our interactions lately.

"Is that supposed to be a compliment?" She huffs out a soft laugh, her gaze lingering on my mouth, and I lean in, so close, my lips brush hers when I speak.

"Yes."

We stand there like that for what feels like minutes. Hours. In reality, it lasts only a few seconds tops before she's pulling away, taking her delicious floral scent with her. My hands fall away from her waist and she's backing up until her butt hits the wall.

"This is going to be the crudest thing ever, but shit or get off the pot, Camden. I've given you every indication that I want you. I'm not going to make a fool of myself forever," she murmurs.

"Are you coming to Saturday's game?" I'm changing the subject on purpose.

"I haven't got any tickets yet," she admits.

Students have first dibs on the cheap seats, but she doesn't belong in that section.

"Did Knox give you tickets?"

"I haven't spoken to him about the game."

"I'll make sure you have tickets. You want a couple, so you can bring someone? Maybe your roommates?"

She shakes her head, wrinkling her nose. "I'll come alone, thanks."

"You sure?" I hate the idea of her alone, while watching the game. But then again, maybe it'll be good that she's alone. That means her focus will only be on the game.

On me.

I am such an egotistical ass.

"I'm positive. I'm a big girl, Cam." Her gaze goes to the street and she pushes away from the wall, heading for the curb. "My ride is here. I'll see you later."

I watch her head for a black BMW SUV, the passenger side window lowering, and the driver says her name, indicating he's there for her. She opens the back door and slides inside, the door shutting quickly, cutting my view of her.

I stare at the car, willing her to roll down her window and wave at me. Needing just one more glimpse.

It doesn't happen. The car pulls away from the curb and heads down the street, disappearing into the darkness. I watch it until the red taillights are nothing but pinpricks before I finally head for my own vehicle, not caring enough to go back inside and tell my friends and teammates that I'm leaving. They don't care where I'm at. They're too busy trying to pick up girls. Needing their adulation to feed their egos. No judgment. I've done it too. It feels pretty fucking good.

I'm starting to realize that nothing is going to feel as fucking good as Blair Maguire tastes.

And I haven't even tasted her yet.

. . .

Saturday. Game day. Practice has gone great all week. My accuracy has improved. My offensive line is getting stronger. Faster. We're coming together nicely, and I have a feeling we're going to fucking kill it today.

I remind myself of that as I run out onto the field with the rest of the team to a roaring crowd. The stands are already full and I'm scanning the bleachers, looking for one face in particular. She should be sitting pretty low, closer to the sideline, and when I spot her, my entire body shifts into overdrive.

Meaning I feel the need to show off. Look strong. Appear ready to conquer.

Blair doesn't even notice me though. She's too busy talking to two women who sit directly in front of her.

"I see Blair showed up," I say, as casually as I can to Knox, who is currently jogging right next to me. Thought it might be smart to bring her up first.

Knox glances over at me, slowing down, and I do the same. "I didn't give her a ticket."

"Yeah, I know. I did." I brace myself for the blast of questions.

"What? Why?"

"She asked me for one." I shrug, lying. I actually offered it up first, but Knox doesn't need to know that.

"And why didn't she ask me for one?" He seems offended. "When did you see her?"

"I don't know why she didn't ask you. I ran into her last night and we got to talking." Fuck yeah, we did. "She mentioned going to the game and sitting in the student section, and I told her I could get her a better seat, so I did."

"So, you saw Blair at a bar?" Knox doesn't like the idea of his sister at a bar, which is fucking ridiculous, but whatever.

"Well, yeah. She's twenty-one, and she was with her roommates. Don't worry, I kept watch over her," I reassure him, not mentioning the fact that we talked about hair pulling and if we've ever thought about having sex with each other. Not the kind of "watching over" Knox is hoping for.

"Thanks for that. And thanks for getting her a ticket," Knox says as we both swivel our heads in Blair's direction to find her already watching us.

Me.

"No problem." Our gazes connect. Hold. She lifts her hand and offers a little wave, her lips curved into the faintest smile, and my chest expands with pride, knowing that she's here, watching me. "Anything for your sister, am I right?"

I wave at her in return and so does Knox.

"As long as you treat her like she's your little sister and nothing else, I'm good, bro," Knox says, his words a warning.

His words stay with me while we make random small talk. I ask about his knee. We talk about the opposing team's defensive line. My eyes keep going to the stands where Blair sits. How the sun flashes upon her blonde hair, making it seem brighter. She's wearing an Eagles T-shirt that I have no idea where she got, and I'm filled with the sudden need to see her wearing my number.

Fucking stupid.

By the time the first quarter starts, I'm not thinking about her any longer. All I can focus on is the game. The other team is good and they guard my receivers well. They must've studied past games and our fucking playbook because these assholes are hard to shake. Most of my passes throughout the first half are thrown out of bounds, just to get rid of the ball versus risking an interception.

We finally get our moment during the second half. I throw a

forty-yard pass that Knox catches with ease and he runs as fast as he can into the end zone. I throw a couple more touchdowns, which secures our win, and by the time the game is over, I'm fucking exhausted.

But satisfied that I played a good game—which I did.

All to impress Blair.

11

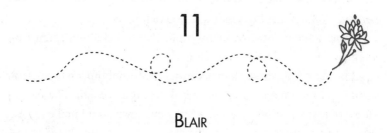

Blair

The game was great and the weather was perfect. I made two new friends and Cam played so well. He got a total of four touchdowns, and I was so proud of him I wanted to tackle him out on the field after the game was over, but I restrained myself. Not like I could talk to him. He was too busy chatting with various reporters and a group of fangirls who all literally screamed when he agreed to pose for photos with them.

I watched with barely-restrained jealousy, ignoring the conversation going on around me. Joanna—the girl from the bookstore that my brother invited to the game, hmm—and her roommate Natalie are chatting it up with Derek, who is a sweetheart, but also a not-so-secret manwhore. He's watching Natalie with keen interest, flirting with her while Joanna shares knowing looks with me, rolling her eyes at one point, like we're in on the secret together.

I can't deny that it's nice—I really like Joanna a lot, and if she can put up with my brother? She's a freaking saint. Natalie would probably love my roommates, since she's kind of loud like they are, but Joanna is more my type. When they invite me to go to dinner with them, I can't resist, and we have a great time talking. Learning about each other. Cracking jokes.

They act so normal, not full of drama like my roommates.

When we eventually end up at Logan's after dinner, I'm on high alert, my gaze scanning the room in search of Cam the moment we enter the bar.

"Can you go first?" Natalie shouts at me when I turn to look back at them. "One of the boys will spot you before us."

True. I know most of them—well, I've heard about them from Knox—and they all know who I am.

I push my way through the crowd, Natalie holding on to me from behind, and Joanna holding on to Nat, forming a chain. The backup quarterback Ace spots me first, waving me down, and I make my way over to the group of guys from the team, who have already taken over a corner of the bar.

Derek approaches us like he's the host, a welcoming smile on his face that is aimed directly at Natalie. He stops directly in front of her, reaching out to touch her arm. "You made it! Want something to drink? Beer?"

Natalie wrinkles her nose. "You have something a little harder?"

"Come on, let's go to the bar." Derek hesitates, his hand still on Natalie's arm, his question now directed at all three of us. As if he was just made aware that we came with Natalie. "You ladies want anything?"

"I'll have whatever Nat's having," Joanna says with a faint smile, her expression nervous.

Hanging out with football players isn't something she normally does. She so much as admitted that to me earlier at Taco Bell. She also told me how she's Knox's English tutor, which I think is cool. My brother doesn't enjoy reading much, and he has dyslexia, which makes reading difficult for him.

My gaze drifts over the three booths the guys are sitting in, noting the pitcher of beer and the empty mugs sitting on one of the tables.

"I'll take a beer."

What in the world am I doing? I hate beer. The stuff tastes awful most of the time, but I stand there pouring myself a cup, slowly becoming aware of someone watching me. I set the pitcher on the table with an unsteady hand, glancing over my shoulder to find Cam sitting at the same table my brother is, watching me with a broody expression on his face, an untouched mug of beer sitting in front of him.

I look away quickly, not wanting to give him the satisfaction of trying to join them at the table. He'll think I'm chasing after him yet again, and I'm tired of chasing.

He needs to chase after me this time.

Besides, Knox is at that table too and he'll be a total pain in my ass, constantly questioning me and demanding that none of the guys even look in my direction. Lame.

I sit at the next table over instead, sliding onto the booth seat and finding myself sitting right next to Ace, who's all smiles the moment I sit down.

"Hey."

"Hi." Okay, this guy is super cute. Golden brown hair and light blue eyes. A boyish face with a wholesome smile. He doesn't look old enough to attend college, let alone be able to drink.

"You're Maguire's sister, right?"

I nod, taking a sip of my beer. It's awful. Too foamy.

His smile brightens. "Your dad is Owen Maguire, and your uncle is Drew Callahan. That's so fucking cool."

"Yeah," I say weakly. "Really cool."

Guys are always dazzled by my family lineup, especially guys who love football.

"And isn't Jake Callahan your cousin? He's, like, the best QB in the NFL right now." Ace shakes his head, seemingly in awe over the thought. He immediately thrusts his hand out toward me. "I'm Ace. You're—"

"Blair," I supply for him. "Nice to meet you. You're the backup quarterback, right?"

"Yeah." He glances in the direction of the other table, where Cam and my brother sit. "He's so fucking good. I doubt I'll get any field time this season."

"You never know," I say, but I don't mean it. Unless something happens to Cam, so he couldn't play, I'm sure Ace won't see much actual field time at all.

Just the mere idea of Cam getting injured and being unable to play makes my heart trip over itself. It's too scary to even contemplate.

"You're just saying that." Ace grins, curling his fingers around his beer mug. "You're pretty."

I burst out laughing at the way he just blurted that out. "Thank you."

"Much prettier than Knox."

I'm still laughing. More like giggling. "I would hope so."

"He'd kill me if he knew I said that." Ace's eyes are twinkling. He seems pleased with himself.

"You should see my sister," I tell him. I'd guess they're about the same age. "She's even prettier than me."

"No way." He rests his hand over his heart like he can't fathom the thought. "I've got a weakness for blondes."

"She's blonde too." I tilt my head, studying him intently. "What year are you?"

His cheekbones turn the faintest touch of red. "A sophomore."

"And you're how old?"

Ace glances around the bar before he ducks down, his mouth right at my ear level. Which means he's really ducking low because he's extremely tall. "Fake ID. Don't blow my cover."

"Never," I vow as I lean away from him with a little smile.

He smiles in return, lifting his beer mug up and I do the same, clinking mine with his before we both take big swallows. He polishes the rest of his off, while I drink at least a third, and it was mostly foam.

I am seriously not a beer drinker. I should've gone with Nat and Derek to the bar and got a mixed drink.

"Noyes! Sit down, brotha!" Ace greets another teammate, who's currently sliding into the booth on the other side of the table, a cute brunette with him. "Join us!"

The girl sends me a helpless look as she settles in, curling her arm around Noyes' arm and leaning her head on his shoulder. Clearly, they're together. Clearly, she's staking her claim on her man and a tiny flicker of jealousy rises up within me, making me wish I could do the same to someone in particular.

A certain someone who chooses to push me away more often than not.

A guy who acts like he's interested, yet insists he wants nothing to do with me.

I contemplate Ace, who's currently engaged in conversation with every guy sitting at our table, telling a story about what happened to him while sitting on the sideline during the game. I'm half-listening, my gaze going to the table to my right, wishing I could hear what they're talking about.

Ace says something that makes everyone crack up and I join in, laughing at something I didn't even hear. I see Knox glance over at me, followed by Cam, and I immediately look away, praying that Knox doesn't come over here and say something stupid to embarrass me.

But it's not Knox who slides into the booth right next to me mere minutes later.

Nope.

It's Cam.

The moment he presses his big warm body right up against mine, I'm done for. I can't hear what Ace or the rest of the guys are saying. All I can focus on is how hard his thigh feels wedged next to mine. And how his arm brushes mine when he settles his beer mug on the table in front of him before turning to look at me with a giant smile on his face.

A smile that I don't recall ever seeing him wear before. It's dazzling. Beautiful. But there's another emotion lying just beneath it, one I can't quite figure out, and I stare at him in confusion.

"What's gotten into you?" I ask.

"I'm your new babysitter." When I don't respond, he continues, "Knox sent me over here to keep watch over you and tell everyone else to back the fuck off."

Cam sends a pointed look in Ace's direction.

Huh?

"I'm just being friendly, QB." Ace lifts his hands up like he's being held at gunpoint, just before he starts laughing.

He doesn't seem to take too much seriously, which is the complete opposite of Cam.

"Friendly, my ass," Cam mutters under his breath, shooting invisible daggers at Ace with his eyes.

"Oh, calm down." I reach out and settle my hand on his thigh, giving it a platonic pat and he quickly settles his hand on top of mine, trapping it there. I lift my gaze to his, suddenly breathless.

He angles his head away from mine, answering a question one of the guys asked him, his grip gentling but not moving. I'm able to splay my fingers out, touching as much of his thigh as I can, marveling at the muscle I feel beneath my palm.

He's rock hard and so freaking hot. I swear my hand is going to go up in flames if I keep it here much longer. But I don't want to stop touching him. In fact, I test him to see how far I can take it before he pushes me away.

I slide my hand inward, my fingers shifting to the inside of his thigh and he doesn't stop me. Keeping my gaze focused on the table in front of me, I stroke my index finger back and forth. Slowly.

Cam doesn't push my hand away. He doesn't stop me either when I shift my hand higher, close enough to touch his crotch. My heart racing, my breaths accelerating. I lift my head, my gaze seeking his.

He's not even looking in my direction, engaged in conversation with his teammates, but there's a tic in his jaw. Like he's barely restraining himself. As if my touch affects him.

Of course, it does. I'm zeroing in on his junk. It doesn't matter who I am, he's going to enjoy it.

Feeling emboldened, I brush the side of my hand against him, shocked to discover that he's…already hard?

I snatch my hand away, my entire body going hot. Blindly, I reach for my mug and chug the rest of it in a couple of swallows, needing the liquid to cool me down. I chance a look at him to find he's watching me, his expression impassive. No emotion noted.

Just before he settles that big hand of his on my knee.

I'm tense. Aware of his hand on me. It's innocent enough yet not. This is all taking place beneath the table, where no one else can see us, and my brother is sitting in the next booth over, which is dangerous. Though I can see from the corner of my eye that Knox is flirting with some random fangirl when he has the sweet and beautiful Joanna sitting right there in front of him.

My brother is such a bonehead.

"You need another beer?" Cam's voice is low, his focus entirely on me.

I stare into his eyes, my lips parting, all the air leaving me when he slides his hand up my leg, his fingers curving, sliding to the inside of my thigh. I clamp my legs together, trapping his hand, he smiles, the look on his face…

Sexy.

Slowly, I shake my head, unable to speak. His hand struggles to move between my locked thighs and I spread them a little to give him room. He shifts closer, his hand sweeping back and forth, getting closer. Closer…

"Hey, Blair! You should come to my frat tomorrow," Ace says.

Cam glares at him, but Ace is oblivious.

"Um, why?"

"We're having a big bash. Chasing away the Sunday blues. Would love to see you there. Already invited everyone else at the table, can't forget Maguire's sister." Ace grins.

"You'd be smart to forget all about her," Cam says like a freakin' threat.

I send him a look, but he's not paying attention to me. Well, with his eyes anyway.

His hand though? That's now firmly lodged directly between my thighs, pressing right against the seam of my jeans.

"Knox doesn't scare me," Ace says.

"He should. I should too."

"Cam," I murmur.

He presses more firmly against my pussy, and I swear I gasp.

"You're invited too, QB," Ace rushes to say. "We'd love to have you there."

Cam turns to face me. "You going?"

I nod, tilting my hips toward his hand.

"Then I'll be there too." He glares at Ace. "Someone has to watch over Blair."

"I don't need a babysitter at a frat party," I murmur, so only Cam can hear.

"I trust you. I don't trust any of those other fuckers that'll be at this party." He removes his hand from between my thighs, and I immediately mourn the loss. "If you're going, I'm going."

"You're so confusing," I tell him, as everyone else at our table starts arguing over a particular football stat.

"Tell me all about it," he mutters, draining his beer in one last swallow before he sets the mug on the table. He glances over at me, his gaze heated. Intense. I can't look away. I don't want to. Something has shifted between us tonight and I don't understand exactly what. "You into him?"

I frown. "Into who?"

"Him." He angles his head to his left, toward...Ace. "I think he likes you."

"He's just flirtatious. It's part of his personality. I don't believe he's into me," I insist, meaning every word I say.

"I don't know about that." There's that tic in his jaw again, and I realize what's changed between us. Changed with Cam.

He's...jealous. Of. Ace.

I'm freaking giddy at the thought.

"Fine. Be my date at the frat party tomorrow. You can stand guard over me all night," I say in challenge.

Cam doesn't even hesitate with his answer.

"Deal. I'll pick you up at your place."

Oh boy.

I think I'm in over my head.

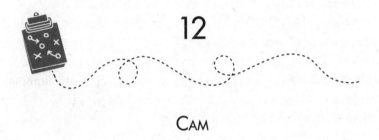

12

CAM

'm so amped up over this "date" with Blair tonight, I went shopping for a new outfit to impress her, and I'm not about to look into any hidden meaning there might be in this endeavor of mine. I'm just accepting it, running with it and telling myself it's no big deal. I needed new clothes anyway.

Uh huh.

I don't come from Maguire wealth, but my father gives me enough money to pay for my college and living expenses, with some left over. He also bought me the Challenger because I needed a car and it was what he called a graduation gift.

More like it makes him feel better to give me expensive things since he wasn't a great dad, but whatever. I'll take it.

I got into Colorado University on a partial scholarship but not a full ride, and that's okay since I was able to cover it. Football takes up most of my time, so it's hard for me to get a job. I don't spend a lot. I try to live frugally.

But tonight's date feels like an event I could splurge on a little.

I ended up at a shopping center in town where I bought an entire outfit for myself, plus a new pair of shoes. Shit, I even bought new socks and underwear, reassuring myself that it was all stuff I needed. I never go shopping, so I may as well take advantage while I'm here.

It's not like I'm trying to impress Blair tonight. That'll just give her hope that I'm taking whatever this is between us seriously, and I'm not.

No way can I actually think I have a chance with Blair.

After exiting the department store, loaded down with two bags full of stuff, I find myself wandering into one of those beauty/makeup stores, the place full of women. I'm the only guy there beyond a couple of employees. I immediately go to the men's cologne section, thinking I might find something new for myself, but somehow, inexplicably, I end up in the women's perfume section instead.

Directly in front of the Gucci display.

Goddamn, they make a lot of different perfumes. I rack my brain, trying to remember the name of the perfume Blair wears, and I'm standing in front of the display, slightly panicked when I hear a sweet voice come from behind me.

"Can I help you?"

I turn to find a woman about my mother's age, standing in front of me, clad in all black with vivid red lipstick coating her lips. "Uh…"

"Are you looking for something in particular?" she presses.

"I can't remember the name of it. I know it's a Gucci perfume." I'm starting to sweat from the pressure and I deal with pressure all the damn time out on the field, without ever freaking out like this.

"As you can see, there are plenty to choose from." She waves her hand at the variety of perfumes on display. "Maybe one of the newer ones?"

"Maybe." I'm hesitant only because, shit, I don't know.

"This one was released recently." She grabs a turquoise blue bottle from the shelf and that's when it hits me. I remember Blair saying it was in that color bottle.

"Pretty sure that's it." I take the bottle of perfume, confused when she also hands me a thin white paper stick. "What's that for?"

"It's a blotter. You can spray the perfume onto it to see if it's the correct one," she gently suggests, waving the blotter at me.

I take it and aim the perfume nozzle at the paper stick before I spray. The scent hits me immediately, before I even bring the blotter to my nose, inhaling deeply. That's it. The scent that Blair always wears.

The scent that practically brings me to my knees every time I catch a whiff of it.

"We offer a variety of sizes. Are you wanting to buy this as a gift?" the woman asks, her delicate brows lifting in question.

She already owns it. I hold the blotter stick to my nose again, taking another deep whiff. Floral and light and perfectly Blair. I wonder how long the scent lasts on paper.

"Sir?" the clerk asks when I still haven't said anything.

"What about that small size." I reach for the bottle that's no bigger than a writing pen, holding it up. "How much is this?"

She quotes the price, and since it's not awful, I somehow find myself at the register making the purchase. I don't know what I'm going to do with this perfume. I sure as hell am not going to give it to Blair because she already owns it and would probably ask me what the fuck is it for. And I'm definitely not giving it to my mom, like I told Blair I would. The last thing I want is for my mom to smell like the woman I am in hot pursuit of, even though I shouldn't be chasing after her.

Hot pursuit. That's not necessarily true. I'm not chasing Blair. Not really. There are a million reasons why it would never work between Blair and me. Yet here I am, buying a perfume because she wears it. Buying new clothes so I can look good for her later tonight when I pick her up.

I'm acting like this is a date when it absolutely cannot be.

What the hell is wrong with me?

Once I've made my purchase, I hightail it out of there and head back to my apartment, jumping right into the shower the second I get home. I think of Blair as I stand under the hot spray of water and scrub my head with shampoo, and what I did to her last night.

Touching her like I did. Though she started it. Resting her hand on my leg. Sliding it up, curling her fingers around the inside of my thigh.

Then I remember how I rested my hand on top of hers to keep it there, and yeah, I'm just as much to blame as she is.

She brushed those fingers right across my cock and it sprang to life.

Kind of like it's doing right now.

Giving in, I wrap my fingers around my dick and start stroking, my eyes falling closed as I imagine a different scenario playing out with Blair last night. Me slipping my hand beneath her jeans. Beneath her panties. Finding her wet and hot, testing her. Teasing her clit. Thrusting my fingers deep inside her tight heat.

My strokes increase. I lean against the shower wall, pressing my lips together to muffle the groan that slips out.

She would've spread her legs wider to give me better access, all while trying her best to pretend it wasn't happening. She'd smile and keep up the conversation with Ace while I was secretly getting her off, but she'd grow weaker. Until eventually, she would give in, her lips parting, her eyes closing, a soft moan escaping her.

That imagined sweet sound makes my muscles grow tight and my balls tingle. I'm on the verge, just like that.

Another image comes to mind. Blair joining me in the shower. Completely naked. On her knees in front of me, drenched by the water, her lush lips parted as I feed her my dick, inch by inch, until I'm hitting the back of her throat. She takes it all, groaning around my shaft, her eyes locking with mine as she pulls me out and licks at just the head with an exaggerated swipe of her tongue.

I'm coming with that visual still in my head, my groans loud, the semen that coats my fingers immediately washed away by the shower. I'm left a shaky mess, glad Knox isn't home, so he can't hear me and give me shit later. I have no idea where he is and I'm just grateful I don't have to answer to him when he asks where I'm going when I try to leave the apartment.

Escorting your hot as fuck sister to a frat house party. No big.

He'll figure it out soon enough, though. Ace didn't just invite us. He probably invited the entire team and I know a few of the guys will show up. Hell, several members of our team are in the same fraternity Ace is. I show up there with Blair tonight? They're all going to be talking about it tomorrow at practice.

And Knox will hear everything from someone else before he hears it from me.

That'll fucking suck.

. . .

"This is a shit idea and I don't think we should go to that party together," I announce to Blair as soon as she opens the door.

She comes to a standstill, her hand on the door handle, her other hand propped on the door frame, a frown on her pretty face. Her hair is curled into loose waves that cascade past her shoulders, covering her chest, and my gaze drops, widening when I take in what she's wearing.

"No way." I shake my head. "Uh uh."

"What?"

"Your...dress." If you can call it that. "You can't wear that to the party."

She glances down at herself before lifting her head, her gaze narrowed. "What's wrong with it?"

It shows off her gorgeous body, and I don't know if I'll be able to control myself around her tonight. It's strapless. White with little pink flowers scattered all over it. The top wraps around her tits and there's a bow in the center of her chest. Like I could pull it and expose her completely. There's a matching tie around her waist, like a belt? I don't know, but the skin below the tie is exposed, meaning I can see her belly button.

I scrub a hand over my face, hating my life.

The skirt is fitted, ending with a ruffle at the hem, and it hits her about mid-thigh. She has on tan, strappy flat sandals, so at least she's not in heels, but fuck.

She's going to give me a heart attack, I swear to God.

When I still haven't answered, her frown deepens.

"I thought it was pretty." Her voice is small and she sounds disappointed, which makes me feel like shit.

"It's pretty. You look gorgeous," I rush to say, noting the smile that appears on her face. I feel like I just got played to admit that out loud. "But there's so much skin exposed."

"Too much?" She lifts her brows, making a face.

Yes, I want to shout. *Way too much. I don't want any other motherfucker looking at you like I'm looking at you currently.* All I want is to undo the ties at her chest and her waist, preferably with my teeth.

"Yeah," I croak, scratching the side of my neck. "Your brother would kill me if I let you go out dressed like that."

"Good thing Knox won't be there then." She pulls the door shut behind her and that's when I notice she's got a tiny purse hanging from her shoulder.

Her scent hits me like a drug as she walks past, floral and warm and sweet. I trail after her like a dog sniffing out a treat, my gaze going to her ass and the way it shifts enticingly beneath the tight fabric of her dress.

I'm going to die tonight. Die of either overwhelming lust or I'll die defending the honor of my best friend's sister when I catch some jackass staring at her when she walks past him.

I pick up my speed as I watch her head for the Challenger, hitting unlock on the key fob, so she can open her own door. I'd open it for her, but the girl is somehow too fast for me, slipping into the passenger seat and disappearing with a gentle slam of the door.

Jogging toward my car, I open the door and slip inside, overwhelmed by the scent of her when I shut it. I glance over at her to find she's already watching me, an expectant look on her face, her hands resting on her bare thighs.

That fucking skirt is way too short, but I keep my mouth shut. Her scent is even more intensified inside my car, and I wonder if she bathed in it. And when I look a little more closely, I swear there's some sort of sheen covering her skin, like her lotion had glitter in it or something, and fuck me running, I am in big, massive trouble tonight.

"Are you ready to go?" she asks when I still haven't started the car.

"Oh yeah." The engine roars to life and I floor it while still in park, enjoying the sound. Trying to concentrate on that versus the beautiful woman sitting mere inches away from me. It would take nothing to reach out and touch her. Streak my fingers down her arm. Across her chest. Toy with the fabric that's tied at the center of her chest.

"Let's go then," she suggests, laughing when I back out of the parking space with squealing tires before I throw the car in drive and blast out of there like I've just robbed a bank and I'm desperate to get away from the cops.

"You're crazy," she says, watching me with laughing eyes.

I smile at her before I pull out onto the street. "I think you like it."

"You don't know how much."

13

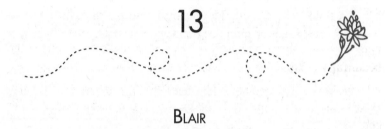

BLAIR

Pretty sure my plan worked. The moment Cam took in my outfit, his eyes practically bugged out of his head. He didn't approve, or so he said.

I think he approved plenty. He wouldn't stop staring at my chest. And he keeps inhaling loudly as he's driving, and I remember when he commented on my perfume before. I think he likes my Gucci Gorgeous scent. I might need to go buy a vat of that stuff. I sprayed so much on myself tonight as I was getting ready, I probably used up most of the bottle.

Not that I mind. It's worth using up a bunch of expensive perfume to get that reaction out of Cam, the man who rarely reacts at all.

The closer we get to fraternity row, the quieter Cam gets. He's quiet enough as it is, so I'm thinking something is seriously bugging him. I just wish I knew exactly what it was.

"Do you not want to go to this party?" I finally ask.

"I want to go. I just—worry what might happen if we walk in together."

"What? Are you embarrassed to be seen with me?" I'm kind of mad he would say something like this.

"No, it's not that. I just know if anyone from the team sees us together—and there will be guys from the team there, I can guarantee it—they're going to tell Knox. And then Knox will ask me about it, and I won't know what to say."

"Just say you came with me to babysit. Isn't that what you said last night?"

He pulls the car alongside the curb, putting the vehicle in park before he turns to look at me. "I don't want anyone getting the wrong idea."

"Like what?"

"Like we're...together." He faces straight ahead, like he can't look at me, which builds the anger within me, slowly but surely.

"It's fine." Leaning down, I grab my bag off the floorboard and slip the strap onto my shoulder. "We can walk in separately."

The frat house we're going to is the next block up. It won't be much of a walk at all.

"I don't know—"

"I do know, and that's fine with me. I'm a big girl. I can walk into a party by myself." I climb out of the car without another word, slamming the door as hard as I can, the car rattling with the force of it. Shaking my hair back, I head down the sidewalk with my head held high, ignoring Cam who's trying to—not so discreetly—call my name.

"Cam." I turn and watch him as he approaches, resting my hands on my hips, annoyed beyond reason. And I'm so tired of being annoyed with Cam Fields. Isn't he tired of this bullshit too? "You don't have to go if you don't want to. Clearly, you're not comfortable being seen with me, or being with me in general. We're wasting each other's time here."

"What?" He sounds completely confused, and I almost feel sorry for him.

Almost.

"I'm walking into that frat by myself, and if you want to show up a few minutes later, looking like we didn't come together, cool. Go for it. But if you really want to leave? I'm okay with that too."

We study each other in silence for a minute, and I take the opportunity to really drink him in. Just like I made the effort to dress up for him, it appears he did the same for me too. He's wearing a fitted navy button-down shirt with the sleeves rolled up to his elbows and jeans, with pristine white Nikes on his feet.

I'm tempted to step all over them with my sandals, but I tell myself to chill.

He looks good. I swear he even got a haircut, his dark hair trimmed neatly on the sides and a little longer on top. His dark eyes sweep over me, lingering on spots that he has no business lingering over, and I stand up straighter, squaring my shoulders. Preparing for a fight.

"Go ahead and walk in first," he says. "I'll wait a few before I come inside."

Without a word, I turn away from him and start walking, my anger growing with every step closer to the frat. He's such a wimp. Is he that afraid Knox will find out we came together to this stupid party? Knox would probably be relieved that Cam escorted me here. At least Knox can trust his best friend not to do anything, ahem, inappropriate towards me.

Ugh that's so annoying.

The closer I get to the house party, the louder everything sounds: multiple conversations happening at once, punctuated by a squeal of high-pitched laughter. The low pulsing bass of music being played. A group of people loudly counting down, right before they all scream, "Chug!"

Ah, welcome to college.

The front lawn is teeming with people, the majority of them male, and all of them looking at me with undisguised interest in their eyes. I offer them a wave as I head up the sidewalk that leads to the porch, carefully taking the steps while all eyes are on me. The moment I'm inside, I breathe a sigh of relief, swallowed up in the crowd.

I didn't like being put on display just now in front of those guys. Made me feel kind of creepy.

There are so many people in this house, it's hard to move. I patiently make my way through the crowd, smiling at familiar faces, wishing someone would say something to me.

Wishing more that Cam was man enough to enter the house by my side.

"Blair, you made it!"

I turn to find Ace leaning against the wall, surrounded by a group of women who are all watching me with suspicious gazes. He's grinning at me and he pushes away from the wall, approaching me with open arms just before he wraps me up in a big hug.

"I'm so glad you came." He rocks me back and forth, and it takes me a minute to extract myself from his hold. And when I finally do break free, I find he's still grinning at me while the women all watch me, looking ready to scratch my eyes out. "Where's Cam?"

"Cam?" I glance around like I'm looking for him. "I don't know."

"Oh. I thought you two were coming here together."

"You did?" I squeak, clearing my throat.

Don't want to give myself away.

"Well, yeah. I saw his hand on your thigh last night so…" He nods, giving me a look that says he's on to us. "I just thought you two were a thing."

I swallow hard, trying to come up with something to say, but I draw a blank. So I just shrug instead.

"You two *are* together?"

"Uh, no." I smile brightly at him. "No. Not really. Not at all. He's just a friend. My brother's friend. And mine. Nothing else. Just friends."

I'm babbling and I sound stupid. I need to quit while I'm ahead.

"Uh huh." The knowing look on Ace's face tells me he's got us all figured out after all. "Do you know if he'll be here tonight?"

"Are you talking about Camden Fields?" one of the girls standing by Ace asks.

He turns his charm on her. "I am. I'm his backup QB. We're friends."

I want to roll my eyes. "He should be coming."

"Really?" Ace asks, at the same time that half of the females he's with do as well.

Nodding, I send all of them an assessing look. I do not want any of these women near Cam tonight. They are all far too good looking and a lot of them are showing plenty of skin. More than I am, and I felt like I was really pushing the limits. "He should be here any minute."

With that, I turn and leave them, heading deeper into the house, in search of the kitchen. I eventually find it, relieved to see that it's not as crowded as the rest of the house and I can actually breathe in here.

There are giant steel buckets full of cans of beer on the floor, a row of bottles of hard liquor lining the counter, and I can see through the window that faces the backyard that there are a couple of kegs outside as well. Plenty of alcohol to get good and drunk tonight, which is rapidly becoming my plan.

I grab a red solo cup and a bottle of flavored vodka and pour myself a drink, taking a sip and grimacing the moment the overly sweet alcohol hits my tongue. Hissing through my gritted teeth, I take another drink, steeling myself, enjoying the sensation of the liquor burning a pleasant trail through my veins, settling into my stomach. Despite the bad taste, I can already feel it working its magic on me.

Magic I desperately need.

"Hey."

I glance up to find a very attractive dark-haired guy approaching me with just the right amount of swagger that makes him seem confident without being too cocky. I glance around quickly to make sure he's actually talking to me before I say, "Hi."

He comes to a stop directly in front of me, standing on the other side of the counter. "I don't think I've seen you on campus."

"I just started here this fall," I offer.

"Ah, that makes sense. I know I'd remember if I saw someone as beautiful as you around here before." He smiles, and it's a nice one, but it can't make up for the cheesy line he just fed me.

I smile in return before I take another sip of the terrible vodka, needing it to carry me through this conversation.

"I'm Cohen." He thrusts his hand out toward me.

"Blair." I shake his offered hand, not feeling a single thing when he touches me. Not a tingle, not a shiver. Nothing.

How unfortunate.

"Nice to meet you." He smiles, reluctantly letting my hand go.

"Yeah. Same." I glance around the room, wishing I would spot a familiar face.

"Are you from around here?"

I meet his gaze once more. "I grew up in Colorado, yeah."

"I'm from California."

"I have family in California," I offer.

"Oh yeah? From what part?"

Shit. I don't want to admit to this guy I'm related to Drew Callahan. That would be a mistake. "Somewhere in the mountains? I don't remember exactly where."

"We have a lot of mountains in California," he says with a nod. "It's beautiful there."

"It is," I agree.

"I miss it. But it's beautiful here, too. The mountains, they're incredible. Great for snowboarding. Do you snowboard?"

I shake my head. "I've done it, but I'm not very good at it."

"Oh, maybe you just need more practice. I'm not a pro. Not even close, but I enjoy it."

My problem is I don't really enjoy it. I'm not very sporty. I'm like my mom in that sense. She loves watching sports—mostly football. She'll support my dad and brother in every way possible. When I was younger, Ruby and I were both in dance, but I was kind of awkward while Ruby was great. She ended up on the hip-hop competition dance team at our studio for a few years in her early teens, and she loved every minute of it.

"You're living in the perfect state to snowboard," I say, glancing into my cup. It's empty and I really don't want to refill it with that shitty tasting vodka.

"You know someone who's in this frat?" Cohen asks, changing the subject. "Or did you crash the party? I won't tell on you if you did."

"I know someone." He sends me a pointed look, so I give him a name. "Ace."

He grins. "You know Ace? Ace is my boy! We were recruited here together."

I'm guessing this means Cohen is the same age as Ace, and Ace is a year younger than I am. "He's nice."

"Yeah, he is. How do you know him?"

This is where I don't want to admit my connections, but Cohen isn't leaving me much choice. "I, uh...my brother is Knox Maguire."

Cohen's eyes nearly bug out of his head at my reveal. "No shit? You're related to Knox?"

"Yeah. He's my big brother."

"He's a fucking great football player. Makes sense, considering who his dad is." Cohen's eyes seem to grow even larger, if that's possible. "That means Owen Maguire is your dad too. And Drew Callahan is your uncle."

"You know your football."

"I'm from California, remember? I'm a Niner fan. Grew up in the Bay Area. San Mateo." Realization dawns. "Is that the family you were referring to that lives in California? The Callahans?"

Oh God. I'm in over my head with this conversation. And Cohen has latched on to it like a baby with a bottle.

"Um, yeah." I laugh, trying to play it off. "We used to go to their lake house a lot. Still do every Thanksgiving."

"Where you play those infamous football games with the family, right? I can't even fucking imagine." He sounds beyond impressed, but I'm a little alarmed.

How did he know about the family football games during Thanksgiving? That's all my Uncle Drew's doing. He loves those games. Pretty sure he enjoys Thanksgiving more than Christmas.

"Right. Uh, how did you know about the family football game?" I sound nervous, but that remark left me unsettled.

"Oh, he mentioned it in some article a while ago. And now everyone asks Jake Callahan about it. And Eli Bennett. He's married to your cousin Ava."

"Yeah," I say weakly, hating how much this guy knows about my family. I know they're in the public spotlight, and it makes sense. Not only was my uncle a revered football player and a game announcer for a few years, but now his son and his sons-in-law all play for the NFL. And my youngest cousin Beck plays college football too. He always brushes it off and says the NFL isn't for him, but we'll see.

My family is a giant dynasty of football players that my brother is most likely on his way to becoming a part of.

Just like Cam. He has the potential to go pro as well. Something we've never really talked about before.

Something I'm not so sure I would be comfortable with, if I'm being real right now. Oh, I know I could handle it, considering my background. My dad wasn't nearly as famous as my uncle, he did have his moments of fame, though he was pretty private about it all. Dad had quite a few endorsement deals, and made great money. But it's a different scenario when you're the famous QB who leads your team to a number of Super Bowl wins.

That could be Cam. He has the potential. I believe he could do whatever he sets his mind to.

Could I handle that though? I'm getting way ahead of myself, but this dude is freaking me out talking about my family, and my brush with fame isn't what I would consider a big deal.

If I were with Cam, though? And he entered the NFL with the spotlight shining brightly upon him?

That might be cause for a potential freak out.

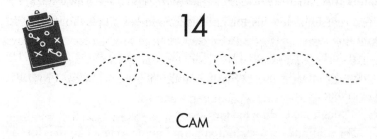

14

CAM

I enter the house minutes after I watch Blair stride inside, and I'm immediately in search of her. The place is packed with people and I can't help but wonder what the fuck would it be like if the party was held on a Saturday night.

It's Sunday and everyone showed up in droves. But a party is a party. The day it's happening doesn't really matter.

"Camden, hi!" A cute girl with half her tits hanging out of her dress greets me, a red solo cup clutched in her hand, her overly bright smile unsettling.

"Hey." I glance around the room, wishing I would spot Blair's familiar blonde head so I could get away from this woman but no such luck.

"How are you?"

"I'm good." I hesitate, staring at her face. Do I know her? Did I hook up with her before? Shit, I can't remember and I feel like a shithead. "How are you?"

"Fantastic. Glad that you're here. You were awesome in

yesterday's game," she gushes before she takes a big gulp from her cup.

"Thanks." I see a blonde in the distance. "Nice seeing you."

I start to walk, the girl calling after me, "Let's catch up soon!"

Yeah. More like never.

It goes on like this for a few minutes. I keep running into women, who are overly familiar with me, and I don't know if they're just acting this way to make conversation with me or if I actually know them. The more this happens, the worse I feel, and when I finally spot a familiar face—Ace's—I'm actually glad.

And I am rarely glad to see this kid. He makes me feel old. He makes me feel like he's gunning for my position and I can't trust him. I hate that.

Though the feeling old part is the worst of it.

If I continue on with football, am I going to feel like that for the entirety of my career? Constantly worried that someone else is eager and ready to take my place? A couple of mistakes and the coaching staff could be ready to get rid of me. A bad season could mean I get traded. An injury could mean I'm out for the season. Or even out for good.

All of that shit is nerve-racking. I've been a lucky son of a bitch the past three seasons. I've had some hard sacks. Been injured a couple of times, but nothing too serious. I need to sail through this season and then I'll be free.

Only to torture myself and hope I get picked up in the NFL draft.

"My number one QB," is how Ace greets me when I get close enough to hear him. He's currently surrounded by a posse of women, and they are all watching him with adoration in their eyes. He slaps me on the back. "Glad you could make it."

"Thanks for inviting me." I smile at the women who are all watching me with interest flaring in their gazes before I return my focus to Ace. "There are a lot of people here."

"Isn't it great? I didn't think we'd have as big a bash since it's a Sunday, but here we are." He spreads his arms out wide, indicating the packed frat house, and I can't help but smile at him. He seems so damn pleased with himself. "Helps that people like you show up. Tried to invite Maguire, but he didn't respond. Was kind of hoping you'd bring him with you."

"He wasn't home when I left." Pretty normal for Knox. Sometimes he holes up in the library on Sunday night to do homework. He did that a lot last year, and it helped him to focus and keep up his grades.

"That's too bad. I'd like to get to know him better. I'd love to get to know you better too, but you guys are always out on the field while I'm sitting on the sidelines." His smile is completely unassuming, and I almost don't know how to take his comment. Is he bashing on us?

Or is he just that freaking nice?

"I saw Blair earlier." He drops the comment casually and that gets my attention.

"Oh yeah?" I try to play it cool, but I'm desperate to find her.

"Yeah." He leans in closer, his voice lowering. "I thought you two were a thing."

"Why would you think that?" I work hard to keep my expression completely neutral, but I feel like I'm going to crack under the sudden pressure.

Why the hell would he assume Blair and I are together?

"You two looked pretty cozy last night."

"We did?"

"I saw your hand on her thigh." He sends me a look, one that says I know what you two are up to. "I get it if you don't want to say anything to Maguire. From what I've observed, he's pretty overprotective of his sister."

Fuck. He saw that? And here I thought we were being discreet.

"It was nothing."

"That's what she said."

My heart drops. "Did she tell you we were together?"

"No. She played it off like you're currently doing." Ace laughs, slowly shaking his head. "It's cool, bro. Your secret is safe with me."

"There's no secret to keep," I protest.

"So, if I told Maguire that I saw you with your hand on his sister's thigh at Logan's, he wouldn't care?"

Knox specifically sent me to sit with Blair to protect her, as he calls it. Yes, he would care.

A lot.

"Best if you never mention it," I say as casually as possible.

"That's what I thought." He reaches out to slap me on the back again, nearly sending me a couple of steps forward. The kid is strong. "Like I said, your secret is safe with me."

"Ooh, Ace, are you saying Camden Fields has secrets?" one of the women asks, her eyes twinkling with curiosity.

"Anything to do with football and strategy? Yeah. I'm taking his secrets to the grave." Our gazes meet and I wish I could tell him thank you, but I just nod my agreement.

I need to get the fuck out of here.

"I'm going to grab something to drink," I tell Ace.

"Everything's either in the kitchen or the backyard. Have fun, bro. Come back by and we can chat some more. I'll be holding court here all night," Ace says with a friendly smile.

I leave him with his harem of babes and make my way to the kitchen, my head spinning. Fucking Ace—he knows. Who else knows? Did anyone notice us? I thought we were being so sly. Ace was sitting right next to Blair on the other side of her, so I guess I should've assumed he might've seen something.

Here I was, overly confident while touching her under the table, and we still got caught. It's fucking worrisome.

I enter the kitchen, appreciating that it's not as crowded, even though this is where all the booze is. My gaze catches on a familiar blonde head and I'm filled with relief to see it's Blair.

Only to be immediately filled with rage when I notice she's with some random guy, who's currently talking to her tits.

Without thinking, I approach them, stopping just behind Blair, my gaze fixed on the dude who's still staring at her chest. Blair glances over her shoulder, doing a double take when she realizes it's me, and she turns her back to the guy, the relief on her face obvious.

"Cam! There you are. I've been looking everywhere for you!" She's louder than usual, her expression overly bright, and I get the sense she's putting on a show.

Probably trying to get rid of the dickhead behind her. Hopefully.

"Oh yeah? Well, here I am." I stare at her beautiful face, entranced for a second too long before I send a scathing look toward the dude. "Who's your...friend?"

"Cohen." The guy holds his hand out for me and I lean across Blair to briefly shake his hand, giving it an extra squeeze to flex my strength because I'm an asshole like that. "You were fucking amazing yesterday, bro."

Bro. I'm not this guy's bro.

"Thanks," I say coolly, my gaze returning to Blair's, who's watching me with pure panic in her eyes. "You two just meet?"

"Yes," she murmurs.

"Maguire's sister," Cohen tells me, like I'm an idiot. Like I don't live with the very Maguire he's referring to.

"Yeah, I know." Blair turns to face Cohen, standing right next to me, and I sling my arm around her bare shoulders, staking my claim as I pull her into my side. Like we're a couple or whatever. "Just a warning to you, Cohen. I'm as protective of her as her brother is. And that's saying a lot."

It's quiet among the three of us, despite the party raging on around us. The music and the constant chatter. The people yelling outside, their good-natured shouts making me wish I was out there. The tension between me and Cohen grows the longer we watch each other. And the look of pure panic on Cohen's face when he realizes I'm not playing is undeniable.

A wave of satisfaction washes over me. God, sometimes I really am an asshole, but this guy needs to get the hint.

"Noted," Cohen says solemnly, his gaze flicking to the right. "Uh, I just spotted my friends over there. I'll see you both later. Nice meeting you."

Cohen is gone in an instant and the moment he is, Blair is shaking my arm off her shoulders, turning to glare up at me.

"You drove him away." Her tone is accusatory.

"And I don't get a thank you?"

"You just did it in such an...intimidating way," she says.

"How else did you expect me to get rid of him? He was all over you." I saw red. I wanted to fuck that guy up. All because he was *smiling* at Blair.

Smiling.

Oh yeah, and staring at her tits.

Why did I get so pissed just now over some dumb guy? Over Blair?

Because you like her, you idiot.

"He wasn't all over me. Not really." I hate that she defends him, but then she adds, "It was kind of weird how he knew so much about my family, though. That was a little off-putting."

She crosses her arms in front of her, which plumps up her breasts, causing them to rise above the fabric of her dress a little. I'm fairly positive she's not wearing a bra and that realization causes my insides to go a little haywire.

"I'm not surprised." I'm more surprised that I'm defending the asshole. "Your family is pretty famous. We all like talking about your dad and uncle. And your cousins."

"Yeah, but you don't feel this constant need to mention them all the time. That guy latched on to it and couldn't stop talking about them. It's just—it's weird sometimes. Still." She drops her arms, shrugging.

"Your dad was famous," I remind her.

"When I was younger. I don't remember a lot of it. And he wasn't nearly as popular as Uncle Drew." She pauses, her gaze meeting mine. "That sort of thing could happen to you, you know. In fact, I think it's definitely going to happen."

I scoff, stuffing down the surge of pleasure I feel at her words. "Yeah, right."

No way can I count on it. Shit changes on a dime. I'll be praised and loved one minute, torn apart and ravaged the next. Everything hinges on how I play this season.

Everything.

"I'm being serious. You'll end up in the draft and you'll get picked up pretty fast. By the third or fourth round at least. And when you take your new team far, which I have no doubt you'll do exactly that, then you'll be famous too. A celebrity. Like my uncle. The quarterbacks always get all the attention." She peers at me, like she's trying to look deep into my mind. My soul. "Are you prepared for that?"

I'm not even focused on her asking if I'm prepared for so-called fame. I'm too caught up on the fact that she has no doubts in regard to my success. She actually believes I'll be in the NFL one day and that I'll be successful.

That feels...good. Fucking awesome, really. No one has that sort of faith in me. My parents are too wrapped up in their own problems to worry about me. My brother probably doesn't even remember my name. My teammates don't say shit like that because we're all so focused on our own selves, and I totally understand that. I get it. I'm too wrapped up in my own shit too.

My coaches tell me I can do it, but they also share their doubts with me. Or they add the word "if" to every sentence.

If you have a good season.

If you don't get injured.

If you make it into the draft.

If you get picked up.

If. If. If.

Blair just flat-out said I'll make it. Her belief in me is that solid.

"I don't know. I guess I'll worry about it when it happens." I shrug, trying to play it cool. Like I don't have a single concern in the world about my future.

"Oh, come on. You know it's going to happen." She reaches out to swat at my chest and I grab her wrist, keeping her hand pinned to my chest. She doesn't struggle to get away. She doesn't make any demands either.

No, Blair just stands there and lets me hold her. Lets me stare into her eyes as I try to quietly convey how much it means to me, what she just said.

That she fucking believes in me when, most of the time, I don't even believe in myself.

"I don't know," I admit. "We'll see."

"So cryptic," she murmurs.

"I have to be." I tug on her wrist, pulling her even closer, her body gently colliding with mine. "I don't believe in myself as much as you seem to believe in me."

15

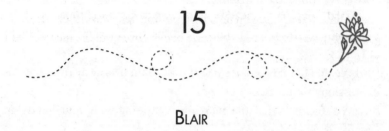

BLAIR

I stare at Cam in disbelief. Is he for real right now? He always acts like he's got everything under control. Like nothing bothers him. He's calm on the field, off the field, everywhere he's at. To hear him say he doesn't always believe in himself is…

Shocking.

What else is shocking is him voluntarily touching me at a frat party. In public. Surrounded by all kinds of people. His fingers are still wrapped around my wrist, his other arm somehow slipping around my waist, and I go completely still when I see the heated look in his eyes.

Like he…wants me.

"This dress is criminal," he murmurs, his gaze sweeping over me, leaving me shaky. His fingers slip just beneath the fabric of my dress' open back, pressing into my skin. "I should've never let you leave the house wearing it."

I glance down at myself, noting the way my cleavage is most definitely exposed, before I return my gaze to Cam's. "What's wrong with it?"

"It shows too much skin." His fingers dip lower, and I suck in a sharp breath. "We should get out of here."

"We barely just got here."

"No one will notice we're gone."

"They'll miss you. Ace was so glad you came."

"Yeah. About Ace." Cam releases his hold on me, dipping his head so he can murmur in my ear, "Did he ask you if we were together?"

I nod, keeping my head bent, staying as close to him as possible. I am enjoying this way too much. "He saw you touch my leg last night at Logan's."

"Yeah. He told me the same thing." Cam lifts away from me, his expression unreadable. "Let's go."

"Yo, Fields! What the fuck are you doing with your hands on Maguire's sister?"

We both whirl around to find Derek striding into the kitchen, a girl under each of his arms, a giant shit-eating grin on his face. Cam springs away from me like I'm diseased, and I run a shaky hand through my hair, flipping it over my shoulder.

"Wasn't touching her." Cam looks at me. "Was I touching you?"

I turn to face Derek and declare, "He had his hands all over me."

Derek laughs, dropping his arms from the girls' shoulders. "That's what I thought. I like this girl, Camden. She's feisty."

Guys who call women feisty should be socked in the gut, I swear. "Derek, I would never let you touch me. Knox has told me too many things about you."

Derek actually appears offended and the girls who still stand on either side of him start giggling. "What sort of things?"

"That you're a manwhore for one." Like how Joanna's roommate Natalie ended up leaving the bar with Derek last night and now here he is at a frat party with not just one but two women hanging off of him.

Derek flicks his chin at me. "Nothing wrong with that. Your brother's one too."

I make a face. "No need to give me details."

"And Cam isn't an altar boy either. He might be the worst out of all of us." Derek waves a hand in Cam's direction.

"Oh, really?" I turn to look at Cam and he's hanging his head, but I can see his cheeks are faintly pink. Like he's embarrassed.

"Yeah, he's a complete dog. He's always hooking up with girls, taking them out to the Challenger. The back seat of that car has seen some major action." Derek chortles. "Hell, he just had some chick back there last week—"

"Shut the fuck up, D," Cam practically snarls, his panicked gaze flitting in my direction for the briefest moment before he looks away.

"Sorry, captain," Derek says morosely, before he grabs his girls and steers them out to the backyard.

More deafening silence follows when Derek's gone and it's just me and Cam, watching each other warily. Derek's words still ring in my head.

"The Challenger sees a lot of action, huh?" I raise my brows.

"Don't listen to him—"

Not wanting to hear his lame defense, I interrupt him.

"I swear I've even heard Knox say that." I cross my arms, trying to fight the humiliation that wants to take over. Feeling stupid and used and just completely...ugh. Why didn't Cam just try and make out with me in the back seat of his car already? I probably would've done whatever he wanted last night. All he had to do was say the word, and like the idiot I am, I would've been rolling around in the back seat at the word go, eager to give him a hand job or whatever.

God, I'm so dumb.

"I mean, it's not a lie, okay? Yes, the back seat of my car might've seen...some action." Cam appears pained by the admission. Good. "But Derek is exaggerating. They all exaggerate. My number is definitely lower than what people claim it is."

"And what exactly is your number?"

He rubs his chin, grimacing. "I don't want to say it out loud."

Which means it's awful.

"I know my exact number." I drop my arms at my side, glaring at him. "It's four."

With that, I turn and exit the kitchen, the volume level increasing twenty-fold when I enter the living room. There are people everywhere. Groups of girls talking and laughing. A cluster of guys doing the same. There are couples blatantly groping each other and couples that are arguing. One girl has tears streaming down her face as she yells at who I can only assume is her boyfriend, her friends standing right behind her in solidarity.

Every single person has some sort of alcoholic beverage in their hand.

I push my way through the crowd, smiling when I make eye contact with anyone, none of their faces familiar. Sometimes I wonder if it was a bad idea, transferring to the same university my brother goes to after spending the last two years at home, attending community college and trying to figure out what I want to do with my life.

I still don't know what I want to do with my life, but I know one thing I want to do right freaking now.

And that's drop-kick Camden Fields across the room.

More like I'm furious at myself. Furious at Cam for being so incredibly good-looking and charming and popular. He's been with so many girls, the back seat of his car should probably be sanitized, possibly even reupholstered, and God, I hate how pathetic that makes me feel.

Maybe I need to change my focus and find a nice guy to fall for. A calm, slightly nerdy, really smart guy, who's quiet and no one notices. Who might not make me shake or tingle every time he so much as looks at me, but that's okay. I can deal with that. As long as he's sweet and kind, I can teach him how to give me an orgasm. It's not that hard.

I'm close to the front door of the house, eager to make my escape, when a big body brushes against my back, an arm shooting out to stop me from opening the door. I recognize the hand that presses against the wood, his fingers splayed. That hand will most likely make him millions someday.

Despite everything I just learned, despite my worry and feelings of stupidity, I still want those same big hands all over me.

Just once. Just so I know what it's like.

"This all feels very familiar," I tell Cam, glancing over my shoulder to find him hovering behind me.

"Where do you think you're going?" Ooh, he sounds mad. Good. I'm mad too.

I lift my chin. "I'm leaving."

"Hey." He rests his other hand on my waist, a ghost of a touch that I can't help but lean into, which means that since the dress has cut-outs, his fingers are now burning into my bare skin. "I'm an asshole."

"You are," I readily agree.

"I didn't have a girl in the back seat of my car last week."

I swallow hard, briefly closing my eyes. That was the part that got to me the most. He could be flirting with me, staring at me, rejecting me and still hooking up with other women.

"I haven't been with a girl in…a while," he admits, his voice low and shivery and doing weird things to my insides. Twisting them all up and making me feel…agitated.

In a good way.

Facing the door, I ask, "Really?"

"B, look at me." I do as he asks, hating how much I like him just calling me B. "Believe me. Don't believe Derek. That guy is an asshole."

"So are you. You just said so yourself."

"True. But when it comes to you, I won't be an asshole. I never want to treat you bad. Or disrespect you."

"Because of my brother?"

"Because of you. I like *you*. Not because you're my best friend's sister, either." He inclines his head toward the open archway to the right of the front door. "Come sit with me. We don't need to leave yet. I'll grab us some drinks and we can just sit around and…talk."

"You want to talk to me? Out in public?" I'm shocked.

His smile is slow. Sexy. Every little part of me lights up and I can't stop staring at his lips when he speaks. "Yeah. Who's going to say anything? We're just friends, right?"

"Right," I echo, letting him take my hand and lead me into the small, cozy room that actually has seating available. There's an overstuffed couch and loveseat that are angled next to each other, both occupied by people on either end. I sit on the loveseat and Cam sits on the couch, a small end table with a lamp between us.

"Save my seat," he orders before he rises to his feet. "I'll be right back."

I watch him leave, startled by the turn of events. Confused by my feelings for him. I glance over at the couple sitting on the other end of the couch. They're completely wrapped up in each other, passionately kissing. I swear I see tongue at one point and I look away, just before I see him touch her boob.

I really hope they don't have sex in here. That'll be super awkward.

Cam is back within two minutes, carrying a solo cup in each hand and when he gives me mine, I check the contents inside—it's blue— before I glance up at him. "What is this?"

"A wine cooler." He shrugs, slightly sheepish. "They always have a few in the fridge for the girls who don't want to drink the other stuff."

"How do you know that?"

"I've been to this frat before. A few times." He settles onto the spot he just vacated, sending a concerned glance toward the groping couple before he takes a swig from his cup. "I wanted to make sure you were drinking something you liked."

"I drank beer last night."

"You barely choked it down."

True.

And I love that he noticed that.

I take a sip from the cup, surprised to find the drink fruity and delicious. I take a bigger gulp, tasting the alcohol this time around, and I make an ahh sound after I swallow.

"You like it?"

I'm a little embarrassed he caught me doing that. "Definitely. Thank you."

"Still mad at me?"

I wince. "A little."

"Can I make it up to you?"

"Definitely." I nod, staring at the contents of my cup once more. "How?"

"Talk to me." It's so simple. But it's all I want.

Just your basic conversation with Cam. No protesting, no telling me, *stay away, you're my best friend's sister* type stuff.

"We talk," he says almost defiantly. He sounds defensive. "Isn't what we're doing right now?"

"I want to have a real conversation with you, Camden Fields. I want to know your favorite season. Mine is fall. Do you have a sweet tooth or a salty one? Did you wear braces, because you have really straight teeth, so I'm going to assume yes. What's your favorite color, your favorite food? What are you scared of? What makes you happy? If you could go anywhere in the world right now, where would you go? When was your first kiss, your first heartbreak, your first job? When did you know you wanted to be a football player? Tell me everything." I prop my elbow on the arm of the loveseat, resting my chin on my fist and wait for his response.

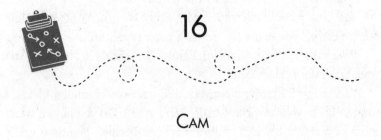

16

CAM

I glance over my shoulder yet again, checking on that couple who are literally all over each other. As in, she's currently dry humping his leg and his hands are on her hips, guiding her, their mouths still locked.

Shit.

"Hey," I call to them, but they completely ignore me. They start moving even faster, and she's panting into his mouth. Jesus. "Hey!"

They break away from each other's lips, both of them glaring at me.

"You two need to take this somewhere else. Get a room," I advise them, and after a few seconds of heavy breathing and straightening their clothes, they scramble off the couch, linking their hands and shooting dirty looks in our direction as they leave the room.

The moment they're gone, Blair laughs, and it's the sweetest sound.

"Glad they're gone." She shakes her head. "They were making me uncomfortable."

Same. Watching them trying to get it on only made me think of getting it on with Blair, and while I would love to do that, I'm definitely not going to make a public spectacle of myself with her.

That I'm even contemplating getting with her is…huge. At least for me, it is.

"Come sit by me." I pat the empty spot to my left on the couch.

Blair frowns. "Are you sure?"

Damn, I hate that she doubts me, but I deserve it. Fucking Derek, opening his big mouth like he did and telling her I'm a total horn dog. What a dick.

But Derek didn't lie. The back seat of the Challenger has definitely seen a lot of action—not last week though. Not for a while. That's where he's mistaken.

"Positive." I pat the empty spot again. "Come here."

She rises from the loveseat and doesn't hesitate, settling in right next to my side. We're so close, you couldn't fit a piece of paper in between us. Her scent swarms me, reminding me that I now own it and can spray it in my room whenever I want. And that realization is making me feel pretty fucking weird, so I focus on the questions she just asked me.

"All right, you want to talk? Let's talk." I settle in deeper into the couch, surprised by how comfortable it is. My weight makes the cushions dip, Blair falling into me a little, and I stretch my arm across the back of the couch, dangling my fingers perilously close to her bare shoulder.

I will be touching that shoulder here in a few. Mark my words.

"Do you remember my questions?" she asks hopefully, peering up at me from beneath her thick lashes.

"I'm going to try." I lean my head back, staring up at the ceiling. There's an old water stain above me, and a thick spider web in the corner. This place has definitely seen better days. "Um, my favorite season is summer. I have more of a salty tooth I guess, but I do like cheesecake. I wore braces. I had terrible teeth. So crooked."

She laughs softly, and I don't need to look at her pretty face to know she's smiling. "Me too."

I glance down at her, drowning in her green eyes for a moment. "My favorite color is green. My favorite food is...pizza. I'm scared of failure. Football makes me happy. My first kiss was with Lara Young. We were six."

"Aw."

"My first heartbreak? Hasn't happened yet. My first job was at McDonald's."

Blair giggles. "McDonald's? Really?"

"Don't knock it." I tap her shoulder with my index finger, leaving my fingers there, savoring her smooth skin. "I worked there the summer before my junior year in high school. I made decent money, but the hours were shit. And I knew I wanted to be a football player when my parents put me in pee-wee football. I was six and wanted to conquer the world."

"You did a lot when you were six," she notes, amusement lacing her voice.

"I've been focused since birth."

"I believe it." She's quiet for a moment. "You skipped a few questions."

"I did?"

"Yeah." She glances over at me the same time I look down at her. "If you could be anywhere in the world right now, where would you go?"

I get a little lost in her eyes for a second, that look on her face. She's waiting for my answer, expectant, and I realize I have to be one hundred percent real with her right now.

"You really want to know?"

"I'm dying to know," she admits.

"I wouldn't want to be anywhere else right now, because I'm perfectly happy right here with you," I answer her, staring into her eyes.

They widen slightly, my answer shocking her, and I know why.

This is not normal for me. I'm the guy who pushes her away. Who tells her it can't happen.

Tonight...fuck it. She wants to have a real conversation with me, so I'm going to be real with her.

"Oh," she finally says, dropping her gaze so she's staring at her lap, where her hands currently rest. "Wow."

I lean into her, inhaling the scent of her hair as discreetly as possible. "I mean it. I like spending time with you, B."

"I like it when you call me B." I see just the corner of her mouth turn up and I know she's smiling. I give her shoulders a squeeze, savoring the feel of her silky-smooth skin beneath my palm.

"Your turn." When she finally meets my gaze, I explain, "I have a few questions for you."

She sits up straighter, but I don't let my arm fall from her shoulders. "Shoot."

"Favorite color?"

"Pink."

"Favorite number?"

"Four."

"Bullshit," I drawl, shaking my head. That's *my* fucking number. The only one I've ever worn on my jersey. Even when I was six, they gave me the first available jersey for a quarterback and it was the number four.

Been my lucky number ever since.

"It's true! It really is my favorite number. Every address I've ever had, there's a four in it. The apartment I live in now is 248. And everywhere I go, I see forty-four. Like, it's everywhere. That's my number. Four," she says firmly.

"That's my number," I tell her, and she grins, briefly leaning into me.

"I know."

"You see forty-four everywhere you go?"

She nods, seemingly pleased with herself. "It's like...a sign."

"You know what day my birthday is, right?"

Blair frowns. "Um..."

I'm not offended she doesn't know. Why should she? I don't know hers either.

"It's April." I pause for full effect. "Fourth."

Her eyes grow so big, I worry they'll fall out of her head. "No way."

"Way." I nod.

"That…that is…wow." I'm pretty sure I stunned her silent, which isn't an easy thing.

We can't linger on that tasty little fact. If I don't watch it, the next thing coming out of my mouth will be that we're meant to be or some other sappy shit I don't mean.

"Favorite food." We need to get back on track.

"Sushi," she answers.

"Yuck."

"Have you ever tried it?"

"Well…no."

"Then you don't know if it's yuck or not."

So logical, this girl.

"First job," I ask her.

"At the hair salon where my mom goes. I worked there every summer and on the weekends during high school until I graduated. I'd answer the phones, greet customers and sweep up hair." She smiles. "It was fun."

I like the fact that she comes from money yet worked a job. That's one thing I can say about the Maguire siblings. They aren't spoiled or pretentious. They all work hard, and they're smart and friendly.

Blair? Sometimes she's a little too friendly.

Ha. What am I saying? I love her kind of friendly.

"Who was your first kiss?" My mind immediately goes to her admitting earlier that she's been with four guys. As in, she's had sex with four partners.

I hate that. First, because it's her so-called lucky number so that's some shit. If we were to…do anything, would that mean I'd be her number five? God, I hate the number five. Like, I seriously hate it. And second, I absolutely cannot stand the thought of her being with anyone else. Just trying to imagine some other guy touching her is like...

Fuck that. I can't stand it.

"Benjamin Lathrop," she admits, and I chuckle. "Why are you laughing?"

"He sounds like a loser."

She lightly slaps at my chest, and I sort of want to ask her to do it again, just to feel her hands on me. "Stop. You're mean. Benji was sweet."

"Benji? Sounds like a dog's name."

"That's what we called him. We were seven! Or was it eight? We were playing spin the bottle because his big sister was playing it with her friends. They were in middle school and having a party, and we were spying on them. So, the younger group of us decided to do it too. I spun the bottle and it landed on Benji, and oh God, I wanted to die. I had to get up and kiss him in front of everyone. And Ruby."

"Your sister?"

She nods, lost in thought. "I was so embarrassed, but then I told myself a game is a game and so I went for it. I leaned in and kissed poor Benji right on the lips. I believe he turned twenty-five shades of red and then ran up to his bedroom."

"Sounds like you rocked his world." I smile.

"More like I embarrassed the crap out of him. Oh well." A sigh leaves her.

I stare at her bent head, the various shades of blonde and gold woven into her hair. There are even thin streaks of light brown. She's got some of the prettiest hair I've ever seen, and I wish I could run my fingers through it. Grip the ends in my hand and tug on it. Right before I...how did she describe it? Smack her ass?

"Was he your first heartbreak too?"

"Who, Benji?" She lifts her head, her green gaze meeting mine, and she slowly shakes her head. "No. That would be you."

My heart sinks into my gut, making me feel like a shit. "Come on, Blair."

I'm tempted to leave. I even position myself like I'm going to leap from the couch.

"Don't you dare try to leave or make excuses." She settles her hand on my thigh, like that's going to keep me in place. I don't move, letting her think it's working. "You're my greatest heartbreak, only because I wish you could see how easy this would be."

"How easy what would be?"

"Us. You and me." She gives my thigh a squeeze and my dick stirs to life. "But you're stubborn and ridiculous, so I'm going to have to be patient."

I hear the disappointment in her voice, mixed with resolve, and I wonder if I'm just a project for her to work on. "I don't know if you should."

"Too late. It's already happening. You don't even realize it, yet here you sit with me, your arm around my shoulders and my hand on your leg." She smiles, like all of this was part of her secret master plan. "Face it, Cam. I'm going to make you fall for me."

I'm about to disagree, but I clamp my lips shut, not wanting to admit the truth.

I've already fallen for her. I'm pretty much gone over her. I just—I don't want to misstep. I definitely don't want to fuck this up.

And I don't want to hurt her.

"So, I'm guessing you have a type then," I say, slightly changing the subject.

"I do," she says tentatively. "I mean, don't we all?"

"Yeah. So, what's your type?" I'm hoping she'll give me more insight into the four guys she's fucked in the past, though that's also a bit of information I don't want to know about.

Fucking torture, is what this all is.

"My type?" She lifts her brows.

"Yeah. Come on, don't be shy. Tell me."

She raises her left hand and forms her fingers into a gun position, aiming it right at my face like she might shoot me. "You," she murmurs.

"You're just saying that because I'm sitting right in front of you."

"I'm saying it because it's true," she counters.

I grab her wrist yet again, keeping her hand where it is—directly in front of my face. Leaning in, I bite the edge of her fingers, keeping it light. Flirty. Fun.

Blair sucks in a breath, her gaze zeroed in on the spot where my teeth just sank into her skin, and she lifts her gaze to mine, that startled expression on her face making me go completely still. "You bit me."

"You didn't like it?"

"I just…I don't get you." She slides her hand up my thigh, drawing closer to my junk. And my dick is pretty damn eager to meet her hand. "You send mixed signals."

I rub at my chest. "It's been a problem my entire life."

"Really?"

"Sort of." I glance around, noting that I don't see a familiar face anywhere. "We should get out of here."

"Should we?"

"Well, yeah. Fuck this party. It's kind of boring."

"We could be like the couple you just kicked out. I could dry hump your thigh," she suggests, her eyes full of mischief.

I groan. "Don't give me any ideas, woman."

"You know what makes me crazy?"

"What?"

She stares at my lips for a moment before lifting her gaze to mine. "How we keep going around and around the subject, yet you never do the one thing I want the most."

"And what's that?"

"I want you to…kiss me."

17

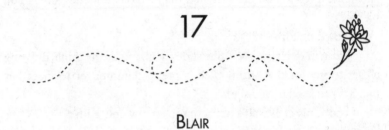

BLAIR

I can't believe I just said that. I wish I could take it back. We keep circling around the subject because he's not interested in me like that. Well, he is, but he isn't. And his mixed signals always leaving me confused isn't good for my soul. I don't need to try and get involved with someone like that.

But the things he admits to me, the way he looks at me...I love every bit of that. His fingers are currently tracing circles on my bare shoulder, and his body heat has seeped into me, leaving me hot enough that I swear I'm going to break out into a sweat.

His intense gaze focuses on my lips and he stares for a beat too long. To the point that it's probably not appropriate, how he's looking at my mouth. As if he's imagining all the things he could stick in it.

Yeah. I just went there.

"You want me to kiss you?"

I nod, unable to speak. Afraid of what I might say.

He licks his lips, and oh my God, that was so...arousing. What is he trying to do to me? "Someone could see us."

I glance around the tiny room. There's a couple standing in the archway. He's leaning against the wall and she's standing in front of him, the two of them engaged in a serious conversation. Otherwise, no one else is around. No one is paying us any attention. "Who? I see no one I know."

"Doesn't mean they're not watching." His smile is slow and naughty, making me melt. I squirm, pressing my thighs together, and when those fingers streak down the side of my arm, I almost slide off the couch.

Okay, I'm exaggerating. A little.

"Let them watch," I whisper as his head descends, his lips drawing close.

Even closer...

They brush mine, light and fleeting, and tingles spread all over my body, making me shiver. He pulls away before I can register that he actually kissed me, his gaze hooded and zeroed in on my mouth. "We need to get the fuck out of here."

The promise in his voice is what has me pulling away from him and rising to my feet. He does the same, heading for the front door, without a word, and I follow him. He holds the door open for me and I exit the frat house, pleased when he keeps pace next to me as we cross the crowded porch. He ignores the guys who shout his name as we descend the stairs. Ignores everyone as we walk down the walkway and turn onto the sidewalk, heading for his car.

Our pace is brisk. Our breathing slightly heavy. Still no words are said and my imagination is going wild with all the possibilities.

He hits the key fob when we draw closer to his car, rushing ahead of me to hold the door open for me. I crawl into the passenger seat, my breath lodged in my throat when he jogs around the front of the car and throws open the driver's door, sliding into the seat and slamming the door hard before he starts the engine, then turns to me.

I stare at him expectantly, still not breathing. I don't know how I'm able to function. He's so close. So tempting. So deliciously Cam. I see the conflict in his gaze. The pain in his expression. He's torn. His loyalty to my brother is admirable but…

I want him to be more loyal to me.

His gaze drops to my chest, lingering there, and I swear my nipples harden the longer he stares. I'm not wearing a bra. It would take nothing for him to tug on the fabric and expose me. To put his hands on me. His mouth…

An agonized groan leaves him, and he leans in, his mouth hovering above mine, but not quite touching. "If we do this, it changes everything."

"Promise?"

He tilts his head to the side, his mouth finding mine with ease. A sigh of total relief leaves me when he kisses me again and again. Soft, sweet kisses. Gentle presses of his lips. As if he's testing me. I kiss him in return, my lips parting more and more with every pass, until his tongue sneaks out, teasing the seam of my lips, sliding past them. I touch his tongue with mine, pleasure rippling through me when he moans.

Cam reaches for me, his hands landing on my waist, lightly tugging. I break away from him first, both of us breathing harder, our gazes meeting. His pupils are dilated and his lips are parted.

He's achingly beautiful. I can't take looking at him for too long. It hurts my heart too much. I never thought this could actually happen.

"We can't do this here."

His dark brows draw together. "Why the fuck not?"

"Anyone can pass by." I wave a hand toward the window. "Everyone knows this is your car."

"No one can see us."

"And I refuse to be just another number in the Challenger," I add, which is the real reason I refuse to make out with Cam in this car.

I'm not going to be a statistic to add to his long list of hookups.

"Let's go." His voice is deep. Quiet. Full of hidden meaning. I stare at him as he starts the engine, puts the car in drive and pulls onto the street with a roar of squealing tires.

I almost want to laugh, but there's nothing funny about the way he's looking at me. He's so intense. So freaking quiet as he drives through the streets, heading God knows where. Just...anywhere but this neighborhood.

Shock courses through me when he turns into his apartment parking lot minutes later.

"Really?" I ask when he parks the car. "Here?"

"Where else?" He shrugs. "Come on."

He's out of the car before I can say another word, opening my door for me and offering me his hand. I take it, loving how it completely engulfs mine when he tugs me out of the car, pressing me against the side, his body pinning me there. I press my hands against his chest before he can kiss me, the confusion obvious on his face.

"Where's Knox?"

Cam glances around the parking lot, frowning when his gaze meets mine. "In our apartment."

"I can't go in there." I shake my head. No way.

"I can sneak you in." His gaze turns pleading. "It's late. He's probably already asleep."

"What if he's not?" Anxiety claws at my chest. This is not how I want my brother to find out about us.

I don't even know if there's actually an *us* yet.

"Come on." He pulls away from me, grabbing my hand and leading me toward his apartment building.

Despite my worry, giddiness rises within me, leaving me shaky. Nervous. I can't believe we're doing this. Even crazier, I can't believe Cam is so willingly dragging me to his apartment. We're taking a huge risk here.

What if Knox is still awake? What then? How are we going to explain ourselves?

When we're in front of their apartment door, Cam places his finger to his lips, making a shushing noise before he shoves his key in the lock and undoes it, opening the door and sticking just his head inside.

"It's dark in here," he whispers to me. "He's asleep."

"You don't know that for sure," I whisper back.

He glances over his shoulder. "Hold on."

Cam leaves me out on the front stoop of their apartment, shutting the door behind him. I wait, wrapping my arms around myself to ward off the cool breeze that washes over me. The chill in the air sobers me up and worry gnaws at my thoughts, making me think a little clearer.

This is way too risky. We're being ridiculous. Knox is going to be so pissed—

"Coast is clear." The door swings open, and Cam is standing there, quickly ushering me inside, an intense gleam in his gaze as he reaches for me.

I follow him into the apartment, my eyes barely having enough time to adjust to the darkness when he grabs my hand and pulls me in deeper. We're quiet. I don't even hear us breathe as he tugs me into his room, shutting the door behind us with a soft click. I hear the turn of the lock…

And then he's on me, as if he's a starving man, his hands on my waist, his mouth finding mine even in the absolute darkness of his bedroom. I reach for him, circling my arms around his neck as I open to him immediately, our tongues gliding together, his hands roaming upward, lightly touching my skin that's exposed, thanks to the cut-outs of my dress.

It's like this for long, delicious minutes. Us kissing and kissing, my jaw growing tired, my entire body on fire from his touch. His lips. I gasp into his mouth when his fingers slide beneath the fabric of my dress, touching the bare skin of my waist, moaning when he shifts to my throat. I tilt my head back, hitting it against the wall when he kisses his way down my neck, licking and sucking my sensitive skin.

I open my eyes, staring into the darkness, my fingers sinking into his hair, clutching him to me. It feels like all of my dreams are coming true, being with Cam like this. His mouth on my skin, his hands on my body. He's solid and warm and I can feel him, hard and insistent against my hip.

"I'm not." He pants against my skin. "Having sex." He sinks his teeth into the spot where my neck meets my shoulder, making me gasp. "With you."

I go completely still, and he lifts his head so his gaze meets mine. Only a sliver of light shines in through the blinds on his window, but I can make out his handsome face. The seriousness swirling in his gaze. This man is incredibly confusing. "Why not?"

"Your brother is in the next room for one."

I wince. Didn't really need the reminder. "Why did you sneak me into your apartment then?"

A ragged exhale leaves him and he presses his forehead against mine, closing his eyes. "Because I had to." The agony in his voice makes my stomach flip. "And you make me fucking insane."

It feels good, knowing he's all twisted up over me, just like I am over him. At least I'm not alone in this predicament, considering for the longest time, I thought I was the only one willing to take it another step.

"Can we cuddle at least?" I trace my fingers down his firm chest slowly, up and down.

"Cuddle?" His voice is hoarse. Raspy. He says the word like a curse.

I nod, rising up on my tiptoes, circling my arms around his neck, my mouth at his ear. "It'll be nice. I promise."

His arms circle around my waist, pulling me completely into him, our bodies molded. Fitting together perfectly. He's solid and hot and hard as a rock, and I initiate the kiss this time, taking from him exactly what I want. Kissing him with total abandon.

He responds, his arms tightening their hold, his mouth becoming more insistent. I let him take over, my tongue tangling with his, our simultaneous moans ringing in the air a little too loudly.

Cam breaks the kiss, his hand slipping over my mouth, covering it lightly. "We can't be loud," he whispers. "Someone might hear."

At least he didn't say my brother's name out loud. Talk about a mood killer.

Slipping out of his hold, his hand drops from my mouth at the same time I duck and make my escape, heading for the bed. It's neatly made with two very flat pillows and I grimace, turning toward him.

"Your pillows…"

"I like 'em flat," he says when I don't finish the sentence. He's reaching for the front of his shirt, undoing the buttons, and I stare, excitement bubbling within me at every inch of skin that's revealed.

"I don't," I counter, my mouth going dry when he finishes with the buttons and shrugs out of his shirt.

I eat him up with my gaze. His shoulders and neck and chest and pecs. His rib cage and that flat expanse of stomach. The ridges there. His navel and the thin line of hair that leads from the bottom of it, disappearing into the waistband of his jeans.

"When you say cuddle, do you mean naked?" His voice sounds so hopeful, I can't help but giggle.

"No." I shake my head. "You're the one who said we can't have sex, Cam."

"Right." He looks like he might regret that decision.

"And I can't give it up to you the first night we kiss."

"All of our conversations have been foreplay, B."

"Don't you think we should continue the foreplay for a little while longer?" I need to make sure he's serious about this. About me. I refuse to let him fuck me and then forget me.

Nope.

His groan is loud, and now it's my turn to rush toward him, slapping my hand over his mouth. "He'll hear you."

He nods, his hand coming up to circle around my wrist and remove my hand from his face. I let him, my mouth popping open when he licks my palm. The sight of his tongue does something to my insides, lighting me up.

Setting me on fire.

Slowly, he pulls away from me, his hands going to the waistband of his jeans, his gaze locked on mine.

"No naked cuddling then?" he asks with an arched brow.

I slowly shake my head, telling myself I cannot be tempted. "Nope."

"You won't take off the dress?"

"There needs to be some mystery here, Cam." I rest my hands on my hips, my tone a little stern. A lot teasing. My resolve is totally weak when it comes to this man.

He's currently taking off his jeans. He is literally stripping right in front of me, kicking off his shoes before he tugs the denim from his body. I wish the lights were on so I could really ogle him. Standing here in the semi-darkness and trying to get a good look at everything is proving difficult.

"I'm all for giving up on the mystery part." He falls onto the edge of the mattress, shoving at his jeans until they're completely off, leaving a denim lump on his floor. "If you want."

"Cam."

"Just saying." He jumps to his feet, moving quickly as he yanks back the comforter and pats the mattress. "Join me?"

I toe off my shoes, nerves making my stomach churn. "Okay," I whisper.

He frowns. "You sound nervous."

"I'm a little nervous," I admit.

"I'll keep my hands to myself." He lifts them up above his head.

That is the last thing I want, though I don't say so. Instead, I tug the covers down on my side of the bed and crawl beneath them, yanking the comforter up so I'm completely covered.

Cam slides beneath it, the heat radiating off his body and reaching toward me. Trying to lure me in.

It takes everything I have to stay on my side of the bed, the comforter tucked under my chin, my entire body covered. I watch him as he pulls the comforter to about mid-chest, his pecs and shoulders on total display. My gaze greedily roams all over his exposed skin, my heart hammering in my chest at having him so close.

Touchable close.

Kissable close.

Wrap myself all around him and melt into his skin close.

What made him change his mind, inviting me into his home? With Knox sleeping in the bedroom next to us?

My heart starts hammering for a different reason.

"Cam?"

"Yeah?"

"What are we doing?"

He's quiet for a moment, the air heavy when he says...

"I don't really know."

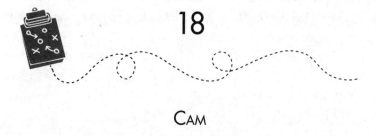

18

CAM

I wake up with a sweet little bundle wrapped up in my arms.

Blair.

It's still dark out. Quiet. I can hear the steady rhythm of her breathing, slow and deep. Her face is pressed against my chest, one long leg thrown over mine, her arm draped around my waist. Mine is around her, holding her lightly, my hand on her ass.

She has a nice one. I've always had a thing for it. And it feels perfect against my palm. Even through the fabric of her dress she wouldn't remove before she dove under the comforter.

This fucking dress.

No, this fucking girl. *Woman.*

She drives me out of my damn mind.

Kissing her felt like coming home, and if that isn't some sappy shit, I don't know what is. But it's true. The moment my lips touched hers, it felt good. More than that, it felt *right*. Like kissing Blair Maguire is what I was made to do. That and football.

And that's fucked up. I can't go around continuing to kiss my best friend's sister. Kissing will lead to other things and I can't do any of those other things with her. Unless I want to get my ass kicked and lose my best friend forever.

Despite everything, I don't regret what happened last night. Does that mean I'm willing to take the chance of possibly losing my friendship with Knox?

A little murmur sounds, Blair's lips moving against my chest as she snuggles even closer, and I close my eyes, bracing myself. She's practically lying on top of me, her hand sliding up my rib cage, lightly tickling my skin.

I give her ass a light tap as a warning and she does it again. Tickles me.

This time on purpose.

So I tap her ass again. Harder this time.

"Pull my hair and call me baby, and I'll be yours forever," she whispers.

The fuck?

Without hesitation, I grab her hair at the base of her neck, wrapping my fingers around it like they're a frickin' scrunchie and tug on it slightly. She tips her head back at the same time I look down at her, her eyes cracking open, a sly smile curling her lips.

"I wondered when you'd finally get around to it," she murmurs.

"You want me to slap your ass and pull your hair?" I am incredulous. She seems like such a sweet little thing.

"I want you to do whatever you want to me."

That is an open invitation I don't think she's aware she's giving me.

I still have a handful of her ass in my palm and I give it a squeeze, which makes her snuggle even closer. My dick—which has been in a perpetual erect state since I started kissing her in my car last night—surges against the front of my boxer briefs, letting me know he's perfectly open to being sprung free.

"You can't say shit like that," I croak, clearing my throat. "I still need to figure out how to get you home."

"You throw on some sweats and you drive me home like a gentleman," she suggests, her voice prim.

Prim, while she's got herself wrapped all around me like a clingy koala bear.

"I can do that." I release my hold on her hair and stroke it instead, my fingers getting tangled in the soft strands. "Just let me...hold you for a few minutes longer."

The moment the words are out, I wish I could snatch them back. Shove them down my throat and forget I even said them. I can't admit things like that to Blair. Leaving myself open and vulnerable for this girl. Worse, I feel like I'm giving her hope.

When I'm absolutely hopeless.

"I don't mind." She sounds so pleased with herself. Pleased with me. She scoots up and somehow presses her face into my neck, her mouth soft and damp against my skin when she speaks. "This feels nice."

It feels better than nice. And she was right. Naked cuddling wasn't the move. Once I got her naked, there would've been no cuddling. It would've been on. So, yeah.

This is much better.

For now.

We lie together for at least another hour, Blair drifting back to sleep while I lie there and savor holding her in my arms. Until the grayish light of early dawn starts to filter through the edges of my blinds, slowly illuminating the room. Allowing me to study her lying on top of me. How good she looks there.

How right.

Clearly, I've lost my damn mind.

Finally, she pulls out of my embrace and rolls over the side of the bed, her head dangling over the floor as she reaches for something. What, I'm not quite sure. When I see the screen light up her face, I realize she's checking her phone.

"It's past five," she says, practically falling out of bed before she stands. "I should go."

Reluctantly, I crawl out of bed and find a pair of sweats, slipping them on before I pull a T-shirt over my head. I shove my feet into some old Adidas slides as she puts her sandals back on and then we're sneaking out of my apartment, quietly creeping past Knox's closed bedroom door.

By the time we're in my car and I'm starting the engine, I'm fully awake and aware of what we just did. It wasn't much in the scheme of things, but I still feel guilty.

I even feel a little remorse.

"Are you regretting it?" she asks when I pull into the parking lot of her apartment.

I send her a quick look, surprised at her perceptiveness. "No."

A little laugh escapes her, but it sounds sad. "Yeah, right."

She's exiting my car before I can barely put it in park, and I call out her name to keep her from slamming the door and walking away completely.

"I'll see you later?" I send her a pointed look, wanting her to know this isn't it. I'll see her again. I want to do this again. Maybe?

Probably shouldn't, but I know myself. When it comes to this girl...

I'm weak.

"Sure, Cam. Bye." She shuts the door and turns, walking toward her building, never once looking back.

I watch her go, my gaze dropping to her ass, the way it shifts and moves beneath the dress. We barely did anything. Some simple kissing that turned into some heavy making out that transformed into cuddling and sleeping together in my bed, wrapped up in each other. Big deal.

I hook up with women pretty often with zero regrets. Always looking to get off and nothing else. Relationships are complicated. Feelings make things difficult. Maybe that's my problem. I actually have feelings for Blair and that's why I'm having a hard time watching her walk away without a backward glance. Like I just pissed her off when I really didn't do anything.

Did I? I don't think so.

Shit. I probably did.

• • •

I toss and turn for the next couple of hours before I finally give up and roll out of bed, taking a shower while jerking off yet again to thoughts of Blair. At least I have more to work with now, like how it feels to lie in bed with her in my arms. Her soft body pressing into mine, her breasts resting against my chest. My imagination goes into overdrive with what she might look like naked. I have a decent visual, but damn, I wish I could see the real thing in the flesh.

I could be so lucky.

Once I'm out of the shower and dressed, I go to the kitchen, a little surprised to see Knox's bedroom door is still shut tight. I go about my business, brewing a cup of coffee with the Keurig, while popping a couple of slices of whole wheat bread into the toaster. I fry up a couple of eggs and settle them on top of the toast, then drench them in hot sauce before I settle into my spot at the kitchen counter when I hear a ringing sound coming from nearby.

Knox's iPad, which is plugged into the charger at the counter. He's getting a FaceTime call from his other sister, Ruby. Her smiling face flashes on the screen, Knox's arm hooked around her neck.

Glancing around, the words *fuck it* drift through my head as I lean over and answer the call. Ruby's eyes about pop out of her head when she discovers who's waiting for her on the screen.

"Camden Fields in the flesh," she murmurs, her lips curving into a smile.

I smile at her in return. "Hey, Ruby."

She's pretty, I can't deny that fact. Both of the Maguire sisters are, but there's something about Blair that just gets me going every time I see her, and Ruby doesn't have it. At least with me, she doesn't.

"Where's my brother?" she asks.

I look over my shoulder at Knox's closed door before I return my attention to her. "Still sleeping."

"What a bum."

"You are a few hours ahead of us," I remind her.

"Only two. Doesn't he have an early class? Did I wake you up?"

"I'm eating breakfast." I hold up my plate to show her.

"I don't want to disturb you, Cam. I'll let you go. Tell Knox to call me when he can if you see him." She's about to disconnect when I stop her.

"I don't mind talking to you for a few minutes," I say, sounding completely lame because why am I wanting to talk to her?

Right, I might want to drill her for info about her sister.

"Oh. Well, what's up? How's school? How's football?"

I fill her in on the usual stuff, telling her what I tell everyone else. School is good, football is great, my life is perfect, blah blah blah. Even though that last part is a lie. My life is far from perfect, but I can guess Ruby Maguire doesn't want to hear about my troubles. Why should she care?

"Dating anyone special?" she asks once I'm done.

"No." I sound defensive, muttering that one word, even to my own ears. "Not really."

"Not really?" Her brows shoot up. "Tell me. Is there someone you're interested in?"

"It's complicated."

Her smile grows. "Oh, now you have to tell me, Camden. I need all the details."

"There are no details to share." I backpedal, needing to change the subject. "What about you? How's school going there? Are you seeing anyone?"

"School is a shitshow. I hate it out here, and no, I'm seeing absolutely no one because all of the prospects here on this godforsaken campus are terrible," she says almost bitterly. "Knox suggested I should move back home and enroll where you guys are at, and I'm thinking about it. That's why I called him. I wanted his input, but you're like Knox, so I'll ask your opinion instead. Do you think I should come out there and go to school? Do you like it there?"

"If you really hate it where you're at, then yes. Life's too short to be miserable."

"Right? I totally agree. Blair, on the other hand, acts like she doesn't want me around." Ruby shakes her head, faintly irritated.

Really? That's surprising.

"Why do you say that?"

"I don't know. She acts kind of weird whenever I bring it up." Ruby shrugs.

"Your sister loves you. I know you guys are close."

"Maybe not that close." Ruby pouts, the look on her face reminding me of Blair.

"Oh, come on. I think Blair would love to have you around again. She misses you," I say, defending Blair because, of course, I am.

"Has she told you that? Do you guys talk? Hang out?" Ruby's brows shoot up and I wonder what Blair has told her.

Shit. I never even thought about that. Girls talk. Sisters share secrets. Maybe Blair has told her she...likes me or whatever. Am I worthy of that kind of conversation?

Probably not.

"We don't hang out." I am lying through my teeth. We did exactly that last night and well into this morning. "And, as a matter of fact, Knox and Blair talked about you a few nights ago when she came over to make us dinner."

"She made you dinner?" Ruby sounds surprised.

"Me and Knox," I clarify.

"Isn't that sweet of her?"

"Isn't it, though?" I see the gleam in Ruby's eye. She's eating this shit up.

"Well, I'm not sure what I'm going to do. But I'll finish out the semester here at least," she says. "I'm no quitter."

Said like a true Maguire. None of them are quitters, that's for damn sure. "You should come out here in January then."

"I might," she says. "Though you and Knox leave pretty much after that."

"Yeah, we do."

"Are you excited?" Her face brightens. "You'll probably get picked up in the draft."

"Maybe," I hedge, not about to get all giddy over it. What's the point? "We'll see."

"Playing it cool?"

"Always."

19

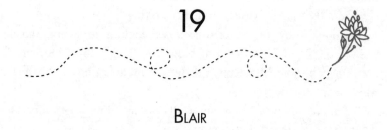

Blair

"Spoke to your boyfriend earlier." Ruby drops that little factoid on me after a few minutes of boring conversation via FaceTime.

It's Monday night and I'm still on a "I cuddled with Cam" high. His big hand on my ass. How he gave it a gentle slap before pulling on my hair. That was kind of.hot. I'm still thinking about it, wishing he'd done more.

Wishing we'd done so much more.

"My boyfriend?" I wrinkle my nose. "Who are you talking about now?"

Ruby is always joking around, calling some poor random guy, *my boyfriend*. The most recent was that guy who worked at the library when I was at community college. He was friendly to me once. I mentioned it to Ruby and said he had a nice smile, which he did. But that was it. I had zero interest in him. But she'd tease me sometimes, asking about my library boyfriend.

She's annoying. The absolute epitome of a pain in the ass little sister.

"I FaceTimed with Camden Fields this morning." The smug look on Ruby's face is undeniable.

I sit up straighter, peering at her closely, like I can see inside her brain, which I so cannot. And wait a minute—this morning? "When exactly did you FaceTime with him?"

I was with him this morning. Well, until around five a.m., when he drove me home, his expression full of regret and misery the entire time.

God, the man is exasperating. Frustrating.

"I don't know the exact time. I was looking for Knox and he answered instead. He was eating breakfast. Eggs with way too much hot sauce on them." It's Ruby's turn to wrinkle her nose. "I can see why you're into him though."

"I'm not into him," I automatically say, as if I'm programmed to do exactly that. Deny, deny, deny.

"Please. You're so into him. And I get it. That man is fine." She draws the last word out, sounding silly.

"Keep away from him," I practically snap. "He's mine."

Ruby bursts out laughing, and I sort of hate how much she's enjoying herself.

"Oh my God, Blair. Calm down. I'm clear across the country, so you have nothing to worry about." Ruby grins. "You're cute when you're jealous though."

Her comment reminds me of when Cam told me I was cute when I was mad and my heart pangs. I wish I could see him. Fall asleep in his arms again, listening to the steady thump of his heart. That had been so comforting. He's like a big ol' teddy bear I can cling to and count on. A teddy bear with an edge.

I want more of that edge. It's there. He reveals it in bits and pieces, and I want to see all of it. I want him to unleash on me, leaving me a trembling, overwhelmed mess.

A shiver moves through me at just the thought.

"I'm not jealous," I mumble, flopping back against my pillows. My hair is wet because I just got out of the shower and I'm tired. I didn't get much sleep last night thanks to Cam, though I'm not complaining. I'd stay up all night with him for days on end, just to spend time with him. "I'm just..."

"Overprotective of your boyfriend?"

My bedroom door pops open in the middle of Ruby's sentence, Rita peeking her head inside, a frown forming on her face. "Wait a minute. You have a boyfriend?"

I glare at Ruby before I turn my attention to Rita. "My sister is just teasing."

"I am not! Blair totally has a boyfriend! His name is—"

I end the call, essentially hanging up on her before I deposit my phone on my nightstand. "What's up?" I ask Rita.

She gives me a strange look but chooses to ignore Ruby's cutoff outburst, thank God. "Um, there's a guy here to see you."

"What? Who?" I sit up straight, running my fingers through my damp hair. I have no makeup on. No bra. I'm in a pair of old shorts that don't really fit me anymore—they're too short to go out in public—and an oversized T-shirt that used to belong to my brother. I cut off the hem and it's cropped. One wrong move and I'll flash a tit at someone. I don't even have to be provoked.

"That cute backup quarterback. Ace?"

What?

"I can't go out there looking like this," I frantically whisper at her, as I hop off the bed and go over to the mirror that hangs over my dresser, checking my reflection. Oh God, I really do look awful. I have one of those zit patches covering the pimple that decided to make its appearance on the bridge of my nose. Oh, and I'm wearing eye gels under my eyes to soothe the bags that appeared, thanks to my lack of sleep.

"I tried to get him to leave, but he said he had a quick question for you and it couldn't wait. Come on." Rita waves her hand at me and with a frustrated sigh I fall into step behind her, letting her lead me to the front door.

It's partially cracked open and I peek around it hesitantly to find

Ace standing on our welcome mat, his gaze fixed on his phone, his fingers flying over the screen.

"Hey," I say weakly, praying he doesn't look too closely at my face.

"Oh hey, Blair." He lifts his head, his gaze zeroing in on me. He doesn't even bat an eyelash at my less than stellar appearance. "Uh, I have a message for you."

"A message?" I frown.

"Yeah." He takes a step closer, his voice shifting lower. "Um, Cam asked me to deliver it. To you."

Say what? "Cam wants you to give me a message?"

What in the world is going on?

"Yeah." Ace nods, but doesn't say anything else. His phone dings and he checks it quickly, typing out a one-word response, that familiar "whoosh" sounding, indicating he sent it.

"Well, what's the message?"

"Um, he's out in your parking lot right now and he wants you to go out to his car and talk to him." Ace jerks his thumb over his shoulder to indicate that Cam is indeed waiting for me out there.

"Did you ride over with him?"

"I did. And he told me I had to walk back to my apartment." Ace grins, as if he's enjoying every minute of this. "I think you got the number one QB wrapped around your finger, Maguire."

I step out of the apartment, pulling the front door shut behind me. "Doubtful. And why would he ask you to come to the door instead of him?"

"He didn't want your roomies to know." He says this so logically, as if that makes all the sense in the world.

"But you're okay with showing your face to my roommates."

"Not like they actually know me. Not yet." He shrugs, shoving his hands into the pockets of his dark blue athletic shorts. "And who are they going to tell?"

True. This is all so silly. Like we're playing some sort of spy game.

But it's also thrilling, not gonna lie. Cam is waiting out in the parking lot for me.

He wanted to see me.

He came here by choice.

"Camden Fields shows up on your doorstep? That's going to cause a scene," Ace continues, shaking his head. "Can't wait to get to that status someday."

I hold up a finger, practically thrusting it in his face. "Give me a couple of minutes."

"Want me to tell Cam that you're going to be a few?"

"You'd do that for me?"

He nods. "For sure. You treat me way nicer than anyone else on the team, and that includes your brother."

I roll my eyes, hating that my brother probably treats him terribly. "Then please tell him. I'll be out in...ten minutes."

Ace beams. "Gotcha. I'll let him know."

He's gone before I can say another word, running down the stairs that lead to the ground floor so quickly, he makes everything rattle, including my head.

But I have no time to worry about any of that. Instead, I dash inside the apartment, coming to a complete stop when I see Rita watching me, her arms crossed in front of her chest. There's a suspicious look on her face and my brain scrambles to come up with something to tell her, because I know she's gonna ask.

"Where are you going?"

See?

"Out with Ace," I say weakly, hating that I'm lying.

"Really?" Her brows shoot up.

"We're just friends." I shrug. "He's younger than me."

"So? He's hot as fuck."

That...isn't a lie. Not that I care.

I have my heart set on someone else.

"Friends," I reiterate. "He wants my advice."

"About?"

What's up with the third degree?

"Football life. You know, my family was and is heavily involved in the NFL," I remind her.

That's all it takes for Rita's gaze to glaze over. "Right. Fun times. I like the money and fame part, but otherwise, no thanks. Football is boring."

Not even offering a response, I leave her standing in the living room and go to my bedroom, my hands already in my wet hair, twisting it into a top knot. Once that's completed, I tear off the undereye gel strips, tossing them in the trash before I stop in front of the full-length mirror that sits in the corner of my room.

A realization hits—Knox didn't give me this T-shirt. It belonged to my ex-boyfriend. I still look like I'm going to bed, which was the original plan.

Screw it. I'm going with this outfit. Not like he's going to take me out. Maybe what I'm wearing will give him easy access to the...parts he'd like to touch. Though I probably shouldn't get hot and heavy in the Challenger.

I am not about to become just another number in Cam's long list of conquests. If anything happens between us, I plan on sticking around.

Once I shove my feet into the Ugg slippers I had to beg my mom to buy me last Christmas, I'm walking out of the apartment, heading straight for the Challenger, which is parked all the way on the opposite of the lot, the engine rumbling as he waits for me.

Giddiness has me running those last few steps, my T-shirt—and my boobs—bouncing somewhat out of control. I go to the driver's side, staring at Cam's perfect profile for a too brief moment before I start knocking on the glass.

He appears to jump out of his skin for a second before he realizes it's just me and sags against the seat. He opens the window, so I can see his handsome face and hear his deliciously deep voice.

"You scared the shit out of me," he accuses.

I'm grinning. "You're the one who's acting like you're a part of some covert operation, sending your spy to the door to fetch me."

He grins, seemingly pleased with himself. "I couldn't just knock on the door and ask for you. I'd cause a scene."

"Do you really think you're that important?"

He tilts his head to the side, contemplating me. "Come on, B. You know how it is."

Dang it, I do.

"Get in the car." He hits a button and I can hear the locks deactivate. "Hurry."

"So bossy," I murmur as I walk around the back of the car before reaching for the door handle, sliding into the seat and shutting the door behind me. "What's going on?"

He stares, his gaze raking over me from my wet head to my Ugg-slippered feet. My skin tingles everywhere his eyes touch and I'm practically squirming in my seat when he finally meets my gaze once more.

"What the fuck are you wearing?"

I glance down at myself for a quick moment before I return my gaze to his. "I was getting ready for bed."

"It's nine o'clock."

"Someone kept me up late last night. I'm tired."

He smiles.

So do I. We're looking at each other as if we share a secret.

Which we do.

"Where did you get this?" He reaches out, fingering the sleeve of my old T-shirt, his fingers coming perilously close to my untethered boobs. "Your old high school?"

I nod, silent. Scared to tell him who the shirt belonged to. It says varsity football team, so he's going to make assumptions.

"Knox's?"

I shake my head, my gaze never straying from his. Trying to telepath who this shirt belonged to without having to say it out loud.

"Then who?" Something must dawn on him because he starts nodding. "Ahh. I can guess."

My smile is sheepish. "It belonged to my ex-boyfriend. I stole it from him. He played football."

"With Knox?" He sounds…pissed off?

"Yeah, but he was in my grade."

"Huh." Cam reaches for the gearshift, his foot tapping the gas, making the engine rev. He slides the car into reverse, and in seconds, we're peeling out of the parking space, roaring through the lot and out onto the street.

I'm literally resting my hand against my chest, trying to breathe through the palpitations his reckless driving is giving me. "What's your problem?"

He speeds through a yellow light, ignoring the car honking at him as we pass it by. "Nothing."

His jaw is clenched, his knuckles white as he grips the steering wheel. He's intense. A little scary.

A lot sexy.

He hits a button, both windows sliding down and the wind whips through his hair. He taps another button and music fills the car. Something loud and vaguely obnoxious at first, though after a while, I realize I'm enjoying it.

Enjoying the moment with the wind in our hair and the music playing so loudly that I can't think about anything else. All I can do is focus on Cam. The way his biceps bulge against the sleeves of his T-shirt. It stretches across his broad chest and I'm filled with the urge to touch him. After having free rein to let my hands roam all over him last night, now it's all I want to do.

My gaze drops and I take in his strong thighs. How they're covered lightly with hair. How I wish I had the right to reach out and settle my hand on his leg and claim him. Like he's mine.

As if he belongs to me.

We end up at a park on the opposite side of town, Cam pulling into a spot that's right next to a massive lake, his car lights shining upon the water before he turns them off, the entire area shrouded in darkness. I can hear bugs chirping and frogs croaking, despite the time of year, and I glance over at Cam to find he's already watching me, his narrowed gaze making me shrink back in my chair a little bit.

"What's wrong?" I know I already asked what his problem is, but he's starting to…scare me.

But only a little bit.

He blows out a harsh breath, running his fingers through his hair as he stares out the driver's side window. I drink in his profile, my gaze skimming over his features. The sharp angle of his nose. The high curve of his cheeks. The strong jut of his chin. He has a finely-made face and I'm tempted to crawl into his lap and run my mouth all over it. Map his skin with my lips. Taste him everywhere I can.

I do none of that. Instead, I grip my hands together in my lap and wait for him to say something.

Anything.

"I hate thinking about you with someone else," he finally says, his head still averted so I can't look into his eyes.

My mouth drops open, only for me to immediately snap it shut. "Are you serious?"

He looks at me, his expression pure misery. "Yeah. You're still wearing his shirt."

"It was in high school," I reiterate. "He doesn't matter to me."

Once upon a time, Travis did, but not anymore. I haven't even really thought about him in years. For God's sake, I even thought I got the T-shirt from Knox.

Cam turns his head away from me, yet again, the breeze filtering through his hair, making it flop over his forehead, and without thought, I do exactly what I've been wanting to do since I got into this car.

Reaching out, I touch his hair, sliding my fingers through the soft strands that are at the back of his neck. He needs a haircut. His hair isn't usually this unruly, but God, it's so soft. I don't want to quit touching him.

He closes his eyes yet doesn't say a word, and I wonder if he's enjoying it.

"Blair." My name sounds like a plea. As if he's in complete agony.

"What are you doing?"

"What's it look like?" I scoot a little closer, thrusting my fingers into the hair at the base of his skull.

"You should probably stop."

I start to pull my hand away from his hair, but his next words make me pause.

"No. Don't stop."

I continue rubbing the conflicted man's head, enjoying every second of it. He leans into my touch, reminding me of our family dog who is the neediest being I've ever known. Remington is a chocolate lab. He's a giant goofball and so affectionate, he could knock you down in his enthusiasm over being petted.

Cam is giving me serious chocolate lab vibes right now. Though he's not sweet and goofy like Remy is, he is acting like he's starved for affection. I'm guessing he probably is.

"Come here," he finally says, still sounding as if he's in agony, but I don't hesitate.

I do exactly as I envisioned, climbing into his lap, curling my arms around his neck, my mouth landing on his. Tonight's kissing isn't tentative or exploratory. No, it slides straight into needy territory. My hands are buried in his hair. His hands are on my bare waist. Sliding up my back, pausing when he tears his mouth from mine.

"You're not wearing a bra," he whispers.

I open my eyes and smile at him. "I'm not wearing much at all."

"Fuck." Those hands come around to my front, fingers brushing the underside of my breasts, and I whimper, thrusting my chest out. "I hate this T-shirt."

"Knox played there."

"I don't care. I hate it." He tugs on the tattered hem, like he wants to rip it from my body.

"Cam."

"Blair." He cups the back of my head, holding me in place so he can stare into my eyes. "I told myself to stay away from you."

Pain filters through my blood. My brain. Why would he tell me that now? When I'm in his arms and I can feel his erection poking me?

"But I couldn't. I can't." His grip tightens, fingers sliding down to curve around my neck. "I can't stop thinking about you."

That admission took a lot out of him, I can tell. By the raspy sound of his voice and the terrified expression on his handsome face. Big man on campus, Camden Fields, doesn't express emotions like this.

He's not outwardly needy. He doesn't want for much.

Yet he wants...

Me.

Finally.

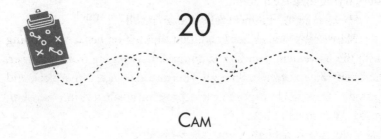

20

Cam

I probably shouldn't have said any of that to Blair, but fuck it. She deserves the truth. And she looks so pleased by my confession too. The way her eyes lit up at my words, her lush lips curving into a faint smile. She touches my face, her fingers sliding down my cheek, and fuck, I can't take it when she puts her hands on me. It feels too good.

My entire life, I've told myself I don't need anyone. Just football and myself. I care about my friends. I care about my parents, even though they never showed they cared much about me when I was growing up.

I vowed a long time ago not to be a selfish bastard like my dad, but when you also tell yourself you don't care about anyone else, you tend to be just that...a selfish bastard. A couple of years ago, I gave into the feelings and told myself it was easier not to care than to care too much. Easier to be an arrogant prick versus an overemotional dickwad.

Staring at Blair's beautiful face, losing myself in her green eyes, I feel like...

An overemotional dickwad.

And that's some scary shit.

"I can't stop thinking about you either," she admits, her voice low, her gaze on me, her fingers still streaking down my cheek, though now they're making their way to my mouth. "We didn't kiss near enough for my liking."

She presses her index finger into the corner of my mouth, like she's trying to make a point.

"Not enough?" I almost take it as an insult.

Blair slowly shakes her head, that topknot on her head bobbing with the movement. Her hair is damp, I'm assuming from a shower, and her skin is fragrant. Smooth. I release the back of her neck and rest my hands on her exposed waist, pressing my fingers into her skin, making her breath hitch.

"Not nearly enough, Cam," she whispers.

I like hearing her say my name. I like the way she seems to savor it. Like it's her favorite word.

I also really do hate that shirt she's wearing. Knowing that her ex-boyfriend from high school gave it to her fucks with my head. Who was that guy to her? Did she love him? Did he break her heart and make her cry? I don't respond well to tears. I've seen enough of them come from my mom over the years, always when she's raging over something my father did to her.

The idea of Blair crying? Or worse, the idea of *me* making Blair cry?

My heart aches just thinking of it.

"Can I confess something to you?"

I meet her gaze, noting how big her eyes look. Almost as if she's scared.

"Tell me," I demand.

"I thought about doing something...very specific to you earlier," she admits.

My dick twitches in excitement. My brain is automatically filled with visions of Blair on her knees and my cock filling her mouth.

Though I am pretty positive that's not what she's referring to.

"What did you want to do?"

"I still want to do it." She sinks her teeth into her plump lower lip, and I almost groan out loud at the sight. "Can I show you?"

"Uh, sure." She can fucking show me whatever she wants. I'm game for all of it.

She sits up straighter, readjusting herself on my lap, her ass brushing against my dick, and I wince, wishing I could readjust myself. At least I'm in shorts and not jeans. It wouldn't take much to free the beast, so to speak.

Blair brushes a stray strand of hair away from her face and blows out a nervous breath while I sit there and wait in anticipation over what she might do.

Grab my junk?

Tear my clothes off?

Grind on my dick?

I am ready, willing and able.

But then she does the most surprising thing.

Leaning in, she brushes her lips against my cheek. It's soft. Sweet. Far too brief. Then she does it again.

And again.

She kisses me all over my face. Tender presses of her lips all over my cheeks, my chin, my forehead. Even my nose. She avoids my lips the entire time, and I'm filled with the need to actually kiss her. Thrust my tongue into her mouth and taste her.

But I restrain myself, my hands clutched into fists and resting on my thighs. I can't touch her. If I do, I won't be able to control myself, and I also can't lie.

I'm enjoying this way too much to stop her or to change our focus. It's...sweet.

Downright innocent.

And none of my thoughts involving Blair are innocent. Not even close.

"You smell so good," she whispers, her mouth right at my ear before she kisses the lobe. "And you need to shave."

Her lips drift across my jaw. Down my neck. I press the back of my head into the seat, my eyes tightly closed, all the air lodged in my lungs. I can't breathe. I can't so much as move for fear she'll stop her exploration of my face and neck with her mouth.

"Bet you've never had a girl do that to you before," she murmurs, sounding smug.

"Woman," I croak out.

She pauses in her exploration, lifting away from me. I crack open my eyes to find her watching me, brows wrinkled in confusion.

"You got mad last time I called you a girl. Said you were a woman. Remember?"

Her smile is slow. Confident. The smile of a woman who knows exactly what she's doing. "You're right. I'm glad you remembered."

"Like I told you already, there is nothing girlish about you whatsoever, B."

We stare at each other for a moment, her eyes glowing, her lips parted. I want those lips back on me. I want that lush body pressed up against mine. I want my hands on her tits or her ass or whatever available part I can grab. And I want to feel her grind on me and hear her moan when I lift my hips.

I want to hear her moan when I first enter her too. I'm dying to hear that sound. Fuck, I'll probably come the moment it happens.

Shit. I am getting way ahead of myself.

She leans in, her delectable scent hitting my nostrils at the same time she presses her lips to the right corner of my mouth. Then the left. She traps my bottom lip with both of hers, sucking for a moment. Tugging. Her teeth sink into my flesh, lightly at first. Testing how far she can go. I let her take complete control, hissing in a breath when she bites a little too hard and she releases my lip immediately, soothing the sting with her fucking tongue.

"Jesus," I mutter, grabbing the back of her head, keeping her close so she can't escape.

"I hurt you?"

"Felt good," I say truthfully before I give in and kiss her, taking away her power and making it my own.

I devour her and she responds just how I want her to. Shifting closer, a needy sound emanating from the back of her throat. Her upper body is pressed firmly against mine, her hands in my hair, her thighs clasped on either side of my torso. It's awkward in the car with not much space. Blindly, I reach for the controls on the side of my seat, sliding it back until we're almost horizontal, Blair on top of me.

She ends the kiss and I open my eyes to find her face in mine, those green eyes shining. Maguire eyes. Knox's are a similar color, but Blair's are much more vivid.

Much more beautiful.

"What are you doing, Cam?"

"Getting comfortable." Reluctantly I let go of her, folding my arms behind my head like I have all the time in the world, a grin stretching my mouth wide. What is it about this woman that makes me feel like teasing her? Laughing with her?

She sits up, her ass resting right on my dick, and stretches her arms out, her hands braced on my chest. At this angle, I can see a gap between the T-shirt and her actual body, catching a glimpse of the underside of her tits.

Of course, they're perfect. A nice round handful that I'm tempted to grab. But I've still got my hands behind my head so I'll wait on that for a bit.

"You're hard." She states the obvious, rubbing her ass against my erection. Playing with fucking fire.

"That's all your fault."

Her smile is smug. "You liked it when I kissed your face."

I like just about anything she does to me.

"It was all right," I drawl, teasing her, my gaze still locked on her chest. That teasing glimpse of plump flesh. The flat expanse of her stomach. The dip of her waist and the sexy flare of her hips.

"I think it was more than all right." She sounds amused, her ass still doing things to my dick, her fingers gathering the fabric of my

T-shirt in her palms before she lets go, one hand going to her face. Picking at something on the side of her nose. "Oh my God. Well, this is embarrassing."

My gaze lifts to her face, watching as she peels off one of those tiny zit patches, holding it up for me to see. "What's the big deal?"

"You—well, Ace—caught me at the worst time. I even had those gel strips under my eyes, but I at least managed to take those off."

"Getting ready for bed?"

She nods, pressing the pimple patch onto the side of an empty water bottle that's sitting in my center console.

"C'mere." I like the idea of watching her perform all of her nightly rituals while I'm waiting for her in bed. Applying zit patches and gel strips to her face. Brushing her wet hair. Admiring her firm body in the barely-there clothes she wears to sleep in. The shorts she's currently got on should be borderline criminal. Her ass is practically falling out of them.

If she were going to bed with me on a regular basis, there would be no need to wear clothes. I'd only strip them off of her eventually.

Blair frowns. "I'm right here."

"Come down here. With me." I unfold my arms, resting my hands on her hips as she dips down, her face in mine, our lips colliding in a soft kiss.

She keeps kissing me until I part my lips, my tongue sneaking out to meet hers. It's on at that moment. Our tongues glide against each other in a subtle rhythm, her body starting to move. Back and forth across my dick, making me groan. She grinds a little, a whimper leaving her when she hits a particular spot and I let her use me to hopefully get off.

I slide my hands up, beneath the offensive T-shirt, cupping her tits. Another whimper sounds and she arches her chest into my palms, as if she wants more.

I'll gladly give her more.

I knead her flesh, rub my thumbs across her distended nipples, playing with them. Her whimpers turn into moans, her hips working, sliding over my cock, rubbing shamelessly. Our mouths are still fused, me swallowing her panting breaths, continuing to let her use my body for her pleasure. I remove my hands from beneath her shirt, her noise of disappointment obvious, but when I grab handfuls of her ass, the sad sound disappears. Replaced by a ragged moan that I swallow.

Slipping my fingers beneath the fabric of her too-short shorts, I splay my hands across her ass cheeks, pinning her in place. Letting her feel what she's doing to me. My cock fucking throbs, it's so eager to get inside her, but I know that's not going to happen.

Not tonight.

Instead, I keep her there for a few more seconds and then I start to move her over me. Establishing a steady pace that has her rocking.

"Oh God." She gasps when she shifts her pussy over my dick. Christ, I can feel her. Hot and wet and dying for it.

Dying for me.

I don't say a word. Just grip her perfect ass and move her back and forth over my erection, my fingers sliding closer and closer to the heat of her pussy. It wouldn't take much to sink my fingers inside her from behind. Test her. See how wet she is.

I imagine she's pretty soaked. I can smell her, for fuck's sake. That musky, sweet scent filling the confines of my car, making me dizzy. Making my mouth water.

I'd love to go down on her. Lick that perfect little pussy from ass to clit and make her shriek with pleasure, having her come in seconds. She'd taste like heaven. She feels like an angel in my arms. Mythical and sweet and eager to please.

Me.

It's not about me in this moment though. It's all about her.

Breaking the kiss, I slide my lips down her neck, sucking and nibbling her skin. I finally give her what I think she wants, my fingers dipping into the heat of her pussy from behind and she cries out. Throwing her head back and giving me better access to her neck.

"Cam." She pants my name when I slip a finger inside her, all the way in. Her greedy pussy swallows my finger, throbbing all around it and I add another. "I'm—I'm going to come."

I start to pump my fingers in and out of her welcoming body, shifting away from her neck so I can watch her beautiful face. Her eyes are closed, her cheeks suffused with color, those perfect lips parted, her chest heaving. Her brows draw together in seeming concentration as she basically grinds her clit against my cock, and I increase my pace, fucking her with my fingers, her chest moving faster. Faster...

"Oh God." The two words fall from her lips on a gasp, her body straining, nothing moving. Like she's frozen. Just before the orgasm sweeps over her, making her shudder and shake.

It fucking kills me to watch her come while wearing that stupid shirt, and without thinking, I remove my hand from her pussy and reach toward her, gripping the bottom of the T-shirt with both hands and giving it a firm tug. It rips easily, the fabric old and soft, tearing in a jagged line straight up the middle, stopping at the neck. It hangs from her, exposing her chest and I sit up, wrapping my lips around one pink nipple before I start to suck.

Another anguished cry leaves her, her hands coming around the back of my head, clutching me to her. I suck and lick one nipple before delivering the same treatment to the other, savoring the taste of her sweet skin, her fingers tugging on my hair. Like all she wants is more.

That's all I want too.

21

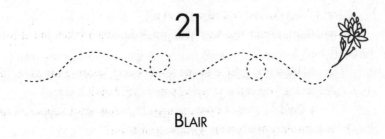

BLAIR

'm a little embarrassed.

The last thing I expected to happen tonight was me grinding on Cam's erection and making myself come. Well, I only had a little bit to do with that orgasm. Cam helped too, thanks to his fingers.

His extremely thick, expert fingers.

Then he goes and tears my old T-shirt like a savage, so now it's basically hanging off of me in two pieces, only connected by the neck and sleeves. How am I supposed to walk back into my apartment like this? There will be no explaining what happened.

It's fairly obvious.

No, what's most embarrassing is that I've now become what I never wanted to be.

Just another girl he's messed around with in the Challenger.

If I could slap myself in the face I so would.

I'm still clutching him to me, his face buried between my breasts, his breaths hot on my sensitive skin. The shivers are mostly gone, just the occasional twitch running through me, and I take a deep breath, exhaling slowly, trying to calm my racing heart.

"You okay?" His lips tease my skin when he speaks, his deep voice vibrating against me.

Nodding, I loosen my hold on his hair, which allows him to lift his head, his dark eyes meeting mine. "Yeah."

His smile is slow. "I rocked your world."

I roll my eyes. He would say something like that. "You tore my shirt."

"Sorry." He doesn't sound sorry at all.

"Something about the way you just said that makes me think you're lying."

"I am." His searing gaze drops to my chest, heating my skin. "I didn't like seeing you come wearing some other dude's shirt."

"Oh my God." I glance down at myself. "How am I supposed to sneak back into my apartment without a shirt on?"

"I have another one in my trunk."

"You do?" I ask.

"Yeah. I always keep a couple extra changes of clothes with me. You never know when you're going to sweat through what you're wearing after an unexpected stop at the gym," he explains.

Only Cam would make a surprise stop at a gym and work out so hard he's sweating through his clothes.

"Besides, you don't need to wear that asshole's shirt anymore," he says vehemently, his gaze dropping to my tattered shirt. "You can wear mine."

Heat sweeps over my skin at the territorial sound of his voice. I should be offended. Cam Fields doesn't *own* me.

Or does he?

"You'll look good in my shirt." His hand slides up, fingers curving beneath my right breast, testing the weight. "Maybe you could wear it for me sometime."

"I can do that," I say without hesitation.

"And nothing else." His gaze lifts to mine, dark and serious, and oh so captivating. I couldn't look away even if I wanted to. "Like tonight. You had no panties on, B."

"I know." I sink my teeth into my lower lip, not feeling bad about it at all. "That's how I dress for bed, remember?"

He nods, his fingers squeezing my flesh, making my core throb again. Already. "Next time, I want you to wear the shirt and nothing else underneath. Got it?"

Now I'm the one nodding. Almost frantically in my excitement. "Got it."

The fact that he wants a next time leaves me breathless.

His hand drops from my body and I fight the disappointment that threatens to sweep over me. Even though I'm still on top of him and can feel his erection beneath me, heavy and insistent.

"We should go," he says.

More disappointment hits. "What about you?"

"What about me?"

"You...didn't get to have your turn." I shift my hips, sliding my pussy over his cock, and I swear his eyes cross. "Let me help you."

"I'm fine," he insists as I crawl off him, plopping into the passenger seat before I reach for him. My fingers eager to slide beneath the waistband of his shorts. He stops me, his fingers curling around my wrist like a steel band, holding me off.

"I'm okay," he reiterates. "Really."

He lets go of my wrist, and I settle into the passenger seat, feeling silly. Worse? Feeling inept. I just came all over his shorts— pretty sure I saw a wet spot I left behind, how mortifying—and now he won't let me finish him off, so to speak. All while I sit here wearing an old T-shirt he tore and a pair of crumpled shorts that barely cover my ass.

Sighing, I slip my feet into my Ugg slippers I left on the floorboard and turn my head so I can stare out the window, feeling silly. Cam starts the car, and for once in his life, he doesn't rev the engine or make the tires squeal when he pulls out of the parking spot. Instead, he drives calmly, pulling out of the park moments later, not saying a single word.

While I'm slowly dying inside.

All my earlier excitement over him saying we're going to do this again evaporates. I'm left wallowing in my confusion and worry, sneaking glances at him every few minutes. He looks no different. He rolled up the window so the wind is no longer blowing through his hair and his expression is calm. Almost indifferent?

God, I can't tell. I haven't spent enough time with him yet to get a good read on him and his facial expressions. And what man turns down a hand job or blow job? I mean, seriously? Why would he say no?

By the time we're pulling back into my apartment parking lot, I'm a twisted-up mess, worried he's going to reject me outright before he kicks me out of the Challenger, once and for all.

"Stay here," he says, his voice firm as he puts the car into park and opens the door, climbing out before he shuts the door behind him.

I'm sitting there feeling stupid with my torn-up T-shirt and my boobs essentially hanging out. I clutch my bent arms to my chest, my fists at my mouth. I part my lips, nibbling on my thumb, nearly jumping out of my skin when he opens the passenger side door and kneels down.

"Here." He holds out a T-shirt and I take it, lifting my gaze to his. He's watching me carefully, another bundle of fabric in his hands. "I brought you a sweatshirt too. You looked cold."

"Thank you," I murmur, taking the sweatshirt from him.

"I'll give you some privacy." He rises to his full height and carefully shuts the door, leaving me alone once again.

Giving me the opportunity to bring the sweatshirt to my face and breathe deep. It smells like him. Spicy and fresh. I get rid of the torn T-shirt, dropping it onto the floorboard before I slip on the T-shirt he gave me. It's huge, fitting me like a dress, and when I pull the hoodie sweatshirt over my head, it fits much the same.

I absolutely love it.

Glancing out the window, I see he's leaning against his car, waiting for me, and so I open the door and go to stand beside him, the T-shirt and hoodie both falling to my knees, almost swallowing me whole.

"Kind of big on you," he notes, his voice laced with amusement.

It's the amusement that gives me hope. If he wasn't interested in me anymore, I'd already be in my apartment and sobbing in my pillow.

"Hey." He grabs hold of the strings of the hoodie and tugs on them, bringing me closer to him. "Sorry about your shirt."

"Stop apologizing for something you meant to destroy," I say, resting my hands on his chest, giddy at the realization that I can touch him whenever I want.

At least in this moment. And God, isn't it wonderful?

"You're right. I'm not sorry. You look better in my hoodie anyway." He tugs on the strings again, bringing me even closer, and when he sweeps his mouth over mine, I revel in the tingles cascading over my skin, leaving me breathless. "I'll see you later?"

I nod, my movements slow. Languid. Like I'm in a trance.

He kisses me again, like he can't help himself, and when he finally pulls away, I ask the question that's been on my mind since the orgasmic haze left my brain.

"I'm not just another girl you fucked around with in your car, right, Cam?"

He blinks at me, seemingly surprised by my question. "Hell no. I don't think of you like that."

"You don't?"

Cam slowly shakes his head. "I don't know what we're doing, B, so all I can say is...be patient with me. I'm bound to say something stupid that'll make you angry."

I appreciate his honesty. It's refreshing.

"That's okay. I'm sure I'll do something stupid too." I rise up on my tiptoes and press my mouth to his, whispering against his lips, "Bye, Camden."

Just before I turn and run all the way back to my apartment.

. . .

Having a sexual encounter with Cam is just the invigorating experience I needed to put some excitement into my life and some hope in my deepest, most secret dreams. The ones that haunt me at night and make me think I might have a chance with Cam after all.

Well, when you end up grinding on his extremely thick dick while he makes you come with his fingers buried deep inside you, that gives a woman a lot of hope.

Especially me.

I spend the next few days in a haze. Doped up on the lusty feelings Cam brought out of me, praying I'll come across him eventually. I spot Derek on Tuesday and dodge out of his line of vision, just before he catches sight of me, not in the mood to put up with the way he stares at my chest every single time we run into each other.

No thanks.

I see my brother everywhere I go and sometimes I even see him with Joanna, my new friend—and it seems like she's his new 'friend' as well. It's so obvious Knox is into her, and I'm pretty sure she's into him as well, though I haven't really talked to her about it.

I'm too busy, always on the hunt for Cam.

I run into Ace at the Student Center on Thursday, his smiling face a friendly reminder that he's a good guy. He holds his arms out to me in greeting when he spots me, surrounded by a bunch of girls, and I walk straight into them, letting him hug me.

The girls are jealous. I can feel their energy radiating toward me when I pull out of his embrace, but I ignore them. I'm not interested in Ace that way. They can have him.

There's someone else that I want.

"Looking good, Maguire," Ace teases, always flirting.

"Right back at you," I return, flirting just as much.

"Uh, just to let you know—your friend has been in an extra good mood lately," Ace tells me.

My heart threatens to flutter right out of my chest at his words. "Oh, really?"

Ace nods. "Extra cheerful. Cracking jokes. Giving everyone shit, which is not his usual style, and always in a good-natured way. Hell, he even shouted encouraging words at me during practice and he normally has a permanent scowl on his face when he watches me play."

Hmm. Cam is threatened by Ace, not that he's ever told me that out loud. It just makes sense, and I understand his feelings. Ace is young and coming up through the ranks. He'll take over Cam's spot once Cam graduates, and of course, Cam wants to leave on top.

But what if Ace goes on to top him?

It won't matter. Cam will be on to bigger and brighter things by then. I just know it.

I'm just not sure if Cam has as much faith in himself as I do.

It's much later in the afternoon when I *finally* run into Cam. I'm out in the school parking lot, ready to jog around the track at the practice field—why did I never think of this idea before?—when I see Cam and Knox leaving practice together, heading straight for me.

I come to a stop and wait for them, disappointment filling me when I realize I came too late. They're already leaving.

"Hey, sis," Knox greets, waving at me.

"Hi." I wave at him in return, my gaze zeroing in on Cam, who's watching me with that intense dark gaze, silently communicating with me the reminder that he's had his mouth on me in lots of places.

He's seen me naked. Well, mostly.

He's had his fingers inside my body.

He's witnessed me come.

My entire body goes hot at the memory.

"Heya, B," Cam drawls when we come to a stop on the sidewalk, his fingers wrapped tight around the strap of his duffel bag.

Knox sends him a look. "B? Is that what we're calling her now?"

"I like it." Cam shrugs, a secret smile curving his lips, his gaze sliding to mine.

I smile at him in return. "It's kind of cute. Don't you think, Knox?"

"If you say so." He studies his best friend before his gaze shifts to mine. "You two are acting weird."

I school my features, trying to appear nonchalant. "You're the weird one, Knox. What's your problem?"

"We were just leaving," Knox says, his voice clipped. He won't hardly look at me, and I can tell I offended him.

Good. He needs to focus on that emotion and not me and Cam giving off weird vibes.

"You have a good practice?" I ask Cam.

He tilts his head toward me, his lips curved into the faintest smile. It's sexy and sets about a zillion butterflies loose in my stomach, making me feel all fluttery inside. "Yeah. You coming to the game this Saturday?"

"Definitely," I say without hesitation.

"I'll get you tickets," Knox says, sending Cam a look that I can't read. "Come on, bro. Let's get out of here. I'm starving."

"You want me to make you guys dinner?" I offer, hating that they're trying to leave.

Well, Knox is trying to leave.

"I'm hungry now," Knox says, his gaze scanning my outfit. I'm wearing a matching dark green tank and leggings that I got at Aerie and I'm feeling extra cute at the moment. "Are you going running or something?"

"Yeah. Trying to work on my fitness." I rest my hand on my hip, thrusting my chest out, praying my nipples aren't obvious because eww, not in front of my brother.

"Looking good, B," Cam says, earning a slap on the chest from Knox.

"That's my sister," my brother oh so obviously reminds him.

"No shit. I can still tell her she's looking good, which she is." Cam's gaze locks with mine. "Been working out extra hard lately?"

The only extra hard workout I've had was with him in the front seat of his car. "Not particularly."

"That's a shame." He whistles low, ignoring how Knox is glaring at him like he wants to tear his head off. "We should meet up at the gym sometime and I can put you through a workout regimen."

"Oh, come the fuck on," Knox groans, "you're trying to piss me off, aren't you?"

"No. I'm serious." Cam glances over at Knox for a moment before sliding that gaze onto me. "I'm always looking for an excuse to hit the gym."

"I'll hit the gym with you," I say like the shameless hussy I am.

"Let's plan something soon then." He thrusts his hand out toward me. "Give me your phone."

Oh, my word. This man is a genius.

I pull my phone from my pocket and open it before I hand it to him, watching as he enters his phone number into my contacts and then sends himself a text from me. "Here. Now you can text me. Or I can text you. We can meet up next week."

Disappointment coats my tongue and I try to remain bright and chirpy despite it all. "Next week sounds good."

"Great."

"You two are full of shit," Knox mutters. "Just trying to get under my skin."

"Well, it worked, so point for me and Blair." Cam's amused gaze meets mine. "See ya this weekend."

"Bye," I call to the both of them, staying in the same spot so I can watch them walk away.

Knox's mouth is moving a mile a minute and I can only imagine what he's saying to Cam. Cam glances over his shoulder one last time before he goes to the passenger side of Knox's truck, his gaze locking with mine.

I waggle my fingers at him, dropping my hand when Knox looks at me too, a puzzled expression on his face.

Turning, I head for the field, not in the mood to run any longer. Mad I wasted a cute outfit when I got to talk to Cam for all of five minutes. I feel like I'm in middle school. Desperate to catch the attention of the popular boy and failing miserably with every chance I get. I remember those days far too vividly.

Can't believe I'm living them again.

I'm stretching out on the field before I run when I feel my phone buzz against my side. I pull it out of the tiny pocket that's in my leggings, smiling when I see the name of the person who's texting me.

Hottest QB Alive.

Giggling, I open our very short text thread, reading the text he sent from my number to himself.

Me: *U r hot.*

I want to roll my eyes. He would send that to himself.

Hottest QB Alive: *Sorry I had to go.*

I send him a quick text back.

Me: *It's fine. Knox is obnoxious.*

Hottest QB Alive: *You look gorgeous in that outfit. Green is your color.*

I'm smiling. Grinning, really. Now I don't regret wearing it. Not one bit.

Me: *Thank you.*

Hottest QB Alive: *See you later tonight?*

The butterflies are back, bigger than ever, their wings flapping and leaving me giddy.

I decide to play it cool.

Me: *We'll see.*

He responds immediately.

Hottest QB Alive: *We'll see? Oh B. You know you want more of this.*

Me: *More like I think you want more of THIS.*

I snap a photo of myself out on the field, a full body shot, and send it.

Hottest QB Alive: *You're right. I def want more of that.*

Me: *Text me later and like I said.*

Me: *We'll see.*

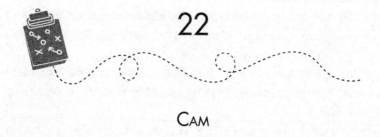

22

CAM

'm fucking horny.

It's bad. All I can think about is Blair. Sexy as fuck Blair gasping and shaking when the orgasm took over her. Hot as hell Blair grinding her pussy on my dick. Offering to take care of me. Wearing my shirt and hoodie, looking cute as hell in my clothes.

The conflict has weighed heavy on my mind since Tuesday morning when I woke up with an aching dick and the memory of her pussy gripping my fingers so damn tight. It was too much. Not enough. I'm totally into her. I shouldn't touch her again.

I told myself I would leave her alone and I did. I spotted her a few times on campus and went right when she went left. Another time, I found her heading straight for me and turned to go in the other direction. It was for the best. Knox is going to murder me. He might murder her too. We don't need to die at the hands of one of my favorite people. I'd rather be his friend than fuck his sister.

At least that's what I kept telling myself until we ran into her only a few minutes ago. Looking hot as shit wearing that green get-up that clung to her body like a second skin. Her hair was up in a ponytail, her eyes extra green, thanks to the outfit, and all I could think about was getting her out of it.

Instead, I talked to her about workouts and got her phone number because my mama didn't raise no fool. I can finally text and call her freely, though I should probably have her contact name say something different than Blair.

I'm staring at my phone right now while Knox drives us back to our apartment, smiling as Blair and I keep texting. She hit me with *we'll see* when I mentioned we should get together.

Yeah, we'll see all right. I'll be seeing plenty of her later tonight because I can guarantee we're getting together. Somewhere preferably with a bed.

"What are you smiling at?" Knox asks out of nowhere, irritation in his voice.

"Nothing." I send Blair a quick response and pocket my phone. "Texting a girl."

Knox grins, all irritation gone, just like that. "Some hottie you met at Logan's?"

"Something like that," I say, purposely vague.

"I'm, uh, seeing a girl tonight." He clears his throat, suddenly uncomfortable.

"Who?" I think I know who. I'm just trying to torture him.

"Joanna."

"Bookstore girl?"

"Yeah."

"She seems nice."

"I like her." I glance over at Knox, catching him swallowing hard, like that was tough to admit. "A lot."

"That's great, man." I'm not going to be a dick and discourage him from seeing her. If that's who he wants, then he should go for it.

"You're not going to tell me it's a dumb idea to start dating someone now? At this point in our lives?"

It is a ridiculous idea for him to start dating someone now. His last year in college, during the most important football season of his life. He's going to be busy as shit—we all are—and next thing we know, he'll be getting drafted and moving on to a professional team. Now is not the time to start a relationship that has more potential to fail than anything else.

But who am I to judge, when I'm thinking about the same thing? And even worse, I'm determined to keep it under wraps because I don't want Knox to find out I have a serious—thing for his sister.

I don't know what else to call it, but Jesus, she's all I think about. This isn't some occasional booty-call, hookup scenario. At least, I don't think it is.

"I'm not," I finally say, keeping my voice neutral. "You do you, bro. I just want you happy. And she doesn't seem to be fucking with your mojo out on the field."

"She's not. It's the weirdest thing. I was always afraid getting with just one girl would make me lose my focus, but I swear to God, I feel more determined out on that field than ever. I am fucking untouchable right now." Knox slaps the steering wheel for emphasis.

"That's great." I'm the slightest bit envious of his ability to freely see whomever he wants, whenever he wants, and to be able to talk about her too.

"I'd recommend you do the same, though I don't know if you're looking for anything serious." Knox chuckles. "A girl will set you straight, bro."

"I'm sure."

"And I'm serious. Though you should probably steer clear of my sister."

Unease slips into my veins, reminding me of what I'm doing, and how mad he's going to be if he ever finds out.

I'm only fooling myself. He's eventually going to find out.

"You two were kind of, I don't know, flirting earlier?" I glance over at Knox to find him sending me quick looks, while also trying to keep his eye on the road. "It was weird."

"That's why you said we were being weird?"

"Yeah. Look, I know I always tell everyone to back off from Blair, even you, but there's a reason for me saying that."

"A reason beyond you just being an overprotective asshole?" My tone is light. I'm teasing.

Not really.

"Ha ha," Knox says, the sarcasm thick in those two short words. "But really. When it comes to Blair, I worry about her."

"Why?"

"When she falls, she falls hard. She's all in. And every single one of her boyfriends did a number on her."

"Seriously?" I do not want to hear this. Nope.

Okay fine. I'm dying for more details.

"Yeah. God damn, it was so bad when her high school boyfriend broke it off with her. I thought she was going to fling herself off a bridge. She was so freaking upset. Crying all the damn time. Mom always having to console her. It was a lot."

I hate hearing that. Knowing she was crying over someone who wasn't worth her tears. "Did you know that loser?"

"Yeah, but I was here when they split. It was their senior year. Little dickhead broke her heart and she was in love with that fucker." The bitter expression on Knox's face would be sweet if I wasn't worried about how he'd react about us. "Dad told me she locked herself in her room and cried for days."

I think of her wearing that asshole's shirt and I'm fucking glad I tore it. Threw it in the trash when I got home too. Fuck the shirt, and the guy too.

"And then there was her boyfriend she had last year. Randy." Knox makes a face.

"What was wrong with that dude?" Oh, I am as casual as I can be, slouched in the seat, propping my feet up on the dash even.

"Put your feet down," Knox chastises, and I do as he says because I'd never allow that shit in the Challenger either. "He was the complete opposite of Travis. Quiet. Kind of nerdy. Really smart. He talked down to Blair. I witnessed it myself when I was home over winter break. Guy was a massive, pretentious prick."

"Why did they break up?"

"I don't know the exact reason, but she was the one who ended it that time around. I gave her a high five when she told me and that was that."

I want more info, but I can't ask Knox without alerting him. He'll wonder why I want all the scoop on his sister's previous boyfriends and I won't have a reason why. More like, I can't tell him the reason why.

I want to know every little thing about her. Even about the guys she's been with before me. Despite the jealousy that courses through me at the thought of her being with some other dude, I want all the details like the sadistic fuck I am.

"Are you really going to work out with my sister?" Knox asks, interrupting my thoughts.

"Yeah. If she's interested." I shrug, playing it off. "You know me. Any time I can get back into the gym, I'm going for it."

"She has zero stamina," Knox informs me. "She always gives up kind of fast. A bit of a wimp if you ask me."

Zero stamina, huh?

I bet I can have her going all fucking night long.

• • •

I finally give in and send her a text at nine o'clock that night. Knox is long gone, off to see his precious bookstore tutor girl, and I'm all alone. With thoughts of an orgasmic Blair and my dick urging me to reach out to her.

Me: *Whatcha doing?*

Bumblebee: *Nothing. What are YOU doing?*

I smile at the all-caps you, and I don't even understand why.

Me: *Want to come over?*

I wait for her response, which takes longer than I like. I probably shouldn't have led with that, but fuck it.

I'm dying to see her.

Bumblebee: *Where's Knox?*

Me: *Not here.*

Bumblebee: *What do you want to do?*

I bark out a laugh.

Me: *What do you think?*

Bumblebee: *I refuse to be the girl you only hook up with in secret.*

My stomach cramps. Not like we can come out and make whatever we're doing public, and she knows this.

Me: *Maybe you shouldn't come over then.*

My phone starts ringing. That familiar tone indicating it's a FaceTime call.

From…

Bumblebee.

I answer her call and her pretty face appears in seconds.

Her pretty, irritated face.

"I don't expect us to come right out with this," she says as her greeting.

"Hello to you too."

She rolls her eyes. "And I don't even know what we're doing."

"Do we need to define it?"

"I just don't want you to think of me as a casual hookup. Like… someone you could toss away like a piece of trash or whatever." She bites her lip, seemingly embarrassed she just admitted that.

"I would never think of you like that." I fucking hate that she worries about it. "You just…have to be patient with me."

She watches me with those big green eyes and my gaze drops for a moment, noting that she's wearing what looks like a black tank. "Patient with you."

I nod. "I've never been in a relationship before."

"Never?"

"Ever."

"Really?"

"Don't act so shocked." I chuckle.

"I can't help it. I am shocked. You're what…twenty-two?"

"Yeah."

"And you've never been in a relationship. Not even in high school?"

"Especially not in high school." Wasn't like I was banging a bunch of girls back then, but I wasn't about to let myself be tied down either. I was a lot angrier back then too. Pissed off at the world and not capable of caring about anyone else but myself.

When you witness your parents' toxic relationship and eventual crumbling marriage, that leaves a lasting impression, especially at the age I was when it all played out. Made me wary of relationships my entire life. I never allowed myself to get close to a girl. Woman.

Until Blair.

She's so damn wholesome—well, outwardly at least. I'm thinking she's got a few kinks tucked away in that devious part of her brain. But when it comes down to it, she's a good person. She comes from a great family. People who actually love each other and take care of each other.

My dad only takes care of me now out of a sense of guilt for all the previous shit he's doled out on me. Mom still apologizes to me out of nowhere, seemingly for no reason, but I get what's happening.

She's trying to unburden herself of all of that old guilt.

This is why I'm not interested in being in a relationship. I've set up all of these personal rules with myself that I can never break. I've been playing by them for a long ass time.

Then Blair comes along and she's got me thinking I should break every single one of those rules.

"Wow." She stares off into the distance, her gaze finally shifting to me. "I've been in a few."

I know, is what I want to say, but I don't. "You've got more experience than me."

"Only in relationships. Not with the...other stuff."

My curiosity is piqued. "What other stuff?"

"You know. The sex stuff."

"Blair."

"Cam," she returns, her cheeks the faintest shade of pink.

"You were doing all right a couple of nights ago."

"That was nothing." Her cheeks are brighter, and she waves a hand, dismissing me. "On my part at least. That was all you."

"You're the one who kissed me all over my face," I remind her, my voice soft.

That had been a sweet moment. And sexy too. No one has ever taken the time to do that to me before and I liked it.

A lot.

"That was probably childish." She ducks her head, her blonde hair falling across her face. It's damp again, much like it was a few nights ago, and I know she must've already taken a shower. Meaning her skin is extra soft and fragrant.

"Not childish," I reassure her. "Not with the thoughts running through my head when you did it."

"You liked it?" She lifts her head, her gaze finding mine once more.

"I like just about everything you do."

Her smile is small. Adorable. "You keep saying stuff like that and make me swoon when I should be annoyed at you for treating me like a casual hookup."

"You're not a casual hookup." The words leave my mouth before I can stop them and I realize in that moment that I mean them.

Blair is so far from casual to me.

I don't know what we're doing, and we've already established I don't like the words serious or relationship, but I do know one thing.

I'm not ready to let her go. I want more.

Her demeanor shifts, her shoulders relaxing, and it's like my words just eased all of the tension out of her. Tension that I caused, which makes me feel like a jerk.

"I like you too," she admits.

"I know I don't have any relationship experience, but I think we're beyond that stage," I tease her.

"You're right. We are." She laughs.

"Are you coming over?"

She sobers right up. "Are you sure it's...safe?"

"Knox isn't here," I remind her.

"When is he coming home?"

"I don't know."

"Where's he at?"

"With a girl."

"Who?"

Am I supposed to tell? I know she buddied up with Joanna and her roommate Natalie at the game, but I don't know how much I should reveal.

"Is he with Joanna?"

Relief floods me at not having to say her name first. "Yeah."

"Oh, I love that. She's so nice."

"She is." I hesitate. "Your brother is into her."

"I can tell."

Frustration ripples through me. "Blair."

I say her name a little too fiercely because now she's frowning. "What?"

"Get your pretty ass over here. Now."

"So bossy," she murmurs, and I'm pretty sure she's said that to me before.

"Please?"

She laughs, tossing her hair over her shoulder. "Fine. Give me a few."

"Don't worry about changing into a different outfit or whatever,"

I tell her. "Just—come as you are. I want to see you."

"Will do." Blair salutes me. "See you soon."

It won't be soon enough, I think after we end the call.

I've got it so bad for her.

Really hope I don't fuck everything up.

23

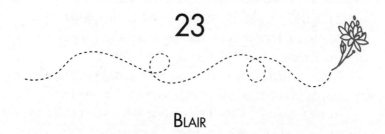

Blair

I do as Cam says and don't bother changing into something else or putting on makeup or whatever. He seems perfectly content to see me in my natural state, which is...nice.

I'm wearing a cropped black tank that's more of a sports bra and a pair of baggy gray Nike sweatpants that have wide legs and make me feel like a cool girl. As in, right on trend. After I brush my hair, I shove my feet into slides and am about to exit my bedroom when I have a realization.

I'm going to need to give a reason to my roommates as to why I'm leaving after nine o'clock at night. Something I haven't normally done since we all moved in together. Rita and Cheyenne are out in the living room right now. I can hear them talking, the low hum of music playing. They were supposed to be working on homework together but that never seems to happen when they do it at home. They get too caught up in chatting and gossiping, which I totally get. This is why I study by myself. At the library.

Struck by my new idea, I grab my backpack from where I left it on top of my desk and sling it over my shoulder before I leave my bedroom and make my way to the living room. The girls stop talking the moment they spot me.

"Where are you going?" Rita's voice is sly, like she knows exactly what I'm up to.

"The library," I say firmly, lifting my chin. Like I'm daring her to defy my words. "I need to study for a test tomorrow."

"At this time of night?" Cheyenne asks, sounding like my mom.

Speaking of, I haven't talked to her in a while. I need to call her. Maybe tomorrow.

I shrug. "The library is open till midnight. I can't concentrate here anyway. I need to go somewhere with no distractions."

"Are we too loud?" Cheyenne's expression turns contrite and she and Rita share a look. "We'll be quiet. Promise."

"It's not your guys' fault. I'm in my room trying to go over my notes and I'd rather watch something on Netflix. Or paint my toenails. Anything but study." I offer them both a smile. "You guys are fine. This is a me problem."

A me needing to see Cam problem, more like.

"Totally understand," Rita says with a nod. "Studying sucks."

Says the STEM major. It's all she does, when she's not chasing after guys or arguing with her best friend.

But I've come to respect Rita. And Cheyenne too. They're a little over the top and when they start yelling at each other, it can be a bit much, but they're easy to get along with. They're clean and respectful too. I have zero problems with them. Right now, I'm the shady one, sneaking out to see Cam and lying to them about it.

"Yeah." I tighten my grip on my backpack strap. "It does. See you guys later."

"Be safe out there!" Cheyenne shouts after I open the door and am halfway out of the apartment.

"Will do!" I shout back, slamming the door behind me.

Damn. I feel like a shit. And if all goes well, I'm not coming back for hours.

Sure hope they don't stay up and wait for me.

. . .

Not even ten minutes later, I'm standing on Cam and Knox's doorstep, raising my fist to knock when the door swings open. Cam is shirtless, clad in only a pair of training shorts that hang perilously low on his hips, and he grabs my raised hand, yanking me into the mostly dark apartment.

"You took forever," he scolds, his hands moving to wrap around my upper arms. He turns me so I'm leaning against the now-closed door, shifting closer. Pinning me with his body. "How did you get here anyway?"

Silly man. He didn't even think to ask when he flipped out over me walking last time. "I have a car now."

It's been in the shop the last couple of weeks because of a recalled part and I didn't really mind because I don't drive far. Everything I need is on campus or close by.

"Good." His voice is firm. "But you should've been here five minutes ago."

I roll my eyes. "I have roommates. They were questioning where I was going." I'm breathless thanks to the wall of heat pressed against me. I'm not even looking at his face any longer. I can only stare at his chest, taking in all of his bare skin on display.

All I want to do is touch it. Touch him. Kiss and lick my way down his chest…

"What did you tell them?"

I tilt my head back to find he's staring at my lips. I lick them with a quick swipe of my tongue and his gaze flares with heat. "I said I was going to the library to study."

"Study." His smile is faint. "Good one."

I settle my hands on his pecs because I have nowhere else to put them, and his eyelids flutter. "You're not wearing a shirt."

"I know." His smile grows. He looks pleased with himself. "Figured I'd give you a good look at my abs. Then you wouldn't be able to resist me."

"You're so arrogant." I slide my hands down over his pecs and his ribs, mentally counting the muscled ridges in his stomach. "I might be able to resist you. I come from a family of athletes, you know. I've seen a lot of firm abs in my life."

"None like mine, babe." He stops my hand just as it reaches the waistband of his shorts. "Let's go to my room."

"Nothing like getting right to it, huh?" Nerves gnaw at my insides, making me feel shaky.

"More like I don't want your brother to come home unexpectedly and catch us," he says, his expression solemn.

Oh shit. I didn't even think of that.

He takes my hand and leads me through the apartment. Even though there isn't any real light on, beyond the one shining through the open doorway of his bedroom, I still try and check out their living space. It's usually clean, but I don't come here that often and this is an unexpected visit. Thankfully, it doesn't smell bad in here—a good sign. Men can be such pigs. And outwardly it appears fairly neat. Just like it did when I was here making them dinner.

Now I brace myself for Cam's bedroom. If it's a total pigsty, that'll be a dealbreaker. I'm a neat freak. Some people view this as a flaw and my sister has accused me of having OCD on more than one occasion, but I don't think there's anything wrong with it.

I like being clean, what can I say?

Cam pulls me into his room, shutting and locking the door behind me, and I'm able to take a casual glance around the mostly clean room when he shoves me against the door and proceeds to kiss the shit out of me.

I know that doesn't sound pleasant, but trust me when I say the man has magical lips and wandering hands, and I'm not protesting when he kisses me for long, tongue-filled minutes. There are lots of sighs and soft groans and a couple of whimpers—those come from me—and the sound of clothing shifting. My clothing. As in, he's got his hands under my sweats and is kneading my butt with his fingers.

Finally breaking the kiss so I can catch a decent breath, I gasp when he lifts my ass, causing me to automatically wrap my legs around his hips. He presses his erection against me, right at my core, and I moan, knocking the back of my head against the door, my eyes falling closed. "You feel so good."

"I could fuck you like this," he murmurs. I crack my eyes open to see his fiercely intense expression as he rubs his hard cock against me. "You're at the perfect height."

He flexes his hips, hitting a particular spot that has me seeing stars, and I thunk my head against the door yet again, overcome by the sensations rolling through me. All we've done is kiss with a little bit of fondling and I'm already on edge. Ready to fall right over it with a few calculated strokes or touches. I swear the man could just look at me and I'd probably spontaneously combust.

"Watch it," he whispers, removing one hand from my ass to slip it behind my head. "Don't want to hurt yourself."

"You sound very proud," I whisper back. "Look at what you make me do."

"I can't help it that I drive you out of your mind." He presses his face into the crook of my neck, breathing deep. "Fuck, you smell good."

"It's my perfume," I tell him. I spritzed so much on myself before I left the apartment, I'm surprised my roommates didn't call me out on it. Who needs to wear that much perfume to go study at the library?

"I love that shit." His lips move against my neck, making me shiver. "Your skin is so soft here."

Before I can respond, he starts kissing me there, blazing a trail with his hot mouth down the length of my neck. I arch my head back, giving him better access, panting louder with every touch of his tongue on my skin. And when he bites me, his teeth making my flesh sting when they gently clamp down, I cry out.

He pauses. "Did I hurt you?"

I shake my head. "Do it again."

He licks and kisses and nibbles on my neck. My shoulder. His fingers slide the strap of my tank down, but it doesn't move much, thanks to it being really tight spandex. A frustrated growl leaves him and he gives it a good shove, my left breast popping out, my nipple aching for his mouth.

Cam covers it with his hand, squeezing and kneading my flesh. Eventually removing all of his fingers but one, drawing it in circles around my nipple, making it grow even harder if that's possible.

When he dips his head and swipes his tongue across the bit of flesh, I immediately clamp my hands around the back of his head, keeping him there. He sucks and licks it, his other hand tugging on the strap on my right shoulder, until my other breast is exposed too.

"Fuck." He groans just as he gathers me in his arms and carries me over to his bed, dumping me onto the mattress, so I land with a little bounce.

"Cam—" I can only choke the one word out before he's on me. Crawling over me, pressing his big, heavy body onto mine. I welcome the weight, savoring the feel of him, a sigh of pleasure leaving me when his mouth finds mine.

We kiss and grind, essentially dry humping each other like we're teens who can't take it too far because we have a curfew, but oh my God, it's glorious, having Cam Fields rub his thick dick against me, showing me what he can do without actually doing it. My skin is electrified, my core aching with the need to be filled, and I seriously can't remember the last time I enjoyed a make-out session so much.

Maybe never.

"We need to get this off you," he mutters after he's ended our kiss. He rises above me, his hands busy, tugging on the bottom of my cropped tank. I throw my hands up, giggling when he struggles, and eventually, I take over, pulling the suddenly too tight tank off and over my head, tossing it onto the floor.

He pauses, staring at me, his gaze skimming over my shoulders.

My chest. My stomach. I just lie there and let him look his fill, not embarrassed. He's the one who's essentially straddling my body and studying me as if he wants to eat me alive. "You're beautiful."

I squirm, vaguely uncomfortable with his compliment.

"You are." Cam drifts his fingers across my stomach, toying along the edge of my sweats. Goose bumps rise on my skin from his touch. "Whatcha got on under those sweatpants, B?"

"Wouldn't you like to know." I suck in a breath when he tugs on the drawstring.

"I would." He slips his fingers beneath the gathered waistband, sliding down. Down… "You are such a bad girl, Bumblebee."

"Bumblebee?" I'm breathless. Unable to think when he's got his fingers so close to my pussy.

"Your new nickname. You like it?" He dips his head, his mouth brushing mine, teeth nibbling at my lower lip before he pulls away. "You're not wearing panties. Again."

"What's the point?" I ask weakly, spreading my legs slightly when his fingers slip lower.

"I like the way you think." He's grinning, his smile devilish, his touch sent straight from heaven when he slides his fingers downward to completely cup my pussy. "We should get rid of these."

The sweats are gone in an instant, leaving me completely naked and still pinned beneath him. He's straddling me, his knees on either side of my thighs, his hands braced on the pillow my head rests on. He kisses me, soft and sweet, his tongue doing a thorough sweep, and when he pulls away, I try to follow him, lifting my head. Needing more.

His smile tells me he knows this, his mouth finding my ear. My neck. Drifting across my chest, my breasts, tongue teasing my nipples. His lips coast across my stomach, kissing one hipbone, then the other. Until I'm a panting, squirming mess, watching him drift his mouth across my lower belly, right above my pubic hair.

"You want me?" His gaze lifts to mine, dark and naughty. "Here?"

His fingers trace the seam of my pussy, never quite dipping inside.

I nod frantically, my heart racing in anticipation.

"I can smell you." He presses his face into my skin, breathing deep. "Better than the perfume."

He has a thing for the way I smell, and it's kind of hot.

"Spread your legs, B." His big hands go to the insides of my thighs, pushing them wide open. "And get ready."

I've had men go down on me before. Most of the time, they don't know what they're doing. As in, they can't figure out what feels good or what's going to make me come. Of course, I'm not the most comfortable when it comes to expressing my needs to a man while I'm having sex with him. I don't moan and scream and carry on like I'm participating in an exorcism.

Look, I watch porn. I've seen the way some of those women 'act.' Heavy emphasis on the last word. They thrash about as if they're having a seizure and sex has never, ever been like that for me.

But the moment I feel Cam's lips on my most intimate parts, I about shoot off the bed. He licks and sucks everywhere, leaving no part of me untouched. It's almost embarrassing, how thoroughly he searches me with his tongue, his big hands braced on my inner thighs, keeping me spread open for him.

It's so fucking hot. I can hardly take it.

His tongue toys with my clit, teasing it. Circling it, sucking it between his lips. He massages my thighs, his hands slipping downward, close to my ass, giving it a squeeze before he slips his hands all the way around my butt, holding me to him as he feasts on my pussy. There is seriously no other way to describe it.

The man is devouring me.

Everything inside me tingles with every stroke of his tongue. My skin is on fire and I'm panting, my heart racing, like I can't catch my breath. I feel like I could black out at any moment, and when he slides a finger inside me, his lips wrapped tightly around my clit, that's it.

I'm coming.

Oh God, I'm *screaming*.

It's like I'm having an out of body experience. Like my soul just slipped from my body and drifted above it for a moment, staring down at the picture we make. Cam's head buried between my legs, my hands gathering the comforter fabric in my fists, like I needed to clutch something or else I'd slip away completely.

When I finally come to, it's only to realize I've now got my hands in his hair and I'm trying to shove him away from me with my feet on his shoulders, and he's chuckling.

Laughing.

I swear to God, he's Satan wrapped up in a sexy, ab-tastic package.

He's still chuckling, wiping his face against the inside of my thigh because, oh my God, did I like, squirt or whatever? I didn't even think that was actually possible.

"I-I don't normally do that," I finally say to him, once I've found my voice.

"Do what?"

"Shout." I meet his gaze, wincing. "Why? Did I do—something else?"

"Define something else."

"I can't." I cover my face with my hands, suddenly mortified. The man had his face all up in my private parts only moments ago and suddenly I'm embarrassed? What is wrong with me?

He shifts so he's lying next to me, and he peels my hands off my face, his gaze warm and sexy and oh so comforting when I finally stare into his eyes. "Don't be embarrassed."

"I came really hard," I say, my voice small. "I don't think I've ever come that hard in my life."

"Keep talking."

I swat at his chest. "I'm not trying to feed your ego. I'm trying to be real with you."

"Well, you're doing both." He leans in, brushing my mouth with his and I can taste myself on his lips. "And it was hot, the way you shouted my name."

"Cam..."

He kisses me again, essentially shutting me up with his lips, and

I lose myself in his kiss for a while. The expert stroke of his tongue. I can feel his heavy erection press into me, reminding me that the poor man is probably suffering from a serious case of blue balls and I slide my hand down his chest, slipping beneath the waistband of his shorts, pausing at my discovery.

I break the kiss, raising my brows when he opens his eyes. "You're just as bad, Camden."

"What makes you say that?" The defiant tone of his voice tells me he already knows exactly what I'm talking about.

"You're not wearing any underwear either." I am touching warm skin, pubic hair tickling my fingers. I shift lower, my fingers grazing his shaft, and he hisses in a breath. "You're bad, Cam."

"Just like you. Looks like we're a perfect match."

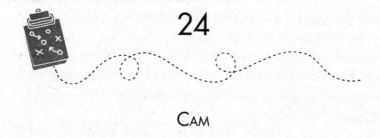

24

CAM

I kiss her before she can say anything, essentially shutting her up, and I enjoy the sensation of her fingers drifting up and down my dick while I continue kissing her, my blood growing hotter and hotter with every pass of her fingers.

Going down on her and making her come was a hot moment. One I won't forget. Does she even realize how sexy she is? How responsive? I barely touch her and she's shaking. I shove a finger inside her tight pussy and she's coming all over me, making a mess.

A hot mess. It didn't bother me at all.

Her fingers curl around my shaft and start to stroke. Slowly at first, trying to find her rhythm, and once it picks up, I lift my hips, ridding myself of my shorts so they don't interfere.

It hits me in this moment that I'm naked in bed with Blair Maguire. I never thought it could happen. Or if it would, I'd immediately regret it.

I have zero regrets. This girl is just…doing it for me right now.

"Lie back," she demands, her sweet voice a little firmer than usual, and I do as she says, folding my arms under my head, much like I did when we were together in my car, watching as she sends me a vaguely dirty look just before she puts her mouth on my chest.

My breath sticks in my lungs as I watch her deliver the same treatment that I gave her only minutes before. Her mouth sliding over my skin, her tongue licking my nipples, nibbling them even. Her lips are warm and soft and they are everywhere. Drifting over my ribs, across my stomach. Her hand is already curved around the base of my cock, gripping it firmly, and I thrust my hips, indicating I want her to start stroking.

She does me one better, sliding downward until she's face to cock, a little smile teasing the corner of her lips before she sticks out her tongue and licks the head of my dick, like it's her favorite ice cream on a hot summer day.

"Christ," I bite out, holding my breath when she continues to lick and suck on the head, her tongue playing with the flared edge, teasing the slit that's leaking pre-cum.

Sweet little Blair is a dirty girl in bed. She's giving me head like she's enjoying every second, sliding my cock deep into her mouth, until I swear I bump against the back of her throat. I prop myself up against the headboard so I can see better, her hair falling in front of her face, blocking my view.

Reaching out, I gather the silky strands in one fist and hold it away from her face. She releases my cock from her mouth, her swollen lips shiny and sexy as fuck when she says, "Pull it."

I frown. "What?"

"My hair." She tilts her head to the side and I tug on it gently, noting her wince. "Remember?"

Pull her hair and slap her ass. I can manage both of those here eventually.

She resumes sucking my cock deep into her mouth, pulling it almost all the way out before sliding it back in. I stare at her, fascinated, fucking growling when she pulls me out and grips my shaft, tapping the head against her stuck-out tongue. Really giving me a visual, which I can appreciate.

"What the fuck are you doing?" I finally ask her.

Blair pauses, her gaze lifting to mine as she releases me from her mouth. "What's wrong? You don't like what I'm doing?"

"I fucking love it, but it also feels like you're just...playing with it. Me."

"Well, it is called foreplay, Cam." She teases the tip of my dick with her tongue and with a growl, I lunge toward her, cupping her flushed face with my hands. "You want me to stop?"

"No way." I rub her lips with my thumb, brushing it back and forth. "I want you to suck it harder."

She nods, her eyes going wide.

"I want to fuck your mouth."

"Okay," she whispers.

I press my thumb between her lips, pleased when she sucks it deeper. "I want to come down your throat."

Blair says nothing, and I wonder if I've taken it too far. But fuck it.

I keep going.

"Do you swallow, Bumblebee?"

She lets go of my thumb from her lips. "I mean...I have."

I tug on her face, pulling her closer, her hands on my thighs, my mouth at her ear as I whisper, "I want to watch you swallow every last drop that drips down your throat, baby. Are you up for that?"

She's trembling. Fuck, did I scare her?

The tiny nod she gives as an answer tells me no, I definitely did not.

"Get on your knees, baby," I command once I've let go of her head.

She scrambles off the bed, falling to her knees on the floor, waiting obediently, her hands resting on top of her thighs. I watch her, my gaze dropping to her tits. Her perfect pink nipples that I'd love to suck on again soon.

Everything about her is perfection. Like she was made for me.

Just looking at her leaves my skin tight and itchy. Like I might burst out of it at any given moment. Such a sexy little thing.

Does she know what she does to me? Probably not.

I crawl off the bed and stand directly in front of her, my erect cock waving in her face. She reaches for it and I shift away from her hand at the last second, settling on the edge of the mattress, leaning back to rest one hand on it, my other hand wrapped around the base of my dick.

"Let me feed it to you," I tell her, and she parts her lips automatically.

Slowly, I shove my cock between her lips, inch by inch. She takes it, her mouth open wide, until the head bumps the back of her throat and she makes a slight gagging noise. Reaching out, I draw my fingers down her throat, murmuring, "Relax."

She tries, I'll give her that, but it's not easy. I'm basically gagging her with my cock and that's not normally my scene. There's something about seeing her like this, though. All choked up.

Literally.

"Brace yourself, B," I warn her before I start to lift my hips, then pull back. Within seconds, she's got it handled, her body still, her mouth suctioning around my cock as I fuck her mouth. All the kissing and pussy licking and watching her suck my cock has already sent me closer and closer to the edge and I'm not too far from blowing my entire load in her mouth. But fuck.

I want to witness it.

"Part your lips," I tell her, and she automatically does what I demand of her. I pull almost all the way out of her mouth and wrap my fingers tight around my shaft, starting to stroke. "Keep 'em open."

I'm frantic, desperate to make myself come. My breaths are harsh. Ragged. My chest is tight. A strangled groan leaves me at the exact time the first splatter of semen hits her lips, right at the corner of her mouth.

She licks it away quickly, the white substance disappearing on her tongue and I fucking groan, making a mess all over her open mouth.

But she swallows it all, her eyes closing, her lips curling up in the faintest smile. As if she's enjoying herself.

I think she might be.

When I'm finished, I collapse backward on the bed, staring up at the ceiling as I try to calm my racing heart. My erratic breathing. Within seconds, she's crawling onto the bed to join me, snuggling up next to my side. I curl my arm around her shoulders and drop a kiss on her forehead, holding her tight, and she rests her hand low on my stomach. Close to my still twitching dick.

"Was I too mean?" I ask after a few minutes of silence.

"No." She tilts her face up just as I look down, our gazes meeting. "I liked it."

"You liked me coming on your face?" I lift my brows.

"You didn't come on my face." She rolls her eyes, feisty as ever. "You came on my lips."

"Hot as fuck, Bumblebee." I kiss her.

"I don't know how to feel about this new nickname," she mumbles against my lips.

"I call you B, right? And I wanted to give you a nickname in my contacts on my phone, so your brother wouldn't see that I'm actually texting you, so I came up with what I thought was the next best thing." I kiss her temple, my lips lingering. "Kind of clever, am I right?"

There's no response, and for a second there, I think she might've fallen asleep until I hear her whisper, "We need to tell him. Eventually."

We do. I know we do.

But I don't want to. Not yet.

• • •

I'm woken up to the sound of insistent knocking on my bedroom door, followed by the handle rattling. Oh, and the insistent sound of my phone alarm going off.

"Wake the fuck up, bro. Your alarm has been going off for twenty minutes," Knox yells from behind the door.

"Oh shit." My eyes crack open and I turn my head, grabbing the phone off my nightstand to check the time, turning off the alarm. I'm late. I have class in fifteen minutes.

But I have a sweet little blonde bundle wrapped up in my arms, her face snuggled right against my chest. I'm not getting up yet.

Looks like I'm skipping class.

"Why the hell is your door locked anyway?" Knox keeps on shouting, and I wish I could throw a pillow at his big head, but I can't. That means I'd have to open the door and show him who's in my bed, and that's a problem I don't want to deal with anytime soon.

"Go away," I yell back at him, causing Blair to stir. "And it's locked to keep you out. Otherwise, you'd just barge in and yell in my face."

"Whatever man." I can hear him walk away, and I sink back into the mattress, giving Blair a gentle squeeze.

"He still has no clue, huh?" Blair murmurs against my chest.

"About what?" I kiss the top of her head. It's like I can't stop touching her.

"You and me. Us. I mean, I already know he doesn't know. I just had to ask." She tilts her head back, her expression sleepy, her eyes tired. I lean in for a kiss, and she swerves left, not giving me the opportunity. "You can't kiss me."

"Why not?"

"Morning breath."

"I don't give a damn."

"Yeah, you will. No kissing." She keeps her head averted.

"You're being ridiculous. I'll take care of the morning breath problem. At least for myself." I grab her, pulling her up. She yelps and I rest my finger against her lips, indicating I want her to be quiet and she nods, those green eyes of hers even bigger.

Next thing I know I've got her gripping the headboard, her knees on either side of my head, her pussy right above me. I wrap my arms around her waist and start licking, letting her grind all over my face, my tongue touching every part of her that's within reach.

It takes nothing to make her come. Might've helped that I streaked my finger across the tiny puckered hole between her plump ass cheeks. Did that a couple of times and she was coming with a muffled shout, her hand over her mouth preventing her from getting too loud.

Fucking hot.

I drag her into my connected bathroom once she's come down from her orgasm, pulling her into the hot shower with me. I soap up her body and she does the same to me, our wandering hands making our skin slick from the suds. She won't leave my dick alone, but it is hard and constantly getting in the way between us. And when she drops to her knees and takes me into her mouth, it doesn't take me long to come either, sending it all straight down her throat.

"What are you doing to me?" I ask her once she's gathered up in my arms, our bodies soaked, our skin wrinkled from being under the water for too long. She's even shivering, her teeth chattering slightly.

"W-what do you m-mean?" she asks.

I press her against the slick tile wall, trying to warm her with my body. I'm so hot I feel like I might burst out of my skin and she's shaking from being too damn cold.

"If you don't watch it, I'm going to become addicted to everything you do," I admit, about as real with her as I've ever been.

Her smile is faint, her eyes glowing. "Promise?"

25

BLAIR

The FaceTime call comes out of nowhere, just as I'm about to settle into bed and fall asleep. I'm exhausted after last night's extracurricular activities with Cam and I've been sluggish all day. Despite how much coffee I've chugged, and I even skipped class.

It didn't help. None of it. I'm so tired. I guess this is what happens when you get with a man with an enormous sexual appetite. And we haven't even had actual sex yet.

I'll probably end up dead, but at least I'll pass with a smile on my face.

The photo flashing on the screen indicates it's my mom and so I answer the call, offering a little wave and hello when her face appears.

Her brows immediately draw together in concern when she sees me. "Blair. You look exhausted."

"Gee thanks." I hide a yawn behind my hand and the look she sends me tells me she's overly concerned.

"Are you doing too much?"

I'm not about to go into detail about what exactly I'm doing, so

I just smile at her instead. "No. I'm fine. Just stayed up too late last night."

"With school work? Or having fun."

"Having fun." Way too much fun.

"I'm glad you're making friends. Your brother mentioned you were," she says.

"You talked to Knox?"

Mom nods. "Earlier. Saw Cam as well and we chatted."

My heart is in my throat at her mentioning Cam.

"You spoke to Cam too?" There's a faint edge to my voice I'm afraid she'll notice, but thankfully, she doesn't.

"Yes. He's a darling. Such a flirt." Mom laughs. "Your brother got mad at him and said 'stop trying to make a pass at my mom.'"

"He would never," I say.

"No, he wouldn't. I am old enough to be his mama and he knows it. Besides your father would kick his ass." Mom cackles, and I can't help but laugh too. "Tell me about school."

I give her the usual rundown, letting her know about my class load and how it's going. Giving her an update on my roommates and how much I'm starting to like them. I even mention going to the home game and getting to know Joanna and Natalie.

"The tutor?" Mom asks, interrupting me mid-conversation.

"Yes. Did Knox tell you about her?"

"Sort of. When I reminded him that's how I met your father, he sort of blew me off." Mom smiles. "He doesn't want to think about getting in a steady relationship. He's always been so independent."

More like he's been a complete manwhore, but I don't need to rip on him to our mother.

"I think he might like her," I say, giving her a little info. Mom always complains about how tight-lipped Knox is with her, but right now, I'm the one who's feeling tight-lipped about my own situation so...

I'm throwing Mom a bone.

"Oh really? I love that."

"And she's really nice." I smile. "I approve." So far.

"That's great. He deserves happiness. Your brother is such a sweetheart."

I snort. "To you."

"He's nice to you too, and you know it. Just a little overprotective sometimes."

"All the time," I add.

"All the time. Sometimes. You know what I mean." Mom laughs. "How was the game?"

I give her some details, frowning when I finish.

"Why haven't you and Dad been to any games lately?"

"We've been busy," she chirps, reminding me of...me.

I get chirpy when I'm feeling awkward or nervous.

Hmm.

"Busy with what?"

"Well, your father and I went to visit your aunt and uncle in California a few weeks ago. And then we went to see Ruby too, last week. It was parents' weekend so of course we had to go. Not too sure how much longer she's going to last there, though."

The tone in Mom's voice tells me she's worried. "She mentioned something to me as well."

"That she's not happy? No, I don't suppose she is. She's so far away. That's tough. You just can't come home for the weekend. Not like you and your brother can."

"Right," I say softly, my heart suddenly aching.

I miss my mom. My dad too. I need to see them. Soon.

"I think she might come home over winter break and possibly transfer somewhere else. Maybe even go to the community college like you did for the next semester and start where you're at in the fall," Mom says.

"Wow, really?" I can't believe Ruby is making the switch. I figured she wanted out of this area, this state. She always talked about how stifling it felt here, which is something neither Knox nor I ever experienced.

We like it here. Colorado is beautiful. And if I were to go anywhere else, it would most likely be California, because we already have family there, even though it's expensive.

"I wanted to call you not to just catch up but also to let you know that your father and I will be out there soon. We're flying too. We don't want to deal with the drive," Mom explains.

My sadness evaporates, replaced with joy at the thought of having them here.

"Oh, that's great. It'll be so nice to see you guys."

"There's a home game that weekend too so we'll go to that and hang out. It'll be fun, but I wish Ruby could be with us." Mom offers up a little pout.

"Me too," I admit.

My thoughts immediately go to Cam and wondering where he might end up if he gets drafted. His choices are endless. He could end up anywhere in this country, and then I wouldn't get to see him anymore. Only on TV while watching a game he's playing in.

So weird to think about, but then again, it's not. I watch my family play all the time. My cousins and their spouses. Back in the day, when I was younger, I remember watching my dad. My uncle. I don't remember the NFL *not* being in my life. It's that ingrained in me.

What a great little NFL wife I would make, am I right?

I am so getting ahead of myself.

Mom and I talk for a little while longer and I'm just about to end the call when I get a notification that I'm getting another FaceTime call.

From Cam.

I don't answer him right away, finishing my chat with Mom first, not wanting to rush her off the phone. All of my exhaustion evaporates though, knowing that he's trying to get a hold of me. On a Friday night, no less.

Right as I'm saying good night to my mom, a text notification comes through.

Hottest QB Alive: *I want to see you.*

"Mom, I really have to go." Another yawn, this one fake, and I cover my mouth at the last second. "Talk to you later?"

"Of course. Love you, sweetie. Good night!"

"Night." I finally end the call and immediately send Cam a text.

Me: *See me how?*

He responds immediately.

Hottest QB Alive: *See you now. Preferably naked.*

My skin goes hot at his words.

Me: *Where's Knox?*

Hottest QB Alive: *In the living room.*

Me: *I can't come over.*

Hottest QB Alive: *What's going on at your place?*

Me: *I thought you didn't want to cause a scandal or whatever if you ended up coming over?*

My phone lights up with a FaceTime call and I answer him, smiling when I finally see his face pop up on the screen. Ugh, he's so gorgeous. His hair is damp and he's not wearing a shirt, which I think is a purposeful move on his part. Like he's trying to drive me wild with lust.

It's working.

"Where are your roommates?" he asks.

"They're out."

His brows shoot up. "Where?"

"The bars. Most likely Logan's."

"Perfect. I'm coming right over." He starts to move, like he's going to get off his bed and jet over here in minutes.

"Wait a sec." He flops back onto the bed at my words, frowning. "I'm actually...really tired."

"You are?"

I nod. "Someone kept me up late last night."

He grins, looking pleased with himself. "That guy is such an asshole."

"He's something all right." I'm teasing. So is he.

This is fun. Sweet even. Relationship-type banter, though if I said that out loud, Cam would deny it.

"Maybe I could come over and give you a massage," he suggests. "Help you fall asleep."

"A massage?"

"Yeah." He grins, lifting his hands and waggling his fingers. "I've been told I have magic hands."

"You do." Now I'm frowning. "Who told you that?"

I imagine all of these gorgeous girls he's been with over the years cooing at him, telling him he has magic hands, fingers, whatever. *Ugh.*

"The media." He laughs, making like he's going to throw a football. "They're referring to how I throw a football, Bumblebee. So get those dirty thoughts out of your head."

I scowl at him while he continues to laugh.

"Look, if you'd rather not get together tonight, I understand," he says, once his laughter has died down. "If you're too tired, maybe we can make it happen some another time."

Why do I feel like this might be my only opportunity to see him? All of these moments we share seem so fleeting. Like I need to grab hold of them and grip them tightly. Probably because Cam isn't the type to keep seeing the same woman for an extended period of time. I know he said he wants to see where this takes us, but what if it takes us straight to nowheresville? What if I end up getting dumped next week?

It could happen.

"You should come over," I tell him, my voice soft, my heart aching to have him close.

"Really?" He sounds excited and he immediately clears his throat, his expression shifting into impassive. Oh, he's trying to play it cool. That's cute too. "Are you sure?"

"I'm sure. Just—no strenuous exercise tonight, okay?"

"My workout routine last night was too rough on you?"

"Yeah. I'm more in the mood for some cuddling."

"You and your cuddling." He tries to make it sound like an insult, but I know the truth.

He likes it.

A lot.

Minutes after we end our call, there's a knock on the door, and I go to answer it, sucking in a sharp breath when I find Cam standing in front of me, looking delicious in a pair of charcoal gray joggers and a long-sleeved team T-shirt that fits him like a glove. Showing off every muscle he's got in his arms and shoulders. His chest and torso and stomach.

Seriously, I think he's trying to slay me dead.

"Hey." He's rubbing his chin, his gaze drifting over me.

I'm wearing his hoodie and nothing else. Not a drop of clothing under this gargantuan sweatshirt. I hurried up and changed into it the moment I knew he was coming over.

"Hi." I sound breathless, and my skin is starting to overheat, thanks to the lust I see flashing in his gaze. "Come in."

I hold the door open wider and he strides right on in, resting his hands on his hips as he checks out my apartment.

"This is nice."

"Thanks." I shut and lock the door, leaning against it while I watch him. "You were fast."

He turns to meet my gaze. "I have an early day tomorrow. Can't waste time."

"Are you saying I'm a waste of time?" I know that's not what he means but...

It sort of sounds like that? Or am I just being way too sensitive?

Probably the latter.

"You? A waste of time?" He starts walking toward me, slowly shaking his head. "I don't think so."

My worry evaporates at the look in his eyes. My heart starts to pump a little harder, my breaths come a little faster, and when he stops directly in front of me, his hands going to my waist, I inhale sharply.

"Whatcha got on under my sweatshirt?"

I tilt my head back, smiling at him. "Why don't you check and see?"

His big hands gather up the fabric of his sweatshirt, pulling it up. His gaze drops, focused on my lower half as he slowly exposes me. Revealing that, yep, I'm naked. He stares at me silently for so long, I start to feel restless. And when he finally settles his hot gaze on my face, I feel scorched.

"I feel like I created a monster," he murmurs, and I can see it in his eyes. His expression.

He's pleased. He likes that I did this for him. And he's not too far off the mark. He's totally created a monster. My entire body aches from what we did last night, and even though I told him I was tired, I can't wait to do it again.

From the look on his face, I'm guessing he feels the same way.

Dropping my sweatshirt, he glances over his shoulder toward the hallway that leads to our bedrooms before he returns his gaze to me. "Where's your bedroom?"

"Down there." I incline my head toward the hallway he just looked at.

"Wanna show me?" He lifts his brows.

"Yes," I whisper, shrieking when he grabs hold of me and swings me over his shoulder, my head dangling upside down.

Cam carries me like he's some sort of caveman down the short hallway, pausing in front of the first open doorway. "Your room?"

"Yes." Another shriek escapes me when he lightly slaps my exposed butt. "Cam!"

He strides into the bedroom, depositing me onto the bed. I land on my side, immediately sitting up, shoving my hair out of my face. "You spanked me."

"So?" He checks out my bedroom, walking over to my dresser and picking up a framed photograph of my family. It was taken last year, after one of Knox's football games and he's still in uniform, looking pretty beat. The rest of us surround him, my parents standing on either side, Ruby and I directly in front of them. "I remember this game."

"You do?" They won, I remember that. Even back then I admired Cam out on the field. He was so good, so confident and quick, playing like a professional. That's what my father said as he watched him, and I couldn't help but silently agree.

"You looked cute that night." He glances up, his gaze meeting mine. "I noticed."

How long has he noticed? "You did?"

"I noticed you that summer Knox brought me to your house and you followed me around all weekend." He sets the frame back on the dresser, turning to face me. "Take off the sweatshirt."

I gape at him, shocked by his fierce tone. Also aroused, I can't lie. "I didn't follow you around that weekend."

He's grinning. "You definitely did. Wore the tiniest bikini too. Trust me, I noticed."

Damn it, he's right. I was shameless, while trying to gain his attention, and all of these years I thought it didn't work. Now it sounds like all the effort I put into myself that weekend actually had results. "Why didn't you do anything? Say anything?"

"First of all, you weren't even eighteen," he reminds me.

"I was close."

"Not close enough. And second, I just met Knox and we were getting along great. I wasn't about to fuck around with his sister and make him hate me."

"So, what's the difference now?"

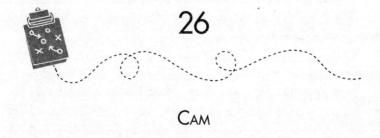

26

CAM

Her words ring in my head, and I stare at her, enjoying how good she looks in my hoodie. Wishing she'd taken it off when I told her, so we wouldn't be having this conversation.

"I didn't know you then," is what I finally say, and I can tell my response pleases her.

"And you know me so well now?"

"I know you well enough to see that you're kind. Compassionate. Smart. Sweet. Well, sometimes." She glares, but I don't acknowledge it. "You're sexy as fuck. You're relentless."

"Relentless?"

"You never let up on me."

"Only recently." She shrugs, her shoulders looking extra small in my sweatshirt. That thing is giant on her. "You were blind."

"Blind to what?"

"Us."

She says the word without any fear. Like it's so logical, us being together. While it's difficult for me to wrap my head around the possibility of us still, I'm starting to see it.

Believe it.

Clearing my throat, I lean against the edge of her dresser, crossing my arms. "You didn't do what I told you earlier."

Blair blinks at me, her expression one of pure innocence. "Do what?"

"Take off my sweatshirt."

"You're not wearing a sweatshirt," she points out.

"But you are. And that sweatshirt belongs to me." I incline my head in her direction. "Take it off."

"Cam…"

"Do it, B."

Heaving a big sigh, she rises up on her knees and tugs the sweatshirt up, revealing her beautiful naked body to my gaze. She tosses the hoodie onto the floor but remains on her knees in the center of the bed, spreading her legs a little.

Fuck, what a sight. Smooth skin and heavy breasts topped with dark pink nipples. Slender waist and sexy hips. A neat little landing strip of dark blonde pubic hair leads to her pussy. She's gorgeous.

Blair runs her hands down her thighs and I'm hit with a thought. "Touch yourself."

Her hands pause on her knees, her eyes widening. "What?"

"Touch yourself," I repeat. "Show me how you like it."

"Camden…"

"Do it. Don't be shy." I raise my brows. "I like to watch."

"You do?" Her voice is a little shaky and I wonder if I'm freaking her out. But shit, this isn't a big deal, is it? She should show me how she likes to be touched. I have an idea, but it's always fun to watch.

Not that I've ever been much of a watcher in the past. I'm more of a doer. But when it comes to Blair, I'm up for anything.

Everything.

"I like to watch you," I clarify, which gives her the boost of confidence I'd hoped. Squaring her shoulders, she straightens her spine, her hands still gripped tightly on her knees. "Show me,

Bumblebee. Get yourself off knowing I'm watching your every move."

Her lips part, her eyes seeming to glaze over, and she lifts her hands, cupping them around her breasts. "Like this?"

I nod, my cock already responding. "Keep going."

She lifts her tits up toward me like an offering, brushing her thumbs back and forth across her hardening nipples, and I lick my lips, tempted to say fuck it and jump on her.

But I don't. I remain where I'm at, leaning uncomfortably against the damn dresser, my cock already straining the front of my boxers. She lets go of her breasts until it's just her thumb and index finger tugging on her nipples, so hard she hisses in a breath.

"Hurt?" I ask.

Blair slowly shakes her head, her blonde hair sliding over her shoulders. "Feels good."

This girl.

Pardon me, *woman*.

Everything about her is perfect. As if she were made for me.

She lets go of her nipples, sliding her hands down her torso. Along her ribs, her stomach, hands pausing at her hips, her fingers fanned out, pointing toward one of my favorite parts of her. "I feel a little silly," she admits.

"You don't look silly," I rush to say, not wanting her to stop. "I think you look fucking sexy."

Her fingers come together and she slides her hands down farther, almost covering her pussy completely and she pauses, bending her head to study herself as she keeps one hand in place while the other slips down, a single finger parting her lips.

Oh fuck.

A shuddery sigh leaves her as she explores her sensitive flesh with just her index finger, her head still bent, her hair covering her pretty face. I can hear her finger slicking through all of that wet heat, and I bark out a command without thought.

"Look at me."

Blair lifts her head, her eyes wide, her mouth hanging open, her finger on pause.

"Keep touching yourself."

She starts stroking again, her knuckles bending as she begins to rub her clit. Her teeth sink into her lower lip, a low moan sounding, and her eyelids start to waver. Like they're going to shut.

"Don't close your eyes." She blinks at me. "That's it. Add another finger."

Without hesitation, she does as I tell her, the scent of her starting to fill the room. I try to remain calm, but my hands are curled into fists. My heart is thundering in my chest and my dick is reminding me that he's a needy bastard and he's dying to get inside her.

Not yet, I tell myself—and my dick. We need to see this through first.

"Fuck yourself, B," I tell her, and she goes still. "Lie back on the bed and spread your legs. Let me see you do it."

She gets into position without a word, lying back, her upper body propped against her pillows. Spreading her legs wide, she lets me see everything she's got, pink glistening flesh on display as she drifts her fingers along the edge of her pussy, toying with herself.

Hot.

Slowly, she sinks a finger inside her, pulling it out before sliding it back in. She does this a few times, eventually adding another finger, and I watch, mesmerized as she lifts her hips and arches her back. Her eyes are closed, her long blonde hair spread across the pillow, and fuck me, she is the sexiest thing I've ever seen.

"Roll over," I suddenly tell her, and she frowns, her busy fingers pausing. "Do it."

Removing her fingers from her pussy, she rolls over as I tell her, "Get on your hands and knees."

She shifts into position, wagging that perfect ass at me, offering a sweet glimpse of her pussy between her thighs, and I go to the bed, taking my shirt off as I make my way toward her, crawling onto the mattress, so I'm directly behind her. I'm close enough to see that she's trembling, her skin shining with the thinnest layer of sweat, and damn if she isn't the sexiest thing I've ever seen.

Going on pure instinct, I slap her ass, making her jolt. I rise up above her and grab hold of her hair, gathering it in one hand and giving it a gentle tug. She throws her head back, panting as she whispers, "Harder."

I pull harder, enough to yank her head back, her lips parting on a moan.

"Jesus, Blair," I mutter, leaning over her as I cover the smooth expanse of her back with my upper body. "You're a fucking dirty girl."

"N-not n-normally," she stutters out, whimpering when I tighten my grip on her hair. "I swear you bring it out of me."

Pausing, I stare at her profile, the way her lids are at half mast, her lips parted. Looking like a sex goddess straight out of my darkest dreams. "Yeah?"

She nods, her head barely moving since I've got such a strong hold of her hair. "I want to do whatever you want me to, Cam. I-I want to please you."

I tug on her hair until she's just on her knees, pressing my chest to her back, curling my other arm around her waist while keeping a hold on her hair. Her ass is snug against my cock, her entire body trembling, and I let my hand drift down her stomach until I'm cupping her between her thighs. She's hot and wet and when I gently swipe my thumb across her clit, a jolt rocks her body, her ass brushing against my dick.

"I haven't even fucked you yet," I murmur close to her ear, licking her lobe. "And look at you. Always so eager to please me."

She nods but doesn't say a word, her body seeming to melt into mine. I let go of her hair and reach around her to grab hold of her breast, rubbing and kneading her supple flesh, my thumb tracing around her nipple. She turns her head toward mine, her mouth landing on my jaw, breathing into my skin, and I angle my head so I can kiss her.

Consume her.

I turn her around so we're facing each other, her hands in front of my sweats, her fingers curled around my dick. I've got my fingers between her legs, rubbing and searching, our mouths fused, tongues battling. I can't get enough of her and I think she feels the same about me. We're out of control, hands wandering everywhere, as if we're trying to get under each other's skin. I take over the situation, wrangling her into position, so she's lying on the mattress beneath me, her legs spread and me lying between them. She breaks our kiss to stare up at me, her breaths coming quick, and I wait for her, dipping my head, running my lips across her collarbone.

"I-I want you," she whispers, her hands coming up to sink into my hair.

I smile against her skin. "I know."

"I want you inside me," she continues, tilting her head so she can stare into my eyes when I lift my gaze to hers. "Now."

"You think you're in control of this?"

"No." She laughs, and the sound warms my goddamn soul, I swear. "I just wanted to let you know how I feel."

She wants me, I think as I resume kissing a path along her skin. She wants to have sex with me, and fuck, I want to be inside her too. This will change everything between us.

Every single thing.

Not that it hasn't already changed. We've messed around enough to shift the boundaries past the point of no return. We're involved— sexually. She's all I can think about. Not when I'm on the field, I can still focus, thank God, but once I'm off and able to do whatever I want? All I want to do is...

Her.

Blair.

My sweet little Bumblebee.

I don't give nicknames to girls. I don't tease them or laugh with them while they're naked in my arms. I'm a serious motherfucker. I get it done and get the hell out, every single time I'm with a woman. Emotions are messy and I'm not about to clean up anyone's mess. Including my own.

That's all changed since I started spending time with Blair.

And fuck, I'm in too deep now.

Her legs shift beneath me and I can tell she's restless. Needy. I shift up until my face is in hers once more, taking her hands and stretching her arms above her head, holding her wrists together with one hand. I lift my body away from hers, my knees on either side of her hips, my gaze locked on her beautiful flushed face. "You want this?"

I thrust my hips nice and slow, dragging my covered erection across her wet center and she instinctively arches beneath me, rubbing her wet pussy all over the front of my sweats. "Yes," she whispers.

"Take it out then," I urge her, her eyes lighting up with excitement. "Show me what you can do with it."

Eagerly, she reaches around me and shoves at my sweats, taking them down along with my boxers, exposing my ass. My cock. She drags them farther until they stop about midthigh, one hand curling around the base of my shaft as she begins to stroke.

She handles me so expertly, I swear my eyes fucking cross, her touch feels so damn good. Squeezing me in all the right places, her grip is firm, sliding up and down my shaft in a perfect rhythm that brings me closer and closer to blowing in a scarily short amount of time.

Fuck that. I need to draw this out.

Reluctantly, I pull out of her grip, noting the pout on her face. I'm relieved and grateful when she helps me get rid of my sweats and boxers, until I'm just as naked as she is. When I resume my position, my cock probes at her pussy and she grabs hold of me once more, squeezing the base.

"You need to get a condom," she practically croons, her strokes putting me in a near trance.

"Got any nearby?" The words scrape against my raw throat and I glance over at the nightstand, praying she's a safety girl and has a couple stashed in the drawer.

"In my bathroom—"

I'm up and out the door, buck-ass naked and crossing the hall, flipping the light on in her bathroom. "Where?"

"The top drawer on the right," she calls.

I jerk the drawer open, rifling through the various products inside, relief smacking me square in the chest when I spot two condom packets. I grab them both, slam the drawer closed and quickly bail out of the bathroom, shutting and locking her bedroom door behind me before I rejoin her on the bed.

She's still lying there where I left her, lazily drifting her fingers back and forth across her tits, and I stop, watching her. Her gaze lifts to mine and she smiles, cupping her breasts like an offering.

One I cannot refuse.

27

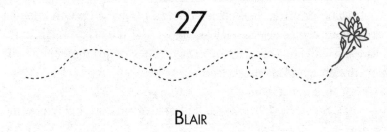

BLAIR

Cam drops the condoms on top of my nightstand and crawls onto the mattress, my gaze dropping to his erect cock, quietly marveling at its size. He is probably the biggest guy I've ever been with and Travis was no slouch. He just didn't know what the hell he was doing. We were so young, so inept.

And Randy? He was flat-out selfish in bed.

Not that I need to think about my exes during a moment like this, but it sort of can't be helped. The other two I've been with were random hookups. One over the summer when I was feeling lonely and ended up just feeling used.

Sex makes things so complicated most of the time. And it's never as great as I hoped. At least, until I started messing around with Cam.

Now it's all I can think about. Everything he does to me, everything he says, even when he just looks at me…sends me into this pre-orgasmic, blissful state. When he demanded I touch myself earlier, I knew I would. It had been hot, stroking myself while he watched, his gaze tracking my every movement. I felt powerful in that moment. Like I could do anything and he'd approve.

The feminist in me should rise up and boldly state that I don't need this man's approval, but it's so much more than that. Even when he's telling me what to do, I feel...powerful. Like a woman whose man is completely enthralled with her.

That's heady stuff, knowing Camden Fields, campus legend and quarterback of the football team, is in my bed. Currently on top of me, his championship-winning hands running up and down the outside of my thighs, making me shiver. I reach out for him, cupping his beautiful face between my hands, staring into his eyes. His touch slows, coming to a complete stop and resting on my hips, and I drift my thumb across his cheek, smiling at him.

"This is going to be so good," I whisper.

"I'll do my best," he says, full of sudden modesty, but I know the truth.

He will do whatever it takes to ensure I have my orgasm before he has his. He is the furthest thing from selfish, and I know, without a doubt, that it'll be better than good. Most likely earth-shattering, if I'm being real right now, not that I want to say that out loud to him.

No need to freak him out.

Cam dips his head, his mouth finding mine, delivering a sweet, tongue-filled kiss that is slow and delicious. He takes his time with me, his hands wandering, mapping my skin. I release his face and slide my hands down his back, running my fingers over his muscles, enjoying the way they flex beneath my fingertips. His body is absolute perfection. Strong and capable and all mine to touch and explore.

But our slow, savoring moment turns into hurried, frantic touching, and I'm suddenly too eager to feel him move inside me to want to linger much longer. Instead, I'm reaching for him, curling my fingers around his cock, bringing him where I want him, dragging just the head against my wet center. He nudges my clit and I moan, the sound swallowed by his greedy mouth, until he eventually breaks the kiss, slapping my hand away from him while he leans over and grabs one of those condom packets, tearing the wrapper open.

I rise up on my elbows to watch him roll the condom on, my lips parted as I take in his thick shaft. The vein that runs down the side of it. The flared head that was dribbling with pre-cum. I lift my gaze to find he's already watching me, his fingers still wrapped around the base of his shaft. He gives himself a stroke and something tugs deep at my core, wishing I would've asked him to touch himself in front of me.

Next time, I think as he repositions himself, coming down over me, his face in mine. He kisses me and I keep my eyes open, running my hand over the side of his head, my fingers sinking into his soft hair. Everything about this man is beautiful.

I'm starting to realize his heart is beautiful too.

His cock probes, seeking entry, and I lift my hips, eager for the same. He guides himself inside my body, filling me with just the tip at first, pausing and hanging his head. Breathing deep. Like he needs to regain some semblance of control.

Like the greedy girl I am, I tilt my hips, sending him deeper, and he groans. His eyes are tightly closed and there's a vein throbbing in his forehead. The man looks like he's going to lose it at any moment.

"You feel so fucking good, B," he whispers, his voice harsh.

"You're barely inside me," I protest, wiggling beneath him.

He clamps his hand on my hip, keeping me in place. "Stop moving. You're going to make me come too fast."

I make him feel like he's going to lose control and that knowledge is powerful too. I savor the sensation of his fingers pressing into my skin, pinning me in place, and I wait breathlessly for him to start moving again.

With a deep, even breath, he pushes his way inside me, inch by delicious inch, until I'm full to the very hilt. We go still the moment we're fully connected, his breathing matching mine. I'm staring at his face, smiling when he opens his eyes, his arm curved around the top of my head, his fingers in my hair. We don't say a word to each other, but he dips his head, his mouth finding mine in another one of those slow, sweet kisses. Communicating to me without words that he cares.

That this moment means something.

Oh God.

He starts to move, slowly at first, that delicious drag of his cock pulling almost all of the way out of my body before he pushes back in, making me moan with his every thrust. I run my hands down his sides, curving them around the hard muscles of his ass, pushing there. Wanting him as deep as I can get him.

Soon enough, we lose all patience, our bodies moving in tandem, our pace increasing. Until we're both straining, his hand slipping between us, his fingers toying with my clit, sending shivers up and down my spine. Our skin is sweaty, slapping against each other, and he presses his forehead against mine, swallowing hard before he begins to thrust with earnest. It's a steady, unrelenting pace that sends me closer and closer to the edge, my orgasm hovering just on the horizon…

And then I'm reaching for it, just…right…there…

The shivers roll over me in waves, my mind going blank, my body one hundred percent focused on the pleasure sweeping through me and nothing else. The waves take me under and I cling to him, shaking, crying out when he thrusts extra deep, my name on his lips as he goes still, just before his own orgasm takes over.

I hold him close, soothing him as he shudders and shakes above me, my hands running up and down his back. I've never felt this connected to another human being ever, and when he kisses me, I can tell.

He feels it too. The connection.

It's undeniable.

• • •

I wake up to soft lips on my forehead and a whispered goodbye, my eyes popping open, vision needing to readjust in the darkness to find Cam leaning over me, fully dressed.

Pushing my hair away from my face, I ask him, "Where are you going?"

"I have a game today." His smile is rueful. "Gotta go, B. Get some real sleep for at least a couple of hours."

"No. Stay with me." I sit up, reaching for him, and he comes to me, sweeping me into a hug, my bare torso pressing against his T-shirt. He's warm and firm and I wish he was still naked with me, but I understand. He needs rest.

And we haven't been doing any real resting since he came over last night.

"Can't." He leans in and gives me a kiss. "But come to the game later, okay? We can meet up after."

"We can?" I sound hopeful. Way too hopeful, really. Like some sort of dumb fangirl or worse...a groupie.

"Definitely. Come to Logan's. We'll be there after the game. Hopefully celebrating." He smiles, kisses me one more time and then he's gone.

I fall back asleep the moment he's gone, not waking up until I hear a knock on my door before one of my roommates barges into my room. I crack open one eye to see it's Rita, standing by my bed with her hands on her hips, studying me.

"Are you naked, Blair?"

I slide farther under the covers, praying nothing was on display while I was sleeping. Rita doesn't need to see my bare ass. "Go away."

"Did you have a guy over last night? Oh my God, you DID. Cheyenne!" Rita is screaming, so I tuck my comforter around my head to block the sound. "Get in here! We need to question Blair."

"Please don't question me," I croak from beneath the covers, hoping they'll leave me alone.

But no such luck. Within seconds, Cheyenne is in my bedroom too, and I peek over my covers to see her completely dressed and ready for her day, munching on an everything bagel slathered with cream cheese.

"Blair." Rita tries to tug on my comforter, but my grip is too firm. "Talk to us."

"There's nothing to tell," I say from beneath the mound of covers.

"There so is. You're naked under there. And I swear I could smell men's cologne lingering in the air when I first woke up. You had a fine ass man in this house and you didn't bother to tell us!" Rita sounds pissed. Excited but mad.

Yanking the covers down so only my head is visible, I contemplate my roommates, who are both watching me with curiosity lighting their eyes. They want all the scoop and normally I would spill every damn detail, but I don't know...

Cam might not want me to. He hasn't said anything about keeping us a complete secret, and he knows that would trigger me, but I don't feel right blasting our—whatever it is we're calling it—to my roommates. Not yet at least.

Though I suppose they do have some right to know who was in their apartment last night.

"Rita, leave her alone. Maybe she's trying to keep it quiet for now. Doesn't want to jinx anything." The knowing look on Cheyenne's face tells me she has her suspicions and they're probably correct.

"Jinx what? The fact that she's having sex with some random?" Rita yells.

"He's not random," I say. "I *know* him."

"How well?" Cheyenne asks.

"If it's one of your brother's teammates, I'm going to explode with jealousy," Rita says.

"Boom." My voice is quiet and I can't help but start giggling.

Rita frowns. Cheyenne eventually gets it and starts to laugh too, which only adds to Rita's confusion.

"Looks like you just exploded, Rita," Cheyenne says.

"Oh shit!" Rita throws her arms up in the air. "You have to tell us, Blair. It's not fair, keeping such a juicy secret to yourself."

"It's not that juicy," I start to protest, but they're not having it.

"Nope. No way. You're spilling your guts!" Rita jumps on my bed, reaching out so she can tickle me. I dodge her hands, laughing harder, and when she touches my bare skin, I let out a scream.

"You do not want to put your hands on me," I warn her. "I'm naked!"

"Oh, you whore." She flops backward onto my mattress, her tone light. I know she doesn't mean anything by calling me that. Her head is at the foot of the bed and her feet are practically in my face and I scoot away from them, sighing when Cheyenne plops onto the edge of my mattress too.

Looks like they're going nowhere soon. I'm going to have to explain myself. Somewhat.

"Just give us a couple of details and we'll leave you alone," Rita says.

I sit up, propped against the pillows, my comforter wrapped all around me. Cam's hoodie is still lying on the floor nearby in a heap and I wish I could pull it on. "He came over last night. We've been sort of seeing each other when we can lately."

"Define lately," Rita says.

"The last couple of weeks."

"And what's his name?"

I press my lips together. It feels so...final, if I say his name out loud. There's no turning back once it's out there. My roommates will know, and they might make a scene the next time they run into him, which I absolutely do not want. Us being together—if that's even the right word—and becoming public knowledge is overwhelming. This is just so weird and awkward and truly unchartered territory.

And I haven't even thought about what we will do once Knox finds out. He might lose it. He might be really pissed, and what happens then? Are we done? Will Cam back away out of respect for my brother? What about me and my feelings?

It's too much to even think about.

"I'm not ready to reveal that information yet," I say, keeping my voice even. "I'll tell you when he's cool with it."

"Why wouldn't he be cool with it?" Rita sounds suspicious, and I don't blame her.

"I just don't want to put him on blast, without consulting him first. I'm trying to be considerate of his feelings," I explain.

Rita's mouth opens, ready to protest when Cheyenne cuts her off.

"Leave her alone, Rita. She'll tell us when she's ready."

With a sigh, Rita leaps to her feet, studying the two of us, though her gaze comes back to me, extra shrewd. "You better come clean as soon as possible, Blair. I'm dying over here. I need to take a shower."

With that, she strides out of my room and holes up in her bathroom, the crank of the shower turning on obvious less than a minute later. Cheyenne is still sitting on the edge of my bed and she finally stands, a knowing smile on her face.

"If I asked if his initials were CF, would I be correct?" she asks.

I shrug, trying to play it off, but I feel the way my cheeks heat. I'm sure they're bright pink.

"That's what I thought." She taps her index finger against her lips. "Your secret is safe with me."

I watch her leave, softly closing the door behind her, and I sink under the covers, pulling them over my head.

I hope I can trust her to keep my secret. If this gets out now?

There might be hell to pay. And I'm not referring to my brother either.

I'm talking about Cam.

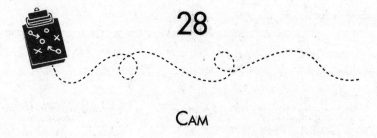

28

CAM

'm not playing well.

The opposing team has been hard to beat every damn season since I started here and today's game is no exception. The weather is for shit too. Gloomy with a cold wind that feels as if it's taking every ball I'm throwing and whipping it in a different direction. I've thrown two interceptions in the first half, which isn't like me. We're still up by a touchdown at halftime, but I don't feel good about anything I've done out on that field today.

Not a single thing.

"You all right?" Knox asks me as we enter the locker room.

I send him a look, not wanting to discuss my problems in front of the entire damn team. They're all already in the locker room, watching us—me—with expectancy in their gazes. Like they want an explanation and hope I'm going to come out fighting in the second half.

Shit, I hope I can manage it.

"Fields? A word." Coach Mattson hooks his finger at me,

indicating he wants me to come into his office and talk privately.

Great.

I follow him inside, shutting the door behind me, bracing myself for a barrage of questions and not so gentle slams on my lack of skill this afternoon, but he says nothing like that.

"I'm going to put Ace out there. He's going to start the third quarter."

My jaw feels like it's going to hit the floor and I snap it shut, taking a deep breath. "Seriously?"

"Yeah. You're slipping today. I don't know what it is and you don't have to explain anything, but you're not on top of your shit and it's...worrisome, son."

I'll say.

"Fine. Start him." I stand up straighter, ready to be done with this conversation. "Are we finished?"

"If he does shitty, we're pulling him, so don't get too comfortable on the bench." Mattson opens his office door, ready to tear into everyone's asses. "And yeah, we're done."

I follow him out of the office, hating the excitement that lights up Ace's eyes when Coach tells him he's starting the second half. Ace gives me a quick glance after that announcement was made, checking on me. My reaction.

I give him a nod, appreciating that little gesture of respect. The kid looks up to me and I can't be a shit to him, just because Coach is giving him a chance. We have to play all our options, and right now, I'm a bad one.

Fuck, that hurts to admit.

I mostly ignore the inspiring speech Coach and the rest of his staff give us, zoning out. I'm tired, my mind filled with images of Blair. A naked, sweet Blair lying in bed, sleeping peacefully. I should've just left her there without a sound, sneaking out of her room and her apartment like a thief. Like the casual hookup I should be to her. To myself.

But I didn't. I had to touch her. Kiss her forehead and whisper her name. Just to witness her slowly wake up, her eyes filling with a mixture of joy and confusion at finding me standing above her, at the one sweet word she murmured to me.

Stay.

Fuck, I wanted to so badly. When I first woke up, I was aware of her warm body wrapped all around me. That delicious floral scent of hers tickling my senses. She smells good. She feels good. She is inherently good. And I don't deserve it.

I don't deserve her.

"Don't let this fuck with you," Derek says after Coach's halftime speech. He slaps the back of my head lightly, a show of affection for him. "You're having an off-moment. It happens to all of us."

The problem is…it never happens to me. All I can think is it has something to do with Blair.

She's a distraction, and I can't focus when I'm with her. Spending all my time with her is dangerous for my future. What if I'm playing so shitty, I get injured? My season is over, just like that. My possible NFL career, done for.

Can't risk it.

I'm in a shit mood when we head back out onto the field, the only thing making me happy are the boos everyone shouts when they mention that Ace is playing quarterback and not me. At least I'm loved by the fans.

Then I immediately feel like shit for not supporting Ace. When he approaches where I'm sitting on the bench, all suited up with his helmet on, looking nervous, I almost apologize to him.

"I'm fucking scared, boss, but I've got you," he tells me, his tone earnest. As if he means every word he says. "I won't let you down."

I say nothing, just stare at him in shock and wonder, until a whistle blows. Ace starts to leave and before he gets too far, I call his name, causing him to look back.

I give him the thumbs-up signal with both hands and he grins, putting his hands around his mouth and hollering, "Got you, number one QB!"

Out on that field, Ace plays with his heart, putting his all into it, his decision-making fast, his reflexes quick. He throws a forty-yard pass that Knox catches with ease, running into the end zone and making a touchdown like they were born to play with each other.

I leap to my feet along with the rest of my teammates, who are sitting with me on the bench. And I don't sit down for the rest of the quarter, watching as Ace goes back out there and scores another fucking touchdown, while our defense keeps the opposing team from scoring shit. All they get is another three points on the scoreboard, thanks to a field goal, and that's it.

End of the third quarter, with our offense out on the field, Coach approaches me, his voice gruff when he asks, "You want another shot during the fourth quarter?"

"Yeah," I tell him with a curt nod.

"Get ready."

Knox approaches me at the top of the fourth, while our defense is out there, holding back the other team. "You all right?"

I shrug. "Shitty day."

"We all have them."

"I don't." When he sends me a look, I shrug. "Not really."

"Can't keep up the perfect façade forever, bro. You're human like the rest of us."

That is really fucking hard to admit.

"Coach said you're playing," Ace says, appearing right by my side. I turn to look at him. "You'll get it."

"Get what?" I ask him.

"The win."

"I think that's all thanks to you."

"Whatever. We're just taking care of each other. Doing it for the team. Right?"

His words linger when I'm out on the field, reminding me that sometimes I get a little too caught up in my bullshit when I should be focusing on the big picture.

The team. All of us as a cohesive unit versus just me and my position. My future.

That's all coming, but none of it will work if we don't work on it together.

I refocus my energy on the field and let it all happen naturally. Pushing everything out of my brain, even Blair—especially Blair—and I'm back. In charge and living large, as Derek shouts at me after I throw the ball, and Knox, yet again, runs it into the end zone.

Once the game is over and we've won, I jog over to Knox and give him a hug, slapping the side of his helmet while grinning at him.

"It's your game today, motherfucker. You're a superstar," I tell him.

He grins back. "You weren't so bad yourself once you came out of your fog."

My smile slips. My fog can only be blamed on his sister.

Which really fucking sucks.

• • •

A bunch of us from the team finally arrive at Logan's, much later after the game, and we're greeted like kings. Plenty of shouting, raised mugs in the air as if they're toasting us. I'm surrounded by my teammates, purposely placing myself in the center, so I don't have to deal with anyone's questions about the game.

I avoided the media after it was finished, hiding away in the locker room, showering way longer than necessary. Not that anyone actually wanted to talk to me. They were too busy chatting up Knox, who deserved the attention, or fawning over Ace, who also deserved the recognition.

I felt easily forgotten, which is stupid because I wanted to avoid the media. The reporters and the local news stations. That one chick from ESPN, who is a goddamn stalker sometimes, following us all over the field after a game when we're usually trying to avoid her.

Now they want nothing to do with me and I'm butthurt. It's stupid. I'm being ridiculous, but sometimes, it feels good to sulk.

Blair sent me a text that I didn't see until I was in the locker room, saying she'd be at Logan's later, and like a shithead, I ignored it. Didn't bother to reply, which also has me feeling miserable. I hate having a rough game, and it's been a while since it's happened. It would be easy to blame her for everything. Hell, when I was in the thick of it, I *did* blame her. Was coming up with twenty different ways to let her down easy, not a single one of them sounding possible.

It's hard to admit I'm the one who's at fault sometimes. I can't keep blaming my mistakes and fuck-ups on other people. Having Blair in my life is a good thing.

I need to remember that.

Hopefully, she'll show up here and I'll get a chance to apologize. And hopefully her brother won't be anywhere around when I do make that apology. I don't need him ruining this. I already feel bad enough.

We sit in our usual spot in the back of the bar, taking over three of the booths that line the back wall. Knox ditches us almost immediately, and I watch as he finds Joanna, giving her a kiss in front of God and everybody, not giving a damn who sees them. She smiles up at him, slinging her arms around his neck, looking proud.

Envy curls through my blood, and I mentally tell myself to get over it. Our situations are different. I don't even know if Blair is feeling anything toward me right now. Probably not pride, not after the shitty way I just played that game.

It doesn't matter if I threw a touchdown during that last quarter. I'm still reveling in my shitty gameplay, which is normal for me. It'll take about four beers before I'm pulled out of my bad mood.

I'm on beer number one so I've got a long way to go.

A group of girls approach our table at one point, and while we're making small talk, one of them comes right up to me.

"Great game today, Cam," she says, her tone overly familiar. As if she knows me.

She wishes.

"Thanks." I take a swig of beer, wishing she would leave. She's cute enough, but her hair is the wrong color and her face is just…the wrong face. I don't want to talk to this woman.

I want Blair.

"Feeling down?" she asks, her frown more like a pout. Bet she thinks that's sexy.

"Not particularly." I grab my phone and bring up my text thread with Blair, shooting her a quick one.

Me: *You at Logan's?*

She doesn't respond right away and I lift my head to find the girl who was trying to chat me up is now talking to someone else. Good.

I'm almost finished with my second beer when my phone finally buzzes.

Bumblebee: *Just got here.*

Bumblebee: *I'm pissed at you though.*

I smile. I love her honesty. It's like a Maguire trait.

Me: *I should be put on time out.*

Bumblebee: *Where are you?*

Me: *The usual spot.*

I set my phone on the table and wait, ignoring the conversations going on around me, focusing on the front of the bar, searching for that familiar blonde head I like so damn much. I drain the last of my beer, grateful when one of my teammates swipes the mug from me and refills it from the fresh pitcher that was just delivered to our table. I lift my mug at him in a cheers gesture and take another sip, right as Blair appears.

Swear to God, a beam of light follows her wherever she walks, like she's an angel sent from heaven. I watch her make her way toward our table, taking in her outfit. She's got on black leggings that mold to her skin, reminding me just how long they are. And she's wearing my T-shirt I gave her. It's way too big and she's got it knotted on the right side, resting just at her hip with a zip-up gray hoodie thrown over it. Her hair is down and her lips are slicked in some glossy stuff that I want to see all over my dick later, and fuck, I am so relieved to see her I feel like I could collapse.

Thank Christ I'm sitting down or I'd probably make a damn fool of myself.

She stops at the front of our table, a beautiful smile on her equally beautiful face, her gaze scanning everyone I'm seated with before those pretty eyes settle on me. "Hey, guys. Great game today."

They all greet her with friendly hellos, respectful because she's Maguire's sister, and I tip my head toward her, scooting over a bit and patting the now-empty spot right beside me.

With no hesitation she settles right in, her warm, soft body nestled close to mine and I lean in, inhaling as subtly as possible, breathing her delicious scent.

"Camden," she murmurs.

I lift my glass toward her. "Bumblebee."

Her eyes are sparkling, I swear to God, though she's trying to look stern. And failing—miserably. "Are you drunk?"

"On my way there."

Her façade cracks a little, her eyes now shining with worry. "Oh, Cam. You had a rough go of it today."

"Bad," I agree with a nod, taking a giant swallow. I just want to forget tonight. Forget my troubles and the stress and the worry. Just focus on getting shitfaced and spending the night with this pretty girl sitting next to me. Will she let me lose myself in her? Just for a little bit?

Fuck, I hope so.

"You played great in the last quarter," she says, trying to turn a negative into a positive.

"Thanks." My voice is clipped and I feel like a dick, but there's still sympathy in her eyes, so I didn't totally fuck it up.

Yet.

"What do you need from me?" she whispers, her hand settling on my thigh, warm and reassuring.

"Nothing." I meet her gaze, hoping she sees how serious I am. "Just having you here sitting next to me so I can look at you is enough."

Her smile turns tremulous and she squeezes my thigh, leaning in slightly so she can murmur, "I wish we were alone."

"Me too." I pause. "I'd kiss you if we were."

Her cheeks turn pink. "How long do you have to stay?"

"I can leave whenever the hell I want." I announce this loudly, causing a few heads to turn in my direction. "You ready to go?"

An awkward laugh escapes her, and when no one is paying attention to us, she rests her finger against her pursed lips. Damn if that doesn't make me want to lean in and kiss that pretty mouth of hers, right here in front of everyone. Fuck it.

I sway toward her, my head swimming from the beer, and she presses a hand against my shoulder, keeping me from getting any closer. I know exactly what she's doing and she's only respecting my wishes, but that hurts too.

"Let's go," I practically growl in her ear.

She shakes her head, refusing to look at me, her nails digging into my thigh. Good thing I'm wearing jeans or she might draw blood. "You're trying to cause a scene, Cam, and that's not like you. Let's get you to calm down first and then I'll go. A few minutes after I leave, you can leave too and come back to my place." Her head angles toward mine. "Okay?"

Leaning back in my seat, I nod, settling my hand over hers and giving it a squeeze. I don't mean to be a dick. I'm just frustrated with myself and a little drunk.

Doesn't help that I consume more beer, despite the disapproving looks Blair sends in my direction every time I take another swig. I choose to ignore her, polishing off my fourth beer and finally forgetting all of my troubles regarding the game.

Now I'm just flat-out drunk. And more than a little sloppy.

"Should we get an Uber?" I whisper to Blair, needing her to talk to me. She's too busy laughing over something Derek says, and I tell myself not to act like a dick. He's got a girl with giant tits sitting on his lap, who's totally into him. He doesn't give a damn about Blair.

Yet, I'm jealous. I see green on the edges of my vision and I feel like slinging my arm around Bair's shoulders and hauling her into me, proclaiming to everyone that she's mine.

She belongs to me.

But my girl barely glances in my direction, whispering out of the side of her mouth, "I drove myself here."

"Are you sober?" I burp. Loudly.

Blair winces. "Someone needs to be."

"I thought you were drinking?"

"The same someone also has to drag your drunk ass out of here," she drawls.

Derek perks up and I realize that he heard her. "You brave enough to give Fields a ride home, Blair?"

Blair blinks at Derek, her body going stiff. Like she's embarrassed we just got caught talking about it. "Um, yeah. My brother asked me to."

"She's such a good sister, don't you think?" I ask Derek, leaning over Blair and giving into my urges, sliding my arm around her shoulders and giving her a squeeze. She tenses beneath my touch, but I don't give a damn. "The perfect little sister to Maguire."

She says nothing, her body language screaming *I'm extremely uncomfortable*, but I choose to ignore her vibe.

"Blair's pretty great," Derek says, and my heart turns black at his words.

"What do you know about her?" I'm growling. Feeling territorial. Glaring at Derek like I want to tear him apart with my bare hands.

"Whoa, calm down there, buddy. I've got someone to distract me already. Right, Sheena?" He looks at the girl in his lap with the giant tits.

"It's Sheila," she corrects him, wrapping her arms around his neck and practically shoving his face in her cleavage. "And yes, baby. I'm here to distract you all night long."

They laugh and kiss, not trying to hide their interest in each other, and I'm jealous yet again. Everything makes me jealous tonight.

"You're being a jerk," Blair tells me, shrugging my arm off her shoulders and shoving my hand off her thigh. Like she doesn't want me touching her. "You need to calm down before people start getting suspicious."

"Suspicious of what?" I play dumb on purpose and she scowls at me, slowly shaking her head.

"You're acting like a child." Before I can stop her, she rises to her feet, staring down at me with disappointment written all over her face. "Get your shit together, Fields."

She leaves, and I watch her retreating form, feeling like an absolute dickhead.

"Hey, baby, go get me a tequila shot."

Sheila pops up off Derek's lap, snatching the twenty-dollar bill from his fingers. "Sure thing, sexy."

We both watch her head for the bar, Derek turning to me the moment she's out of earshot.

"What's the deal with you and Maguire's sister?"

"Nothing," I say too quickly.

Derek snorts. "Fuckin' liar. You got a thing for her?"

"No."

"She got a thing for you?"

"Possibly."

"You kiss her yet?"

I remain quiet.

"Fuck her?"

The look on my face must say it all. Derek whistles low, slowly shaking his head. "You're in serious trouble, my dude."

"I don't need your input if you're just going to sit here and make me feel like shit."

"Just stating facts, bro. You're gonna get in over your head. Actually, I think you're already there. That girl is sweet. And a Maguire. She's not someone you just casually mess around with." Another low whistle. "Her daddy is a fucking professional, man! A legend! And her brother is your best friend."

"Thanks for telling me what I already know." I reach for my beer, realizing too late that it's empty, as only drops hit my tongue when I try and drink from it. I set it on the table with a loud thunk. "There is nothing going on between Blair and me."

Derek's brows shoot up, the doubt written all over his face. "Keep telling yourself that."

Blair doesn't come back to the table. Sheila reappears carrying two tequila shots, and Derek nestles his between her tits, grabbing it with his lips and tilting his head back to swallow it while she laughs and laughs. I just scowl at them the entire time, annoyed with their antics. Even more annoyed with their freedom to do whatever the hell they want with no judgment, except from me.

But right now, I don't count because I'm just a jealous fuck who wishes he could be as free as they are. But I can't.

Worse? There's no one to blame. I could say it's Knox's fault but that would be a lie.

It's my fault too.

After about thirty minutes of me sitting there talking to no one and not drinking anything but water, I finally get up from the table to go use the bathroom. I make my way through the thick crowd, nodding and smiling at everyone who greets me as I pass by, noting that most of them are women. Women whose gazes are full of interest. Who give me a full body scan with their eyes, like they're thoroughly checking me out.

In the past, I would've chosen the cutest one and singled her out. Made conversation with her. Brought her back to the table, much like Derek did with his chosen one for the night. I would've flattered her and flirted with her and touched her here and there. On the arm. Her leg. Maybe even her hair. She would be totally into me and I'd be into her and I'd bring her out to my car and let her do whatever she wanted to me. Usually a blow job.

Most of the time, I wouldn't give them anything in return because I'm selfish like that. They never complained. But they'd always leave with the hope that I would reach out again. They'd give me their phone number and practically beg me to hit them up sometime.

I never did. Most of the time, I'd delete their number and forget all about them. I was a dick.

I still am.

But I'm not tempted to do any of that tonight. I hate how they check me out. I hate the way they make a simple word like, "hey," sound suggestive. As if they look at me and think of only one thing. It makes me feel used.

And I'm the user in this situation. I'm aware of what I am.

Damn it, Blair Maguire has really fucked with my head.

After I handle my business, I'm walking out of the bathroom when I spot Blair standing at the bar, talking with some random guy. I go completely still, my focus only on Blair. The faint smile on her face, her friendly expression. She's completely open to what this guy is saying to her and I hate that.

I should walk away. Let her go. Find my own ride home and deal with the consequences later.

My gaze shifts to the guy who's talking to her and I realize it's not just some rando.

It's fucking Ace.

29

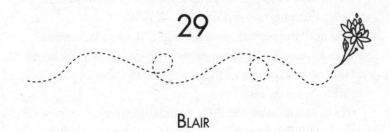

Blair

It's downright refreshing, getting away from the brooding, angry Cam for a bit. He's drunk. Miserable. Grumpy. Also a little...

Jealous?

Yes, definitely jealous. Which is surprisingly thrilling, I can't lie.

But his mood is spreading like a dark cloud over me and I don't want to end up mad too. Especially at him. Though I was before I arrived at Logan's. I didn't like how he just ignored me after the game, though I also knew that he was hiding after playing so poorly. Licking his wounds.

Cam is moodier than usual, thanks to how much alcohol he's consumed tonight.

Not sure I approve of the drunk version of Cam either, but he's not a big drinker overall, which is a good thing from what I can tell.

This is why I gave myself—and him—some space. I chatted up my brother and Joanna for a little bit, but I could tell they wanted to be alone so I left them. Found my roommates and ignored Cheyenne's pointed remarks. Decided to grab myself a soda so I looked like I was drinking something and ended up running into Ace.

I like him. He's sweet, friendly and so excited about everything. He's also smashed but friendly about it. Like right now, explaining to me exactly what happened on the field when he threw his first touchdown.

"Swear to God, the ball pretty much slipped out of my fingers a little early and I thought I fucked it all up. The terror that ran through me." Ace shakes his head, his hair flopping with the movement. "If I threw an interception I was done for."

"You would've been dead in the water," I agree with a nod.

He sends me a look, his head tilted as he contemplates me. "I forget that you come from a long line of football players."

"I do."

"That's so...unbelievable." He sounds awestruck.

"It's just life." I shrug. "I don't know anything different."

"That's wild to think about. You just...grew up going to NFL games. Do you go to any now?"

"I've been to a couple. Mostly just to watch my cousin. It's kind of weird when you think about all of the professionals I'm linked to now."

"Guess it just runs in the family."

"More like some of my family end up falling in love with football players." I frown the moment the words leave my lips. Do I know Cam well enough to think I'm actually in love with him? I like him. I'm attracted to him.

I care about him. A lot. My heart ached for him during the game. I know he was frustrated with himself. He wasn't playing well, and I know that had to have been hard on him. All I wanted to do was comfort him, but from the way he's currently acting, he's making it difficult.

"What the fuck are you doing?"

Oh God. Speaking of Cam...

Both Ace and I turn our heads at the same time to find Cam standing in front of us, his hands clutched into fists at his sides,

his expression about the meanest I've ever seen him look. He is...
furious.

But why?

"Who are you talking to, buddy?" Ace is trying to keep it friendly
and I'm grateful for it.

"You." Cam turns to stare at me. "And her."

"We're just talking," I start, reaching for Cam, but he jerks his
arm away from me, taking a step backward.

"First you come for my position and now you're coming for her?
This is some bullshit." I shift in between Cam and Ace, pressing my
hands against Cam's chest to keep him from lunging toward Ace.
"Stay away from her."

"We're just friends, QB. Don't worry." Ace throws his hands up
in the air, confusion written all over his face. "I'm not interested in
Maguire's sister. That's way too risky."

My heart sinks at Ace's words. At the way they sink into Cam's
brain, as if he's having that same realization. That yes, being with me
would be too risky.

Damn it.

I practically drag Cam from the bar and toward the front door.
He tries to tug out of my grip, though weakly. "Where are you taking
me?"

"We need to leave." I send him a look. "You need to sober up. Go
to bed. Whatever."

He lets me lead him out of the bar, plenty of people cheering
him on when he walks through the door. He raises one fist in victory,
earning more cheers, and I sort of want to bop him upside the head.

Luckily enough, I was able to find a parking spot relatively close
to the entrance, so I hit the unlock button on my key fob, guiding
Cam toward the passenger side door.

"You driving me home?" he asks, slinging an arm around my
shoulders and leaning heavily into me.

I nearly sag under his hold. God, he's heavy. "I told you I would."

"Right. To help Knox out." He's sneering. It's not a good look on him. "Such a good sister."

"I'm not doing this for Knox." I open the door and shove him inside, pleased when he falls into the seat with a startled expression on his face. Like he can't believe I just pushed him around. "I'm doing this for you."

I slam the door before he can say anything and take my time walking around the car, inhaling deeply with every step. I get a tiny thrill out of him acting so territorial over me, but it's also irritating. He's just drunk. Sloppy. Emotional. But it's also...

Kind of awful.

Finally, I'm in the car and starting the engine, not saying a word. He remains quiet as well, staring out the passenger side window once I start to drive. We don't speak at all, the tension growing between us so thick that by the time I pull into the parking lot of his apartment, I'm ready to scream.

"I'm sorry," he murmurs after I put my car into park.

I stare at the back of his head because he's still looking out the window. As if he can't face me. "For what?"

"For all of it. The whole night." He turns to look at me and I see the remorse written all over his handsome face. "It was a shit day and I turned it into a shit night and...I'm sorry."

I get this sense that Camden Fields doesn't apologize for much. Not because he doesn't want to or has a hard time saying the words, but because he's the type of guy who just does things and doesn't have to answer to anyone. He keeps his circle extremely tight. And somehow...

I wormed my way in. Just like I hoped.

"I drank too much and I rarely do that. Not anymore." He inhales deeply, averting his gaze, so he can stare out the windshield this time around. "I was pissed when I saw you with Ace."

"I don't like Ace like that."

"I was mad at Knox too."

"Why?"

"Because he can do whatever he wants with Joanna and doesn't have to worry about someone else finding out and losing their shit over it." He sounds miserable and my heart aches for him.

For me too.

When I say nothing—because what can I say to that?—Cam continues talking.

"Derek can be with whomever he wants. Everyone can. And I can't." He bangs the back of his head against his seat, closing his eyes. "I don't like how I feel when I drink."

"And how do you feel?"

"Like I've lost control. Like I'm marinating in my feelings and it's freaking me out." He turns his head, cracking his eyes open to look at me. "I don't deserve you."

"Cam—"

"I don't. I've told you this before and I'm realizing it right now. All over again. Especially with everything that's happened. You're like...fucking perfect for me and I'm not for you. I'm far from it. All I'll do is break your heart. You know what scares me?"

"What scares you?" I ask gently, trying to keep up with him changing the subject.

"That I'll turn into the same piece of shit my dad is. He's a drunk. An alcoholic who cares about no one else but himself. That's going to be me." He jerks his thumb at his chest, tapping it right in the center. "I'm afraid I'm going to turn into him and it fucking sucks."

"You won't." I give in and reach out to thread my fingers in his hair at his temple, wanting to soothe him. He doesn't react. He doesn't even flinch. "You're not like him. You're kind and you're good. You're a great leader. Your team adores you."

"Not today." He presses his head against the seat and I feel like I'm witnessing the real Camden. The man who feels the weight of so much responsibility on his shoulders, and who struggles with it. Struggles with himself. He's not as cocky as my brother is, not really. It's a quiet confidence that radiates from Cam, but that's not happening today.

Today he's feeling less than, and that hurts my heart.

"Hey." He turns at my whisper, his brows drawing together. "You never gave me that massage."

Realization dawns and he shakes his head. "Are you trying to collect now?"

"No." I shake my head. "But I'd like to give you one."

"You would?"

I nod as I glance around the parking lot, looking for my brother's truck. "You think Knox is here?"

"No. He's still with Joanna."

"Then sneak me into your bedroom and I'll rub your shoulders," I offer.

He stares at me for a long moment, his gaze roaming over my face. "Why are you so good to me?"

"Because someone needs to be. You beat yourself up far too much." I smile at him.

He smiles in return.

And in that moment, I know that everything is going to be all right.

• • •

We're in his bedroom less than five minutes later, Cam shutting and locking the door behind him, while I go into the connected bathroom. I stare at myself in the mirror while I wash my hands, drying them quickly, once I turn off the water, then run my fingers through my hair.

I'm not dressed to impress. Not really. He didn't even notice that I'm wearing his shirt, but that's okay. It was my secret gesture to show that I was rooting for him. Not like I can wear his jersey or paint his number on my face. That would bring up too many questions I don't want to answer.

But I wanted to show support in any way I could and this was my only way.

I go through his cabinets, feeling like a creeper when I'm just looking for lotion. I find a travel-sized bottle of Vaseline Intensive Care and don't want to know what he uses it for, but I'm using it to rub his back. I'm sure he's got some tense knots in his shoulders and a good rubdown will help him. Relax him.

Maybe even put him to sleep.

I've let go of all thoughts of having sex with him tonight. I don't think he's in the mood. And he's still a little drunk, though he's sobered up somewhat. Not enough to make much sense, the poor, rambling man.

Tucking my hair behind my ears, I grab the lotion and exit the bathroom to find Cam sprawled out across his bed on his back, covering nearly the entire space. He has no shirt on. The jeans are gone too. He's just in his boxer briefs—they're red—and his arms are curved up, over his head, his face turned to the side, so all I can see is his profile. His eyes are closed and his feet are dangling over the edge of the mattress and lord help me, this man is so fine.

Even when he's hurting.

Only when I press my knee onto the mattress does he open his eyes, watching me as I climb onto the bed. "Roll over," I tell him, surprised when he does what I say without arguing.

"What are you doing?" His deep voice is muffled against the comforter and I smile at him.

"I'm going to give you that massage."

He turns his head, pressing his face into the mattress. "Now I'll owe you two."

"And I'll collect." I crawl over him until I'm straddling his back, my butt resting on his. I pop open the cap on the lotion and pour some into my palm, rubbing my hands together before I apply them to his back. The moment I start digging my fingers in, he's groaning.

"What are you using?"

"I found some lotion in your bathroom." I rub and knead his tense muscles, working on one particular spot at the base of his neck. "You're tense."

"No shit." He hesitates. "I use that lotion to jerk off sometimes."

That was my exact thought when I found it. "No shit?"

He chuckles and the sound is warm. Hopeful. The first laugh I've heard out of him all night. "Yeah. Sometimes I even jerk off to thoughts of you."

My entire body flushes hot and I drift my hands down his back, along his spine, my touch light. "Dirty thoughts?"

"You don't even want to know."

I press my elbows into his flesh, earning a grunt. "Actually, I do."

Cam remains quiet as I continue massaging him. He's so big and my hands really aren't, so I have to put my all into it. Pounding on him with my fists. Working those knots out with my elbows. I'm getting tired because he's nothing but a solid wall of flesh, but I feel like he needs this. Someone giving him something and not expecting anything in return.

"Sometimes I fantasize about you in the shower with me, taking it further than last time. Remember what happened?"

His deep voice vibrates against me and I go still, wanting to hear more.

"Or I think about you on your knees and I'm standing in front of you, fucking your pretty mouth, like I did that one time." He exhales when I squeeze his side, right above his hip. "You have a pretty mouth, B."

"Um...thanks?" His words are turning me on and I didn't plan on that. Doesn't help that I'm sitting on top of him, straddling his big body. Rubbing all of those glorious muscles.

"You make me want things I shouldn't," he admits, his voice low.

I pause, my hands braced on his back, my heart beating a little faster. "Like what?"

"Like you. Like a relationship. With you." Another groan leaves him and this one has nothing to do with his aching muscles. "I should've never said that."

Hope is a flickering flame in my heart and I tell it to knock it off. "I'd make a great girlfriend, you know."

He laughs. "I know."

"I'd be supportive of your football career. More than that, I understand it. I have lots of experience."

"No one else would understand it like you do." His voice is solemn and I know he means it.

"And I'm a decent cook."

"A great one," he corrects. "Wish you'd stop by and make us more dinners."

"Noted. Only if I get massages as payment."

"I'll pay you in sexual favors," he teases, and I smile.

"I'm sort of decent with the sex thing." My words are hesitant. I don't think I'm necessarily decent, but I'm not bad either. Cam is helping me in that department. Helping me gain more confidence, being open to trying new things.

"You're better than decent. I've got a boner right now."

"You do?" I'm shocked.

"You're rubbing lotion all over me, your hands are all over my skin and I'm basically naked. Of course, I've got a hard-on." He suddenly starts to roll over, his hands going to my waist, basically lifting me as if I weigh nothing before settling me back down on him, my ass now snug against his very hard erection. "Wanna fuck?"

I burst out laughing and shake my head. "That wasn't my plan for tonight."

"Really?" He sounds surprised. "It's all I've been thinking about since I got to Logan's."

"Even before I showed up?"

He nods, his hands squeezing my waist. "Then you came in wearing my shirt and I was done for."

I sit up straighter. "You noticed."

"How could I not? Did you do that for me?"

"Yeah," I admit on a whisper.

"Come here."

I lean over him, my face aligned with his. His gaze is zeroed in on my lips, his parting, his tongue sneaking out to lick at the corner of his mouth and I dip my head, lightly kissing him. "You should go to sleep."

"No fucking way." His hand tunnels beneath my shirt and up my back, fingers teasing along my bra, lingering on the snap. "We need to get you naked."

"Cam..."

"Unless you just want to cuddle," he suggests, using my favorite word. "I'd be down for some naked cuddling."

"Is that your new code word for sex?"

"Well, yeah. Whatever it takes, Bumblebee."

He kisses me then and I drown in his taste. In the firm strokes of his tongue and the way his hands drift all over my body. He's sweeter tonight, not as commanding, and I fall for it.

Of course, I do.

Next thing I know I'm naked and he is too, and I'm still sitting astride him with his hands on my breasts and his already condom-covered cock poking my ass. I lift up, trying to align him so he can slide in easily, and he reaches around us, guiding himself inside my welcoming body, until I'm completely filled.

"Ride me," he says, his hands on my hips, his hooded gaze on the spot where our bodies are connected.

I do as he says, slow at first, trying to find my rhythm, straining against him when he nudges a spot deep within me that sends imaginary sparks all over my skin. We're moving together, slow and deep, our hips rocking, his cock filling me again and again. I close my eyes, lost in the moment. Swept up. Carried away by the throb of him deep within me, the sensation growing. Building. Spreading outward, racing through my veins.

We don't say much. We barely look at each other, too caught up in the way we're making each other feel. He's groaning. I'm whimpering with his every thrust. He hits that spot again and I see stars. The orgasm rushes through me, my inner walls clamping tightly around his shaft, strangling his orgasm out of him as well. We come together like some sort of miracle just happened, and when it's over, when I collapse on top of him and press my lips to his neck, the racing beat of his pulse pounding against my lips, I realize that I lied to myself.

I might be in love with Camden Fields after all.

30

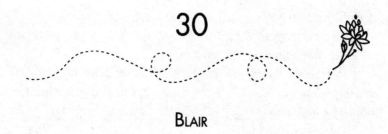

BLAIR

It's a Tuesday. The one day when Cam gets out of class early and I wait for him in his room at his apartment because Knox won't be there. Cam rushes home from his class and we mess around for an hour before he goes to practice.

It is the best hour, ever. I enjoy myself immensely. The clever things the man comes up with to do to me in such a limited amount of time...

My body trembles just at the thought.

Since that game a few weeks ago, Cam and I have seen each other as much as possible, but have not clued anyone in on what we're doing. It's hard, keeping it a secret. I want to tell Knox. I want to tell everyone, but Cam isn't ready. Why, I don't know, and if I think about it too much, I get mad.

And that's...that's bad.

Especially because my parents are coming to this weekend's game and I would love to tell them that Cam is my boyfriend. Even though we haven't defined exactly what we're doing, I don't know how else to describe it. My hook-up partner? My booty call? No one says it's a booty call anymore.

I'm at a loss.

I hear the front door open and close, and seconds later, Cam is opening his bedroom door, a smile on his beautiful face. He shuts it behind him and crosses his arms, watching me.

"Hi." I wave at him.

"What are you doing?" He makes his way toward the bed, his steps slow. Methodical.

"Waiting for you." I tuck the comforter closer to my body, only my arms and shoulders exposed. "Naked."

"Just the way I like you." He leans in, nuzzling the side of my face before finding my mouth, kissing me hard. I drown in his lips for a moment, pulling away to tug at the hem of his sweatshirt.

"Take your clothes off."

With a chuckle he does exactly that, slipping beneath the comforter with me, rolling me over onto my back, so he can kiss me.

Devour me.

I let him, kissing him in return, letting my hands roam all over his bare skin. It's like this for a few minutes, until he becomes impatient and starts issuing orders, which always work in my favor.

"Get on your hands and knees."

I get into position, wriggling my ass at him, yelping when he gives it a light slap. He soothes the sting with his palm, then bends over and drops a kiss on the spot where he smacked me.

I feel the touch of his lips on my skin to my very core, making me quiver.

The last couple of times we've had sex, we've included him fucking me from behind in our roster, and oh God, it feels so damn good, how deep he gets. How easily I come when he slams into me again and again.

When he finally slides inside me, I suck in a deep breath, savoring the feel of him buried so deep. His thick cock pulsing inside me, making me shiver all over. I remain still, hanging my head, taking in the moment like I always seem to do. He does the same, his big hands kneading my flesh, all the encouragement I need to start moving.

It's his turn to stay still as I slide up and down his cock, slow at first, gasping at the friction, how my body drags along his shaft, eventually picking up speed. Until he grips my hips hard and slams into me, that guaranteed orgasm hovering in the near distance, making me reach for it…

I cry out his name the moment it hits me, falling forward so I can whimper into the pillow in front of me, clutching it to my face while he continues to fuck me. Another orgasm builds, this one smaller but still intense, and when it's all over, I collapse onto the bed with Cam wrapping me up in his arms, my face pressed against his chest so I can feel his thundering heart.

"I wouldn't be surprised if they eventually find me dead on a Tuesday," he says once he's caught his breath. "You right next to me. Dead as well."

"What are you talking about?" I lightly slap his chest, hating the visual.

"I mean that if we keep this up, I don't know how we're going to survive it." He kisses my forehead. "I have news."

I frown. "What is it?"

"There's no practice today. Some sort of coaches' meeting is happening instead and they told us about it at the last minute." He smiles down at me when I tilt my head up to look at him. "I'm free for the rest of the afternoon."

"That's great," I breathe. "But what about Knox?"

"What about him?"

"Is he coming home eventually too?"

"Oh yeah. Probably." Cam's gaze turns distant and I wish I could read his mind.

Or maybe I don't want to know what he's thinking. I'm not sure.

Eventually we climb out of bed and get dressed, Cam protesting that he's hungry. We put together a snack in the kitchen for him and I join him on the couch, where he turns on some action movie that he cranks up the volume on, leaning back against the couch to eat his nachos, flashing me a smirk every once in a while.

"What is your deal?" I finally have to ask him.

"Life is good, you know? Got you sitting by my side after banging our brains out. Eating nachos. Catching up on the Fast and Furious franchise. No practice. I can't complain." He holds his arm out to me and I snuggle in close, leaning my head on his chest.

Thinking of all the things I could complain about, though I keep my mouth shut.

It's starting to get to me, all the sneaking around. He acts like he's totally into me, but he doesn't seem in any hurry to let people know we're even together.

Specifically, my brother.

How hard is it, to just come clean and tell Knox the truth? I'm getting to the point where if Cam doesn't do it, I will. I'm not scared of Knox. He's all show anyway. He'll put up a fit, yell that Cam isn't good enough for me but then eventually settle down. Then we'll be able to move on and actually be in a public relationship.

But Cam doesn't take the initiative. He always puts it off. And I'm growing impatient.

Like the *I want to smack him*, kind of impatient.

The movie bores me and I start to drift off to sleep at one point, when suddenly Cam sits up, causing me to practically fall off his chest, rousing me.

"Knox is on his way home." He leaps to his feet and starts gathering up the mess we left behind on the coffee table after eating our snacks, gathering the empty soda cans. "Maybe you should…"

"What, you want me to go?" I stand, brushing my hair out of my face, the annoyance growing as he dashes about the apartment, looking to trash any evidence that shows he might not be alone. "I'm so tired of this."

He takes everything to the kitchen and dumps it in the trash. "Tired of what?"

"Being your secret."

He enters the living room, a little slower this time, resting his hands on his hips. "I don't think now is exactly the right time to tell him."

"There will never be a better time." I throw my hands up in the air, exasperated. "This is getting old, Cam. I feel like I don't matter to you as much as you matter to me."

Cam stares at me, as if he needs a moment to allow the words I just said to him to sink in. "Give me—just give me a couple more days, okay?"

"How many more days do you need?"

"I don't know. I definitely don't want to tell him right now." The pleading look he sends me has my heart cracking. Ugh, I need to be stronger. "But don't leave yet. Go hide out in my room for a few."

"This is ridiculous." I grab my phone and march into Cam's room, shutting and locking the door behind me before I flop onto the bed and stare at the ceiling.

I'm fuming. This is not how I imagined my relationship with Cam playing out. He's being a complete wuss if he can't explain to my brother that we're two consenting adults and if we want to see each other, there's nothing he can do about it.

Nothing.

Instead of lying on the bed and waiting him out, I eventually creep toward the door and press my ear against it, straining to hear Knox and Cam's conversation when I hear my brother arrive at the apartment. Of course, I can't hear anything, but a few chuckles, and Knox saying the name Joanna once or twice. Of course. He's completely sprung over her and in love and doesn't give a damn who knows about it.

I envy him that.

Eventually I hear a door shut and then there's a soft knock sounding on Cam's bedroom door before he jiggles the handle. "Let me in."

I turn the lock and step back, crossing my arms the moment he strides in, shutting the door behind him.

"Where's Knox?"

"Taking a shower."

"Did you tell him?" I already know the answer. I don't know why I even bother asking.

"No, of course not. When am I supposed to fit that into our conversation when he just came home? 'Oh hey, bro. By the way, Blair is in my room and we just fucked. We're together now. Hope you're cool with it.'"

"God, you're crude." I drop my arms and march past him, opening the door and exiting the bedroom with Cam hot on my heels.

"Where are you going?" he asks.

I whirl on him, poking his chest with my index finger. "I'm leaving. And I'm not coming back until you tell him that we're doing—whatever it is we're doing."

"See, you can't even define it."

"Because you won't let me!" I practically yell, taking a deep breath to calm myself. I don't need to cause a scene and bring Knox back out here. "This is dumb."

"Just be patient with me for a little bit longer, okay? I'll take care of this with Knox. I swear."

Collapsing on the couch, I lean my head back, staring at the ceiling. Contemplating all the ways I could torture this man. Withholding sex from him might work, though what if it doesn't? And how petty is that? I don't want us to play games with each other. That is not the answer.

Sneaking around and continuing to do what we're doing now is definitely not the answer either. I know it isn't, but if I cut him off, I'll only be hurting myself too.

And I don't want to do that. I may think Cam is weak when it comes to admitting we're together, but I'm weak too when it comes to him.

"Bumblebee, don't be sad." He settles onto the couch next to me. Reaching for me. I try to resist, remaining in place, but the next thing I know, he's got his hands on me, and his mouth on mine. His lips are persuasive, and so is his tongue, and I fall into his kiss, reaching for him right back.

Only to hear the front door start to open.

Shit!

We leap away from each other so fast, I don't know even how it happened. I'm sitting there staring at the TV screen blankly, Cam just out of reach, his left arm stretching toward me, resting on the back of the couch. Both of us pretending to watch this stupid movie.

Oh yeah, we're not obvious at all.

Joanna comes to a stop in front of the door, her delicate brows drawn together, her gaze going from Cam to me and then back to Cam. "Hey, you guys." She waves at the both of us, all friendly-like.

I'm sure she can feel the tension hanging heavy in the air.

"Hey." Cam keeps his gaze fixed on the TV, his expression sulky. He won't even look at her, and the frustration boiling inside me is now threatening to show itself in the form of tears.

"Hi, Joanna," I offer, trying not to sound as sad as I feel.

She draws closer to me, her gaze locked on my face. "How are you?"

Before I can answer her, Cam is talking.

"I'll let you ladies chat. Knox is in the shower. He'll be out soon." He turns off the TV with the remote, rises from the couch, and leaves the two of us alone, slamming his bedroom door behind him a few seconds later.

What the hell?

A sigh leaves me and I shake my head. "He is such a prick."

"He is?" Joanna sounds shocked.

I nod, letting my annoyance bleed into my words. "The worst, but please don't mention this to Knox, okay? He doesn't even know I'm here."

Now Joanna seems extra confused. "He doesn't?"

I stand, grabbing my tiny bag that's on the coffee table in front of me that I bet money on Knox didn't even notice, and sling the strap over my shoulder. "I need to go."

"Are you sure you don't want to talk about it?" Joanna follows me all the way to the door, and I hurry my steps, desperate to get out of here.

Away from *him*.

"There's nothing to talk about. And please..." I turn to face her. "*Please,* don't mention this to my brother. It's really none of his business."

I don't even give Joanna a chance to respond. I stride right out of the apartment, shutting the door behind me and marching my way toward my car. Not giving in to my emotions until I'm sitting in the driver's seat with the engine running.

Only then do I break down and cry.

31

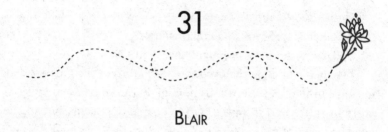

BLAIR

"Sweetheart, you look so good!" Mom leaps to her feet, Dad looming just behind her as I approach their table, where they've been waiting for me at the restaurant.

I met them for lunch. They came in a little earlier to have a few days with us, flying in last night—plus Mom didn't want to deal with the long drive, she said—and when Knox and I went together to the airport to pick them up, Dad announced that they're selling the family house and moving to California to be closer to my aunt and uncle.

And I sort of had a meltdown.

Okay, there was no sort of about it. I had a complete meltdown and I can't even explain exactly why. Change is hard. Knowing that our house, where we grew up—mostly—is up for sale and my parents are moving out of state threw me for a complete loop. Knox said I was acting like a selfish brat, which only pissed me off more, but I can't help it.

The idea of never being able to go back to what I consider home is upsetting.

It doesn't help that I haven't really talked to Cam since I left his apartment earlier this week. I'm mad at him still. I currently feel mad at the world. Even at my parents, who I love and adore. Who are giving me matching, *are you okay* looks that make me feel bad for holding a grudge.

Once I hug them both, I settle into the chair across from them, watching as they share a glance before turning their attention to me.

"About last night," I start, readying to face the problem head-on. Unlike some people I know.

Another shared look, Dad talking first.

"We know our news last night upset you," he says.

I study his familiar, beloved face. My father is the greatest dad, and I mean that. He's shown us nothing but unconditional love our entire lives. Retired from the NFL a couple of seasons early so he could be there for us, and for Mom. I've heard the story before, where he said he had enough money, and he didn't need to make anymore. We've always lived comfortably, nothing too outrageous. Eventually Dad became a coach at one of the local middle schools, and he even got a degree and became a counselor.

Meaning he's really good at the counseling talk. Which is what I'm bracing myself for.

"It did upset me," I say, keeping my voice calm. "It's just hard, to hear your parents are selling your house."

"We probably should've told you in a different way," Dad says. "And I understand why you might feel like that. It's really the only home you remember, and there are a lot of fond memories we created there. But we can create new ones somewhere else. You'll end up moving out on your own when you graduate college, living your own life."

I nod, forcing myself not to think about the future. Only a few days ago I firmly believed Cam would be in it, but now?

I don't know what's going to happen. Or if I even want to keep him around.

That thought makes my stomach feel hollow and I push aside the menu, unsure of what to order. Nothing sounds good. I haven't eaten much in the last few days and I was nauseous when I first woke up this morning. Not that we have anything to worry about. Cam and I have been practicing safe sex since we first started this…whatever you want to call it. I think it's more that I feel sick over the way everything has played out the last few days.

It's been nothing but pure misery.

"There's been a lot on my mind lately and I overreacted last night. When my response really had nothing to do with what you told me." I glance over at my mom, who's frowning at me. "I just wanted to say I'm sorry. It's been…a rough few months since I got here."

"Oh, Blair, why?" Mom reaches out, settling her hand on top of mine, and I give it a squeeze. "Is it your classes? Are they giving you trouble?"

"They're not so bad." They're actually pretty easy.

"Is it your brother? You two were arguing quite a bit last night," Dad says with a frown.

No, it's definitely not Knox's fault. He may be overprotective, but he would do anything for me. Despite the argument we had last evening. I deserved the name-calling because he was right.

I was acting like a brat.

"What is it then?" Mom asks.

"It's just an adjustment, living here." Dealing with my roommates, who I adore, but wow, they're a lot. And then there's dealing with Cam. Hating how everything feels so uncertain all the time. I like to stay in control of all aspects of my life, but since Cam has come into it, I can throw all that control I thought I had right out the window.

"Your sister is having a difficult time too," Mom murmurs, her gaze filling with worry. "I don't know what Ruby is going to do."

"I just spoke with her earlier, right before we entered the restaurant, when you were on the phone with Fable. She's going to finish out the school year where she's at, and then transfer here in the fall." Dad smiles. "She's already filled out her admission application. She submitted it last night."

"Oh, thank goodness. We've all been telling her to do exactly that. Glad she agreed." Mom turns to me. "Isn't that wonderful? Maybe you two can get an apartment together."

I paste on a wan smile, trying to find some enthusiasm. "Sounds great."

Look, I adore my sister. We fought a lot growing up, but we've become closer over the years. In the family lineup, I am the classic middle child. Always fading into the background, while Knox as the oldest got all the attention, or Ruby, the baby, stole the show.

Me? I'm the independent one. Doing her own thing, who can't be bothered by anyone else.

Giving up on trying to make conversation with my parents when all I really want to do is cry in my mother's arms and confess my feelings for and issues with Cam, I let them do most of the talking. I nod and interject my opinion in all of the right places, laughing when necessary, though it feels forced. They tell me how they met with Knox and Joanna earlier for breakfast, and Mom can't stop talking about how great she is, which I readily agree with. Joanna is pretty great and she seems so good for my brother.

"She mentioned you two are becoming fast friends," Dad adds after Mom waxed on about Jo.

"We are. We've spent some time together here and there, mostly during the games. Sometimes out at the bars."

"Ah, the bars." Mom smiles fondly. "We used to do that, huh, Owen? Go out all the time?"

"Uh, not really, babe. Though we did spend a lot of time chasing each other." Dad laughs when Mom nudges him in the side with her elbow.

Ugh, they're still so cute together, even after all these years.

"We're all getting ready for the football game together tomorrow. I'm going over to Joanna's apartment and hanging out with her and Natalie." Though I don't really want to go to the game. Why sit there and watch Cam the entire time while I'm still angry with him? I'll just end up frustrated, like usual.

But I'll go. There's no way in hell I'm going to miss that game. I guess I'm just a glutton for punishment or however that old saying goes.

"That's so nice, that you two are friends. And I'm glad your brother is happy. That he's finally found someone." Mom ducks her head, like she's trying to peer inside my brain, and my smile freezes on my face. "What about you? Have you met anyone yet?"

"Nope," I say with a finality that feels downright ominous. "No one worthy of my time, at least."

Mom frowns. "Oh, that's too bad."

I offer her my first real smile of the day. "Yeah. Isn't it?"

• • •

The game was an absolute nail-biter.

It took everything in me not to overreact at certain moments. Like when Cam got sacked. Or when he threw that interception that had the entire side of our stadium gasping out loud—including me. He never let any of it get him down, playing with a determination that was nothing but admirable. All while I sat in the stands silently willing him to look in my direction at least once. He knows where I usually sit. We've made eye contact before when I've been at a game.

But he doesn't look in my direction. Not even once, and it quietly kills me. Though I'm trying my best to understand. The weight on his shoulders, the pressure he has to deal with trying to win this game—I know he needs to focus.

By the time the game is over—they pulled out a win at the end, thank God—and we're let out on the field, I go in the opposite direction of my friends. Joanna goes in search of my brother. Natalie is just out there for a good time, not caring who she's going to run into. While me?

I'm in search of Cam, even though I don't want to be. Even though I tell myself it's a big mistake, talking to him. It's as if my body has a mind of its own, seeking him out when I mentally tell myself I need to get off this damn field.

My body doesn't listen, honing in on his location as if I'm using GPS and he's the item that's gone missing. I come to a stop a few feet away from where he's standing, giving an interview with a gorgeous blonde holding a microphone to his face with the ESPN emblem on it. He's talking about the game, his deep voice rumbling, drifting toward me, and I watch and listen, my entire body aching to give him a hug. Congratulate him on a game well-played.

At one point during the interview, I must catch his eye because he does a double take, though that's his only visible reaction. Once their chat is over, the reporter fawns over him for a bit before she finally takes her leave, in hot pursuit of some other football player. Cam remains standing where she left him, his helmet dangling from his fingers, looking at a loss.

Sighing, I approach him, noting how much bigger he looks when he's in his full gear. The pads bulk him up, and the dark slashes still painted under his eyes are giving warrior vibes. His white uniform that they wear for home games is streaked with grass and dirt. I swear I even see a couple of drops of blood on it and I can't help but worry that it came from him. Is he hurt? Does he even realize it?

God, I really need to stop worrying about this guy.

"Blair. Uh, hey." He scratches the back of his head, and I sort of wish I could smack him at his greeting.

"You sound surprised that I'm here."

"I am."

"I had to come to the game. My parents are in town."

"I heard. In fact, I'm…supposed to go to dinner with you all tonight." He winces and seems to brace himself for my reaction.

"Are you serious?" He has got to be kidding me. I don't want to spend the next couple of hours listening to my parents drill Cam for information, and he and Knox act all nonchalant about their lives while I'm sitting there in silence, suffering.

That sounds like my own personal hell.

He nods. "They invited me and I couldn't turn them down. Your dad is willing to give me some advice, and I need as much as I can get."

"About what?"

"The draft."

Oh. Right. When he moves on and lives his life without me.

"Look." He glances around, as if he's checking to see who's paying attention to us before he takes a step closer, his voice lowering. "I'm sorry about what happened."

I tilt my head back, staring into his dark eyes. "Oh yeah?"

He nods, his expression grave. "But I gotta be real with you."

"What do you mean?"

"I can only give so much right now, B. Everything feels like it's closing in on me, all at once, and the pressure—it's a lot. I don't know how much more I can stand." He scratches the back of his head again, staring off into the distance. "I care about you."

My heart cracks wide open...

"But I don't know if I can be enough for you."

Only to shatter into a bazillion pieces, falling at my feet.

"Look." I smile at him, though it feels like I'm snarling, so I clamp my lips shut. "Why don't I make it easy on you."

He frowns, his brows drawing together. "How?"

"I'll walk away right now. I don't need anything else from you. Not a single thing. It was fun while it lasted, right?"

Cam studies me for a moment, his lips parting slightly. "If that's how you want to go about this."

"That's exactly how I want this to play out. Look, you were always honest with me from the start, right? You told me you weren't worthy of me. That you didn't do relationships, and I ignored all the signs. You were waving all the red flags in my face, and I'd constantly tell myself, red is my favorite color."

"You think I'm a red flag?"

Oh, he seems offended. I am sort of enjoying this after all the torture he's put me through.

"You are a walking red flag, Camden Fields," I tell him, my

voice firm. "You really need to get your shit together for the next girl. *Woman.*"

"Fuck, Bumblebee. You're brutal," he mutters, his gaze full of pain.

"Don't call me that." I shake my head. "Not anymore, okay? It feels too…"

My throat closes up and I can't get any more words out. I'm choked up, afraid I might cry, and I close my eyes for the briefest moment to stave off the tears.

"If you don't want me to go to dinner with your family, just say the word," he says, his voice faint. "I can come up with an excuse and get out of it."

"No, it's fine. You need to talk to my father. You need his advice. Besides, he adores you." I swallow hard, hating the broken look on Cam's face. He just won a really tough game and he should be on top of the world. Instead, I'm bringing him down and insulting him when it's all my fault.

I walked into this scenario with my eyes wide open and I still went and fell in love with the asshole. In the end, whose fault is that?

All mine.

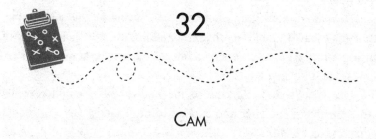

32

CAM

I am such a dickhead.

I've thought it a bazillion times. Said it out loud more than once, specifically to Blair. After she walked out of my apartment and didn't bother trying to reach out to me, I was so pissed, I did the same thing to her, like a toddler on the verge of a major tantrum.

Lots of, *I don't need her. Fuck women*-type chants on repeat in my head these last few days, which is stupid.

The moment I saw her out on the field, all I wanted to do was touch her. Pull her into my arms and kiss her. Tell her how much I missed her over the last few days—which is a lot. Blair Maguire became a regular part of my life that I didn't expect, and when she disappeared, I felt the loss.

Hard.

I probably shouldn't have told her I didn't have it in me anymore to continue what we were doing. I saw the hurt on her face and it made me feel like shit, so what did I do? I pushed her away, which is my usual reaction. If I can't be there for someone, I just shove them out of my life. That's what's easiest on me.

When I started talking to her like the awkward fuck I am, she called me a walking red flag and told me I couldn't call her by her nickname anymore.

I've lost the right. And fuck all if she isn't one hundred percent correct. I did lose the right. As soon as I told her that I couldn't be what she wanted, she let me go. She told me she was done and damn, that hurt.

Now we're at a restaurant together, sitting at the same table, though at least I'm on the other end and not directly facing her. I'm sitting with the guys, locked in an intense conversation with my hero, Owen Maguire, and Knox.

But I can't stop thinking of the many ways I could possibly get Blair to see me later and explain to her exactly why I'm such a complete dickhead.

But how can I explain any of that without her rolling her eyes, calling me a red flag, yet again, and dismissing me completely? I'd deserve all of that treatment and more. Which circles right back to the 'I'm not worthy' statement I love saying to her all the time.

Christ. Even I'm sick of myself.

Instead of sneaking looks at Blair down at the other end of the table every chance I get, I focus on Owen. Taking into consideration his time and his willingness to share all his tips and tricks. The fact that he's willing to share so much valuable information with me while also pushing his son into the NFL draft is huge. It shows that he cares enough that he wants to help me, and I appreciate it more than he could ever know.

I'm a lucky son of a bitch, and I tell them exactly that.

"You're not lucky," Owen says with a faint smile. "You've more than proven yourself. You're worthy of the chance."

I blink at him, absorbing his words, while Knox continues talking. Maybe Owen is right. I am worthy. I worked really hard to get where I am, and now I should reap the possible benefits. I might not get drafted, but what if I do?

My entire life will change. I won't take the opportunity and toss it aside. I'll continue working, striving toward being the best that I can be. I will lead a new team and hopefully find success again.

"I think I'm gonna head out," Knox announces about halfway through dinner, pushing back his chair.

Owen stops mid-conversation, his gaze going to his son. "We just started eating."

"And I'm already done." Knox points to his empty plate. The guy is always starving. I've never seen anyone eat as fast as him.

"Let him go," Chelsea Maguire says, a fond smile on her face as she studies Knox. "He probably wants to go see Joanna."

"I do." Knox doesn't even hesitate with his answer. Just leaps to his feet, an anxious expression on his face. "Do you guys mind if I leave?"

"You should go," his mother says without hesitation.

"What about Cam?" Blair asks.

I'm shocked she'd even say my name. She hasn't acknowledged me since we showed up at the restaurant.

"Do you mind giving him a ride home, Blair?" Knox sends his sister a pleading look. "Mom and Dad are just going to walk across the street to their hotel after dinner, right Dad?"

"I can leave with you now," I start to say but Knox shakes his head.

"I want to go straight to Joanna's. Something's wrong. She won't answer my texts." He sounds worried.

"You really care about her, don't you?" his father asks.

"I do," Knox says solemnly.

A sigh leaves Owen and he sends his wife a look. "When you know, you just...know. Go to Joanna. Tell her we're sorry we didn't get to say goodbye to her."

Knox hesitates, his gaze shifting between his mom and dad. "Are you sure I can leave? I know you're flying out tomorrow."

"We'll take an Uber," Owen reassures him.

I sit there uneasy, while Knox hugs his parents and eventually takes off. Leaving just me and the Maguires and Blair, who still won't look at me. Not really. Everyone is still eating, but my appetite is gone, and I push my plate away from me, checking my phone real quick.

Derek is blowing up my line, sending endless text messages about me showing up at Logan's later. I send him a response.

Can't. I'm having dinner with the Maguires.

Derek proceeds to send me a long string of emojis that include eggplants and peaches and the one that looks like something is blowing up. I figure out quickly that he's asking in emoji-speak if they know I'm banging their daughter.

The fucker.

I send him a single emoji in response.

The middle finger.

I pocket my phone, glancing up to find Blair watching me, her gaze filled with an unfamiliar emotion. She looks away the moment we make eye contact and disappointment floods me. I hate that she doesn't even want to look at me. That I've ruined everything that was good between us.

We finish dinner in strained silence and the Maguires bail on us after paying the bill—I tried to hand them money to pay for my dinner, but they refused my offer. They head back to the hotel after hugging and kissing Blair for a few minutes. All while I stand at the entrance to the restaurant and pretend I'm scrolling on my phone.

It's painful, pretending like what's happening doesn't matter. When all it does is matter—so damn much.

The moment her parents exit the restaurant, I make my offer.

"I can find my own ride home."

She visibly flinches, like my words hurt her. "No way. You're stuck with me."

"More like you're stuck with me," I remind her.

An aggravated noise leaves her just before she pushes her way out of the restaurant and into the cold, dark night.

I follow after her, jogging to keep up with her hurried pace across the parking lot. I don't say a word, worried I might say something to piss her off and I'm not in the mood to feel the full wrath of Blair.

She unlocks the car and slides into the driver's seat, without hesitation, and I jog around the back of the car, entering on the passenger side. The moment the doors slam shut, I'm assaulted with her scent. That one I keep sniffing covertly from the travel-sized perfume I bought a while ago that I keep in my nightstand like some sort of creeper.

I have issues and every one of them begins and ends with this woman sitting in the driver's seat of her car.

We drive in silence to my apartment, the only sound is the music coming from the stereo. She's got a Spotify playlist on and the moment a certain song starts with the gentle tinkling of a piano, she cranks it up, listening to it at full blast, singing along with every single word.

The screen says the song is called "Mad Woman" by Taylor Swift.

Fuck. I'm doomed.

There's nothing like a mad woman, the lyrics say.

Tell me all about it.

She pulls into a parking spot close to my building, throwing the car into park and turning down the music, glaring at me.

"You know what's infuriating about you, Camden Fields?"

I brace myself, about to respond when she talks right over me.

"Your 'oh poor me, I'm not worthy of you' bullshit that you always spew. Like I'm supposed to feel sorry for you? Or just agree with you and leave you alone? It's like you can't see yourself for what you really are, and I'm tired of trying to convince you of it."

Inhaling deeply, I try to come up with something to say, but her words are a jumble in my brain, hard to decipher. Hard to make sense of.

"I know what you're thinking. By me saying I'm tired of convincing you is exactly what you want to hear. It feeds into that whole 'see, I told you I'm not good enough' crap you'll spew next. Well, guess what?"

"What?" I whisper, slowly turning to face her.

God, she's beautiful, especially when she's mad. Her cheeks are flushed and her eyes are wild, and she looks like she wants to strangle me.

"You're *right*. You're not worthy. You don't deserve me. I'm pretty fucking great and if you can't see that, then that's your loss. You may win at football and you'll probably get into the NFL and make a bazillion dollars and have this amazing career. As a matter of fact, I'm positive that you will do exactly that. Women will make thirst-trap posts about you on social media and everyone will think they want you, but they won't know the *real* you and that's a good thing. Because you're awful. And so fucking blind. You wouldn't know the love of a good woman if she slapped you in the ass and called you sexy."

I almost laugh at her slapping my ass comment. What the fuck is she even saying?

Wait a minute. Did she just admit that she's in love with me?

"I believe in you more than you believe in yourself, and I don't know why I waste my time. You don't care about me. Not really. You're too wrapped up in your own shit to see what's really happening right in front of your face."

"Blair—"

"No, don't bother trying to talk your way out of this. My mind is made up. I'm done with you, Cam. I'm tired of wasting my time on someone who is so blind that he can't see—"

"Can't see what?" I interrupt her.

She's breathing hard. Glaring at me. Her chest rises and falls, her eyes are wide and she blinks at me, like she can't answer my question.

"Me," she finally whispers. "You're so wrapped up in your negative thoughts, so focused on your faults, you can't see the good things that make you who you are. And you can't see *me*. I'm right here, Cam. Waiting for you. And you still can't see it."

Her disappointment is thick, filling the close confines of her car, making it hard for me to breathe. I don't even think when I make the next move.

I lunge for her, cupping her beautiful face, tilting it up and forcing her to look at me. She's trembling, her lips parting, surprise flaring in her gaze. Just as I dip my head and kiss her.

The kiss is wild. Fucking feral. Our tongues do battle and she's shoving at my chest, like she wants me to stop, yet she keeps kissing me like she can't get enough.

I feel the same way. The need to push her away yet pull her in close. It's fucking confusing.

She tastes amazing.

Feels even better, despite the layers of clothing she's got on. The puffy black coat, the sweatshirt, her jeans, all of it is denying me access to what I really want, but I'm a determined motherfucker and I'm not going to stop until I can touch actual skin.

My fingers eventually find her waist and when I press them into her warm, smooth skin, she sighs into my mouth, melting into me.

That's it. That's all it takes. I help her get rid of her jacket and she's shoving my coat off. I tug on her, encouraging her to come over to the dark side and she does exactly that, crawling over the console, her lips never slipping from mine, until she's in my lap. A warm, sexy bundle who's straddling me, her hands in my hair, my hands under her sweatshirt, my fingers skimming over the lacy bra covering her breasts.

"I hate you," she murmurs against my lips at one point, when I've got her jeans unzipped and my fingers are pressed against the front of her panties. "I do."

"I don't hate you," I return, sliding my fingers beneath the cotton to find her wet and hot and ready for me. "I couldn't hate you if I tried."

She curls her hand into a fist and lightly socks me on top of my shoulder. "We shouldn't do this."

I go completely still, pulling away slightly, so I can stare into her eyes. "You want me to stop?"

I refuse to force myself on any woman, especially this one. She means too much. I respect her too damn much.

Blair says nothing, but I see the way she swallows. The uncertainty in her gaze. I start to withdraw my hand from her panties, but her own hand shoots down, fingers curling around my wrist and stopping me. "No," she whispers, her head bent, so I can't see her face anymore.

With my other hand, I slip my fingers beneath her chin, tilting her face back up so our gazes meet once more. She tilts her head to the side when I slide my fingers up her cheek, and she leans into my palm, closing her eyes. I press my fingers against her plump lips, whispering, "Come inside with me."

She slowly shakes her head. "I can't."

I frown. "I don't have a condom with me."

A shuddery breath leaves her and she's quiet for too long.

"I don't have the heart to go through with this," she finally admits. "I can't do this again."

She's quiet for a moment and then she adds...

"With you."

I withdraw my hand from her panties, but she doesn't crawl off my lap. Instead, she presses her forehead against mine, a ragged sigh escaping her, and then I feel it. Wetness.

Her tears.

"I'm tired, Cam. I can't be with you like this, giving more of myself to you while knowing you're just going to push me away yet again when we're done. I refuse to be your consolation prize." Finally, she climbs off my lap, falling back into the driver's seat. She grips the steering wheel, staring straight ahead, the tears now flowing freely down her cheeks.

"Blair—"

She turns on me. "Go. Come back to me when you're ready, because I think you're close. We could be so good together. So good for each other. But I'm not going to wait forever. The clock starts now. Think you'll figure it all out in time?"

"I don't know," I croak, needing to be honest with her.

Her eyes close and she leans her forehead against the steering wheel for a moment, like what I just said tore her completely apart.

It probably did.

"That's what I thought you'd say." She waves a dismissive hand. "You need to leave."

I get out of the car, leaning my head back in before I shut the door. "You're stronger than you think."

I don't know why I said that, but I wanted her to know that she doesn't need me to be any stronger than she already is. She was a badass with that speech she just gave me, even if it fucking hurt to hear her say the words.

"So are you," she murmurs. "Too bad you can't see just how strong we'd be together."

33

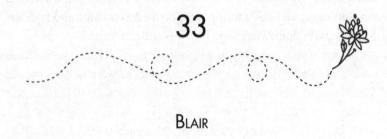

BLAIR

ONE MONTH LATER

Whoever said time heals all wounds is a fucking liar.

The wounds Camden Fields left are like open, gaping ones that I can't repair. They only get uglier the longer I go without him. What makes it worse?

He's everywhere. Everyone's talking about him. Them. The football team. They've gone on to the playoffs. They're projected to be in the championships, and I wouldn't doubt for a minute that they're going to win. Knox tells me Cam's never played better—the entire team is in top form. They haven't lost a single game yet.

They're breaking school records, causing a commotion in town and on campus. In the entire state. They recently set up banners on the light poles on campus with photos of all the best players—my brother. Cam. Especially Cam. It pains me to walk around campus and see his handsome face glowering down at me, a football clutched in his hand. Even the banners where he's wearing his helmet, I can still see his eyes. Like he's watching me everywhere I go.

I hate it.

I love it.

He still hasn't reached out.

The clock is ticking, but time's almost up. I can't wait much longer like some pathetic loser, who's hoping the idiot love of her life will see the light and realize he needs her by his side. I've confessed all to Rita and Cheyenne, and while they're supportive and give me good advice, they also both think I'm giving him way too much time.

"I would've fucked someone else by now to forget him. Get back at him," Rita admitted to me last night, when we were all hanging out in the living room together and passing around a bottle of Peppermint Schnapps.

Why were we voluntarily drinking that again? It's like chugging straight mouthwash.

"Rita, stop," Cheyenne admonished, and all I could do was stare at her, trying to imagine myself with someone else.

I couldn't. Just the idea made me nauseous.

The majority of their football games the last four weeks have been away games, which was the perfect excuse for me not to attend. Joanna asked a few times if I wanted to tag along with her and Natalie. I felt bad for turning her down, but I couldn't do it. I just...couldn't sit there and cheer them on, knowing I couldn't actually talk to him afterward. And I wasn't about to approach him either. This is all on him. The ball is in his court, so to speak.

I don't know what he's been up to beyond football, and I refuse to talk about him with Knox. Not that my brother ever brings him up. We barely talk anyway, considering he's always with Joanna, spending every free moment he has with her.

Honestly? I don't blame him. I would do the same thing with a certain someone, if he'd only get his head out of his ass.

I'm currently sitting in the living room, contemplating getting drunk again like we did a couple of nights ago. Rita is taking a shower. Cheyenne is making a salad for us for dinner, and while I said yes to her offer only a few minutes ago, I'm not really that hungry.

Pretty sure I've lost at least ten pounds on the *he broke my heart* diet I'm currently on.

Cheyenne eventually enters the living room, handing me a silver bowl filled with the salad she made and a fork. I take it from her gratefully, saying thank you before I ask, "Hey, is there any more alcohol in this place?"

She settles into the overstuffed chair across from where I'm sitting on the couch. "No. That's why we polished off that nasty peppermint Schnapps last night. It was all we had left."

I make a face, staring at the contents of my bowl. This is a beautiful salad, full of all of my favorite things and I start gathering a few items with the fork. Lettuce, cucumber, a crouton. "We should Door Dash some vodka and orange juice."

"God, no. Alcohol is not going to solve your problems, Blair."

"I know," I say morosely, chewing for a while. Lost in thought.

Cheyenne remains quiet as well, both of us eating for a few minutes until she finally says, "Is he worth it?"

I pause in my eating, staring at her. "Who?"

"Him. Cam. Is he worth your sadness while you wait for him? What if he never comes back around?"

The possibility is there. The longer he takes, the worse I feel. I'm wasting my time. I'm being such a wimp right now. A doormat. The type of woman who will sacrifice everything for a man who gives her nothing. That's the worst.

If I told my mom this, she would be so mad at me. So disappointed. And the last thing I want to do is disappoint someone.

Truthfully? All I'm doing is disappointing myself.

"Then I guess I move on." I shrug and resume eating.

"I figure that's what you're doing right now. Moving on."

"Am I?"

"I don't want to sound mean, but you probably should."

Cheyenne's gaze is full of sympathy. "Don't wait for him forever."

"I'm not." I mean, I am, but I'm also busy with school. The semester is almost over and finals are coming up. We only just got through Thanksgiving and now the holiday season is upon us. Christmas decorations are up everywhere and holiday music is playing in just about every store I enter lately, but I'm not feeling it.

This is my favorite time of year and I can't even enjoy it.

I'm halfway finished with my salad when my phone dings with a text notification. I check to see who it's from, surprised to find it's Knox, asking me where I'm at.

Me: *Home.*

Knox: *Why are you at home?*

Me: *Where else would I be?*

Knox: *Come hang out. We just got to that pizza place across from the library.*

They have the best pizza there.

Me: *I don't want to.*

Knox: *Why not? You've become really boring lately. You never want to do anything.*

I don't want to do anything if it involves his best friend.

Knox: *Just come out and hang tonight. It'll be fun. I miss you.*

Me: *You're full of shit. Who put you up to this?*

My heart is hammering so hard against my ribs, I swear it's going to burst out of my chest.

Knox: *Fine, Joanna asked about you. She wants you here. She misses you.*

I call him, tired of texting. I just want to finish my salad in peace. He answers immediately.

"Please just stop bugging me, Knox," is how I greet him, not worrying about being polite because he's my brother. "I don't want to go out tonight."

"Come on, B. Just get your butt over here," Knox encourages, and I can tell he's got me on speaker.

Alarm races through me at Knox calling me B. Something I

don't think he's ever really done before. That's a Cam thing. "Who are you with?"

"Who else would I be with? Jo Jo and the Duke of Camden." I can tell Knox is smiling, happy to be with his girlfriend and best friend.

That sounds like torture. Not the Joanna part.

The Cam part. Duke of Camden. Only my brother has ever called him that.

"Oh." I go quiet, thinking, glancing over at Cheyenne, who's watching me with curiosity. "I don't know. I don't feel like pizza."

"Give me a break. You love pizza."

"And I look terrible." I'm in sweats. No makeup. My hair needs a good wash.

"It's just us, Blair. We don't care what you look like." He's quiet for a moment, asking either Joanna or Cam, "You don't care what my sister looks like, right?"

I hear a slam, like the sound of something hitting a table. "Nope. Don't care at all."

Oh shit. That was Cam.

"Really?" I'm pissed. "Are you drunk, Camden?"

"I've had one beer, Blair. Give me a fucking break," Cam mutters.

"Hey, language," Knox says mildly.

"I'm not a baby, Knox. I can handle it when Cam drops a fuck here and there," I say snippily.

I'm guessing Cam doesn't want me there. I'm sure he'd run away with his tail between his legs if I showed up at the restaurant.

"Ouch, okay, sorry." Knox sounds defensive. Typical. "Are you coming or not?"

Don't do it, don't do it!

"You know what? Yes, I'm coming. I'll be there in ten minutes." I end the call and leap from the couch, taking my bowl to the kitchen and dumping it into the sink before I head for my bedroom.

"Where are you going?" Cheyenne asks.

"You don't want to know," I tell her at the same time I receive a text from my brother reminding me of the name of the restaurant they're at, even though I already knew.

Can't wait to show up and I hope seeing me strikes fear in Cam's heart.

It's the least he deserves.

• • •

'm entering the restaurant fifteen minutes later, the scent of cheese and oregano and tomato sauce hitting me, making my stomach growl. That salad didn't even put a dent into my suddenly ravenous appetite.

I'm starved.

Knox spots me first, lifting his hand in a wave and I make my way toward the table, confidence flowing through my veins. I revitalized my hair with dry shampoo and it flows down my back in slight waves, bouncing as I walk. I slicked on some of those glow drops on my face, giving myself a dewy finish as they say in the ad. I'm wearing my favorite straight leg jeans and a black turtleneck that makes my boobs look huge, and all I want to do is make Cam swallow his tongue.

At the very least, choke on it.

I approach their table, stopping at the head of it, smiling at all of them, even Cam.

"Hey, guys," I say brightly.

Knox and Joanna greet me while Cam stares at my chest like he's never seen a pair of tits before.

Triumph flowing through me, I tell him, "Scoot over," and he does without saying a word, allowing me to slide onto the bench beside him.

This is probably going to hurt me in the end, but for now, I'm going to try and enjoy every single minute of this interaction with the man who's too big of an idiot to see that I'm in love with him.

Because, yes, it's true. I'm in love with Cam and I believe he's in love with me too. He just doesn't realize it. Doesn't believe he can actually feel that emotion, which is the dumbest thing ever. All of us are capable of love.

We just have to believe in it.

"It's good to see you, Joanna," I tell my brother's girlfriend, and she smiles at me when I reach across the table and squeeze her arm.

I refuse to look at Cam. I hope it's killing him.

"It's been forever," Joanna agrees with a faint smile. "What have you been up to?"

"Nothing in particular." I'm purposely vague. "School has been kicking my butt lately."

Well, that's not a lie.

"Mine too."

"Not mine," Knox chimes in with a smug smile. "Thanks to Joanna. She's a huge help."

I roll my eyes. "Yeah, yeah. You two are so lucky and in love. Blah, blah, blah. I've heard it all before already from you."

"Don't knock it till you try it." Knox glances over at Joanna, all gooey-eyed. "I don't think I can stop talking about you."

Cam makes a derisive noise mixed with a snort, and I glance over at him, noting the annoyance on his face.

The pain in his gaze when it quickly meets mine before he looks away.

"They're gross," I tell him, feeling like I'm twelve.

"Tell me all about it. I have to deal with them all the time," he mutters before bringing the beer mug to his lips.

"They hang out at the apartment a lot?"

"Every damn day." He grimaces. "A constant reminder."

"Of what?"

"Of what a relationship could be like when it works out." His gaze holds mine for a second before it drops to my mouth for a brief moment. "You look good, Bumblebee."

I can't even lash out at him for calling me that. It feels too good to hear the nickname fall from his sexy lips.

God, I am so weak when it comes to this man, when I need to

remain strong.

I don't need him. I don't even like him.

Liar, the little voice inside my head whispers.

"Blair, your timing is impeccable," Knox says.

I turn away from Cam to find a server at our table with the pizza, setting it on the little silver stand before passing out paper plates to us. Her gaze lands on Cam and her mouth pops open, her eyes going wide.

"Wait, you're—"

"No, I'm not," he tells her, taking the plate she offers. "Could we get some ranch dressing, please?"

"S-sure." She looks at me, her eyes going wide. "You need anything else?"

"I'm great. This is perfect. Thank you." I smile sweetly at her and she scurries away from us, glancing over her shoulder a couple of times, in awe of Cam.

"Is this how it always is with you since your face got slapped on every banner around campus?" I ask, my tone just as sweet as it was to the poor starstruck server.

"I'm not on every banner," he points out, reaching around me to grab himself a slice of pizza.

He sets it on my empty plate instead.

"Thank you," I murmur, reminding myself politeness shouldn't be impressive. This is the very least he can do. "And you're essentially on every banner."

"No, I'm not." He grabs his own slice, taking a bite and breathing around it because it's so hot. Once he's swallowed, he says, "Right Knox?"

Knox tears his mouth away from Joanna's. "Right, what?"

"I'm not on every banner on campus."

Knox snorts. "You're on most of them."

"You're on a few," Joanna says, nudging into his side.

He wraps his arm around her shoulders, ignoring the pizza and nuzzling her face. "Thanks for noticing, babe."

Cam and I share another look, and I realize I'm enjoying this moment far too much with him. "They really are disgusting."

"Right?" He lifts his brows, taking an enormous bite of his pizza.

"Watch it. You're going to burn yourself."

"You still care?" His voice is low, his expression...ugh...sexy.

"Always," I admit, hating that I just said that. "Though it has more to do with me possibly encouraging you to go ahead and do it anyway since you never listen to me in the first place. So go ahead, keep eating that extra hot pizza and burn the roof of your mouth. I'm not your mama."

"No." He grins. "You're definitely not."

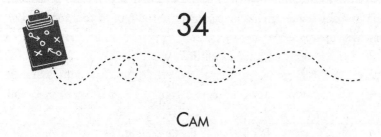

34

Cam

I t's so good to have her sitting close to me. Smelling her familiar heady scent. Staring at her beautiful face. She looks great. Bright-eyed and smiling. Not being too hard on me, when we both know I deserve it.

I'm walking on fragile ground here and I don't want to piss her off. She doesn't know what I've been up to the past month. How hard I've worked. On school, on myself. Both physically and mentally. I wish I could tell her. I want to.

Will she listen to me? Or did my time finally run out?

It's been a month. Pretty sure time's up.

The four of us keep up easy conversation as we polish off the pizza, Knox doing most of the demolishing while I hold my own. I've been eating better these last four weeks after connecting with a nutritionist our offensive line coach hooked me up with. I've been working out more too. Joanna made some crack about me never being around before Blair showed up, and I know they're thinking I'm going out all the time. Getting drunk and getting laid.

Not even close. I've been going to the gym. Going to the library to get my homework done or some extra studying in. After this semester, I only have one left to go and then I graduate. I want to leave school on top in all the ways I can.

Including academically.

After spiraling into a dark pit of despair after that blowup with Blair in her car, I realized I had to do some real soul searching. My mood was affecting everyone on the team, and Coach eventually pulled me aside after one particular brutal practice, telling me I needed to get my shit together.

I broke down. Hell, I cried. It was bad. But my coach gave me zero shit for it. He was his usual stern self, but I saw compassion in his gaze as he told me that maybe I should look into working on my mental health.

"This is as much a physical game as a mental one," he'd told me as I wiped away my tears. "And you gotta get your mental game stronger, son. I think you might need some help."

I did. I still do, though I'm working on myself. After I left his office, Coach sent me some mental wellness info and told me to look into it.

I've now been going to a therapist twice a week. Our campus offers free mental health services, and after so many years of suffering with horrible self-worth and believing I'm not good enough for anyone, I already am feeling better. And I've only met with Betty, my therapist, a handful of times.

It feels good, talking to someone I don't know. Who will listen without judgment and ask me those tough questions. I told her about my parents. My worries about my future.

About Blair.

Only a little bit of Blair. She's not the problem in my life.

I am.

A month probably isn't long enough to heal myself, but it's a start, and I wish I could just declare to Knox right now that I'm in love with his sister, but he'd probably cause a scene.

And Blair would call bullshit because we haven't talked since that night. The night she was so fucking harsh toward me, and I deserved everything she said. Her belief in herself is inspiring. If I had half of her self-confidence, I'd be unstoppable.

"Should we get another pitcher?" Knox asks me after he's had his fifth slice of pizza.

I shake my head. "I'm done. I just want water."

"I notice you're not drinking as much," my friend says, his expression turning serious. "You laying off it on purpose?"

Blair is quiet and I can tell she's waiting to hear my answer.

"I'm not drinking near as much, yeah. My dad is an alcoholic. I don't want that happening to me," I say, just laying it all out there.

"He is?" Knox frowns. "You've never told me that."

"It's hard to admit." I send Blair a quick look to find she's watching me, her gaze soft. "I don't know why. It's not my problem. It's his."

"At least you're self-aware," Joanna says with an encouraging smile.

"I'm proud of you," Blair murmurs, and my heart feels lighter at hearing her words.

That's what I wanted to hear. What I needed.

Blair's approval.

We hang out for a while, Knox finishing off the rest of the beer and the last skinny slice of pizza, and when he and Joanna share a sly glance, I know they're going to bail on us.

"We're gonna get out of here. But that doesn't mean you kids need to run off." Knox slides out of the booth, Joanna following him. "I'm glad you met up with us, Blair. You need to do it more often."

"Thanks for including me," Blair says, smiling at Knox and Jo. "Let's hang out again soon."

They say their goodbyes, and the moment they're gone, I turn to her. "You want to leave, I get it. I should go too."

Blair frowns. "Where are you going?"

"To the gym." My bag is always in my car, ready at any moment to go and work out for an hour. Or two. "I've been working out almost every night."

"Even after practice?"

"Yeah. Sometimes before, too. I need to be in top playing form, you know?"

She smiles. It's faint, but it's there and seeing it gives me way too much hope. "Did my dad tell you that?"

"He did." I nod. "I've been working on...a lot."

"Like what?"

I study her face, noting the genuine curiosity there. No hostility in her gaze either, which is a positive sign. "Eating better. Getting more sleep. And like I said, working out. Increasing my stamina. I've been running too. Waking up earlier than usual to get a couple of miles in before class."

"Wow. Sounds like you're working on yourself."

"I am. Plus I've been focused on my classes. Getting all that handled between games can be a lot, especially with finals coming up." While I've missed her, not having her around as a complete distraction has helped.

More like I'm working on all of this for her. To be better. For myself. For her.

For us.

"School has been rough the last couple of weeks," she agrees, her gaze staying on my face. "It sounds like you're doing well, Cam. I'm happy for you."

"Thanks." I duck my head, feeling...what? Shy? Bashful? That's some bullshit. I've been more open with this woman than anyone else I know. She knows everything. All the bad. Hopefully all the good too. "After everything that happened that night between us, I couldn't stop thinking about it."

"Thinking about what?"

"What you said and how it made me feel." I let myself look my fill of her, taking note of her every little feature. The shape of her eyes, the delicate brows above them. The gentle slope of her nose. The angle of her cheekbones and those pretty pink lips I still fantasize about kissing.

I'd kiss her right now if she'd let me.

"I said some—harsh things." She winces.

"It was all the truth," I remind her. "I deserved to hear all of it."

"I'm glad you're focusing on yourself." She grips the edge of the table, like she's going to slide out of the booth and leave, and panic claws at my throat, making me want to reach out and stop her. "Like I said earlier. I'm proud of you. I mean it."

I don't want her to go. I haven't even told her I'm going to therapy yet. That I'm working on myself in all ways, not just football. That I'm doing this not just for myself.

But for her too.

"Thanks. I appreciate that." I take a deep breath, panic filling me when she pushes her way out of the booth, just like I feared.

"I should go. It's been nice catching up with you, Cam." Her smile is sad, and her eyes are too.

Fuck.

"Can I ask you one more question before you go?"

She shrugs one shoulder. "Sure."

"Is the clock still ticking? Or is my time up?"

35

BLAIR

Oh God. How can he ask me that right now? Here in the pizza place, surrounded by all sorts of strangers?

But what better place to ask, right? I can't go off on him, not that I want to. There's a new sense of calmness to Cam tonight that wasn't there before. When we were seeing each other, sneaking around, there was always this sense of underlying urgency about him. He was anxious. Hurried.

Like he knew it was all going to blow up in his face so he had to get every second with me that he could.

Now though? He seems very…centered.

I don't know what exactly has changed about him, but from what I see, I like it.

Do I like it enough, trust it enough to give him another chance though?

"Can I ask you a question?"

"Answer mine first." He lifts his brows. "Please?"

It's the please that gets me.

"Time's almost up."

A slow smile spreads across his face. "So, you're telling me there's still a chance."

"A lot depends on how you handle this."

"Tell me what I need to do." He sits up straighter, paying close attention, like I'm the teacher and he's the student.

"I love that you're working on yourself." I slide back into the booth, running straight into him since he scooted farther across the bench after I vacated it, and now that I'm back, he doesn't move. Meaning I'm pressed right up against him. All that warm, solid muscle smashed into me is enough to leave me lightheaded. "I was afraid you were going to drown yourself in alcohol and women after my—blow up."

"There is no other woman for me," he says, deadly serious.

My heart rate ratchets up. "Don't say things you don't mean."

"I mean every word I say." He watches me, not reaching out to touch me. Not doing anything else but letting those words sink in, his gaze intense. He means it.

I can tell.

And, oh God, that leaves me feeling all giddy and fluttery inside.

Taking a deep breath, I mentally tell myself to calm down. "Before we—do this, you have to tell Knox."

"Tell Knox what, exactly?"

"Whatever it is you feel about me. You don't have to say it to me right now, but you need to tell Knox about us." I hesitate. "Sooner rather than later."

"I'll tell him," he readily agrees.

"You will?" I sound full of doubt.

I *am* full of doubt.

He nods, pushing against me like he wants me out of the booth. "Let's go now. I'll tell him when I get home."

"But he just left with Joanna."

"Pretty sure they're going back to our place."

Is he purposely being dense? "I think they're going to be...

involved in other activities with each other by the time you get there."

"I'll tell them after they have sex then," he says, sounding perfectly logical. "When he's all mellow and more willing to listen to me."

"Eww." I make a face, and he chuckles. "Maybe you should wait and tell him tomorrow."

"Whatever. Just know that I will tell him." He stops trying to push me out of the seat. "What else do I need to do?"

"Accept the fact that I want you for who you are and stop trying to push me away by saying you're not good enough." My voice is soft, and I'm hoping he doesn't take offense. That is my biggest pet peeve with him. I don't like how he does that. If a man keeps telling you that he's wrong for you, then eventually, he's only proving the point.

"I can do that too." His gaze is imploring as he stares into my eyes. "I've been talking to a therapist."

"You have?" I'm surprised. And relieved.

He nods. "Twice a week. Betty's cool."

"Betty?" I lift my brows.

"My therapist. She's sixty-five and a hottie." He starts to laugh, and I can't help it.

I do too.

"She's helping?"

"A lot. Look." He angles his body more toward mine, and I wish I could snuggle with him. Press my face against his neck. Absorb his warmth. His strength. Feel those thick arms wrap around me and hold me close. "I know it hasn't been long, only a month. And you probably think I'm a giant asshole for not contacting you these last four weeks, but I was doing everything I could to focus on me. I needed to work on that before I could work on us, you know?"

I nod, trying to fight back the tears that want to fall at his using the word 'us.' He notices my reaction. My trembling chin and shiny eyes probably give me away, and he makes like he's going to reach for me, holding back at the last second. "Don't cry, B. This is a good thing."

"It is," I murmur, one tear slipping down my cheek.

He gives in to his urges and stops the tear with his thumb, lingering on my skin. "Come to my game this Saturday."

"It's an away game."

"So? Ride with Joanna. I want you there." He streaks his thumb across my cheek. "I wanna see my number right there."

"What?" I'm gasping, shocked he'd even suggest it.

"A big ol' four on your cheek. I'll give you a jersey with my name on the back if you want to wear it."

"You want me to wear your jersey?" I would love to wear his jersey. And his number. I want to shout and cheer him on and not worry what other people are thinking. I want him to smile at me and tell everyone that we're together. That's all I've ever wanted.

Acknowledgement of his love. Because, deep down, I know it's true.

Camden Fields loves me.

His nod is slow, and he reluctantly drops his thumb from my face. "I'll make sure it all comes together like you want it to. I'll talk to Knox. Your dad."

"My *dad?*" Oh God. I don't think he needs to take it that far. Not yet.

"I'll ask for permission from him to date you."

I'm shaking my head. "You don't have to do that."

"I don't?"

"No. Please don't. They don't need to be involved yet." I'm not ready to deal with all that.

"They'll be involved someday," he says almost ominously.

A sigh leaves me and I finally give in, touching his arm. "One step at a time, okay?"

His smile is hopeful. "Wanna go back to my place?"

"Absolutely not," I say, though my body is screaming a resounding yes.

"I had to try." He's smirking. Reminding me of the Cam of old. The one who flirted and tempted me all the time.

"Aren't Knox and Joanna there?"

"It might be a great way to let them know that we're…"

His voice drifts, and my brain fills in the word he didn't say.

Together.

"Nope."

"Your place then?" He won't let up, and I appreciate his persistence.

"My roommates wish bodily harm upon you on a daily basis. I don't think that's the move," I tell him.

"They know?"

I nod. Shrug. "I had to tell someone."

"I'll earn back their approval." He sounds determined.

"You're going to have to work extra hard, Camden Fields."

His grin is devastating. "A little hard work has never scared me before, Blair Maguire. Trust me on that."

I stare at him in wonder. "Is this really happening right now?"

"You're in control of this entire scenario, B. I know I fucked up. I have to earn my way back into your heart," he says, and I almost want to laugh.

Earn his way back into my heart? Doesn't he realize he's still there?

That he never left?

"Well, it's working." I shouldn't cave, but what's the point of torturing him any longer.

Or torturing myself? I care about him. More than that, I'm in love with him.

If he does everything he just promised, it's going to be okay.

But he needs to come through first.

After that mind-blowing conversation, he walks me out to my car, ever the gentleman while he holds the door open for me at the restaurant's entrance. A group of guys who are just about to enter the place offer up high fives to Cam, all of them calling out his name in greeting when they spot him, and he slaps their hands. Even poses for photos with them, smiling for the camera as they all surround him, offering their congratulations and support before they walk inside.

I just watch it all with a faint smile on my face. I even took the photos so the entire group could be in them with Cam. He's a bit of a superstar in town and on campus, and he takes it all in stride. As I've told him from the beginning, I'm used to this sort of thing, thanks to my family, but then again, it's a little different when it's all happening to the man I'm in love with.

It feels so good, thinking like that. Again. Not going to lie, I'm wary. Who could blame me for feeling that way? I bet even Cam would want me to be wary.

But I'm also…

Happy.

This might work between us.

Maybe.

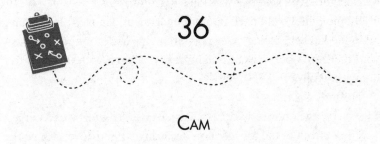

36

CAM

I t's the day after my talk with Blair at the pizza restaurant and I've been running on nervous energy ever since. I stayed up late into the night texting with her, both of us keeping up the conversation and sharing what's happened in the last month. I had a lot more to tell her and she let me. At one point, we FaceTimed because it was so much easier for me to just talk to her instead of typing it all out.

I was in the dark and so was she. Only the glow from her phone screen illuminating her beautiful face. She was wearing some sort of tank top to bed and I saw plenty of skin, which filled me with the urge to just…be with her. So I could touch her. Hold her.

Kiss her. Strip her. You know.

The usual.

Normally, I pack my day with so much activity I'm exhausted, meaning I fall asleep quickly every damn night. It's easier that way. Gives me less time to think. The more time I have on my hands, the worse my thoughts get. Even with therapy. Even with repeating to myself all of the mantras and self-affirmations Betty's supplied for me.

I used to think that sort of thing was nothing but horseshit, but I've come to realize it actually works.

Last night, I couldn't sleep to save my life. I was too anxious, too excited. I finally gave in and crawled out of bed at five in the morning, layered on a bunch of clothing and went to the gym where I ran around the indoor track for a solid four miles. My lucky number.

Hers too. And isn't that just some crazy shit?

By the time I walk back into our apartment, Knox is already up and in the kitchen, frying an egg. I stare at his back for a moment as I shut the front door, my chest tight, ready to burst with the need to tell him my truth.

This is it. It's time.

Shoving the door fully closed, I stride into the kitchen and come to a stop in front of the refrigerator, declaring, "I'm in love with your sister."

Knox flips the egg onto a paper plate and turns off the stove before he faces me, a confused look on his face. "Huh?"

I clear my throat, wondering if this was the wrong tactic. He still looks half asleep while I've been awake for hours. "I've been keeping a secret from you and I'm sorry. Blair and I—we're together."

Hopefully.

Knox is frowning so hard, I wonder if the wrinkles in his forehead hurt him. "Are you fucking for real right now?"

I nod, bracing myself for impact. His gaze is filled with some sort of emotion that doesn't look so good and I wonder if he's pissed. I wonder if he's going to take a swing at me. I'll let him. I'll let him get one in, at least. If he keeps swinging, he'll have a fight on his hands. That's not how I want this to go down, but he has to know that whatever I say about Blair, I mean. I'm in love with her.

And I haven't even told her. I'm telling her brother first.

Jesus, that's messed up. Too late now.

He contemplates me, remaining silent for way too long. I'm

growing uncomfortable, clenching my jaw, dying for him to do something when finally he says, "We knew it."

My mouth hangs open. "What?"

"Jo Jo and I were talking about it last night. You two were acting so weird together. There was all this tension. That's what Jo said at least." Knox forks up some of his egg and shoves it into his mouth.

I stare at him, shocked that's the only reaction I get. "Aren't you pissed that I kept it from you?"

"I'm not thrilled, but I get it. I would've gone ballistic on your ass and told you to back the fuck off."

"And now you won't say that?"

"If you love her, how can I be upset?" He peers at me, his gaze narrowing. "Are you telling me the truth? You're in love with Blair?"

I nod, my throat going dry. "Yeah," I croak. "I'm in love with her. But I haven't even told her yet."

"You two been sneaking around for the last couple of months, huh?" Knox keeps eating while standing at the counter.

"The last couple of months? No. We kind of had an—argument about a month ago and I've been keeping my distance."

"Really?" Knox frowns. "But you're never around. You said you go out all the time."

"I lied." I shrug. "I mean, I do go out. But I'm going to the gym or to the library or whatever." I don't feel like telling Knox about my mental health journey. I know he'd support me no matter what, but I'm still a little too raw over it.

It's hard to share the details, but I'll get around to it.

Someday.

"You're not sneaking around and hooking up with Blair?" He sounds shocked.

"I was. We were. But for the last month? No. I've been working on myself."

"Oh." Knox seems taken aback, his gaze running over me from head to toe. "Where have you been?"

"The gym. I just ran four miles."

"No shit?"

"Yeah."

"You're looking good, bro." He polishes off the last of his egg and then immediately goes to the fridge, pulling out a loaf of whole wheat bread. "Gonna make some toast. Want some?"

"No thanks." I watch him move about the kitchen, surprised this supposed confrontation went so easily. "You're really okay with this?"

Knox drops two slices of bread into the toaster and hits the button before turning to me. "You're my best friend and she's my sister. It's kind of weird, not gonna lie, but I know you're a good dude. You're not going to fuck her over." He pauses. "Are you?"

"No way." I shake my head.

"Good. That's all I need to know."

"But you always said I wasn't worthy of her."

"I only said that shit to keep all of you away from her. The last thing I wanted to imagine was my friends and teammates chasing after my little sister. That's just weird." Knox grimaces.

"So, you really have no problem with me being with Blair." I'm just making sure.

"I have zero problems with it. What can I say?" He spreads his arms out, a cheesy grin on his face. "Love has mellowed me out."

I pretty much said the same thing to Blair last night.

"We talked. Me and Blair. After you guys left."

"Yeah?"

"And later. We FaceTimed." He needs to know this. "I just—I want to do right by her. I don't want to fuck it up."

"Be real, be honest, and be open with her, and you won't have a problem, my friend. Keep the communication flowing, treat her right and tell her you love her every chance you get." Knox's gaze grows hazy and I know he's thinking about his girl. "It'll all work out if you keep that up."

"Yeah. You're right." I nod, wishing I was with her right now.

But then I remember what I promised her and I know I have one more thing I need to ask Knox to do.

"Will you tell her I told you about us? Sometime today?"

"Sure." Knox nods. "I'll send her a text here in a bit. Or maybe I should tell her in person."

"Thanks, man." He wouldn't even be able to comprehend all the reasons I want to thank him right now.

"Hey," he calls out as I'm about to leave our kitchen.

I stop. "What's up?"

"I'm glad you told me. I was going to be offended if you kept it from me much longer. Jo reminded me that I can get a little overprotective sometimes when it comes to Blair."

"A little?"

He chuckles. "Right. A lot."

"I'll protect her now," I tell him, meaning every damn word I say.

"I'm counting on it."

• • •

'm in my room digging through my closet, looking for an old jersey for Blair to wear. I find a couple, one from my freshman year, so it's not as ginormous. I was thinner then, not as bulky, and I hold it up to my nose first to make sure it smells clean before I drop it on my bed with the back showing. I spread it out so it's nice and straight, then grab my phone and take a photo of it before I send it to her.

She answers almost immediately, surprising me.

Bumblebee: *Is that for me to wear to the game?*

Me: *Yeah. It's from freshman year so it's not as big.*

Bumblebee: *You're bigger now?*

Me: *I'm pretty sure I'm even bigger than the last time you saw me naked.*

She sends me a string of shocked face emojis, making me laugh.

Bumblebee: *Are you serious? What do you mean, bigger?*

I send her three eggplant emojis. In response, she sends me the monkey covering his eyes.

Me: *I'm talking about my arms, shoulders and chest. I've been working even more on my upper body strength. Gotta maintain the arm strength to throw all them damn touchdowns.*

Bumblebee: *That makes sense.*

When she doesn't say anything else, I start to get antsy.

Me: *You'll wear my shirt to the game then?*

I don't get a response for at least another five minutes. Maybe longer.

Bumblebee: *Definitely.*

Bumblebee: *Sorry I was in the shower.*

I don't want to think of her in the shower, but my mind instantly goes there. Imagining her naked with steaming hot water pouring all over her bare skin.

I've got a hard-on, just like that.

Me: *You have class soon?*

Bumblebee: *Yeah. In less than an hour.*

Me: *Me too. Catch up later?*

Bumblebee: *Sounds good.*

She sends me a red heart emoji and I do the same, feeling like we're in middle school.

But then she sends me a bunch of peach emojis, followed by an actual ass pic with just a thin pair of pink lacy panties barely covering it and I realize...

We are most definitely not in middle school.

37

Blair

'm approaching the Student Center, about to grab a coffee for myself when I run into Knox.

"Oh hey. I was going to text you," he says, walking along beside me as I head for the small coffee shop on campus.

"What about?"

"I talked to Cam this morning."

My steps slow and so do his. "Oh yeah?"

"Yeah. He told me. Everything." He pauses, holding the door open for me as we both walk inside the building. "And that you two are together."

Now I come to a complete stop, turning to face my brother as he turns toward me too, towering over me in his usual intimidating way.

The expression on his face isn't intimidating whatsoever though. He seems pretty open. Pretty loose.

Pretty, dare I say, happy, about it?

"And you're okay with that?"

"Why wouldn't I be?" He shrugs. "My best friend and my sister are dating. I'm cool with it."

"Dating? Is that the word Cam used?"

Knox winces. "Not quite. Something like it."

"What did he say?"

"He said that you two are together. That he's—into you." Knox rubs at the back of his neck, vaguely uncomfortable.

Meaning he's lying. Or at the very least, holding something back.

"He didn't say that. I can't hear Cam saying that he's 'into me.' That doesn't sound like words he would use." I tap the center of Knox's chest. "Tell me what he really said."

"That should be for him to say to you, not me, Blair."

Alarm races through me. "What? Was it something bad?"

"No. Of course not. It's just, if he's going to admit his feelings for you, I don't think you need to hear them secondhand from me first."

Realization hits me. I think I know what Cam said to Knox.

He told him that he loves me.

"Okay. Sure." I play it cool, not about to go crazy-girl on him. "That makes sense."

Knox rolls his eyes. "Don't give him shit for this, okay?"

"I would never!" That wasn't part of the plan. I just love that Cam was one hundred percent real with my brother about his feelings for me.

Hmm, maybe I'm going completely overboard, but come on. Cam declaring his love for me to my brother is the logical conclusion here.

"Promise me." Now it's Knox's turn to beg. "Cam seems like he's in this—fragile state, and I get it. Being in love is hard, man. Oh shit."

He covers his mouth, his eyes wide, his expression horrified.

"I didn't mean to say that," he says, his voice muffled by his palm.

"It's okay. That's the conclusion I already came to." I let my giddiness fly free and start to hop up and down, while standing in line waiting to order my coffee, Knox grabbing my hand and trying to hold me down, though it doesn't work.

"Calm down. You're making a scene."

"I'm happy, okay? I'm allowed to act like a fool right now."

Oh, I wish Cam were here to see me like this, after receiving confirmation that he's in love with me. This almost doesn't feel fair.

"He seemed shocked that I was cool with you two being together."

"I don't blame the guy. There was a reason we kept it from you."

Knox swivels his head to look at me, frowning. "Was I really that bad?"

I roll my eyes. "You were the freaking worst. You told everyone to leave me alone."

"Can you blame me? They're all jerks," he practically growls.

"Oh my God, you probably gave Cam a complex over it." Though really, I know a lot of Cam's behavior stemmed from his own insecurities and not my brother telling him he wasn't worthy.

"Nah. They all knew I was joking." He pauses. "Mostly." Another pause. "Though I wasn't kidding."

"We know."

"But now that I have Joanna…I'm cool with it."

"Why does that make a difference?"

"Because I'm in love with her. And I know what that feels like." He smiles, appearing pleased with himself.

"You really love her, huh?"

"I do." His gaze meets mine. "You in love with Cam?"

I make a dismissive noise. "I'm not telling you that."

Knox doesn't get to hear those words first.

Cam does.

It's my turn to order coffee, and I get one for myself and for Knox, paying the cashier before we go and wait at the pick-up window. Knox is texting someone, pocketing his phone when he's done.

"Dad will approve," Knox says out of nowhere and I frown at him. "Of Cam with you. He'll love that. He likes Cam."

My heart goes soft. All I want is my family to accept Cam with open arms, and I believe firmly that will happen. "What about Mom?"

"You know she likes him. She's always asking about him when I talk to her." He laughs. "Now she'll ask you."

"I need to tell them."

"You haven't?"

"Of course not. We haven't really told anybody about us. It was all kept under wraps."

Knox's expression shifts into misery. "That's all my fault."

"No. Well, at first, yes." I pat my brother's arm, wanting to console him. "But so much of this has to do with Cam's issues more than anything else. He was sort of a mess."

"I know sometimes he struggled, but I never thought it was bad. I wish he would've asked for help."

"Sometimes we don't even know we need help." And I think in Cam's situation, he had to come to that realization on his own.

I'm so grateful he did. It sounds like he's on the right path. Like we're on the right path.

Hopefully.

• • •

It's Saturday morning and way too early, but here I am, showing up at Joanna's apartment, so we can get ready before we hit the road. I'm driving us to the football game, and luckily enough, the school we're playing is only a couple of hours away. The weather isn't the best, but at least snow isn't in the forecast so we should be good.

Joanna answers the door immediately, already dressed in a football jersey that I know has our family name on the back, with a long-sleeved T-shirt underneath it. Her long dark hair is pulled into a high ponytail and she's got a white ribbon tied in a bow around it. She looks adorable.

"Blair!" She yanks me inside and crushes me in a tight hug, clinging to me a little too long and shifting me back and forth. "I am so glad you're here."

She lets me go and I shake my head once, a little taken aback at her enthusiastic greeting. "Good to see you too."

"So, Knox told me something pretty...interesting." She goes to the small kitchen table and grabs a bag that's sitting on top of it, bringing it to me with a knowing smile. "Cam's jersey for you."

"Thanks." I take the bag from her, my cheeks growing hot. Why, I don't know. Of course, Joanna would know. Knox told her. It makes sense.

Though it still feels weird, making everything public after hiding it for so long.

"I've been saying this for a while. That I thought the two of you were together," Joanna says as she heads for the kitchen. "Want something to drink?"

"No, thank you." I set the bag on the couch and pull the jersey out, flipping it to the back, so I can stare at his name and number.

Fields, in all caps, with the number four below it. My lucky number.

The man was born on 4/4, for God's sake. Talk about a sign.

"Anyway, I knew you two were up to something. Remember when I walked in on you guys in the living room?"

How could I forget? Not our best moment.

"Yeah," I croak.

"You were acting so suspicious. You were so upset! I knew then he did something to make you the type of mad that only a man you're—involved with could do."

"You are very perceptive," I tell her as she rejoins me in the living room, one of those Stanley cups in her hand. It's a pretty light pink shade and I love it. But those things are near impossible to get.

"And your brother is a bonehead. I don't know how he missed it." Joanna takes a sip from her cup, and I laugh.

"He was too in love with you to notice." I'm sure that was the case.

Now it's Joanna's turn to blush and she waves a dismissive hand. "Do you need to change?"

"Yeah." I drop the jersey back into the bag. "Um, do you have any of that face paint still?"

"I do." Joanna's eyes are sparkling. "Want to use some?"

"I need a couple of number fours painted on my cheeks." I frown.

"Or is that too high school? Maybe I'm being a little too over the top."

"Nooooo. You need to do it. The first time I painted Knox's number on my face, he about keeled over he was so happy."

Hmm. I wonder if "keeled over" is code for my brother wanting to jump her.

Ugh. I'd rather not think about it.

I slip the jersey on over my long-sleeved T-shirt and then follow Joanna into her bathroom, where she already has the face paint spread out on the counter. She gets right to work, drawing a four onto my left cheek, then my right, taking her time to make it look good. She even adds all of the school colors, giving the number layers, and when she steps away from me, so I can check it out in the mirror, I'm impressed.

"It looks so good." I turn my face from side to side, pleased with the results.

"He's going to love it," Joanna declares as she starts to put away the face paint.

"I hope so." I sound worried, though I don't feel worried.

"What do you hope?" Natalie appears in the bathroom doorway, her hair still damp from the shower.

"That Cam likes his number painted on her face," Joanna answers for me.

Natalie rolls her eyes. "He's going to love it. He might even jizz in his jock strap when he sees you."

"Gross, Nat!" Joanna yells, but I just start laughing.

"You never know," I say when I can catch my breath. "He might."

Joanna starts giggling.

So do I. Eventually Natalie joins in too.

It's nice to talk about Cam with friends. It makes what we have feel much more real. Like it's not some fairy tale in my head. It's real.

Well, I think it is. I still feel a little unsure. I haven't seen Cam in person since the night at the pizza place. He's always busy, and so am I, but he's never really asked to get together, which is a little unsettling. He texts me every day though, and we've FaceTimed the last couple of nights. That means he's into me.

Right?

God, I hate feeling unsure. And that's been the gist of our so-called relationship since it started. The way he kept me a secret. How he kept me in the dark about his feelings too. After a while, I thought I was losing my mind.

Seeing him after the game will help. Hopefully, we'll talk. And maybe do...other things?

A girl—excuse me, a woman—can dream.

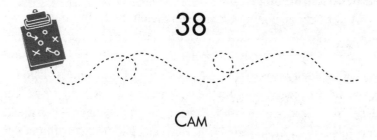

38

Cᴀᴍ

I'm nervous.

Not about the game or the other team or what the stakes are in regards to this game. Whoever wins today goes on to the conference championship. This is huge.

This is our moment to shine bright.

And all I can think about is seeing Blair after we win. Playing for her. Proving to her that I've got what it takes, both on the field and off. I'm going to win this game for my team. For myself.

For Blair too.

We left at the butt-crack of dawn, and somehow, despite how amped up I am, I was able to sleep on the bus. By the time we arrived, I was wide awake and raring to go. Out on the field during practice, I could feel the love surrounding me from my teammates. From the coaching staff. I know it sounds cheesy as shit, but they've got my back and I've got theirs, and it's the vibe I've been seeking all my fucking life.

To belong. Truly. To be wrapped up in love and respect and know it's for real. All these people who are involved with our team, they care about me. We care about each other. Deep down, I knew this. I did. But it was tough to realize when I let all the noise in my head drown it out.

Not anymore. I can't. I refuse to. I'm reveling in the confidence we're feeling. We're on top and we're going to continue this all the way to the championship.

I feel it in my bones.

The stadium is pretty much completely filled by the time we run out onto the field, eager to warm up. We're in our away game uniforms, which are red with white and gold and Knox and I took photos together prior to running out. Shit we even made a video for social media, other guys from the team joining us, including Ace. I'm the one who dragged him into the frame and I'm glad I did it. Instead of acting like a jealous little bitch, who can't handle competition, I'm embracing the kid because he's going to step into my place when I'm gone.

And those are some pretty big shoes to fill.

We're hanging out on the sidelines waiting for the game to start, Coach Mattson talking to us though I'm tuning him out. My gaze is focused on the stands behind us, scanning every face, looking for the one that makes my heart speed up.

I see her. Blonde hair flowing with a white beanie on her head, wearing my jersey with a thick black coat on that's open at the front so everyone can see it. It's cold, meaning she can't show off my name that's on the back of it, but she's reppin' that number four proudly and it makes me swell with pride.

She's got my number painted on her cheeks too and she looks adorable. This is the first time a girl has done this—a girl that I want to do this, that is. Because she is mine. And I'm not scared to say it.

Her gaze finds mine and she smiles, waving at me, practically bouncing in her seat. She shakes Joanna's arm, and she looks in my direction as well, waggling her fingers.

I slap Knox on the arm. "The love of your life is looking at you."

He whips his head around, lifting his hand in greeting to Joanna. "She's sitting next to the love of your life. How fitting."

My breath stalls in my lungs, and Knox and I share a look.

"Too soon?" he asks.

Slowly, I shake my head. "Nah. I'm not scared."

"Good. Don't fuck it up." He slaps my shoulder, repeating the words he said to me earlier.

Even a few days ago when he said that to me the first time, it caused fear to trickle through my blood.

Not anymore. I'm feeling pretty confident.

Cocky even.

Nothing's going to keep me down.

The announcer starts talking and we huddle together, me delivering a rouse 'em up-type of speech to get the team going. It works. We're all roaring and pounding our chests and acting like warriors about to take the field, and I glance over at the stands one last time before we run out there to start the game to find Blair's gaze fixed on me, a look of pride on her face.

Her lips part when our eyes meet and like the lovesick fool I've turned into, I blow her a kiss. She laughs, then does the same thing, and I pretend to catch it, closing my fist around it.

Who am I, and what has she done to me?

"What the fuck are you doing?"

This comes from Derek, whose head swivels between me and Blair up in the stands.

"None of your damn business," I growl.

"Did you just catch the kiss she sent you?" Derek is grinning, trying to hide it behind his meaty hand, but there's no use. He's loving every minute of it. "With her brother standing right next to you? You're brave, Fields."

"I already know," Knox interjects. "So mind your business, Big D."

I'm chuckling. "He wishes he was Big D."

"You guys wouldn't know a big dick if it slapped you in the face." Derek readjusts his junk, which is currently covered by a cup. "You finally official with her?"

I nod. "Sort of. I will be."

Derek frowns. "What does that even mean?"

"You'll see."

. . .

The game is over and we won.

No surprise. I was that confident going into it and it was an easy accomplishment. They fumbled the ball in the first two minutes of the game, allowing one of our defensive linebackers to snatch it up and run that ball all the way in for a touchdown. That set the tone for the entire game. We felt unstoppable.

We became unstoppable.

It was great and I'm still feeling high from the game, but I'm nervous. I'm out on the field in search of Blair, but when I spot the ESPN reporter heading in my direction, I come to a stop, realizing this is my chance.

The moment where I can make my declaration.

"Camden, great game today. You were on fire," she says in greeting, signaling to her cameraman to come closer. She thrusts the microphone she's holding in my face. "Tell us what it feels like, being one step closer to the divisional championship."

"The team came together and we played like a well-oiled machine." The words fall from my lips and I don't even have to think about them. I should probably coach Ace on this sort of thing. He'll have to deal with it next year.

"Your accuracy was stronger than ever," the reporter points out.

"I've been working on myself," I say truthfully, resting my hands on my hips, my gaze still scanning the people milling about. "But this isn't all about me. We're a team and they pulled it out today.

Especially Rhoades. Did you see that catch he made? He's the MVP of this game."

The reporter laughs, a gasp escaping her when Joey Rhoades himself appears by my side, throwing his arm around my neck and giving me a squeeze. "You bragging about me, Fields?"

"You know it."

The reporter talks to Joey for a few, while I stand there and nod, adding my opinion here and there. I spot the familiar face just when Rhoades is about to take off and the reporter is ready to wrap it up.

I glance up at the screens that hang above the field, my face on it, recording this moment live. It's time.

Clearing my throat, I send the reporter a pleading look. "Can I say one more thing?"

She shoves the mic back in my face, eager to get more film for their aftertime show. "Go for it."

"This is something a little more personal." I tilt my head to the side, coughing a little like I'm a nervous wreck.

Which I am.

The reporter frowns. "Where are you going with this?"

"I just—I need to tell everyone how I'm feeling and what better shot do I have than right now?" I swipe the mic out of the reporter's hand and turn, so I'm looking straight at Blair, who's about twenty feet away, watching me with confusion in her eyes, Natalie right by her side. "Blair Maguire, I'm in love with you."

The reporter gasps. Blair's mouth drops open. Natalie grabs her arm, her eyes wide.

Even the stadium seems to go quiet, and it's still full of a lot of spectators. All of them with their eyes on me.

Shit.

"I know I've been a jerk to you and you've had to put up with a lot, dealing with me, but just know that over these last few months, I've changed for the better, and it's all because of you. You've made me realize that there's more to life than just myself. There's you, and you make my world so much brighter when you're in it. When you're with me. I don't want to do this without you, and I swear on everything I've got that I will be the best man I can be for you." I pause, letting the words sink in, my gaze on her and no one else. I bring the mic closer to my mouth and murmur, "I promise."

"Blair Maguire?" the reporter asks. "You mean Knox's sister? Owen's daughter?"

"The one and the same." I hand her the mic. "Thank you for letting me do that."

And then I'm off like a shot headed for my girl—woman—the reporter yelling after me, "I want an exclusive interview with you two, Fields!"

I ignore her, but she'll get her interview. It's the least I can do for her letting me say what I just did.

It's only when I'm standing directly in front of Blair that I realize everyone is cheering. They're as loud as if we just scored a touchdown or won the game—and we're not even at home. I stop and take it all in for a moment, absorbing their shouts of encouragement. Seeing the smiling faces of my teammates, even Knox, who's got Joanna wrapped up in his arms not too far away from where we are. He lifts his arm, giving me a thumbs up, and when I finally meet Blair's gaze, I see that she's teary-eyed, her lips trembling.

"Bumblebee," I start, and a sob escapes her, cutting me off.

Worrying me.

"I can't believe you just did that," she practically wails. "You told everyone."

I'm frowning. "Was that a bad move?"

"You said you loved me on national TV."

"I wanted everyone to know how I feel about you."

"They all definitely know now." She wipes at her face and I go to her, moving her hand aside, so I can gently wipe away her tears. "Cam."

"Blair."

"You said you loved me."

"I do. I love you." I grab her hands and hold them against my chest, my heart thundering. "I'm in love with you."

"I'm in love with you too," she whispers, and I can't hold back any longer.

I grab hold of her face, smearing the already streaked face paint on her cheeks, and kiss her.

39

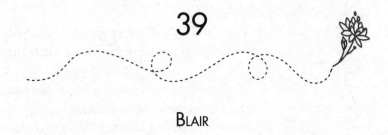

Blair

The team went out for dinner after the game in celebration of their win and I went too. So did Joanna. Even Natalie came along because, where else was she going to go, and she was having the time of her life, surrounded by football players and flirting it up with every single one of them. Even Cam, though I didn't mind.

I've basked in his love and attention all evening. Out of nowhere, he'd just lean over and kiss me on the lips, not caring who was watching. At first, the gesture always set off a reaction from someone on the team, usually Derek. But after he did it a couple of times, it's like they all grew used to it and didn't even acknowledge Cam's gestures of affection.

Me? I'm not used to it at all. I'm a little shocked every time he leans in, those delicious lips finding mine in a soul-stealing kiss. He's the sweetest man.

And he's all mine.

When dinner is over, we cling to each other in front of the bus,

Cam seemingly reluctant to let me go.

"I have to ride back with the team," he murmurs close to my temple before he kisses it.

"I understand. I get how this works." I tilt my head back, smiling at him. "I've got a lot of experience with this sort of thing."

"How'd I get so lucky?" He kisses the tip of my nose and I squeeze him tight.

"Will I see you later tonight?"

"I'll text you when I get back to the apartment. Actually, just go there with Joanna. She has a key." He smirks. "Knox made the suggestion."

"This is weird," I immediately say, not wanting to think about Knox with Joanna in any sort of way while they're alone.

"Get used to it," Cam says. "They're together. We're together. And Knox and I share an apartment. Things are bound to get awkward."

Ughhhhhh.

"Fine. I guess I can handle it." I shrug, acting nonchalant, and Cam starts tickling me, which has me giggling.

"Fields!" One of his coaches is standing in the open doorway of the bus and I realize Cam is the last one still outside. "Get your ass on this bus so we can head home."

"Wait for me." He kisses me, his mouth shifting to my ear to whisper, "Naked in my bed. Preferably."

He pulls away and I'm blushing. I can't help it. It's been a while since we've been together, and I'm a little anxious. Things have shifted between us. He's completely on board. We're in love. I get the sense things might be a little intense later.

But I'm more than okay with that.

Joanna, Natalie and I make the long drive back together, listening to the game-time playlist I put together only last night, singing along with the songs as loud as we can, the music playing full blast. We're laughing and screaming as we sing, and once the playlist ends, another song starts playing.

"Mad Woman" by good ol' T. Swift.

"Oh my God, I love her." Joanna turns it up even louder, making Natalie groan.

"Me too." But we already know this about each other. I know about the Taylor Swift lyrics tattooed on her skin and think they're perfection. "But this song isn't it."

It was it a month ago, when I was so pissed at Cam I couldn't see straight. Couldn't imagine wanting to be with him. I was that frustrated. That mad.

That hurt.

Joanna's gaze meets mine, her expression serious. "Let's change it."

She hits next and the most perfect song starts playing instead. It's on the dirty side, but I love it. Plus, Brent Faiyaz's voice is so smooth.

The song is called "Dreams, Fairytales, Fantasies" and oh my God, that's exactly how I feel when I'm with Cam. Like he's my very favorite dream come true.

Natalie is singing along with the rap parts, impressively knowing every single word, and Joanna is laughing, bopping her head to the beat. It's only when the song gets to the chorus for the second time that I realize I'm crying.

Bawling, really.

"Oh my God, Blair! Are you okay?" Joanna's voice rings with concern and she turns down the music, the only sound in the car my sobs.

"Holy shit, get it together girl," Natalie mutters, making me laugh in the middle of my sobs.

"I'm j-just s-so h-happy," I explain.

"Yeah, you sound thrilled," Natalie says.

Joanna reaches over and tries to smack her, which ends with them struggling. Natalie reaches around me from the back seat, a couple of tissues clutched in her fingers and I take them from her, murmuring thank you as I wipe at my face and nose.

"I'm serious, guys," I say once I've got myself together. "I'm happy. I swear. I just—that song got to me. The lyrics."

"Was it the 'I'll put you on a leash' part? Or the 'hit it from the back' part? Because that one is my personal favorite," Natalie says.

I'm laughing again, and so is Joanna.

"I know it's not what anyone would consider a romantic song, but the entire chorus is just so good. That's how I feel when I'm with Cam. It's like a dream."

"A fairytale," Joanna says.

"A fantasy," Natalie finishes.

We all sigh dreamily, and I know Joanna is thinking about my brother, while I'm sitting over here dreaming about Cam.

"I need to find myself a steady man," Natalie finally says. "You two are convincing me it's the right move."

"Despite my total emotional breakdown?" I ask, teasing.

"Hey, what he did for you today was pretty sweet. And a little overwhelming," Natalie points out. "I'd be a wreck too."

"I'm a wreck in a good way," I admit.

"Totally," Joanna chimes in. "I know what you're going through. It's the best."

I smile to myself, thinking of seeing Cam later. In his room. Waiting for him naked in his bed. Clutching the steering wheel, I bounce in my seat, giddy with excitement.

Joanna turns the music back up to a normal decibel and we continue chatting, Natalie making us laugh when she keeps telling us stories about the guys during dinner. How she came on to Ace and scared the shit out of him. How she thinks the assistant offensive line coach is hot.

"He graduated a couple of years ago. Knox and Cam played with him when they were freshmen," I tell them, which, of course, only excites Natalie even more.

"I should go after that dude. He's only a couple of years older.

And hot as hell." Natalie leans in between our seats, fanning herself.

The music stops, Siri letting me know I have a text from Hottest Quarterback Alive.

Oh hell.

"Hottest Quarterback Alive says, 'can't wait to see you later'."

"Ooooh," Natalie croons. "You going to answer him?"

"Do you want to reply?" Siri asks.

"Yes!" Joanna shouts.

"Okay, what do you want to say?" Siri asks.

Before I can respond, Natalie screams, "Can't wait to see you too, hot stuff."

I'm dying. "Hot stuff?"

"Let it happen," Joanna encourages. "Send it."

I tell Siri to send it when she asks and we're all still giggling. I don't think I've laughed this much since...when? Forever?

A few minutes later and there's another text from HQA.

"Hottest Quarterback Alive says, 'I've changed my mind. Don't wait for me in bed naked. Keep my jersey on and nothing else.'"

Oh God.

I'm beet red.

My entire body is hot.

This is so embarrassing.

But also funny.

And a little bit sexy.

Joanna and Natalie are howling in near hysterics. I check on Nat in the rearview mirror and she's literally rolling around the back seat, clutching her stomach. Until our gazes meet and she sits up straight, her laughter dying.

"That's hot. I want that in my future." Natalie is dead serious.

Joanna and I share a look. Even though I want zero details, I think we both have that already.

"Do you want to respond?" Siri asks.

"Yes," I tell her, clearing my throat as she asks me what I want to say. "We'll see."

"Ooh, playing it cool," Joanna teases.

"It's an inside joke," I tell them, wondering if he'll get it.

Deep down knowing without a doubt…

He will.

40

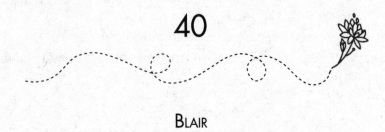

BLAIR

It's late and I'm half-dozing, half-awake when I hear Cam's bedroom door open. I crack open my eyes to watch him creep into the room, closing and locking the door behind him before he leans against it and just watches me.

My heart threatens to burst. This man.

I pretend I'm asleep as he makes his way to the bed, removing items of clothing as he does. He bends over me, whispering my name, and I shift a little but otherwise don't respond.

I want to see what he's going to do to wake me up.

More clothes are removed and he rounds the bed, climbing under the covers until he's directly behind me, yanking the comforter over us. He's big and warm and mostly naked, his chest pressing against my back as he carefully slips his arm around my waist, his big hand slipping under his jersey and pressing against my stomach.

I rest my hand over his, letting him know I'm awake, and he nuzzles my neck, his lips moving against my skin as he murmurs, "You wore my jersey."

His hand slides down lower, over my bare ass.

"And nothing else," I whisper.

"I've missed you," he confesses.

"It's only been a couple of hours."

"No, I mean over the last month." He pauses. "I thought I lost you."

His voice is so serious, and I'm wide awake now. "You didn't."

"Thank you for waiting for me, even when I probably didn't deserve it."

I go stiff in his arms. "Don't start with that kind of talk."

"You're right." He kisses my neck. Then my shoulder. "Hard habit to break."

I slowly turn in his arms until I'm facing him, streaking my fingers down his bare chest, impressed with all the hard muscle I feel there. I scoot backward, wishing the light was on so I could really check him out, but I can tell. "You are bigger."

"I told you." He sounds proud of himself. "I'm working out all the time."

"It shows." I trace my fingers down the center of his pecs. "Are you tired?"

"Exhausted." He kisses my forehead. I like how he can't seem to keep his lips off me. "But never too tired for you."

"We don't have to—"

"I have been thinking about you in my jersey, waiting in my bed and nothing else for the entire ride home. We're doing this." His voice is firm and he sits up, reaching over to turn on the lamp that sits on his nightstand.

I hold my hand up in front of my face like I'm a vampire. I'm even hissing. "That is so bright."

"I wanted to look at you." His touch is gentle when he grips my wrist. "Come on."

He removes my hand from my face and I let my arm drop to my side, sitting up. Letting him look his fill. His gaze roams over me. My messy bed hair, my sleepy face. The jersey hanging on me. I probably don't look great. I wonder if he's disappointed.

"You look sexy wearing my number," he practically growls.

Oh. Wrong assessment on my part.

"Even though it's gone from here." He reaches for me, his thumb streaking across my cheek.

"I had to wash my face."

"I know." He cups my cheeks, bringing me in for a kiss. "You're so pretty. I love you."

The tears threaten and I try to blink them away. But it just feels so good, hearing him say the words so easily. "I love you too."

He frowns. "Why are you crying?"

"I'm emotional." I take a heaving, shuddery breath. "It's been an emotional day. We're back together. You won your game. You told me you loved me on the Jumbotron."

"Pretty epic, am I right?" He raises his brows, his thumbs drifting across my face as he still holds it in his hands.

I nod, my gaze locking with his. "You didn't really check to see what I was wearing under the jersey."

His frown returns. "Yeah, I did."

I'm teasing. "Maybe you should check again."

He grins.

So do I.

Right before he reaches for me, making me shriek, and I press my face into the pillow as he tickles my waist. My stomach. His touch gentles, his fingers drifting over my hip bone. My butt. Slowly flipping me over so I'm lying on my back, Cam hovering above me, shoving at the hem of the jersey and pushing it upward until my breasts are exposed.

"Should we take this off?" His gaze lifts to mine, his fingers clutched around the hem of the shirt.

"I thought maybe you'd fuck me while I'm wearing your number."

"Oh, Bumblebee." He shakes his head. "Just when I think I've got you figured out, you go and say something like that."

"I thought you might like it," I whisper as he lets go of my shirt, shifting so he can kiss me.

"I love it." He kisses me deep, his tongue doing a thorough sweep. "I love you."

We kiss and touch each other, my hands eager this time around because it's been far too long and his body has turned into an even more beautiful work of art. I put my hands on him everywhere I can reach, purposely ignoring his erection, which is currently threatening to pop out of the front of his boxer briefs. He groans when I trace the waistband of his boxers, trying to grab my hand, but I pull away every time, always just out of reach.

Always driving him wild.

It's nothing but kissing and thrusting and rubbing and grinding and finally, he's whispering in my ear, "I want to fuck you from behind."

"Okay," I readily agree, breathless with anticipation.

"So I can see my number on you," he continues.

"Sounds hot."

"It will be." He reaches around me, palming one ass cheek, his fingers close to my pussy. When he brushes against it, I moan and he snatches his hand away from me, filling me with disappointment.

Looks like we're both playing that game.

More kissing and stroking and teasing, and it's only when we're panting against each other's mouths he finally says, "Get on your hands and knees for me, B."

I press my hand against his chest, his eyes opening to study me. "No condom?"

His brows draw together. "That's some risky shit, baby."

"I'm on birth control." I swallow hard. "It won't be as risky."

"I'm clean," he says, his voice low. "They just ran a bunch of tests on me."

"I want to feel you," I whisper. "Please?"

His kiss is fierce, his tongue doing a sweep of my mouth before he murmurs against my lips, "I want to feel you, too."

I get into position, on my hands and knees in the center of the mattress, still wearing the jersey. I'm hot, the back of my neck sticky with sweat, and when the mattress dips, I can feel him behind me just before he rests his hand on my hip.

And slaps my ass with the other hand.

"Oh!" I jolt against his palm, shocked and aroused. "Pull my hair."

He starts to laugh. "You're fucking wild, B."

"I swear only you bring it out of me," I confess, leaning into his soothing palm as he rubs it all over my ass.

"Keep it that way, okay?"

Within seconds, he's sliding inside me, his thick cock filling me completely. We stay in that position for a few seconds, adjusting to the connection, the way his erection throbs deep within me. I start to move first, slow and steady, his hands gripping my waist, helping me increase my pace.

"Fuck, this is hot, watching my cock disappear inside you," he whispers, his voice harsh.

I squeeze my inner walls around him, making him groan and I lean forward, resting on my elbows, my ass in the air as he continues to thrust. Driving himself inside me again and again.

I moan every time he slides inside, my eyes tightly closed, one hundred percent focused on how he's making me feel. Tingles race across my skin, gathering in my stomach, radiating outward, flowing through my blood. I'm sweaty. Mindless. Weightless. And when he presses his thumb against my back hole, increasing his pace at the same time, that's it.

I'm coming.

Crying out into his stupid flat pillow, I clutch it to my face, my inner walls rhythmically squeezing, pulling the orgasm right out of him. I can feel him come inside me, filling me up, and I realize that's the first time I've ever felt that before.

"Fuck," he says once he's come back down to earth, his voice rough. He clears his throat and pulls out of me carefully. "That was…"

"Incredible?" I offer as a suggestion.

"Yeah." He touches me, his fingers drifting across my pussy and making me shudder. "Hold on. Stay right there. I'll be back."

He dashes into his bathroom and I hear water running. I scoot forward, staying in position, and pull open the nightstand drawer, hoping I'll find some tissue when my fingers curl around something else instead.

I pull it out, holding it up. A travel-sized perfume.

The scent I wear.

Huh.

He returns to the bed with a warm, damp washcloth in his hand and proceeds to clean me up, his touch gentle. Arousing. Until I'm feeling needy all over again and his fingers slide in between my thighs, a questioning look on his face.

I shove the perfume under a pillow, nodding frantically.

He strokes me. Soft and slow. Hard and fast. Slides a finger inside me. Then another. Fucking me with his fingers, his thumb brushing against my clit. I come again, the pulsing waves making it hard for me to speak. To think. His touch gentles, pulling the rest of the orgasm out of me, until I'm a clingy, sweaty mess, wrapped all around him.

Cam runs his hand up and down my back, murmuring comforting words and reminding me why I love him.

He's gentle when he needs to be, and dirty too. I love the contradictions. The way he treats me. The way he loves me.

"I still can't believe you did that," I tell him later, when we're snuggling together in his bed, my head on his arm and his finger drifting back and forth across my stomach.

"Did what?"

"Told me you love me on national television."

"It wasn't really on television," he protests.

"Yes, it was. Check your phone and see."

He reaches over and plucks his phone off the nightstand, opening it up and going right to the ESPN app to find that our story is on the main page.

College QB Declares His Love for His GF Live!

"Oh God," he groans. "Our entire relationship has been reduced to a headline."

"I think it's fun."

"You would," he teases, depositing his phone back on the nightstand.

Which reminds me.

"Oh hey. I found something." I keep my voice purposely nonchalant.

"What did you find?"

I turn and reach beneath the other pillow, pulling out the travel perfume and thrusting it in his face. "This."

His face falls. "Oh."

"Yeah. Why do you have it?"

He's wincing. "It's hard to explain."

"I have all night." If this is some other girl's perfume, I'm going to be livid.

But something is telling me that's not the case.

A sigh leaves him and he launches into it.

"Remember that night I picked you up and took you to the frat party?"

"Yes."

"I went shopping. Bought myself a new outfit."

"To impress me?" I tilt my head back, kissing the underside of his jaw. "It worked."

He squeezes me closer. "I ended up in that one makeup store. That starts with an S?"

"Sephora?"

"That's the one. I was looking at the perfumes. Gucci makes a lot of them. I remembered you told me that's what your scent was. Gucci. And that the bottle was turquoise. I was spraying some of them and the lady was helping me, and then I recognized your scent." He pauses. "So I had to buy it."

"For yourself?" I'm confused.

"Well…yeah. Sometimes, especially for the last month, I'd just spritz it in the air and pretend you were there." He groans, pressing his face against my hair. "That's fucking pathetic."

"No, that's the sweetest thing I've ever heard." I rest my hand on his cheek, forcing him to look at me. "I love you."

"I love you too. Enough to confess when I do something embarrassing."

I kiss him. "It's not embarrassing. It's—romantic."

"Oh God, I don't know what's worse."

"Face it, Camden Fields, you're a romantic at heart."

"Only for you."

Only for me.

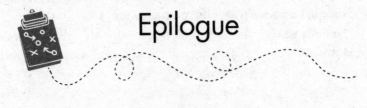

Epilogue

Cam

New Year's Eve

Knox and I decided to throw a party to ring in the New Year. A lot of people are gone for winter break, but we came back early for training, and so did a few of the other seniors. Plus, some of our teammates who are taking on bigger roles for the upcoming season.

Like Ace. His ass came back early too. And his ass is currently in my apartment, hanging out on our couch and throwing back beers with a big ol' smile on his face. Not a single care in the world.

Blair approaches me, clad in a tiny black dress that shows way too much skin and barely covers her ass. I hate it.

Lies. I love it. I just don't want anyone else looking at her.

"Are you having fun?" she asks.

"I am." I have to shout over the music to be heard. "Why do you ask?"

"You're scowling." She pats my chest, both of us turning when her sister approaches.

Ruby is here for winter break. She's going back to college on the East Coast and will complete the next semester there before she'll enroll here. She's already filled out the application. She's ready to come back to Colorado. She made sure to tell us at Christmas.

Multiple times.

I'm glad she'll be going to school here. I know her and Blair are close. It kills me that I won't be on campus next year, but I feel better knowing the Maguire sisters will be together.

"Look at him." I point at Ace, who's currently got a girl under each arm, all three of them laughing. "Is he trying to start a harem in my living room? That shit is not gonna fly."

"Oh, simmer down. He's just having fun. You're so hot and cold with Ace sometimes, I swear. Kind of like you were with me." She snuggles up close, sliding her arms around my neck and kissing me.

I rest my hand on her hip, gently pushing her away so I can watch everyone from where I'm leaning against the wall. "You're blocking my view, B."

"You're supposed to be looking at me." She mock pouts, and I do what she wants.

Taking a good, long look at her.

Wearing that dress should be a crime. It dips low in the front, showing off the tops of her breasts and making me think all sorts of dirty thoughts. Like how I wouldn't mind coming all over them.

Don't think we've done that before. Wouldn't mind trying it out later tonight.

Ruby and Natalie magically appear, their arms curved around each other's, matching grins on their faces. Once they met, they clicked, and they've been running around together ever since. Ruby has to go back to school in less than a week, and I know those two are going to miss each other.

"What's going on?" Blair asks her sister.

"I want to talk to that one." Ruby's gaze slides to Ace.

I groan.

Blair grins.

"I think you two might be cute together," my delusional girlfriend says.

"No fucking way. Look at him. He's currently sitting with two girls." I wave a hand at him like Ruby has no idea who I'm talking about.

She rolls her eyes, bumping her hip into Natalie's. "Duh, Cam. He'll take one look at me and forget all about them." Natalie high fives her while I mutter curse words under my breath.

"I wish I had an ounce of your confidence," Blair tells her.

"You were pretty confident in your pursuit of me," I say.

Blair glances over at me. "You think so?"

"Oh yeah. You wore me down." I lean down to kiss her and she reaches out, pinching my lips together instead. "Ow."

"Wore you down," she mumbles. "More like you couldn't resist me."

"Same difference."

"Hey." We both turn our heads to find Ruby glaring at us. "Introduce me, future brother-in-law. I want to meet that guy."

"Ruby." Blair's eyes are wide, like she hates that Ruby just said that.

But I don't mind. It has a nice ring to it. Being a part of the Maguire family wouldn't be a hardship. They're so close, so obvious with their love for each other, and I come from the complete opposite type of family. I spent Christmas with them since my mom spent the holiday with her new boyfriend, and I loved every second of it. Her parents treated me like I'm already a part of their family, and that was the best gift they could've ever given me.

Besides Blair, of course.

"Come on," I tell Ruby, removing my hold on Blair, so I can escort her sister over to where Ace is currently sprawled out on the couch. One of the girls already left, so he only has a cute redhead under his left arm, a red solo cup clutched in his right hand. When he spots me, he grins, lifting the cup up in a toast.

"Number one QB! Who's the hottie?" Ace's gaze runs up and down Ruby, and I can tell she likes it.

Behind us, Blair groans.

"This is Ruby Maguire. Ruby, I'd like you to meet Ace Townsend." I pause. "The number two QB."

"And about to become number one." Ace rises to his feet, forgetting all about the redhead. "Nice to meet you, beautiful."

They shake hands, Ruby giggling, the redhead glaring from her perch on the edge of the couch.

"You did hear me say her last name, right?" I ask him.

"I caught it. Maguire. You a cousin?"

"She's my sister," Blair pipes up from behind us.

Ace lets go of Ruby's hand as if it were a snake. "I forgot Knox had two sisters."

"Is that a deterrent?" Ruby asks. "That Knox is my brother?"

"It makes you off limits," Ace says, sending a smile in the redhead's direction. What a schmuck.

"Ooh, I love a challenge," Ruby says, making Natalie laugh.

"That might be a mistake," Blair tells me minutes later, when we're alone, watching Ruby and Ace, who are still talking. He's back on the couch, the redhead long gone, Ruby standing directly in front of him.

"Ace and Ruby?"

"Yes." Blair makes a face. "They sound like cartoon characters."

"I think they kind of go together."

Blair swats at my chest. "You do not."

"I'm just giving you shit."

"I know." She beams up at me and I kiss her. "Are you going to kiss me at midnight?"

"Definitely." I kiss her again. "Can't wait to see what the new year brings us."

"Me too." She slings her arms around my waist, peering up at me. "I love you, Camden."

"I love you too, Bumblebee."

She reaches for the necklace I got her, with the tiny gold bumblebee pendant. She hasn't taken it off since Christmas morning. "I sort of hated the nickname at first, but now I love it."

"You hated it?" I whistle. "Those are strong words, baby."

"I was just feeling sassy—and annoyed by you. I wanted you to think of me by my real name, not some made-up nickname." She scowls, and it's adorable.

"I always know exactly who I'm thinking about no matter what I call you. Blair. B. Bumblebee." I kiss her again. "Baby." Another kiss. "Love of my life."

"You've turned into a real sap, Camden Fields," she tells me, her eyes glowing.

"And you love it." I smile.

She smiles in return. "I do."

Epilogue 2

BLAIR

APRIL

I walk into Knox and Cam's apartment just in time to witness Knox whooping at the top of his lungs before he grabs Joanna and lifts her up high in his arms, spinning her in a circle as she laughs. He sets her gently down on her feet and kisses her.

For so long, I have to clear my throat to make them aware of my arrival.

Knox breaks away from her, a giant grin on his face when he spots me. "I got the call."

I grin at him in return, knowing exactly what he's referring to. "Oh, Knox."

"I know." He punches his fist into the air. "Let's fucking go!"

The call he's referring to is an invitation to the NFL draft. We've been waiting for this. Well, Knox and Cam have, while Joanna and I are the supportive girlfriends, anxious over their future.

Cam and Knox both participated in the NFL Scouting Combine in February, where only a select number of athletes are invited for a four-day evaluation of their playing skills, based on medical, mental and physical criteria. It's a grueling endeavor, but it's one step closer to what they want. Knox blew through it with ease, according to him. He's been ready for this moment his entire life.

Direct quote.

For Camden, it was a little harder. After he returned, he admitted to me he struggled. He's worked so hard on himself these last few months, and he worried he wasn't strong enough.

Not everyone who participates in the Scouting Combine gets to participate in the draft. The number shrinks from one step to the next. And while I'm excited that Knox received a call to attend—this means they predict he'll be drafted within the first couple of rounds—I wonder where Cam is.

Did he get the call too?

"I'm so happy for you," I tell my brother as I rush toward him and give him a big hug. He squeezes me hard, letting go of me so he can wrap Joanna up in his arms once more.

"Thanks, Blair. This is like a dream come true." He presses his lips against Joanna's temple and she leans into him, her eyes shiny with tears. I'm sure she's relieved. It's been so tense around here lately. Lots of waiting. Agonizing. Knox always acted confident. Like he had this in the bag, but deep down even he was stressed.

Everyone knows Cam has been stressed. He hasn't been shy about admitting it either.

"Where's Cam?" I ask, glancing around the room for evidence that he's already home. "He texted me a while ago and told me to meet him here."

"I don't know where he is." Knox lets go of Joanna and scratches at the back of his neck, seemingly uncomfortable.

Uh oh.

"You don't?" I send him a hard look, wishing I could read his mind.

He drops his arms to his sides and lets out a ragged exhale. "He went out for a run. He didn't want me to say anything."

Alarm makes me stand up a little straighter as I yank my phone out of my bag. "Why did he want you to keep it quiet?"

"Because we both knew what today could bring. Good news or bad. We didn't want to be together until the end of the day, you know? I don't want to crap on his parade and he doesn't want to crap on mine either," Knox explains.

A semi-rational explanation but I still don't like it.

"Have you told him your news yet?"

"I just found out." Knox slowly shakes his head. "And what if he didn't get the call?"

"That doesn't mean he won't get drafted," I point out.

It just means he'll stay home and watch it on TV. His chances are still really high to get picked.

Right?

"How long ago did he leave?" I ask.

Knox winces. "Two hours ago? Maybe three?"

"Three?" I immediately open my phone and send him a quick text.

Me: *Where are you?*

When he doesn't respond quick enough for my liking, dread coats my stomach, making me nauseous. "Shit, Knox. Where did he say he was going to run?"

"I don't know." He shrugs, sending a quick, worried glance in Joanna's direction. "He was dressed for it already. Didn't have his gym bag with him but that doesn't mean anything since he keeps it in his car. I just thought he was going for a quick run around the neighborhood and campus like usual and coming right back."

"I thought you just said you two planned on spending the day away from each other," I point out.

An aggravated sound leaves my brother. "I don't know what's going on, okay? I'll send him a text too."

He does exactly as he says, frowning when he doesn't get an

immediate response either. He lifts his head, his expression somber when he says, "It doesn't say delivered. Like his phone might be shut off."

Oh my God. I don't mean to sound like a stalker girlfriend, but it would be really nice if I had Find My Phone right now so I could track Cam's every move.

"Don't freak out," Joanna tells the both of us, her voice calm. "We know Cam likes to retreat sometimes. I'm sure he's fine. Probably turned his phone off so he can have a peaceful run."

"For three hours?" I sound incredulous.

I feel incredulous.

Where the hell is Cam?

As if conjured up by my mere thoughts, the apartment door swings open and there's Cam. Standing in the doorway clad in black running shorts and shoes, wearing nothing else. His skin glistens with sweat, he's got AirPods in his ears and he's holding up his phone, the screen black.

"Sorry, my phone just died." He slams the door behind him and strides inside, his expression impassive. Normal, neutral Cam. "What's going on? Why are you all looking for me?"

He cannot be serious.

"I, uh, I just got the call," Knox admits, sounding nervous. Like he doesn't want to admit that something really freaking great just happened to him. "They invited me to the draft."

"No shit?" Cam glances around the room, his gaze lingering on me. "So, you get to be there for the weekend?"

"First day, bro," Knox croaks, clearing his throat.

"Meaning they believe you're going to be a first-round pick? Or second?"

Knox nods.

Cam's gaze never strays from mine as he says, "No shit?" The slightest pause. "Same."

We're all silent for a moment, absorbing Cam's simple statement, the word echoing in my brain.

Same?

Same.

SAME.

"Oh. My. God!" I throw myself at him, not caring that he's all sweaty. My arms circle his neck and I grab hold of his hair, forcing him to look me in the eyes. "You are such a shit, playing it off!"

His arms wrap around my waist, gathering me closer as he lowers his head so his mouth hovers above mine. "Gotcha, huh."

"You're mean," I whisper.

Cam kisses me. "I couldn't help myself. And I'm sorry. I didn't mean to freak you out."

"You totally freaked us out," Knox says as he approaches us, yanking Cam toward him so he has no choice but to let go of me and get hugged by my brother. "We fucking did it!"

"We did," Cam says with equal enthusiasm, the both of them clinging to each other for a moment.

Joanna and I share a look, both of us glassy-eyed now. They're going to get drafted. They're both going to play for the NFL.

But what does that mean for us?

• • •

"Stop. I can't take it anymore." I push Cam away from me, not really meaning a word I say as I roll over on my side with my back facing his front. And he knows it. He scoots across the mattress and gathers me in his arms, dropping a kiss on my bare shoulder, his hands pressing against my stomach. "No more sex for a while."

He nudges his lower body against mine. "I'll let you rest for a few."

"Gee thanks." I laugh when he pinches my side.

After we called our families and friends, the four of us went out for a celebration dinner, and it was just what we needed. Food and drinks and lots of laughter and discussions full of what-ifs.

The good kind of what-ifs.

Everything has been so much heavier the last few weeks, waiting for word from the NFL. All the back and forth. The mixed emotions. The fear. The anxiety. The excitement.

It's a lot.

The moment we came back from dinner, Cam dragged me into his bedroom and had his way with me. In a variety of positions and acts. To the point that I'm now exhausted and need a break. I can already feel his growing erection nudging my ass though. He's going to want to do it again soon.

Not that I mind.

It's like a giant weight has been lifted off his shoulders, and I can literally feel it. Sense it. He's lighter. Happier. He can't stop smiling. It's the best thing ever.

"I love you," he whispers against my neck, and I rest my arms on top of his, pressing my head against his.

"I love you too."

"Don't worry about what's going to happen next."

I tense up slightly. "What do you mean?"

"I mean that wherever I end up going, whatever team I end up playing with, just know it changes nothing. I love you. I'm in love with you. If I had my way, you'd go with me, and we could be together when I start on this new adventure. But I don't want you to give up your dreams for mine."

I'm quiet. So is he.

"Look, I'm trying not to be a selfish bastard. I know how I operate. I can still get a little self-centered here and there. I just want you with me. All the time. This life of mine, this new career I'm about to embark on, it doesn't mean shit if I don't have you with me. By my side," he says, his voice low.

Slowly I turn around so I'm facing him. I tilt my head back to find him already watching me, his gaze, his expression sincere. "What are you trying to tell me, Camden?"

He swallows hard, then reaches behind my pillow, his hand and arm bumping into my head as he...what? Grabs something?

Then he pulls a box out. A little black box.

My heart lodges in my throat when he offers it to me.

"What is that?" I whisper.

"Open it and see," he whispers back.

I crack the box open with fumbling fingers, sucking in a breath when I see the thin gold ring nestled inside, a tiny diamond in the center.

"It was my grandmother's," he murmurs, his gaze stuck on the ring, just like mine. "My mom gave it to me when she visited a couple of months ago."

It was nice, meeting his mom. She was very kind towards me, and I got the sense she was pleased to see that Cam seemed so happy. Plus, he resembles her. They have the same eyes. The same hair color, too.

"Why did she give it to you?"

"Because I asked her if she still had it. And if she would be willing to give it to me so I could give it to you."

"And why do you want to give it to me, Cam?" I just…

I want to make sure of his intentions.

"Because I want to marry you, Bumblebee."

I stare at him, speechless.

And then I promptly burst into tears.

"Aw, baby. Why are you crying?" He pulls me in for a crushing hug, holding me close. Making soothing noises as I continue to cry. I'm getting tears and probably a little bit of snot on his chest but he doesn't seem to mind. He tangles his fingers in my hair, smoothing it away from my face, and when I finally pull away to stare up into his dark eyes, I can see the torture in his gaze. "You're acting like this is a bad thing."

"N-no." I shake my head, hiccupping and sobbing at the same time. "It's t-the b-best th-thing ever."

"Put it on your finger then," he practically demands, swiping the box from my hand. He pulls the ring out and grabs my left hand, sliding it onto my ring finger. It's a little big but not too much, and I stare at the ring on my finger, my smile tremulous.

"It's beautiful," I whisper.

"It's not much, but it comes from the heart," he says. "Think of it as a promise ring."

I lift my head. "So, it's not an engagement ring?"

"Oh, it is." He grins. "Just—I can get you something bigger once I sign the contract. If you want."

"I don't think I need something bigger." I scoot closer, lifting my head up as he tilts his down, our lips meeting at the same time. "I like this one."

"I like you," he murmurs against my lips.

"I like you too," I return with a soft laugh. "I might even love you. So much."

"I definitely love you." He rolls me over onto my back and proceeds to show me exactly how much he loves me.

Over and over again.

Exclusive

BONUS

CONTENT

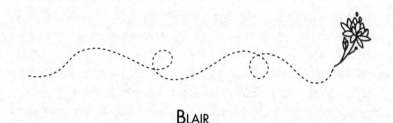

BLAIR

"Oh my God." I'm groaning. Loudly. I might even be making a minor scene, considering how quiet it is in this room.

"You gonna be okay, B?" The concern in my man's voice should actually concern me, but this is his usual way. Especially lately. He thinks I'm as fragile as spun glass, and while I usually appreciate how attentive he is, tonight I'm a little irritable.

"There, there," the instructor croons, her soft voice annoying me. Clearly, I'm in a mood. "Breathe deep, even breaths. Support her, partner. Count those breaths out for her."

The music starts, and it's slow. From the nineties , I think? It's awful, though it's supposed to calm us down, and I immediately feel Camden go tense behind me.

We're in a childbirth class, our second one, and tonight is all about the actual act of labor. We're supposed to pretend that it's actually happening, and I know Cam is freaked the hell out.

I am, too. I can't lie.

"Okay now, push. As hard as you can," the instructor continues.

I just sit there, hunched over my burgeoning belly, feeling dumb. Cam is sitting behind me, his hands rubbing my lower back, his chin settling on my shoulder. "I don't feel you pushing."

His deep voice so close to my ear makes me shiver, and I wish we weren't in this classroom. I'd rather be at home, cuddled up to him.

"I'm afraid if I do that, I could end up farting in the middle of class," I mutter, shaking my head.

Cam buries his face in my shoulder, chuckling. He knows it's true. Since I've become pregnant with his child—a strapping baby boy that's probably going to split me wide open considering Cam was over nine pounds when he was born—I've been a mess. An over-eating, getting-fatter-by-the-minute, burping-and-farting-uncontrollably mess. Hormonal and sad, hormonal and grouchy, I'm just flat-out hormonal, and I seriously don't understand those women who say they love being pregnant.

I most definitely do not.

"Let's pretend we're trying, at least," he encourages me, and I nod, scrunching up my face like I'm actually doing the thing while I fake push, which the instructor just loves.

"Oh yes, just like that, Blair! You're doing wonderfully. And Cam, you are such a big help to your wife. This is wonderful!" the instructor says, clapping her hands.

Cam and I share a look once she's walked past. I mouth the words *get me outta here*.

He just shakes his head and laughs. The jerk.

Twenty minutes later and we're exiting the hospital where the class is—where I'll have our baby—and Cam grabs my hand, pulling me into him. "You're sexy."

He rests his hand on my belly and gives it a fond rub.

I roll my eyes and try to get away from him, but he won't let me go. "I am not. I'm fat."

"You're sexy to me." He raises his brows. "And you're not fat. That's my baby inside you."

"It's all your fault," I grumble, rubbing my belly absently. The baby kicks beneath my palm, like he knows I'm grumpy.

"You were a willing participant," Cam points out, and I send him a dirty look. "Babe. I can't take it when you're in a bad mood. Tell me what I can do to make you happy."

"Give birth instead of me?" I ask hopefully.

He makes a face. "I wish I could, but that's impossible."

"Stop by McDonald's and get me a hot fudge sundae?" I suggest instead.

"Done."

• • •

We each have a hot fudge sundae while sitting in his car in the parking lot of the fast-food restaurant, arguing over baby names. I want to name him Jett. He'll be a fast little fucker like his dad on the field, and what better name than Jett Fields? But Cam doesn't love it.

"I want to name him…Earl."

I send him an incredulous look. "Please tell me you're lying."

"How about Stan?"

"How about no?"

"Grover?"

I burst into laughter, nearly spilling hot fudge down the front of my shirt. "Are you freaking serious? *Grover?*"

Cam shrugs, grinning. "I'm not serious. I just wanted to see you laugh."

"Oh." My laughter dies, and I swirl my spoon in the container, over and over, trying to catch any stray fudge sauce. "I haven't laughed much lately, have I."

"You haven't." He pauses. "I feel bad. Like I'm responsible for this."

"Well, you did remind me I was a willing participant. I guess that means we're both responsible." I leave the spoon in the container and set it in the drink holder in the center console. "You know what my problem is?"

"What?"

I turn to look at him, our gazes locking. While I'm over here growing like a house, Cam has the nerve to get better-looking. I swear every day he wakes up more attractive, and I don't know how he does it. "I'm...horny."

He's grinning. "I did just tell you you're sexy."

"I wasn't sure you meant it," I admit.

"Bumblebee, I would never lie to you." He reaches for my hand and grabs it, bringing it up to his mouth so he can kiss it. "You are the sexiest woman I know."

"Even looking like this?"

"Especially looking like that." His eyes take on a particular glow. "You're going to have my baby."

"It's crazy, right?"

"In the absolute best way." He tugs on my hand, and I have no choice but to practically fall into him. The only thing that saves me is the center console—and my belly. "I love you."

"I love you—"

He swallows my words with a deep kiss, his tongue swirling around mine. His tastes of chocolate and vanilla, and I lean in, trying to get closer, but God, it's awkward in the car.

"Take me home," I murmur against his lips.

Those three words spur him into action as he pulls away from me and starts the car, staring straight ahead. "Get your seat belt on, baby."

I've barely got it clicked into place and we're taking off at high speed, the tires squealing on the road as he turns onto the street. He's speeding, and I'm laughing, and the next thing we know, there are lights flashing behind us. Sirens blaring.

"Fuck," Cam mutters, pulling the car over.

I can't stop laughing.

The cop saunters up to the driver's side of the car a few minutes later, peering down at us as Cam fully rolls down the window. "Do you know how fast you were going— Wait a second. Are you Camden Fields?"

"Guilty," my husband mumbles, and I can't help but think his word choice is bad considering who he's talking to.

"No freaking way. I love you, man. And you had a stellar season." The cop appears thrilled. "Think you can take it all the way next year?"

"We're going to try," Cam says, which is his usual answer when someone asks him that type of question.

"I'm going to let you off tonight, but you need to slow down. And wait— That's your wife, right? Aren't you pregnant?" The cop bends down to study me.

I pat my belly. "Due in two months."

"Congratulations." The cop wags his index finger at Cam. "Be careful. You've literally got a baby on board here."

"Sorry, officer. I'll drive slower." The sheepish grin on my husband's face is adorable, and seeing it just makes me hornier.

I love him so much. How did I get so lucky?

Acknowledgments

Guyyyys this book! Camden Fields! What a moody, down on himself character he was. I love him though. I wrote it really REALLY fast because my schedule got really complicated and I had this urgent need to get Cam and Blair out. These two just poured out of me. I adore them. And I cannot wait to write the next book - I'm guessing you already know who it's about...

Can I just say how excited and overwhelmed I was by the positive response to *Playing Hard to Get*? I didn't expect so many of you to love Knox and Jo Jo and I just want to say thank you. I appreciate each and every one of you and I'm so grateful you want to read my sports romances. I love writing them - they're a nice break from all the intensity that a Lancaster book brings, ha!

This is where I thank everyone at Valentine PR for taking care of me - Nina, Kim, Valentine, Daisy, Sarah, Amy (my child), Kelley - you ladies are the best! Nina, as usual you helped make this story shine and I appreciate you for it!

Thank you to my editor Rebecca for all that you do. Thank you to Sarah for the proofread and keeping the details straight.

If you enjoyed *Playing by the Rules*, it would mean the world to me if you left a review on the retailer site you bought it from, or on Goodreads. Thank you so much!

*Don't miss the exciting new books
Entangled has to offer.*

Follow us!

f @EntangledPublishing

⊙ @Entangled_Publishing

♪ @EntangledPub

AMARA
an imprint of Entangled Publishing LLC